ALICE CAMPBELL
SPIDERWEB

ALICE Campbell (1887-1955) came originally from
Atlanta, Georgia, where she was part of the socially
prominent Ormond family. She moved to New York
City at the age of nineteen and quickly became a
socialist and women's suffragist. Later she moved to
Paris, marrying the American-born artist and writer
James Lawrence Campbell, with whom she had a son
in 1914.

Just before World War One, the family left France for
England, where the couple had two more children,
a son and a daughter. Campbell wrote crime fiction
until 1950, though many of her novels continued to
have French settings. She published her first work
(*Juggernaut*) in 1928. She wrote nineteen detective
novels during her career.

MYSTERIES BY ALICE CAMPBELL

1. *Juggernaut* (1928)

2. *Water Weed* (1929)

3. *Spiderweb* (1930)

4. *The Click of the Gate* (1932)

5. *The Murder of Caroline Bundy* (1933)

6. *Desire to Kill* (1934)

7. *Keep Away from Water!* (1935)

8. *Death Framed in Silver* (1937)

9. *Flying Blind* (1938)

10. *A Door Closed Softly* (1939)

11. *They Hunted a Fox* (1940)

12. *No Murder of Mine* (1941)

13. *No Light Came On* (1942)

14. *Ringed with Fire* (1943)

15. *Travelling Butcher* (1944)

16. *The Cockroach Sings* (1946)

17. *Child's Play* (1947)

18. *The Bloodstained Toy* (1948)

19. *The Corpse Had Red Hair* (1950)

ALICE CAMPBELL

SPIDERWEB

With an introduction
by Curtis Evans

DEAN STREET PRESS

TO PATIENCE, WELL NAMED, AND TO GUIDO, WHOSE
KIND HAND GUIDED ME THROUGH A MAZE OF
DIFFICULTIES

ALICE IN MURDERLAND

Crime Writer Alice Campbell, The Other "AC"

In 1927 Alice Dorothy Ormond Campbell—a thirty-nine-year-old native of Atlanta, Georgia who for the last fifteen years had lived successively in New York, Paris and London, never once returning to the so-called Empire City of the South, published her first novel, an unstoppable crime thriller called *Juggernaut*, selling the serialization rights to the *Chicago Tribune* for $4000 ($60,000 today), a tremendous sum for a brand new author. On its publication in January 1928, both the book and its author caught the keen eye of Bessie S. Stafford, society page editor of the *Atlanta Constitution*. Back when Alice Ormond, as she was then known, lived in Atlanta, Miss Bessie breathlessly informed her readers, she had been "an ethereal blonde-like type of beauty, extremely popular, and always thought she was in love with somebody. She took high honors in school; and her gentleness of manner and breeding bespoke an aristocratic lineage. She grew to a charming womanhood—"

Let us stop Miss Bessie right there, because there is rather more to the story of Alice Campbell, the mystery genre's other "AC," who published nineteen crime novels between 1928 and 1950. Allow me to plunge boldly forward with the tale of Atlanta's great Golden Age crime writer, who as an American expatriate in England, went on to achieve fame and fortune as an atmospheric writer of murder and mystery and become one of the early members of the Detection Club.

Alice Campbell's lineage was distinguished. Alice was born in Atlanta on November 29, 1887, the youngest of the four surviving children of prominent Atlantans James Ormond IV and Florence Root. Both of Alice's grandfathers had been wealthy Atlanta merchants who settled in the city in the years before the American Civil War. Alice's uncles, John Wellborn Root and Walter Clark Root, were noted architects, while her brothers, Sidney James and Walter Emanuel Ormond, were respectively a drama critic and political writer for the *Atlanta Constitution* and an attorney and justice of the peace. Both brothers died untimely deaths before Alice had even turned thirty, as did her uncle John Wellborn Root and her father.

Alice precociously published her first piece of fiction, a fairy story, in the *Atlanta Constitution* in 1897, when she was nine years old. Four years later, the ambitious child was said to be in the final stage of completing a two-volume novel. In 1907, by which time she was nineteen, Alice relocated to New York City, chaperoned by Florence.

In New York Alice became friends with writers Inez Haynes Irwin, a prominent feminist, and Jacques Futrelle, the creator of "The Thinking Machine" detective who was soon to go down with the ship on RMS *Titanic,* and scored her first published short story in *Ladies Home Journal* in 1911. Simultaneously she threw herself pell-mell into the causes of women's suffrage and equal pay for equal work. The same year she herself became engaged, but this was soon broken off and in February 1913 Alice sailed to Paris with her mother to further her cultural education.

Three months later in Paris, on May 22, 1913, twenty-five-year-old Alice married James Lawrence Campbell, a twenty-four-year-old theatrical agent of good looks and good family from Virginia. Jamie, as he was known, had arrived in Paris a couple of years earlier, after a failed stint in New York City as an actor. In Paris he served, more successfully, as an agent for prominent New York play brokers Arch and Edgar Selwyn.

After the wedding Alice Ormond Campbell, as she now was known, remained in Paris with her husband Jamie until hostilities between France and Germany loomed the next year. At this point the couple prudently relocated to England, along with their newborn son, James Lawrence Campbell, Jr., a future artist and critic. After the war the Campbells, living in London, bought an attractive house in St. John's Wood, London, where they established a literary and theatrical salon. There Alice oversaw the raising of the couple's two sons, Lawrence and Robert, and their daughter, named Chita Florence Ormond ("Ormond" for short), while Jamie spent much of his time abroad, brokering play productions in Paris, New York and other cities.

Like Alice, Jamie harbored dreams of personal literary accomplishment; and in 1927 he published a novel entitled *Face Value*, which for a brief time became that much-prized thing by publishers, a putatively "scandalous" novel that gets Talked About. The story of a gentle orphan boy named Serge, the son an emigre Russian prostitute, who grows up in a Parisian "disorderly house," as reviews often blushingly put it, *Face Value* divided critics, but ended up on American bestseller lists. The success of his first novel led to the author being invited out to Hollywood to work as a scriptwriter, and his name appears on credits to a trio of films in 1927-28, including *French Dressing*, a "gay" divorce comedy set among sexually scatterbrained Americans in Paris. One wonders whether in Hollywood Jamie ever came across future crime writer Cornell Woolrich, who was scripting there too at the time.

Alice remained in England with the children, enjoying her own literary splash with her debut thriller *Juggernaut*, which concerned the murderous machinations of an inexorably ruthless French Riviera society doctor, opposed by a valiant young nurse. The novel racked up rave reviews and sales in the UK and US, in the latter country spurred on by its nationwide newspaper serialization, which promised readers

> . . . the open door to adventure! *Juggernaut* by Alice Campbell will sweep you out of the humdrum of everyday life into the gay, swift-moving Arabian-nights existence of the Riviera!

London's *Daily Mail* declared that the irresistible *Juggernaut* "should rank among the 'best sellers' of the year"; and, sure enough, *Juggernaut*'s English publisher, Hodder & Stoughton, boasted, several months after the novel's English publication in July 1928, that they already had run through six printings in an attempt to satisfy customer demand. In 1936 *Juggernaut* was adapted in England as a film vehicle for horror great Boris Karloff, making it the only Alice Campbell novel filmed to date. The film was remade in England under the title *The Temptress* in 1949.

Water Weed (1929) and *Spiderweb* (1930) (*Murder in Paris* in the US), the immediate successors, held up well to their predecessor's performance. Alice chose this moment to return for a fortnight to Atlanta, ostensibly to visit her sister, but doubtlessly in part to parade through her hometown as a conquering, albeit commercial, literary hero. And who was there to welcome Alice in the pages of the *Constitution* but Bessie S. Stafford, who pronounced Alice's hair still looked like spun gold while her eyes remarkably had turned an even deeper shade of blue. To Miss Bessie, Alice imparted enchanting tales of salon chats with such personages as George Bernard Shaw, Lady Asquith, H. G. Wells and (his lover) Rebecca West, the latter of whom a simpatico Alice met and conversed with frequently. Admitting that her political sympathies in England "inclined toward the conservatives," Alice yet urged "the absolute necessity of having two strong parties." English women, she had been pleased to see, evinced more informed interest in politics than their American sisters.

Alice, Miss Bessie declared, diligently devoted every afternoon to her writing, shutting her study door behind her "as a sign that she is not to be interrupted." This commitment to her craft enabled Alice to produce an additional sixteen crime novels between 1932 and 1950, beginning with *The Click of the Gate* and ending with *The Corpse Had Red Hair*.

Altogether nearly half of Alice's crime novels were standalones, in contravention of convention at this time, when series sleuths were so popular. In *The Click of the Gate* the author introduced one of her main recurring characters, intrepid Paris journalist Tommy Rostetter, who appears in three additional novels: *Desire to Kill* (1934), *Flying Blind* (1938) and *The Bloodstained Toy* (1948). In the two latter novels, Tommy appears with Alice's other major recurring character, dauntless Inspector Headcorn of Scotland Yard, who also pursues murderers and other malefactors in *Death Framed in Silver* (1937), *They Hunted a Fox* (1940), *No Murder of Mine* (1941) and *The Cockroach Sings* (1946) (*With Bated Breath* in the US).

Additional recurring characters in Alice's books are Geoffrey Macadam and Catherine West, who appear in *Spiderweb* and *No Light Came On* (1942), and Colin Ladbrooke, who appears in *Death Framed in Silver*, *A Door Closed Softly* (1939) and *They Hunted a Fox*. In the latter two books Colin with his romantic interest Alison Young and in the first and third book with Inspector Headcorn, who also appears, as mentioned, in *Flying Blind* and *The Bloodstained Toy* with Tommy Rosstetter, making Headcorn the connecting link in this universe of sleuths, although the inspector does not appear with Geoffrey Macadam and Catherine West. It is all a rather complicated state of criminal affairs; and this lack of a consistent and enduring central sleuth character in Alice's crime fiction may help explain why her work faded in the Fifties, after the author retired from writing.

Be that as it may, Alice Campbell is a figure of significance in the history of crime fiction. In a 1946 review of *The Cockroach Sings* in the London *Observer*, crime fiction critic Maurice Richardson asserted that "[s]he belongs to the atmospheric school, of which one of the outstanding exponents was the late Ethel Lina White," the author of *The Wheel Spins* (1936), famously filmed in 1938, under the title *The Lady Vanishes*, by director Alfred Hitchcock. This "atmospheric school," as Richardson termed it, had more students in the demonstrative United States than in the decorous United Kingdom, to be sure, the United States being the home of such hugely popular suspense writers as Mary Roberts Rinehart and Mignon Eberhart, to name but a couple of the most prominent examples.

Like the novels of the American Eber-Rinehart school and English authors Ethel Lina White and Marie Belloc Lowndes, the latter the author of the acknowledged landmark 1911 thriller *The Lodger*, Alice Campbell's books are not pure puzzle detective tales, but rather broader mysteries which put a premium on the storytelling imperatives of atmosphere and suspense. "She could not be unexciting if she tried," raved the *Times Literary Supplement* of Alice, stressing the author's remoteness from the so-called "Humdrum" school of detective fiction headed by British authors Freeman Wills Crofts, John Street and J. J. Connington. However, as Maurice Richardson, a great fan of Alice's crime writing, put it, "she generally binds her homework together with a reasonable plot," so the "Humdrum" fans out there need not be put off by what American detective novelist S. S. Van Dine, creator of Philo Vance, dogmatically dismissed as "literary dallying." In her novels Alice Campbell offered people bone-rattling good reads, which explains their popularity in the past and their revival today. Lines from a review of her 1941 crime novel *No Murder of Mine* by "H.V.A." in the *Hartford Courant* suggests the general nature of her work's appeal: "The excitement and mystery of this Class A shocker start on page 1 and continue right to the end of the book. You won't put it down, once you've begun it. And if you like romance mixed with your thrills, you'll find it here."

The protagonist of *No Murder of Mine* is Rowan Wilde, "an attractive young American girl studying in England." Frequently in her books Alice, like the great Anglo-American author Henry James, pits ingenuous but goodhearted Americans, male or female, up against dangerously sophisticated Europeans, drawing on autobiographical details from her and Jamie's own lives. Many of her crime novels, which often are lengthier than the norm for the period, recall, in terms of their length and content, the Victorian sensation novel, which seemingly had been in its dying throes when the author was a precocious child; yet, in their emphasis on morbid psychology and their sexual frankness, they also anticipate the modern crime novel. One can discern this tendency most dramatically, perhaps, in the engrossing *Water Weed*, concerning a sexual affair between a middle-aged Englishwoman and a young American man that has dreadful consequences, and *Desire to Kill*, about murder among a clique of decadent bohemians in Paris. In both of these mysteries the exploration of aberrant sexuality is striking. Indeed, in its depiction of sexual psychosis *Water Weed* bears rather more resemblance to, say, the crime novels of Patricia Highsmith than it does to the cozy mysteries of Patricia Wentworth. One might well term it Alice Campbell's *Deep Water*.

In this context it should be noted that in 1935 Alice Campbell authored a sexual problem play, *Two Share a Dwelling*, which the *New York*

Times described as a "grim, vivid, psychological treatment of dual personality." Although it ran for only twenty-two performances during October 8-26 at the West End's celebrated St. James' Theatre, the play had done well on its provincial tour and it received a standing ovation from the audience on opening night at the West End, primarily on account of the compelling performance of the half-Jewish German stage actress Grete Mosheim, who had fled Germany two years earlier and was making her English stage debut in the play's lead role of a schizophrenic, sexually compulsive woman. Mosheim was described as young and "blondely beautiful," bringing to mind the author herself.

Unfortunately priggish London critics were put off by the play's morbid sexual subject, which put Alice in an impossible position. One reviewer scathingly observed that "Miss Alice Campbell . . . has chosen to give her audience a study in pathology as a pleasant method of spending the evening. . . . one leaves the theatre rather wishing that playwrights would leave medical books on their shelves." Another sniffed that "it is to be hoped that the fashion of plumbing the depths of Freudian theory for dramatic fare will not spread. It is so much more easy to be interested in the doings of the sane." The play died a quick death in London and its author went back, for another fifteen years, to "plumbing the depths" in her crime fiction.

What impelled Alice Campbell, like her husband, to avidly explore human sexuality in her work? Doubtless their writing reflected the temper of modern times, but it also likely was driven by personal imperatives. The child of an unhappy marriage who at a young age had been deprived of a father figure, Alice appears to have wanted to use her crime fiction to explore the human devastation wrought by disordered lives. Sadly, evidence suggests that discord had entered the lives of Alice and Jamie by the 1930s, as they reached middle age and their children entered adulthood. In 1939, as the Second World War loomed, Alice was residing in rural southwestern England with her daughter Ormond at a cottage—the inspiration for her murder setting in *No Murder of Mine*, one guesses—near the bucolic town of Beaminster, Dorset, known for its medieval Anglican church and its charming reference in a poem by English dialect poet William Barnes:

> Sweet Be'mi'ster, that bist a-bound
> By green and woody hills all round,
> Wi'hedges, reachen up between
> A thousand vields o' zummer green.

Alice's elder son Lawrence was living, unemployed, in New York City at this time and he would enlist in the US Army when the country entered the war a couple of years later, serving as a master sergeant throughout the conflict. In December 1939, twenty-three-year-old Ormond, who seems to have herself preferred going by the name Chita, wed the prominent antiques dealer, interior decorator, home restorer and racehorse owner Ernest Thornton-Smith, who at the age of fifty-eight was fully thirty-five years older than she. Antiques would play a crucial role in Alice's 1944 wartime crime novel *Travelling Butcher*, which blogger Kate Jackson at *Cross Examining Crime* deemed "a thrilling read." The author's most comprehensive wartime novel, however, was the highly-praised *Ringed with Fire* (1943). Native Englishman S. Morgan-Powell, the dean of Canadian drama critics, in the *Montreal Star* pronounced *Ringed with Fire* one of the "best spy stories the war has produced," adding, in one of Alice's best notices:

> "Ringed with Fire" begins with mystery and exudes mystery from every chapter. Its clues are most ingeniously developed, and keep the reader guessing in all directions. For once there is a mystery which will, I think, mislead the most adroit and experienced of amateur sleuths. Some time ago there used to be a practice of sealing up the final section of mystery stores with the object of stirring up curiosity and developing the detective instinct among readers. If you sealed up the last forty-two pages of "Ringed with Fire" and then offered a prize of $250 to the person who guessed the mystery correctly, I think that money would be as safe as if you put it in victory bonds.

A few years later, on the back of the dust jacket to the American edition of Alice's *The Cockroach Sings* (1946), which Random House, her new American publisher, less queasily titled *With Bated Breath*, readers learned a little about what the author had been up to during the late war and its recent aftermath: "I got used to oil lamps. . . . and also to riding nine miles in a crowded bus once a week to do the shopping—if there was anything to buy. We thought it rather a lark then, but as a matter of fact we are still suffering from all sorts of shortages and restrictions." Jamie Campbell, on the other hand, spent his war years in Santa Barbara, California. It is unclear whether he and Alice ever lived together again.

Alice remained domiciled for the rest of her life in Dorset, although she returned to London in 1946, when she was inducted into the Detection Club. A number of her novels from this period, all of which were published in England by the Collins Crime Club, more resemble, in tone and form, classic detective fiction, such as *They Hunted a Fox* (1940). This event may have been a moment of triumph for the author, but it was also something of a last hurrah. After 1946 she published only three more crime novels, including the entertaining Tommy Rostetter-Inspector Headcorn mashup *The Bloodstained Toy*, before retiring in 1950. She lived out the remaining five years of her life quietly at her home in the coastal city of Bridport, Dorset, expiring "suddenly" on November 27, 1955, two days before her sixty-eighth birthday. Her brief death notice in the *Daily Telegraph* refers to her only as the "very dear mother of Lawrence, Chita and Robert."

Jamie Campbell had died in 1954 aged sixty-five. Earlier in the year his play *The Praying Mantis*, billed as a "naughty comedy by James Lawrence Campbell," scored hits at the Q Theatre in London and at the Dolphin Theatre in Brighton. (A very young Joan Collins played the eponymous man-eating leading role at the latter venue.) In spite of this, Jamie near the end of the year checked into a hotel in Cannes and fatally imbibed poison. The American consulate sent the report on Jamie's death to Chita in Maida Vale, London, and to Jamie's brother Colonel George Campbell in Washington, D. C., though not to Alice. This was far from the Riviera romance that the publishers of *Juggernaut* had long ago promised. Perhaps the "humdrum of everyday life" had been too much with him.

Alice Campbell own work fell into obscurity after her death, with not one of her novels being reprinted in English for more than seven decades. Happily the ongoing revival of vintage English and American mystery fiction from the twentieth century is rectifying such cases of criminal neglect. It may well be true that it "is impossible not to be thrilled by Edgar Wallace," as the great thriller writer's publishers pronounced, but let us not forget that, as Maurice Richardson put it: "We can always do with Mrs. Alice Campbell." Mystery fans will now have nineteen of them from which to choose—a veritable embarrassment of felonious riches, all from the hand of the other AC.

Curtis Evans

CHAPTER ONE

CATHERINE did not at first know what to make of Geoffrey Macadam. Did his stiffness betoken mere British reserve, or was he trying to hide a natural annoyance at having a stranger thrust upon him, threatening the peace of his journey to Paris?

If the latter, she longed to tell him how hotly she shared his resentment, how for eight days across the Atlantic she had been fleeing from the officious patronage of the lady now needlessly effecting the introduction.

"It's no fault of mine," her eyes strove to convey. "I promise not to take advantage of it!"

The very next instant she caught that curious, almost startled look on his face which set her wondering, asking herself if he were really as wooden as she had imagined.

That look one may take as the starting point of the story . . .

Mrs. Hugh Tyler Pope—the Hugh rendered as Huge by some of their fellow-travellers—was no more to be denied than the forces of nature. She overcame by sheer weight of fatuity, and having constituted herself Catherine's proctress on the voyage was determined to see matters through. Useless for the girl to protest that she wanted no assistance in finding her seat. Overborne by the pressure of a mighty bust she was propelled the full length of the train, while a voice richly-oiled with kind intentions shouted for the benefit of all and sundry:

"Now, if only we'd met you sooner, dear, we could have had your piece reserved along with ours. Such a pity! It's just too dreadful to think of you travelling all this way by your little lonesome? Still it cant be helped now, the train's so jammed. Is this your seat? So it is. At any rate it's a corner one. *Porter! Mettay le grand sac de Mademerselle ploos au coin, il y a un carton aussi.* These foreigners don't give a hoot for your convenience, you have to show 'em everything."

It was at this precise moment that, clogging the aisle with her immense mink coat and treading on one pair of toes after another, she had spied the retiring male in the opposite corner and shrilled with recognition.

"Why, if it isn't Mr. Macadam! Now, what do you know about that? Been up to Havre on business? Well, well! Catherine, my dear—I want you to meet the very nicest man in all Paris, Englishman. Mr. Macadam, let me present a little friend of mine I've met on the boat, Miss West, from Boston. She's on her way to visit a relative in the Avenoo Henri Martin—you know, Mrs. Harry Belmont Bender, whose husband was killed last year in that awful motor accident in Massachoosetts. So sad!"

Extremely painful, nor was this the end. Not content with entrusting her young friend to the Englishman's care ("As though I were a congenital idiot," thought Catherine bitterly), she had dragged her victim back into the corridor and confided a parting message at the top of her lungs.

"Now wasn't that luck? Such a nice man for you to know. Macadam and Langtree. Lawyers. Everybody knows them. This one's the son, quiet, you understand, but such perfect manners. Be nice to him . . . Well, au revoir, dear! Don't forget to ring me up, and come to my very next At Home."

So saying Mrs. Hugh Tyler Pope careened up the swaying corridor and out of Catherine's life. Her part was played, nor did Catherine, inwardly cursing her, suspect what an important part it was.

Self-consciously, now, she sank into her seat. To her relief the Englishman had retired behind his magazine, so that she was able to settle herself calmly and collect her scattered thoughts.

To tell the truth, they needed collecting. Various uneasy qualms, hitherto stifled at birth, rose anew to trouble her, growing more insistent with each repetition.

Had she done right to come?

A guilty voice whispered that she had been unwisely precipitate over the whole affair, and might live to regret it.

"Yet why?" she argued crossly. "Germaine certainly wants me with her. There's no doubt about that."

Yes, Mme. Bender's letter, for all its characteristic vagueness, had expressed an earnest wish for her company. She would have bothered no more about it if it had not been for this other, rather odd epistle now hidden in her bag, a communication she had shown to no one.

Ah, there she had been wrong, there was no blinking the fact. She ought to have confided in her married sister Barbara and her sober brother-in-law, John. Catherine made her home with these two, and usually asked their advice on matters. Only sometimes, when she foresaw the result, she omitted the formality.

To be frank, she had been feverishly eager to leave Boston behind and with it the irksome associations of an engagement just terminated. She felt she could not walk down Boylston Street or across the Common without encountering a certain injured young man or some member of his family, in bitter league against her. Yes, she had dashed off instantly to secure her passage, and when later this curious missive penned by a complete stranger had arrived, she had kept silent about it for fear of shipwrecking her plans.

Oh well, it was done now, there was no looking back. Besides there was nothing definite on the letter, no fact that one could get hold of, in spite of its emotional tone. Who was the woman, anyhow? Probably some excitable friend of Germaine's, prone to exaggeration. The hysterical note spoke for itself. Naturally that accident last year had dealt poor Mme. Bender's nerves a shattering blow, but there could be nothing worse. She would put the whole thing out of her mind. . . .

Why did her *vis-à-vis* keep stealing those furtive glances in her direction? The covert survey, always quickly withdrawn, disturbed her like the prickings of her own conscience. There was a queer look of interest in his face, the same expression she had noticed a little while ago.

Discreetly she took stock of him. He was of slender build, wiry and muscular, his skin ruddy with health, features unremarkable, and eyes grey and keen, beneath strong bushy brows. His whole appearance had an air of restraint, extending to his clothing, which was well-cut, not too new, and by no detail claimed attention. Altogether he looked a man who would do nothing rash. Like John, she decided. John, too, was a lawyer. No, in a situation like her present one, he would undoubtedly have weighed the pros and cons carefully, and then—she was sure of it!—stayed at home . . .

"I beg your pardon?"

She started out of her reverie.

"Yes?"

He coloured in confusion.

"Nothing. I fancied you spoke."

"No, I was only thinking." Then she added with a little laugh, "You didn't overhear my thoughts, did you?"

A glint of humour was her only answer. Still, a thaw had set in, and from now on the glances became more frequent and less furtive. Soon she was sure he had something to say, but that his reticence was fighting against it. Twice he cleared his throat, then at last the question came forth.

"I beg your pardon, but did I understand Mrs. Pope to say you are a relation of Mme. Belmont Bender?"

He had leaned forward, voice lowered, as though the matter were a private one.

"Mr. Bender was my cousin," she replied in surprise. "Mme. Bender is French."

"Yes. Oh, yes, of course!"

"Perhaps you know Mme. Bender?" she suggested.

"I have met her," he said cautiously. "Not in a social way. You see," he went on after a pause, "my firm—we happen to be solicitors—has had the handling of the Benders' affairs for a very long time. Your cousin was one of our oldest clients."

"Oh! So that's it!"

Catherine's eyes lit up, transforming her entire appearance miraculously. Her eyes were her most striking feature. Rather sombre in repose, with a brooding melancholy recalling the famous portrait of Beatrice Cenci, they had a trick of flaming up with the rise of any sudden emotion and becoming twin lakes of liquid fire.

"That's extremely interesting," she exclaimed, and bent towards him, flecks of red straining her cheeks. "I—I wonder if you'd mind telling me just how she seemed to you when you last saw her? I'd rather like to know."

He was gazing straight into her eyes now, as though fascinated, half against his will, by their molten glory. He took a moment to reply.

"It was some time," he answered slowly. "Before Mr. Bender's death, in fact. Few people have seen her recently, and I am told that she's by way of being a complete—" he hesitated, choosing the right word—'"invalid. Probably you know more of her than I do."

Her face fell.

"I know very little indeed," she said uncertainly. "Except for one short note, I've had no news for almost a year. . . . You see, I have never known her very well. She and Cousin Harry were seldom in America, and it wasn't till after the accident, when she was ill in a sanatorium—"

"Sanatorium?" he repeated quickly.

"She was injured, you know—a bad concussion."

She thought he looked a trifle embarrassed.

"But do you mean to say," he ventured gravely, "that her mind was affected?"

"Certainly not!" she retorted with energy. "Why do you ask that?"

He reddened again.

"I'm sorry! In England a sanatorium usually means a home for mental patients."

"Oh, I see! With us it's simply a private hospital."

It was odd, though, his suggesting such a thing. Suppose, after all . . .

"I interrupted you. Please go on."

"I was only about to say that while Mme. Bender was recovering I used to go and see her every afternoon. She seemed so alone, so helpless and so crushed. You know, she had always depended on Cousin Harry for everything, gone everywhere with him, let him act for her, think for her even. Why, she's never bothered to learn English properly. There was no need, her husband spoke such beautiful French."

"I recall that he did."

"She was so overwhelmed by grief and shock that she was utterly incapable of making any plans. She even turned to me for advice, like a little child, perhaps because I could talk French with her, and scarcely anyone else could. She wanted me to go back to Paris with her then, but it wasn't possible."

There was a far-away look in her eyes as she thought of her broken engagement, rejoicing that the ring she had worn for a year—its stone cut like a piece of rock quartz because her fiancé had thought it bad taste for diamonds to sparkle—was no longer on her finger.

He was watching her closely.

"But was Mme. Bender entirely alone in Boston?"

"Oh, no! There was a maid, a most excellent woman, who had been with her for years and understood her perfectly. Indeed, there were two servants, a man and a woman, who used to travel with the Benders wherever they went—Egypt, Biarritz, Cannes, all those places. The man was a sort of courier-valet, spoke a dozen languages—very efficient . . . I wonder if those same servants are still looking after her?" she added, "because, poor dear, she had such a horror of strangers!"

"The servants? Oh, yes, they are still there," he assured her quickly; then in reply to her look of surprised inquiry continued by way of explanation, "At least I saw them at her apartment a few months ago. Mme. Bender sent for me on a business matter, but when I arrived she was too ill to see me, so that the maid you mention had to speak to me instead."

Inexplicably Catherine felt that he was withholding some item of importance. Moreover his interest in her had become so pointed that she grew positively ill at ease, and saying no more, resolutely directed her attention to the flying landscape.

They were in the heart of Normandy, which early spring had garnished with rainwashed tints delicate and vague. Through a mist of green, thatched cottages appeared, each with its little rectangle of farmyard, walled in by slender poplars. There was a flash upon the budding hedges, and here and there showed the pink bouquet of a flowering almond.

Catherine feasted her eyes, but her soul was troubled. The letter in her bag suggested anew such alarming possibilities that she was impelled to run through it again, hoping to fathom the writer's real meaning.

No use. It was a tangled mass of contradictions, framed in extravagant phraseology which left her baffled and irritated. She sat staring at the blue pages as though they contained some strange hieroglyph she had not the wit to decipher.

Minutes passed. The other occupants of the carriage had lapsed into whole or partial somnolence, with the exception of the Englishman, who having donned a pair of horn-rimmed spectacles was frowning sternly at the cover of his magazine.

Suddenly Catherine addressed him.

"Do you happen to know anyone in Paris by the name of Cushing—Hermione Cushing?" she inquired.

He started violently, the copy of *The Bystander* sliding to the floor.

"Hermione Cushing?" he echoed, obviously to gain time.

Their eyes met, and in a flash Catherine realized that there was something in the letter after all.

CHAPTER TWO

DURING the pause which followed, Catherine had time to reflect that this young man was a lawyer, and as such would be extremely unlikely to part with information. Her brother-in-law belonged to the legal profession. She thought she knew the breed.

"Hermione Cushing?" he repeated again with a sort of negative inflection. "Oh, yes! You mean the singer."

"Do I?" she demanded bluntly. "I didn't know she was a singer."

The gleam in his eye was altogether human.

"Perhaps it would be more accurate to say that she was a singer," he amended. "In any case, she's a country-woman of yours."

"You do know her, then?"

"Very slightly. Every one knows Miss Cushing. She's a well-known figure in Paris."

That was all. He had shut up like a clam.

"Oh dear!" fumed Catherine inwardly, "he's going to be tiresome like John! And yet he must know something, or why did he jump like that when I mentioned her name?"

There had been no doubt about his confusion. Even now he was watching her warily, as though dreading a direct attack. She decided to lay her cards on the table.

"Mr. Macadam," she began, glancing hastily at their comatose companions, "just before I sailed I had a queer sort of letter from this Miss Cushing, who tells me she is an old and dear friend of Mme. Bender's, and a such feels it her duty to warn me about something. Is it true? I mean, is she really my cousin's friend?"

He considered briefly.

"Oh, yes. I believe—indeed, I know that she is."

"Then there's nothing wrong about her? Nothing odd?"

She fancied his smile was reminiscent.

"Nothing," he replied discreetly. "Beyond a certain excitability, which one may put down to the artist temperament." Yet even as he spoke she detected a trace of reservation which further mystified her. Why couldn't he be more open?

"Perhaps that explains things. You see, I have been frightfully bothered to know what to make of this." She filtered the pages with hesitation, then suddenly made up her mind. "If you won't think me stupid. I'd like to ask you to read her letter and tell me whether I ought to take what she says seriously or not. You can understand my feeling nervous about it."

She finished the sentence hurriedly, rather ashamed of her boldness; then, as he took the sheets from her and gave them careful attention, she held her breath, studying him anxiously."

Secure behind an expressionless mask, the young solicitor perused the pages to the final flourish. Catherine, watching, could obtain no clue to his thoughts.

"You see what she says about the maid believing Mme. Bender to be out of her mind," she put in presently. "And about it's being an undeniable fact that the poor thing is behaving queerly. Does she herself think my cousin is unbalanced, or doesn't she? That's what I can't make out. The very vehemence with which she denies the suggestion makes me wonder if where there's so much smoke there mayn't be a little fire? Do you understand what I mean?"

"Of course," he assented, "it puts the idea into one's head."

"That's precisely it. I never dreamed of such a thing before, and it's naturally very upsetting."

He folded the pale blue sheets and handed them back to her.

"If it's not impertinent, may I ask if anyone else has seen this?"

Catherine blushed.

"No," she confessed guiltily. "I had made my plans, and frankly I didn't want to give up the trip. Besides, I had heard from Mme. Bender herself."

"Oh, she wrote to you, did she?"

"Certainly, and her letter seemed perfectly rational. She's always a little wandering and impractical, you know, but as a matter of fact, on this occasion she was less so than usual. She urged me to come as soon as possible, and told me to send a wire from Havre, so that Eduardo—that's the manservant—could meet me with the car and see me through the customs."

"You are sure she wrote the letter herself?"

Catherine stared at him astonished.

"Of course! I know her handwriting well. Besides, who else could have written it?"

Somehow his manner filled her with apprehension. How she wished he would offer some opinion, or if he had any secret information that he would let her share it!

"Besides," she argued, to justify herself, "it is not as though Miss Cushing were trying to prevent my coming. It is only that she apparently thinks I ought to be prepared for what to expect. Indeed, she seems most anxious for me not to change my mind. Don't you get that idea?"

"Very much so," he agreed. "She appears to think she will have a better chance of seeing Mme. Bender if you are there."

Catherine gave a quick nod.

"Evidently she's had some sort of shindy with the maid, Jeanne. Here—what is it she says?—'She detests me, *cette femme là*, and will go to any lengths to prevent my seeing her mistress.' I wonder what is at the back of that?"

Macadam stood uncomfortably and took out his cigarette case.

"Oh, I expect the maid is of a jealous disposition. You know what these old servants are like. Will you smoke?"

"Oh, thanks!" She paused while he held his lighter to her cigarette, then puffing thoughtfully remarked: "That probably explains it. But it occurred to me—what if Mme. Bender herself doesn't want to see Miss Cushing, in which case the maid is merely carrying out her orders?"

"Oh, perfectly! I see your point."

Indeed, he saw only too clearly. This possibility had impressed him so strongly during his one memorable interview with the lady in question that even now he could not be sure Miss Cushing was not making a nuisance of herself, forcing her attentions where they were not wasted. Various information, all emanating from the singer herself, disposed him to this opinion. He wished now that he had investigated the matter more thoroughly, but in all justice he had done the best he could. . . .

"Of course, it is not always easy to tell if a person is insane," he remarked with apparent irrelevance. "Often there are completely lucid intervals, so that two observers might easily have different opinions."

"That's what bothers me. I can't help thinking that this maid, who has known Mme. Bender for so many years and is her constant companion, must be in a better position to judge of her mental state than someone who sees her occasionally. Similarly, if Jeanne objects to admitting Miss Cushing, she is likely to have a good reason for it."

She stopped suddenly, realizing that she was putting into words all the doubts she had been trying not to admit. Perhaps she was driven to do so by her companion's evasiveness.

Macadam let his gaze dwell upon her sensitive, troubled face. The eyes were pensive now, clouded with doubt, the corners of the mouth drooped a little. It was a fairly wide mouth, generous, and with a look of firm sweetness, which accorded well with the high-bridged, delicately modelled nose. One would not call her pretty, he decided. Pretty was too trivial a word. No, there was a sort of high loveliness about her, showing as much in her expression as in the fine lines of her body. When her eyes ran over with that golden, liquid fire it was as though emotion had suddenly fused something clear and intense in her very soul. It made one think she had a greater capacity for feeling than most of the women one met. Now, because she was looking downcast, he longed to find some way of relieving her anxiety. But how?

"At any rate," he said, "I don't see that you need worry. I happen to know that your cousin is under the care of a reputable physician who probably understands her case."

"An American?"

"No—French, I believe."

"She's changed, then. Cousin Harry always had an American doctor. Oh, well, I suppose it's all right my going to stay there. Anyway, I hope so."

So did he. The truth was he was finding himself quite concerned over the thought that this singularly attractive girl was about to become the sole companion of a woman whose sanity was in grave dispute. She might be letting herself in for something unpleasant. He himself had known at least one case of so-called "circular insanity," where the patient after a long period of normal conduct, had veered with startling abruptness into homicidal mania, and ended by inflicting a knife-wound upon a member of his family. Miss Cushing's account of things, garbled and difficult to follow, rushed into his mind so forcibly that for an instant he opened his lips to utter a guarded warning. Then, simply because he had long been trained in grooves of discretion, he decided that it was no business of his to interfere.

When the train pulled into the Gare St. Lazare dusk was deepening into night. Doors banged open, porters swarmed into the carriages clamouring for hand-luggage, there was a confusing surging exodus of passengers on to the grimy platform.

Catherine felt a thrill of happy excitement. Paris at last! How she had longed to be here, ever since her single brief visit four years ago? The staccato babble filling her cars had an exotic sound, heralding an era of freedom and romance. How stupid of her to upset herself over imagined difficulties? Everything was going so be perfect. . . .

What was Mr. Macadam saying?

"Shall you be able to recognize this butler who is coming to meet you?"

"Eduardo? Oh, certainly! I'd know him anywhere. He's a sort of mongrel Portuguese, looks as though be ought to have rings in his ears and a knife between his teeth, but quite decent, really. He must be somewhere among the crowd."

While a blue-clad brigand fastened her bags together with a strap and slung them over a nonchalant shoulder, she scanned the platform with an eager eye.

"I'll stay with you, if you don't mind, till you find him," suggested her companion tentatively.

"Oh, thank you, though it's not at all necessary. He's sure to be here."

She accepted the hand outstretched to assist her down the awkward step and, looking this way and that, followed her porter's slouching figure towards the customs enclosure. Humanity jostled her, raucous voices shouted *"Attention!"* and more than once she was glad of the protecting pressure on her arm as some heavily laden truck trundled ruthlessly towards her, bent upon destruction.

Somewhere amid this seething mass her cousin's servant must be searching for her, but although she peered into every masculine face she could descry no one faintly resembling him.

"Probably he's been held up by the traffic. Better let me see you through all this business so as not to waste time."

She turned grateful eyes upon him, her brow faintly furrowed with uncertainty.

"It is too good of you! But aren't you in a hurry to get away?"

"I've nothing to do but go home to dinner," he assured her. "Here we are. Your trunk ought to be down near the end of the line."

It was comforting to be looked after; she let him guide her through the chaos. Already upon the long benches trunks lay open, their contents jumbled together under the inspectors' appraising eyes.

"Like the Last Judgment—the graves giving up their secrets!" she laughed. "I hope they don't paw my possessions about. I've nothing to declare."

It was finished. Certainly Mr. Macadam knew how to get things done with ease and dispatch. Once more, amidst the turbulent scene, her eyes sought expectantly for the familiar, squat figure of the Portuguese, only to meet with disappointment.

Eduardo was not there.

CHAPTER THREE

IN THE open space taxis honked and porters jostled each other with the peculiarly vicious abandon characteristic of Paris. A few private cars were drawn up, and each of these they examined searchingly, sure that one among then must be Mme. Bender's. However, in turn they were claimed, and drove away.

"You say you sent a telegram?" inquired the Englishman.

"Certainly, as soon as the boat docked. Of course it may have gone astray."

"Possibly. That does, of course, occasionally happen."

She glanced at him with indecision. Twenty minutes had now passed, and there was no sign that anyone was coming to meet her. She could not deny feeling disappointed.

"Oh, well, there's no good hanging about. I'll just get into a taxi and go along by myself."

He had not noticed in the train how young she looked, and how slender, almost fragile. Standing now against the dingy building with the cold draught whipping her squirrel coat about her silk-clad knees, she seemed to him altogether unfit to be venturing across a strange city unescorted.

He found himself suggesting solicitously:

"Perhaps you'll let me drop you at the apartment? I'd very much like to."

She shook her head quickly.

"Oh, no, I shouldn't dream of it! You've been too awfully good as it is."

She was conscious of a warm appreciation, more pronounced then if the offer had come from one of the cheerful, less restrained youths of her acquaintance. She had begun by considering him stiff and severe. Now she was not so sure.

"Here's a taxi. I don't in the least mind going alone, really. It's not as if I didn't speak French."

Her manner brooking no argument, he somewhat reluctantly handed her into the waiting cab and gave directions to the driver. Then, not quite satisfied, he hung on to the sill, looking in at her.

"You're sure you're all right?"

"Oh, absolutely! I'm not a baby, you know. I've been looking after myself for years,"—and she laughed, wrinkling her nose.

"It's this question of your cousin, Mme. Bender. I daresay you'll find everything as it should be, but if it isn't—if for any reason you don't want to stay there"—here he floundered a little not sure as to what he wanted to say—"well, perhaps you might let me know."

"I will, if you like," she agreed readily, though a little astonished.

"I'll give you my telephone number—both my numbers, in fact. The first is the office, the second my home."

He scribbled on a card and handed it to her through the window.

"You won't forget, will you? I shall be rather anxious to hear how you're getting on."

For an instant his two hands rested on the ledge. She noted that they were unexpectedly large and sinewy for his medium build, and that there were dark brown hairs on the backs. A detached part of her brain reflected that they were utterly unlike the pale smooth hands of Miles Waring, her late affianced—hands which for some inexplicable reason had always roused in her a faint repugnance.

She thanked him with a grateful smile, and the taxi lunged away, leaving him upon the kerb, gazing after it with doubt in his eyes.

Beastly annoying of these people to let a young girl arrive like this with no one to meet her. Nothing in it, of course, but all the same he ought to have told her plainly the things Hermione Cushing had said to him a few weeks ago. As it was, he had let her go to her destination totally unprepared. Well, it was too late now. . . .

Meanwhile, at breakneck speed the taxi hurtled along crowded thoroughfares. Lights twinkled through the violet dusk, cars flashed past, the air was heavy with the distinctive scent of French petrol, so oddly thrilling because of its associations. Intoxicated by the well-remembered odour, by the hurrying people and the gay shop windows, Catherine sat upon the edge of her seat, keyed up with anticipation of all that Paris was going to mean.

Presently she glanced at the card in her hand. "Mr. Geoffrey Blair Macadam," she read, with the address in the corner, 99, rue d'Assas.

She recalled the rue d'Assas. It was across the river, by the Luxembourg Gardens, a delightful place to live. How thoughtful he had been! She wondered if she was likely to see him again.

With a lightning swerve the taxi rounded a corner, and behold, the Champs-Élysées, broad and darkly glistening like a ballroom floor. Far ahead, in the evening gloom, rose the shadowy Arc of the Étoile, grandly beautiful, the climax to a perfectly planned vista. Beyond it spread the Bois de Boulogne, full of mystery, with its young bare trees, and over the Seine to the left lay the heights of St. Cloud forest. The thought of the myriad slim poplars, pale green even to the mossy stems, pierced her heart with a joy that hurt.

Ah, here was the Avenue Kléber! Two minutes more and she would reach Mme. Bender's magnificent apartment, where four years ago she had spent a few pleasant days. At the thought sudden stage-fright chilled her exultation. She was quite forgetting the possible state of her hostess, and a qualm of self-reproach assailed her. Still, in spite of last year, she felt almost a stranger to her cousin's widow, that intangible creature, so extremely difficult to know. One pitied rather than loved her, but that was inevitable. Ardently Catherine hoped that these rumours about her mental condition were exaggerated. Until she had actually seen her she would feel a bit nervous.

She recalled her first, childish impression of Mme. Bender, long years ago. Always there had been something unreal, a clinging, orchidaceous quality, suggesting that she was constitutionally incapable of existing alone. In the positive personality of her American husband she had taken root, but recently, torn from that support and sustenance, her entire character had wilted and sagged, a fact pathetically apparent a year ago. What would she be like now? With age creeping pitilessly upon her, it was hopeless to expect her to build for herself an independent life.

They turned into the Avenue Henri Martin, a spacious street with a double row of chestnuts down the central parkway. The handsome building on the left contained the Benders' two-floored apartment. There, just round the corner in the side-street, was a private door, through which one might go without passing the concierge's loge; but naturally now she would use the main entrance.

Queer for that telegram, properly addressed, to go astray. Would her arrival take them by surprise?

The driver descended, unstrapped her trunk, and dumped it unceremoniously within the flagged court. Catherine got out, paid the fare, and started to enter the archway.

Then an incident occurred which in itself meant nothing at all, and which would have been speedily erased from her memory if subsequent happenings had not served to emphasize it. As she crossed the pavement she collided forcibly with a lounger who, idling along, head upturned towards the windows above, had not observed her approach. She recoiled with the impact, straightening her disarranged hat, as a muttered apology met her ears.

"*Pardon, mademoiselle!*"

"*Pas de quoi, monsieur,*" she replied mechanically, still tingling with the blow, which had all but knocked the breath from her body.

He drew back to let her pass, and to her slight discomfiture favoured her with a long, penetrating stare. How like a Frenchman, she reflected indignantly. She lowered her eyes, but her brief glance had shown her a slight, meagrely-built person, execrably dressed in black, with a wide-brimmed hat upon his head. Above an old-fashioned winged collar with a cravat rose a small, pasty-white face, the skin recalling the unwholesome pallor of a fish-belly, while pale, red-rimmed eyes, one of them marked with a black triangular blemish, gazed forth with so unwinking fixity.

He was still standing there behind her on the pavement when she reached the high glass doors of the concierge's loge, the official occupant of which came forth to greet her, grudgingly, after the manner of her class. A dried, spare little woman with a nut-cracker countenance and a buck crocheted shawl about her shoulders, she bent on the newcomer a vulture-eyed look of mingled curiosity and suspicion.

"*Bonsoir, mademoiselle!*" she accosted Catherine with metallic precision. "*On desire—?*"

"Madame Bender," announced Catherine briefly.

A quick change came over the hard old features. Eyebrows and shoulders hoisted themselves with one movement, and the sharp eyes narrowed for a closer inspection of the young girl's face.

"Ah!" breathed the concierge with an upward, insinuating inflection. "Madame Bender! I was not informed that madame was expecting a visitor. However, that is no affair of mine." She made a curt gesture with her gnarled hand, at the same time jerking her head towards the octagonal court beyond the covered way. "*Montez, mademoiselle. L'ascenseur est à droit.*"

Catherine thought her manner definitely unpleasant. In some annoyance she motioned to her luggage asking to have it sent up as soon as possible, then turned towards the shallow steps at the right side of the court. She had not gone two paces, however, before the hard voice called out with what sounded like malicious enjoyment:

"Mademoiselle has chosen an unfortunate moment for her visit. If she expects madame to receive her in person, she must prepare for a disappointment."

Catherine looked around.

"What do you mean?" she demanded quickly. "Is anything wrong?"

There was a second meaning shrug.

"I cannot tell you. I know nothing, I! All I can say is that the doctor was summoned for madame last night at nine o'clock, and that he has only this instant gone out of these doors. Almost twenty-four hours he remained there, but everyone has been in too fine a state of excitement to tell me what has happened. Mademoiselle will soon know the truth, though. She has only to inquire."

She turned her back and thrusting her scrawny neck in through the glass doors, screamed *"Gaston!"* in a strident voice.

Her heart pounding, Catherine ran across the court, past the group of trimly clipped box trees, to the big double-doors. A final glance over her shoulder showed her a fat, sluggish old man lumbering out to join the woman under the archway. There the pair stood, planted beside the little pile of luggage and stared after her with a concentration which had something ominous about it. Why should they look at her like that? She was filled at once with antagonism and dread.

A second later she had shut herself into the bronze cage of the lift and was juggling with the automatic buttons. Up rose the *ascenseur* and halted at the *entresol.* She sprang out and with rapid steps crossed the thickly carpeted floor to the imposing mahogany door on the left.

She rang and rang again, but there was no response. Within was complete silence, as though the big flat were untenanted. Really it was incredible that no one should answer the bell! Impatiently, she pressed her finger once more to the bronze button and kept it there.

All at once, without warning, the door opened to reveal the thick, squat figure of a man in conventional butler's attire.

It was Eduardo.

Out of the broad, swarthy face his smallish black eyes stared at her without a trace of recognition. The wide mouth tightened with an expression unfriendly, faintly contemptuous. Was this the suave manservant she knew, this uncompromising person who barred the entrance with his body, making no attempt to admit her? She felt curiously dashed, as though cold water had been thrown in her face.

"Eduardo!" she cried, to jog his memory. "Surely you recall me? I am Miss West, madame's cousin. Madame is expecting me, you know."

Only then did he stand aside, an unwilling smile breaking over his features.

"Oh—Miss West," he mumbled indistinctly. "Sorry, miss, I didn't recognize you."

Then with something approaching his former manner he removed himself from her path and by an after-thought took from her the umbrella and small dressing-bag she was carrying.

Catherine was less annoyed by the nature of her reception than alarmed at what it might indicate. The thought struck her that something had occurred to upset the whole *morale* of the household.

"Didn't madame get my telegram? She was going to send you to meet me. However, that's of no consequence," she added quickly. "The point is, what has happened? Is madame ill?"

In spite of his command of many languages, Eduardo was a man of few words. He muttered something unintelligible in which she could only make out "accident" and "very bad," then after an awkward hesitation he showed her towards the wide doors of the salon.

"Perhaps you'd better go in there, miss," he said, with a jerk of his head. "I'll fetch Jeanne to talk to you—" and without further explanation he vanished, his tread making no sound on the padded carpet.

Catherine was bewildered. Why, he had addressed her with the inarticulate but casual manner he might have used towards one of his own station! Certainly Harry Bender, easy-going though he had been in many ways, would never have tolerated this rude familiarity. Yet she knew that this man had for years been almost indispensable, something approaching a major-domo. Had the accident to which he referred overthrown his customary balance? She hoped it was only that.

She pushed open the salon doors and entered; then, too perturbed to sit down, gazed round her at the rich furnishings. The immense double-room, built on two levels, was divided through the middle by graceful gates of wrought iron and gilded bronze, placed at the head of broad shallow steps. Both portions were filled with exquisite examples of the Louis Quinze period, genuine pieces, fit for a museum, the upholstery of delicate *petit point*. On the left wall hung a large tapestry, and here and there stood vitrines containing collections of miniatures and snuff-boxes. The whole effect was much as she recalled it, yet there was a subtle difference which she was now too preoccupied to define. Probably it was due to the general air of neglect and complete absence of flowers, which, together with a stuffy atmosphere, gave the impression that no one had used the apartment for a very long period.

Minutes went by. She wandered restlessly about, longing for the maid to come and put an end to her suspense. Whatever had occurred, she had perfect confidence in Jeanne, whom she remembered as capable and full of good sense. Sometimes she fancied her a bit too ingratiating, but that was merely a manner.

Why didn't Jeanne come? The prolonged wait intensified her fears. Again and again her eyes strayed towards the doors, but there was neither sight nor sound of anyone approaching.

She walked to the end of the room, where two long windows gave upon a narrow balcony. The curtains of old-gold brocade had not been drawn, and through the opening she could see the trees and glimmering lights of the avenue. Between the windows was a wide fireplace, over which hung an eighteenth-century mirror with a painting in the Watteau style let in at the top. Facing her, flanked by twin lustres with pear-shaped drops, stood a columned *pendule* of white marble with ormolu mounts. Mechanically she compared the time with that of her wrist-watch, then saw that the clock was not going. At the same instant she discovered a thin coating of dust on the delicate surface. Odd! She touched the crystal pendants of the lustres, ran a light finger over the strip of brocade beneath. Dust again. . . .

Suddenly she felt her eyes gravitate upward towards a reflection in the glass. Through the iron tracery of the gates a strange face appeared, sallow and lined, a woman's face, out of which, with a fixed and hostile expression, two opaque eyes stared straight into her own. She gave a little gasp. Who was this person? For a second she gazed back, unpleasantly fascinated. Those black bars between gave her a curious sensation.

It wasn't—it couldn't be—

She wheeled about with a nervous laugh of relief and made an eager movement towards the steps, pushing the gates wide.

"Jeanne!" she exclaimed, "I didn't recognize you! Oh, thank goodness you're here at last!"

She extended an impulsive hand, and the woman took it, after a brief hesitation, and with little answering pressure.

"It is you, mademoiselle. Pardon me for keeping you so long."

Catherine saw that she was indeed altered, her strong features haggard and drawn with fatigue, discoloured semi-circles like bruises under her eyes, the brow deeply furrowed. A year ago she had thought the maid almost handsome with her good white teeth always showing in a cheerful smile, but now, sapped and strangely preoccupied, she appeared actually ugly.

"Jeanne, I am frightened! What has happened to madame?"

The vertical cleft deepened where bristling hairs met over the snub nose.

"How did you know anything had happened to madame?" the woman parried in accents resentful, almost suspicious.

"Why, I heard it from the concierge. She told me the doctor had been here since last night."

A stubborn look settled over the close-lipped face. An appreciable pause elapsed before the reply came, cautious, deliberate.

"Madame is very ill," she said shortly.

A doubt swept into the girl's mind.

"Oh, Jeanne—you don't mean she's—dead?" she whispered, her voice shaking.

"No, no! Certainly not!"

This time she spoke with quick impatience, as though for some reason she were vexed by the suggestion.

"Well, then, tell me what is wrong. I insist on being told."

The idea came to her that there was some mystery in all this. Why couldn't the woman come straight out and tell her?

"Very well, mademoiselle, since you must know, but I warn you it will give you a shock." She came a step closer, glanced over her shoulder, and lowered her voice: "The fact is, last evening madame attempted to commit suicide. There—now you have the truth!"

CHAPTER FOUR

CATHERINE was aghast. Her eyes dilated with horror, while an inner voice whispered that rumour had not lied. Poor Mme. Bender was certainly deranged.

"When—how did it happen?" she gasped.

"It was last evening, Madame tried to drink a glass of strong disinfectant. I only managed to summon the doctor in time to save her life."

For a few seconds the girl remained speechless, her eyes fixed on the maid's worn face.

"What a terrible thing!" she exclaimed at last. "I had no idea it was as bad as then. But"—with a faint glimmer of hope—"are you quite sure she meant to do it? Couldn't it have been accidental?"

Jeanne shook her head slowly and with decision.

"That is what she wishes us to believe," she replied with a shrug and in a leaden manner, as though fatigue had dulled her faculties. "By good luck she had only drunk a little of the liquid when I discovered what she was doing. I seized her arm and dragged it away. To-day, of course, she is ashamed, and pretends she took it in mistake for her sleeping-draught, which I need hardly tell you is extremely unlikely."

"Ashamed, Jeanne? What do you mean?"

"Only that madame in her sane moments suspects that we are watching her, as indeed we are. Invalids with her complaint become cunning."

"Oh, Jeanne, is it true then, about madame's mental condition?"

A shade of reproach almost scornful passed over the other's face.

"In my opinion madame has never been normal since the death of monsieur. Surely you must have realized that last year in Boston, when, ill as she was, she suggested your coming to visit her."

Catherine flushed a little.

"No, Jeanne, she seemed to me perfectly sane at the time. Indeed, I should never have dreamed anything was wrong if I had not heard . . ." Here she checked herself, not sure that it was wise to divulge her informant's confidences.

A look of shrewd intelligence came into the heavy eyes.

"Oh, I see! It was Mademoiselle Cushing who told you," remarked Jeanne rather coldly. "I am not surprised that you have heard from her."

Catherine felt curiously ill at ease, as though she were being accused of some wrongdoing.

"As a matter of fact, Miss Cushing did write to me," she admitted. "But I may as well tell you she doesn't think Mme. Bender is insane—only very nervous and depressed."

A long silence greeted her statement. Then the woman spread her hands outward with an expressive gesture.

"*Eh bien,*" she commented with singular emphasis, as though she had expected this. "There is another who believes what it suits her to believe."

Although Catherine did not grasp the meaning of this cryptic utterance, she felt vaguely disturbed at the under-current of hostility, directed, it seemed, at her as much as at Miss Cushing. What had either of them done to incur the maid's displeasure? Still one must not judge a person who so clearly had just passed through a painful ordeal and had not yet recovered her poise.

"Never mind, Jeanne," she ventured soothingly. "The point is, how is madame now? Is she quite out of danger?"

"Ah, yes! She is sleeping. The doctor ordered her a sedative, and she is not to be disturbed."

"That is good. What a mercy she has you to look after her!"

The Frenchwoman turned on her suddenly with a hint of suppressed passion.

"Ah, mademoiselle, you may well say that!" she whispered, her voice shaking. "Little do you know what I have been through these past weeks. It has been one crisis after another. I live in terror! I dare not leave poor madame, day or night, for fear she will do harm to herself!"

The girl was forcibly impressed by the devotion, almost fanatical, which blazed forth from the sunken dark eyes. Not knowing what to say, she laid her hand upon the arm nearest her with impulsive sympathy.

At her touch a change came over the woman. Pulling herself together she spoke in a business-like tone, almost cheerful:

"And now, mademoiselle, we must think what is to be done about you. Naturally you could not know the situation here, or else—"

Catherine interrupted her reassuringly:

"Don't think of me, Jeanne, I shall be all right. Just show me my room and I'll give you no trouble whatever. You must go to bed and get some sleep."

Her remark was met by a blank stare. She saw the maid's body stiffen slightly.

"Your room? But surely, mademoiselle, you cannot have any idea of remaining here!"

Catherine was taken aback by the almost irritable incredulity of the exclamation. For the second time she felt the blood mount to her cheeks. This was a Jeanne she had not encountered before.

"Why not? I shan't bother anyone. And, of course, I mean to do all I can to help you."

"I do not require help," retorted the maid quickly. "But—visitors, at a time like this! Really, mademoiselle, it is not to be thought of! The apartment is like a *maison de santé*. No, assuredly, it would never do. Eduardo will assist you at once in finding an hotel. There are many small, quite comfortable ones in the quarter."

Her determined manner brooked no contradiction. Catherine was silent for a moment, dashed and puzzled. Then a rush of obstinacy overtook her, and she made up her mind not to be dealt with in so peremptory a fashion. After all, she was not suggesting anything unreasonable.

"Listen to me, Jeanne," she replied, kindly but firmly. "Madame invited me to stay here, and I do not intend to go to an hotel. Show me where I am to sleep, and I will look after myself. Which room is it?"

For a long moment the two regarded one another. The girl felt herself in conflict with a will of steel, but she did not waver. At length she saw that she had won.

"I am not sure that any bedroom is ready," muttered the maid rather sullenly. "But if you are determined to stay, mademoiselle, I must see what can be done."

She turned and left the salon, irate protest in every muscle of her rigid back.

It was a chilling reception. Easy to understand that in the recent crisis no thought could be spared for the coming guest, yet for all that Catherine could not help feeling that Jeanne was assuming an unjustifiable amount of authority. Besides, in an apartment full of servants a single extra person could hardly prove a serious inconvenience.

She felt damped and depressed. What an idiot she had been not to make sure of the situation before plunging into it! Her own fault, too, for she had received a sort of warning. Yet perhaps, after all, she had not done wrong to come; perhaps in some small way she might be able to assist her unhappy relative. It was selfish to think only of her own comfort, which really did not matter very much. She would not have done so but for the fact that she was tired after her journey. Once she could wash and change and have some food, she would take a brighter view of things. A glance at her watch told her it was past eight o'clock. She had eaten nothing since lunch.

All at once a disconcerting thought occurred to her. What if her coming had precipitated this action on Mme. Bender's part? Suppose the poor, tormented woman had brooded upon the prospect of her arrival, yet had not had the courage to put her off? There was no saying what vagaries and exaggerations neurasthenia might attain. For an instant she was half inclined to run after Jeanne and tell her she had changed her mind about remaining. She even went as far as the entrance hall, but before she could carry out her intention common sense pulled her up.

No, it was hardly possible Germaine could feel like that about her. At all events it was better to do nothing till she had seen and spoken with the invalid. It could not possibly matter if she spent the night here. Her cousin would not even be aware of the fact.

She stood looking round the formal hall with its carved chairs and big Sevres vases, the latter bare and a little dusty.

Always before there had been a profusion of flowers, frequently renewed—Madonna lilies, delphiniums, roses. The wide fireplace used to be banked with azaleas, in and out of season, but now it gaped empty, with an unsightly wad of paper thrown carelessly upon the hearth.

Paper? The crumpled fragment, of a pale blue colour, stirred a chord in her memory. She picked it up and straightened it out. Could it possibly be—?

Yes, here it was—the telegram sent from Havre this very afternoon. It had come, then, and been tossed aside as of no account. Queer, that. She studied it abstractedly, and again saw before her the butler's unfriendly stare, the hard, resentful face of Jeanne seen just now in the mirror. Why, it had not looked like Jeanne at all! She still recalled her sense of shock at finding the baleful glare fixed on her.

She shook herself free of disturbing fancies. Why make a mountain out of a molehill? These servants had had twenty-four hours of tension calculated to upset the evenest dispositions. Now things had calmed down, they would come to their senses. They could not bear her any personal ill will.

In the passage which cut across the main hall a whispered colloquy was going on between Jeanne and another maid. She could distinguish no words, but the voices sounded irritable, breaking now and again into smothered exclamations of annoyance. Finally a sentence uttered by Jeanne reached her ears:

"*Alors, la chambre Empire, c'est tout ce qu'on petit faire! Changez les draps, tout de suite!*"

Evidently they were holding a hurried debate as to where they were going to put her. Oh, well, one room was as good as another, if only they would be quick about it.

She caught sight of a blowsy female crossing the archway with an armful of linen. This person, who had a mop of straw-coloured hair and was unsuitably attired in a short black pleated skirt and a blue satin jumper very open at the neck, stared at her curiously. Catherine also stared. Never could she have imagined anyone here going about domestic duties clad in so incongruous a fashion. Even a *femme de ménage* would not be allowed to wear such clothes.

A quarter of an hour elapsed, then Jeanne came to inform her that her room was prepared.

"If you will come with me, mademoiselle, I will show it to you."

She was composed now, still not altogether friendly, but much her usual self. Catherine began to feel more comfortable.

"Thanks, Jeanne, I shall be glad to get off my things."

"You will understand our being a little confused, what with last night's excitement. None of us has slept since the night before last, and it never occurred to me to give orders for you, as I felt so sure you would not wish to stay."

She smiled, showing her very good, white teeth, but her agreeable air did not quite hide the reproach of her last words. Catherine felt unaccountably small and guilty, but she said nothing and followed the brisk figure along the passage which led to the far side of the apartment. Here, turning a corner, she saw ahead of her the stairway which communicated with the ground floor, and just beyond it an open door, in front of which her guide halted.

"I thought it best to put you as far from madame as possible," remarked the maid, signing to her to enter. "Madame sleeps badly, and is apt to be disturbed by the slightest noise."

"Quite right, Jeanne. This will do splendidly."

A glance assured her that her luggage had been brought up, the cabin-trunk placed on a stand at the foot of the bed.

"I hope you will not object to unpacking for yourself," continued her companion with a tentative manner. "The truth is I dare not leave madame for more than a few minutes in case she wakes. Just now is a critical time."

She seemed indeed rather preoccupied and a little restless, as though anxious to get away.

"Certainly, Jeanne—don't let me keep you. I shan't need anything."

A dozen questions regarding last night's affair crowded to her lips, but she decided to postpone them till to-morrow. She saw the maid bow her head in an absent, detached fashion.

"Thank you, mademoiselle. I will wish you good night."

The door was quickly shut, and Catherine was alone.

With a sigh of relief she removed her hat and looked about her. At once she realized that the room, although decent and comfortable, was one of the poorest in the apartment. It was furnished in Empire style, good mahogany with mountings of gilded bronze, the sort of thing now highly prized but twenty years ago picked up for little money. Walls, curtains and covers were alike of a cheap printed *toile* in Empire design, bees and lyres in medallions of rose and yellow. Upon the marble mantelpiece were candlesticks made of gun-metal with crystal drops, while the centre was occupied by a pierced basket of the kind of enamelled iron-work known as *tôle*.

The atmosphere was close, laden with a pungent, cloying odour, suggesting inferior scent. She could not think what it came from, but as she hated the smell she crossed to the curtained window and threw open the casement, letting in the damp night air.

Below lay the narrow side-street, lit by an arc-light at the corner. An occasional motor-car whizzed along the avenue, a section of which was visible. She remained for a few minutes looking out, still shaken by the news lately received. How near this had come to being a house of death! If it had not been for Jeanne's timely intervention, poor Mme. Bender would have breathed her last, no doubt in agony. Yet she found it difficult to grasp the fact of her cousin's suicidal impulses, so cheerful had been the letter written only a few weeks ago. It was frightening to know that a period of gloom could follow so quickly upon apparently tranquil spirits. The thought made her tremble with apprehension. Still she meant to stay. After all, it was only for two months, for she had promised to join some American friends later on and go with them to Italy. These people, a young Harvard professor and his wife, were enjoying a Sabbatical year in Europe, and were to pick her up in May or June, after they had completed the work they were doing at the British Museum.

Gazing absently down, she noticed a small man in a wide-brimmed black hat detach himself from the shadow of the chestnuts and stroll into the circle of light. In him she recognized the lounger she had encountered on entering the building. Still there! What did he want, hanging about like that for almost an hour? He had the appearance of waiting for something.

A moment later the mystery was solved. Below, a few yards to the left, she saw the private door of the apartment open, and a woman issue from it, dressed in a dark cloth coat and a plain pull-on hat. On the threshold she glanced rapidly about, then made straight for the corner, where she joined the black-clad lounger.

In the full glare of the lamp her identity was revealed. It was Jeanne.

Catherine experienced a mild astonishment. After what the maid had said only three minutes ago about not daring to leave her charge alone, it was a little surprising to find her going out, cloaked and hatted. She must be bent on some urgent errand. Hardly unforeseen, though, for the gesture with which she greeted the loiterer—brusquely familiar and charged, it seemed with irritation—showed plainly she expected to find him there. The two exchanged a few words, then hurried away together, down the avenue, out of sight.

It occurred to Catherine that this man, whose rude stare she had not forgotten, must be a relation of Jeanne's, or perhaps an admirer. Of course the woman must have some personal life, difficult as it was to imagine such a thing. For that matter, Catherine had sometimes wondered if there were not some sort of attachment between Jeanne and Eduardo, who for so many years had travelled about together in their service to the Benders. Not that she had ever seen any sign in either remotely suggesting the tender passion.

As she mused thus idly there sounded on the door a sharp rat-tat. She turned with a start.

"*Entrez!*" she called.

CHAPTER FIVE

A SERVANT entered with a tray upon which a meal was set, with silver-covered dishes.

She was none other than the blowsy woman Catherine had seen in the hall, and though she had put on a small, rather absurd apron, she still wore the satin blouse, and her bulging legs, encased in flesh-coloured stockings, ended with patent leather shoes run over at the sides. The mop of bleached hair stuck out unrestrainedly from a vapid, rouged face.

"*Bonsoir, mademoiselle!* As it is so very late, and as mademoiselle no doubt wishes to go early to bed, Jeanne thought it best that I should bring mademoiselle her dinner to her room."

"Oh, thank you! Put it here, on the little table."

The woman set down the tray, and as she bent over Catherine caught an overpowering blast of the same scent already permeating the atmosphere. The creature reeked of it. Instinctively the girl moved away, hoping the abominable odour might not cling to her own person.

Realizing that this extraordinary female was actually attached to the household, she inquired her name, whereupon the blonde vision beamed with a fatuous smile, placed her red hands on her hips, and volunteered a considerable amount of information regarding herself.

She was called Berthe, she was the *cuisinière*, and she had been in her present situation barely two months. The place was not too bad, for although there were only three domestics kept, there was the advantage of no entertaining, and she had all her evenings to herself. She was not much interested in cooking now, since she was going to be married before long, and in company with her prospective husband was planning to start a business of letting rooms in Paris Plage.

"But do you mean to say there are only three servants here now?" Catherine could not help inquiring in amazement.

The creature opened her china-blue eyes wide.

"*Mais si, mademoiselle, il n'y a que trois—Eduardo, Jeanne, et moi. Mais c'est suffisant, puis ce qu'il n'y a pas beaucoup à faire,*" she returned with a friendly yawn.

She added that she had only once seen madame, who kept strictly to her room and issued orders through Jeanne, if indeed she issued them at all. Since the housekeeper left Jeanne was in command. Poor madame dreaded strangers and saw no one, not even her friends when they called, but that was not remarkable as, *bien entendu*, madame was a little odd. Here Berthe touched her forehead with meaning. The poor lady, she went on, had to be constantly guarded, for fear she should do away with herself. Several times she had given them a fright, and last night, *vraiment!* there had been a *scène affreuse*. No one had closed an eye, and she herself had not been able to get out to see her fiancé.

Left alone, Catherine sat down to her solitary repast. It was decently served and not unpalatable, though the cold chicken and galantine suggested a hasty visit to a pastrycook's, while the soup had most certainly come out of a tin. However, she was not disposed to be critical, especially as she felt sure the cook had received no notification of her arrival. Indeed, the woman had assured her that Jeanne was in a state of stupefaction at the idea of anyone choosing to remain here at a time like this.

So Berthe, with her satin blouse and flagrant make-up, was the cook! It was a violent change from the days when Harry Bender's table had been noted, and his chef, in a tall white cap, had on occasions of ceremony been invited into the dining-room to receive congratulations and to partake of a glass of *fine champagne*. She sighed, not because she had expected to find anything approaching the former standard, but simply over things in general—her genial cousin gone, his widow mentally unbalanced and confined to her room, the home in which he had taken so much pride given over to domestics who neglected, if not abused, his cherished possessions. Already her eye had detected small evidences of slipshod management. The best of servants, she reflected, grow careless when left to their own devices.

Oh well, of what importance was it, so long as the invalid herself was properly attended? She had seen a good deal of Jeanne, and felt sure that, however imperfect she might be as an administrative, she would never fail in devotion to her mistress.

Except for the breezy cook, who returned to bring coffee, no one came near her that evening. She might as well have been in an hotel. In half an hour's time she heard Jeanne re-enter the apartment, but saw nothing of her. Somewhere close by she assumed that Mme. Bender was sleeping, prostrated from shock and stupefied by a sedative. She wondered when she would see her, if at all, and the uncertainty as to what to expect filled her with vague discomfort. Easy to picture the clinging woman as rudderless, dependent, her grip of life shaken, but the idea of recurring mania was difficult to grasp. One could not associate the gentle Germaine with any violent action.

She set about unpacking and arranging her belongings, and in so doing made several minor discoveries of a disagreeable nature. First, the enamelled basket on the mantel contained cigarette stumps and ashes; in the dressing-table drawer was a little cheap, red comb, the teeth of which held a wisp of fair hair; the paper at the bottom of the drawer was smeared with grease-paint and powder, at the same time sending forth a wave of the now familiar perfume.

Last she noticed with disgust that the bright pink soap on the washstand was partly used and still moist.

The conclusion was unavoidable. The room until this evening had been used by Berthe herself, who, in her haste to turn out of it, had neglected to remove all traces of her occupancy.

Really this was too much! In an apartment of this size, was there no other room available? How poor Germaine would suffer if she knew! She could not help resenting the advantage taken of a helpless invalid, and most of all she held Jeanne responsible, excellent though she was. For a moment she was conscious of a personal affront, and in order to calm herself had to bring to mind the maid's long and faithful care of her mistress, the undeniable fact that the woman had proved herself both kind and trustworthy.

The hot bath soothed her ruffled temper, and eventually she fell asleep between soft, monogrammed sheets, with the sound of pattering raindrops in her ears. Just before dozing off she thought of the young solicitor she had met in the train. What attentive, serious eyes he had, lighting up now and again with a most agreeable flash of humour! At the beginning there had been a sort of barrier between them, probably because he was English and did not quite know what to make of Americans, but at the last, on the station platform, she had felt suddenly as though he were a real friend. She longed to tell him what had happened here, but she did not know if she would have the courage to ring him up as he had begged her to do. Once more she asked herself if he had known anything about her cousin's condition which he had not seen fit to disclose; but even as the question crossed her mind it was eclipsed by the vision, wholly inconsequent, of his strong, big hands as they had grasped the sill of the taxi. . . .

Morning broke brilliant and windy. It promised well that Berthe, bringing her breakfast, should have had the grace to make herself almost presentable, appearing in a clean print frock, even though her hair was adorned with tiny combs to achieve a "water-wave" and secured in place by a purple veil. The coffee was capital, the croissants crisp and delicious.

Eagerly Catherine inquired news of her hostess, and learned that she had passed a peaceful night and, according to Jeanne, was in a fairly calm state of nerves. Perhaps, after the doctor had paid his call, mademoiselle might be permitted to see her. It all depended on the physician's verdict.

This was slightly reassuring, yet to tell the truth she was nervous at the thought of conversing with a woman who two days ago had tried to take her own life. One never knew when another crisis might occur, or what might cause it. Still, she could ascertain whether or not her visit was welcome, and act accordingly.

As soon as she was dressed she ventured forth, in search of some place to sit and read till the doctor had come and gone. The formal salon oppressed her, especially in its present state of dustiness, but she recalled a small, cheerful room next it, used by her cousin as his study. The door stood ajar, she pushed it wide to enter.

The next instant she gave a faint gasp.

In a big leather chair sprawled Eduardo, legs upon the writing-table, face hidden by a copy of *Le Petit Parisien*. Around him hung wreaths of cigarette smoke, while ashes lay thick on the brown carpet.

Catherine drew back as though struck, but before she could escape the butler had muttered something hardly to be construed as an apology and shuffled out. As he passed her his eyes, muddy like those of an angry bull, surveyed her with abashed but scornful defiance.

Her colour rose, her heart pounded uncontrollably. What insufferable insolence! The man was disgracefully untidy, too, his usually sleek hair bristling rough above the narrow strip of forehead, his chin blue from lack of shaving, carpet slippers on his feet.

After a few seconds she forced herself to treat the matter as a joke. Why work herself up over what did not concern her? Eduardo had simply fallen back to what must have been his original state, a reversion not to be wondered at in the circumstances. After opening the window to rid the room of smoke, she made herself comfortable on the sofa and picked up her book.

However, it was hard to fix her attention. Everything here, from the big mahogany desk to the painting of a favourite race-horse over the mantel, recalled insistently her late relative's presence. Shutting her eyes she could plainly see the tall, blond New Englander leaning back in the chair the butler had just vacated, his silvered hair smooth above keen boyish eyes, his fresh, unlined face so oddly suggesting that of a handsome schoolmaster.

She had always liked Cousin Harry. Her mother's first cousin, the sole heir to a wealthy Boston banker, he had come to France in his youth, married a French wife, and from thence on had pursued a carefree, generous existence, travelling widely, collecting *objets d'art*, and breeding racehorses. In spite of his pleasure-loving instincts he had somehow preserved the backbone of his Puritan ancestry, and had remained singularly unspoiled, never drinking too much, never running after women. His attachment to Germaine had been well known, and for all his popularity he had been happiest in her company. Probably he alone had understood the shy, elusive woman now so shipwrecked by his death.

Thinking of these things Catherine heard a ring at the bell and soon afterwards saw through the crack of the door a heavily-built man with a spade-shaped black beard lumber past, escorted by Jeanne. In the distance a door closed. Then there was silence again, presently broken by subdued whistling which the listener attributed to the cook.

Twenty minutes elapsed, after which the doctor, still accompanied by Jeanne, returned along the hall. Close to the study the two halted for a conference, and Catherine heard a deep bass rumble alternating with the staccato utterance of the maid, whispered and mysterious.

At first there was only a confused babble but eventually after a pregnant pause a few sentences emerged clear. The physician inquired in booming accents oddly puzzled.

"*Vous êtes sûre, entendu, qu'il n'y a pas de souris là bas?*"

To which the reply came, positive and a little impatient:

"*Mais, voyons, monsieur! Un souris, dans cet apartement, parfaitement soigné, tout propre? Elle rêve, la pauvre—c'est évident!*"

"*Ah, la malheureuse! Je crains que vous avez raison.*"

The two moved away.

Catherine knit her brows, perplexed. A mouse? What had a mouse to do with madame, and why should Jeanne make so indignant a denial? She could think of no explanation.

It seemed an age before she caught Jeanne's voice, brisk and business-like, inquiring as to the whereabouts of Mademoiselle West. Without waiting for a reply, Catherine jumped up and ran into the hall.

"I am here, Jeanne. What did the doctor say?"

She fancied the maid looked a little annoyed at finding her at her elbow, but her countenance quickly cleared, resuming its old expression of suavity.

"Ah, there you are, mademoiselle! Madame is much better to-day. The doctor thinks you may be allowed to see her for a quarter of an hour—no longer, for it would not be wise. You will, of course, be careful not to excite her in any way, as she is still in a very nervous state."

"You may trust me, Jeanne."

Keyed up with expectancy, she followed the maid along the transverse passage which communicated with the rooms opening on the court. At the third door Jeanne paused, listened a moment, then grasped the girl's arm and whispered in her ear.

"Another thing, mademoiselle, which the doctor told me to caution you about. Whatever you do, try not to contradict madame. She is apt to get strange ideas into her head, to imagine things which are not true. It is part of her illness, and to oppose her may bring on a *crise*. You will be very careful about this?"

Catherine nodded, and the next instant the maid had slipped quietly into the room, motioning to her to wait. From the other side of the door came a plaintive voice which she well knew. It filled her with surprise to find it so little altered.

"She is there? Tell her to come in—at once, at once! I am longing to see her."

"Yes, yes, madame. I only wished to make sure that madame is ready to receive mademoiselle."

"But of course I am ready! I am waiting! Catherine, my dear child, come in, come in!"

With inward trepidation Catherine opened the door and entered.

CHAPTER SIX

She found herself in a room unexpectedly small and narrow, furnished with sparse simplicity. Nearly everything was white, walls, covers, the bed-hangings, pendent from a sort of crown. The only colour was contained in the dull mauve-grey carpet and in the dark wood of the severely beautiful Directoire furniture. The curtains were drawn, so that although it was nearly midday there was a clear, luminous twilight. On the panel beside the bed, facing the entrance, hung a silver crucifix, under which were wax candles in brackets.

All this was but a general impression. What the girl chiefly saw was the fragile figure in the bed, the grey eyes staring out of the drawn and pallid face, the thin arms outstretched to greet her.

"Catherine! You have come, then! I did not know till a moment ago. My dear—my dear!"

There was strained pathos in the quivering features, a catch in the voice which poured forth its words in a rapid torrent. Tears dimmed the invalid's eyes, the veins stood out on her waxen temples as with feverish intensity she kissed the young girl on both cheeks, then clung to the warm hands with her own transparent ones.

"My darling Germaine!"

Now the first shock was over Catherine felt easier. Until this moment she had nurtured a cankering doubt as to whether or not Mme. Bender would recognize her.

"Madame! madame! Calm yourself! You will suffer for this."

It was Jeanne who spoke, solicitous and reproving, hovering near by as though in readiness to interpose at the slightest warning symptom. Catherine had a fleeting impression of watchful eyes regarding them anxiously.

"No, no, Jeanne, I am quite myself. You need have no fear. Only I am so very, very glad to see this dear child, who has come all the way across the ocean to be with me. Leave us for a little. I promise I shall not become excited."

"Very well, madame, I will go, but I shall not be far away. If madame wants me, she has only to call."

She withdrew into the adjoining room, not without a backward glance full of doubt, and, it seemed to the girl, distrust. Through the half-open door she could be heard moving about, as if reluctant to remove herself from earshot. Evidently, although the patient appeared quite normal, she was not satisfied. Probably experience had taught her not to rely upon these fortunate phases too implicitly.

The Frenchwoman still detained Catherine's hands, stroking them with trembling, quick movements. Her eyes devoured the vivid young face.

"Sit there, my child, in the big chair, quite close to me. Now, tell me everything about yourself. Did you have a good crossing, and was Eduardo in time at the station? You were well looked after?"

"Everything was perfect, Germaine dear! Quite, quite perfect."

On no account must Mme. Bender know what had actually happened. Clearly she had not the least suspicion that her orders were neglected.

"And your room? Do you like it? I told Jeanne to give you my own old one, at the corner. I have lain here thinking how charming you would look against the green and gold. Are you happy there?"

"It is a beautiful room, Germaine. It is like you to think of it."

"No, no. I have nothing pleasanter to think of, here alone. I have always marvelled how, out of that dull, cold New England, where no one has any eyebrows, you could have got that colouring of a Tintoretto. It warms one, like the sun."

She ran on flutteringly in her pure and lovely French, and as the sentences followed one another with rapid irrelevance the girl scanned her features for some sign of aberration. After a few minutes she began to feel less uneasy. Germaine was much as she had always been—aged, of course, and tremulous from weakness, but otherwise little changed. In the haggard features it was still possible to trace remnants of the beauty which had first captivated Harry Bender. The luxuriant hair was streaked with grey, but it retained its natural wave, and was worn as she had always worn it, drawn back from a central parting to show her delicate ears. On the right temple it revealed the end of the ugly scar which marked the injury of last year.

Above all else it was the eyes which held Catherine's attention. Wide, strained and wistful, the eyes of a neurasthenic, they now riveted their gaze eagerly on the girl's face, now darted this way and that with frequent watchful glances towards the open door. They expressed timidity, lack of assurance, and some other less easily defined emotion baffling to the onlooker; yet in them Catherine could detect nothing to indicate loss of reason.

Nor in the rather childish prattle, skipping like a dragonfly from topic to topic, was there anything unusual. At no time had Mme. Bender possessed a keen or logical brain, though fineness of taste and an evasive charm had in a great measure made up for lack of understanding.

Always she had given the impression of being withdrawn in an inner fantastic world, and when it came to practical affairs she had accepted the dictates of her husband without question. Now it struck Catherine that these characteristics had assumed exaggerated form. She had definitely reverted to a child-like state, trusting and fearing without reason, shrinking from reality and claiming protection. Just how far this retirement might extend it was impossible to say.

All was now silent in the next room, though the girl did not remark the fact until upon her companion's face she caught an expression of acute listening. Then she knew that Germaine wished to tell her something, and had been waiting for the maid to go away.

"Catherine, my dear!"

She whispered the words, meantime clutching Catherine's arm in a nervous grasp.

"What is it, Germaine?"

"Yesterday—or was it the day before?—I had a dreadful experience. Something so stupid happened. Have they told you?"

"A little, Germaine. You drank something by mistake. Wasn't that it?" returned the girl, embarrassed to find a suitable reply.

The grey eyes took on an eager glitter.

"A mistake—yes, yes! Just that. So foolish of me—I cannot yet think how it came about." She paused, again listening, then continued earnestly: "I want you to believe me when I say it was an accident. I had here on my table my sleeping-draught in a little glass, and in another glass a solution of carbolic in which at night I put a little dental plate. You understand?" she demanded urgently, her eyes searching Catherine's face.

"Of course. What happened then?"

"You see, one of the glasses is green. That is the one that contains the sleeping-draught. Well, while Jeanne was out of the room getting me a hot-water bottle, I took up the green glass and drank a little. Only a very little, for at once I knew I had taken the wrong thing. Ah!" with a convulsive shudder, her eyes closing, "it was strong, so strong! It burnt my throat. My throat is still raw, though Jeanne declares that is my imagination. You know sometimes my imagination is very vivid. . . . Yet I cannot see how . . ." Her voice trailed off and she pressed her fingers to her throat with a distracted gesture. "Anyhow I screamed. 'Jeanne, Jeanne, come at once!' I called, 'I have taken poison!' But she was at the back of the apartment, she could not hear me. Meantime the drop I had swallowed burnt like fire all the way down. I was in agony. It was a long time before I could make her hear—poor Jeanne! She was terribly upset."

Spent by the recollection, she lay back upon her pillows, while perspiration broke out and lay in heavy drops on the waxen skin. Catherine eyed her in keen distress.

"There, dear, it is all over now. Try to forget about it."

Suddenly the prone figure stiffened, sat bolt upright, staring with a look of terror. At the quick change Catherine realized the fact that she was alone with a patient who a short time ago had suffered an alarming attack. Ought she to summon Jeanne? Yet a second before she had been impressed by the lucidity, the poignant underlying conviction, of the invalid's recital. She watched, uncertain what to do.

"Forget it! Ah, that is what I must not do!" breathed the hoarse voice fearfully. "I must remember it, so I cannot commit so frightful an error again. The great trouble is my memory. I forget things so easily— so easily! I must have forgotten which glass was which, otherwise how could I have done what I did? You see? It shakes one's confidence. It—"

She checked herself with a gasp, eyes dilating. Following the direction of their gaze, Catherine saw that Jeanne had come back, was standing just inside the door. So engrossed had she been by her cousin's excitement she had not heard the light footfall.

The maid approached, anxious and disapproving.

"Madame! madame!" she declared with authority, "this will not do! I implore you not to speak of that affair. Mademoiselle, you see? She is getting into a panic again. Did I not warn you?" she ended accusingly.

Catherine thought it better not to reply. Besides, her attention was transfixed by the instant alteration which had taken place with the patient. Mme. Bender's wan features assumed a timid, conciliatory smile as she relaxed and lay back, breathing hard.

"It is nothing, Jeanne! I was only telling mademoiselle how imbecile it was of me to mistake the plain glass for the green. Never in my life have I done such a thing. It makes me feel quite, quite odd!" She finished with an hysterical laugh of apology infinitely pathetic.

The maid, now on the other side of the bed, nodded at Catherine with grim significance.

"One makes these mistakes sometimes when one is not quite oneself," she remarked soothingly yet with emphasis. "One imagines all sorts of things. Madame knows now that she was wrong, because I showed her the plain glass with the disinfectant still in it. Is it not so, madame?"

"Ah, yes, that is so. You were right, of course," agreed the invalid with eager alacrity. Then she caught the maid's unresponsive hand in hers and pressed it affectionately. "What should I do, where should I be, without my dear, good Jeanne? No one, Catherine, would do for me what she does," she added, as though longing to assure the other of her appreciation.

"You had better go now, mademoiselle," suggested the woman firmly. "This has been quite enough for one day."

The girl rose, but a lightning clutch at her sleeve pulled her back again.

"No, Jeanne, let her stay! I will not excite myself, really I will not!"

With unmoved face the maid bent and loosed the fragile fingers.

"No, madame," she said quietly, then stooping so that her lips were close to the other's ear she whispered in a low, distinct tone: "Madame must try to behave reasonably, if she wishes to be permitted company at all."

At once Mme. Bender gave in with complete docility. "Very well, then, I will do as you say. But she is to come again soon? Catherine, my dear, you will sit with me often, will you not? I am alone so much, and I think and think—such strange, disturbing thoughts . . ."

"But of course, dear, I mean to be with you every day. As long as you will have me."

She kissed the thin cheek and withdrew, gravely nonplussed by the recent scene. Jeanne followed her out, closing the door softly, and when they had reached the bend in the passage spoke in an undertone.

"You see?" she said, and her tone though sorrowful held a touch of triumph—almost, thought Catherine, as if she believed her word had been doubted.

"I don't know what to say, Jeanne," faltered the girl. "Madame was much more rational than I expected. In fact, if I had not been told about this insanity, I doubt if I should have noticed anything. It was only when she mentioned the poison—"

A quick gleam came into the other's eyes.

"Ah, yes, I heard a little of what madame was saying. It is as I told you, she is trying to justify her action and make us think it was unintentional."

"You are quite certain it wasn't accidental?" suggested Catherine doubtfully. "It seemed to me—"

The maid raised her eyebrows.

"Who can say?" she returned after a pause. "But it is strange, is it not, how the mention of it throws her into a fever? No, I am afraid she has lain there making up this story, which she now believes to be true. She is often like that."

"Do you mean, Jeanne," whispered Catherine, recalling the marked discrepancy between the invalid's statement and the maid's, "that what she says about calling you and your not hearing her is an invention?"

A pitying smile broke over the sallow face.

"I am sorry to say, mademoiselle, there is not one word of truth in it," she replied positively. "I was upon the threshold at the time, and snatched the glass from her lips. She did not know, of course, that I was watching. Eduardo, Berthe, both heard me cry out, and ran to see what was the matter."

There seemed no doubt about it. Catherine pondered the matter unhappily.

"But why? Why should she want to take her life?" was all she could manage to say. "A year ago I saw no sign of such a thing, wretched though she was."

"Ah, that is the nature of her malady. Melancholia. It comes in fits, and when the spell is upon her the poor creature cannot be held responsible. Only three weeks ago—but no, I must not alarm you unduly," she broke off, closing her lips with determination.

"Tell me, Jeanne, I would much rather know the truth."

"Well, then," admitted the woman reluctantly, watching her as she spoke, "if you must know, I came into the room there to find madame, in her nightdress, standing upon the window-sill, preparing to throw herself into the court below. If you will look you will see that I have had two bars fastened across the opening, to prevent her attempting it a second time."

Catherine drew in her breath sharply. This was something not easily explained away. Painfully she inquired the details, and learned that after the rescue Mme. Bender suffered from nervous collapse, following which the entire affair appeared to be erased from her memory. Not once had she referred to it, nor asked why the bars were there.

"You understand why it is I have moved my bed into madame's dressing-room," went on the maid. "As I told you last night, it is not safe to leave her for any length of time."

Inconsequently Catherine recalled Jeanne's departure the evening before, but naturally said nothing. After all, her charge had no doubt been sound asleep.

"Of course it isn't," she replied earnestly. "But all the same it is too much for you. Oughtn't you to engage a professional nurse?"

The look of fanatical obstinacy she had seen before tightened the strongly marked features.

"Ab no, mademoiselle. Such a thing might drive the poor creature to desperation. No, I have served her for fifteen years, and I shall continue to do so now that her need of me is so great. Who so well as myself understands her, who would protect her, not only from herself, but"—she hesitated, then finished with slow emphasis—"from those who perhaps might do her injury?"

What on earth could she mean? Catherine stared at her in astonishment.

"Surely, Jeanne, there can be no such person. Why do you suppose there is?"

For a second there was guarded silence. Then the maid, with a suggestion of a shrug, replied:

"I must not make any accusations, mademoiselle. But does it not strike you as strange, to say the least, that on the occasion I have mentioned and also two days ago the attempts at suicide should have followed close upon the visits of an old friend?"

This was news indeed!

"Whom do you mean, Jeanne? I understood madame saw no visitors."

"No one, except"—here she halted and glanced about her, then brought out the name with apparent reluctance—"Mademoiselle Cushing."

Hermione Cushing! Catherine could not suppress a start. She gazed fixedly into the unflinching eyes of the maid.

"Miss Cushing!" she echoed, wonderingly. "But what possible reason is there to connect her visits with—with—"

"There may be no connection. Do not misunderstand me, mademoiselle. Only, since you have put the question to me, I will say plainly that this lady, who calls herself an old and intimate friend, seems to me to exert a bad, a depressing influence on madame. So sure am I of this that I have done my utmost to discourage her coming; but," and she made a gesture of helplessness, "I cannot always keep her away. I know that she persistently speaks of things which are distressing to anyone in madame's condition."

"What sort of things, Jeanne?" demanded the girl curiously.

At the same time she rapidly reviewed the disjointed letter which had so upset her peace of mind, recalling the writer's complaints about the difficulty in seeing her friend. Was there anything behind it all?

The maid's eyes turned from hers secretively.

"Mademoiselle Cushing cannot forget that madame is a rich woman, has been for years her patron and supporter. No doubt she is afraid that madame will die and leave her unprovided for. In short, she thinks always of feathering her nest."

Indefinite as the explanation was, it hinted at unpleasing possibilities. It seemed to her she was beginning to understand in part the problem with which Jeanne had to cope. Had she not somewhere heard the prayer, "Oh, Lord, save us from our friends!"?

She came to herself to find the intelligent brown eyes regarding her shrewdly.

"And now, mademoiselle, that you see what all this is like, do you not think it would be happier for you to leave this sad abode? You can do no good here—you are young, you wish to be gay. It is no life for one whose duty does not call her to it. Believe me, I know what I am saying when I beg you to go elsewhere to live."

Catherine had not expected this renewed importunity.

"On the contrary, Jeanne, I shall be quite content to stay, at least for a few months, and I honestly think I may have a good effect on madame's spirits. She was so evidently glad to see me just now—"

She stopped in time to see an expression of strong displeasure settle over her companion's features. Before she could finish her sentence, however, the silence was pierced by a long ring at the telephone. She found herself listening mechanically to the gruff voice of Eduardo answering the call.

A moment later the butler issued from the study, came a step towards them, then, spying Catherine, halted.

"A gentleman to speak to you, miss," he announced in an offhand manner, more loudly than was necessary. "A Mr. Geoffrey Macadam."

Her friend of the train! The tension snapped, as with a glad sense of relief she hurried towards the study.

She could not say what instinct made her glance back at the two servants, nor why the penetrating look of question passing between them should cause her such poignant discomfort. Certainly it told her that she was an unwelcome alien in their midst, but she half-fancied an additional meaning less easy to interpret.

A tremor shook her voice as she spoke into the telephone.

CHAPTER SEVEN

GEOFFREY Macadam had been going through a struggle. Why this consuming eagerness to acquire news of an American girl whom he had not known existed till yesterday afternoon? Was it genuine anxiety for her welfare, or simply the hankering to hear again a voice which for some inscrutable reason lingered disturbingly in his memory? Suspecting his motives he had fought for an entire hour, during which the telephone drew him like a magnet.

Sheer nonsense, this! She was there haunting him the whole time. Twice last night he had dreamed about her, and even now her dark, shining eyes came between him and the work upon his desk, scattering his ideas to the winds of heaven. There was a kind of spell about it. . . . Not that it would last, of course. This sort of thing never did. In all likelihood after he had looked at the original eyes a time or two . . .

This decided him. He would ring her up, ask her to lunch—not immediately, that was too impetuous—but later, say the end of the week. Then he would see that she was just an ordinary mortal, and as such put her into her proper place.

On firm ground now, his scruples placated, he did what he had been longing to do and put through the call.

Two minutes more, and his prudent resolutions were broken to bits, all because the familiar voice had a catch in it and an undercurrent of excitement vibrating through its guarded replies. Clearly Miss West was upset about something. Lunch at the end of the week became dinner to-night—if she could manage it. Could she? There was a little gasp of astonishment, a pause, then a wavering consent, in which it thrilled him to detect a note of thankfulness. That meant that she really wanted to talk to him about her cousin. Well, he also wanted to talk about her cousin. Only there was no use pretending that Mme. Bender's affairs could cause his pulse to beat in this ridiculous fashion, or rouse in him a thirsty craving like the desire for water after a hectic night. What had come over his well-ordered self? He must take his emotions in hand, or there was no knowing to what stupidity they might lead.

Freeing himself from his reverie, he crossed the reception room to his father's office. He wanted to inform his parent of his meeting with the late Harry Bender's cousin, a fact he had not previously mentioned because the elder Macadam had been dining out last night. Secretly he suspected himself of a fatuous need to speak to someone about the subject of his thoughts.

Blair Macadam was leaning back in his swivelled chair dictating to his secretary, an attractive-looking English girl with well-waved hair and a smart blue serge frock. He glanced at his son from beneath heavy grizzled brows, but went dryly on, now and then running his fingers through the coarse grey hair which stood up stiffly above his furrowed forehead. He was a big, powerfully built Scot, who in his forty years' exile from his native Edinburgh had never lost his accent, noticeable even in his careful French.

Geoffrey walked to the window and looked down upon the busy traffic of the rue Auber. Across the way loomed the square, dingy bulk of the Opéra, round whose island circled a ceaseless stream of hooting taxis and motor-busses, constant menace to the harassed pedestrian. The sun streamed down, spring was in the air.

"*Croyez-vous, cher monsieur, l'expression de mes sentiments*—and so forth. Get those typed as soon as you can. That will be all now, Miss Curwen."

The secretary gathered up her pads and departed, not without an unobtrusive flicker of the eye towards the junior partner's unconscious back. It was characteristic of the old man that he took note of the glance, but paid absolutely no attention to it.

"Well, Geoffrey?" he said, turning over the letters on his desk.

"It's nothing much," replied his son. "Only coming up from Havre on the boat-train I met an American—West her name is—who it seems is some relation of Harry Bender's. I thought you might be interested."

"Going to stay with the widow, is she?" remarked the old lawyer with no evidence of special concern. "What age is she? Responsible woman?"

"No—quite young. Twenty-three, perhaps."

Suddenly self-conscious Geoffrey lit a cigarette, offering his case to his father.

"Thanks, not till after lunch. Well, I daresay it will be dull enough for her." He continued to sort papers. "Odd your mentioning the Benders, though. While you were away that woman came in again to me. Second or third time in six months."

"What woman?"

"Mme. Bender's maid. Seems to have a good deal of authority."

The younger man made a movement of interest.

"Oh! What did she come about?"

"A message from her mistress, who apparently sees to nothing for herself these days. Lost the key of her safety-deposit box at the bank, and wanted to get a duplicate."

"What did you do about it?"

"Oh, communicated with the bank. Told her, of course, that it would be necessary to have a written order, signed by Mme. Bender. However she knew all about that, and produced the paper properly signed. Thoroughly business-like."

Geoffrey frowned suddenly. Had not Miss Cushing, at his one memorable interview with her, made some obscure reference to the contents of the safety-deposit? He was sure, he recalled something of the sort.

"What do you suppose Mme. Bender keeps at the bank?" he inquired.

"Jewels, I should say. You know she seldom wore any, though Bender must have given her some valuable ones."

"Did this maid happen to speak of her mistress's health? Her mental condition, I mean. You know I mentioned it to you some time ago."

"Did you? I forget. In any case nothing was said about it the other day. I gather that she's merely confined to the apartment. She can sign her name, at all events. Why do you ask? Nothing wrong, is there?"— and he glanced up keenly.

His son paused on the threshold.

"I don't know that there is. I happened to hear that she is regarded as rather—well, erratic."

"Always was," murmured his father. "Nothing new about that."

"By the way," remarked the young man, pausing in his exit, "you might tell Elspeth I'm dining out."

Elspeth was his married sister, who lived at Fontainebleau, but who at the moment was staying with his father and himself at their flat in the rue d'Assas. Father and son maintained a bachelor existence they liked to feel was all sufficient, yet both were quick to fall into consulting and relying upon Elspeth during her brief visits to their *ménage.*

At a little before eight that evening Geoffrey drove his Citroën over the Pont de la Concorde, along the Cour la Reine and so past the Place d'Iéna and the Place du Trocadéro to the Avenue Henri Martin. He was conscious of a vivid elation, yet in proportion as this sensation soared within him he felt himself growing each moment stiffer and more awkward. Why, he asked angrily, should anticipation exert so petrifying an effect upon his powers of speech and movement? With his whole soul he envied the easy, expansive youths of his generation, their readiness to pay compliments and to take small liberties without giving offense. Never could he hope to be one of these lucky beings. He was far removed from a prig, nor did he cherish any footling illusions about womenfolk. Except for his school and university days he had spent his life in Paris, a city which does not foster illusions of any kind. No, it was not from ignorance nor prudery if he froze at a glance the exceedingly desirable girl he was hastening to meet. It was some despised quality handed down to him through a long line of Scottish forebears, as inseparable from their fibre as the heather from their hills. He could as easily cut off his right arm as to rid himself of its restraint.

It might have soothed his ire to know that this adamantine exterior carried its own compensations, that a fair number of women, French as well as English, regarded him with covetous interest, feeling as women do that a nut hard to crack must contain a rewarding kernel; but little suspicion of this penetrated his mind, even though for the past year he had been dodging the advances of at least two damsels, well-bred and amply dowered. What vanity was his left him uninformed as to his powers of personal seduction.

He crossed the well of the court and entered the *ascenseur*. Alighting at the *entresol* he became at once aware of angry voices, a man's and a woman's, engaged in turbulent altercation. The sounds came from the direction of the Bender apartment, and as he turned the corner he saw the maid, Jeanne, making vigorous efforts to shut the door upon an intruder, a man in chauffeur's uniform, who, having wedged his foot within the entrance, stubbornly refused to budge.

"I tell you, I am not going to take my dismissal from such as you!" shouted the aggressor furiously. "After five years, to be sent about my business, and by another domestic! No, a thousand times no! It is not done—a serious man, with a family, too, chucked for no reason! I won't have it! I insist on seeing madame, devil take you and yours!"

The woman's features glowered with black rage.

"Must I repeat, dirty pig, that madame is ill, can see no one, by the doctor's orders? I have given you her message. Let that be enough for you. Now take yourself off!"

"Not till I've been told why I'm given the sack. Do you imagine I am going to say to my next patron that Mme. Bender, of the Avenue Henri Martin, has sent me packing after five years, without a character? Name of a pipe, no, you infernal schemer! I intend to see madame in person and get to the bottom of this!"

Here the brawlers caught sight of Geoffrey and lapsed into sullen silence. With slow reluctance the chauffeur withdrew his foot and turned away, breathing hard. Geoffrey had a glimpse of a white, enraged face, chin mutinous, eyes blazing. He was a youngish man of decent appearance, and, contrary to Geoffrey's first impression, seemed to be perfectly sober. He shot a glance at the newcomer as though of half a mind to appeal to him for support, thought better of it, and made off towards the stairs. The woman gave a snort of triumph.

"Another time," she muttered in vitriolic accents, "he will not get past the concierge. I'll see to that! Making a scene like this in a respectable house!"

Then pulling herself together she addressed Geoffrey with courteous composure.

"Monsieur—?"

"Good evening. Will you kindly tell Mademoiselle West that Monsieur Macadam is here?"

On hearing the name a subtle alteration came over the pronounced features. The lips drew back in a mechanical smile, the brown eyes scrutinized the visitor with searching keenness.

"Ah-h-h!" breathed the maid with a prolonged inflection. "It is for mademoiselle! Come in, monsieur. I will inform mademoiselle."

It was needless to do so, however, for at that moment Catherine, ready in her coat and hat, issued from the salon. At once the expression of her face arrested Geoffrey's attention to such an extent his self-consciousness deserted him and he forgot everything except curiosity and concern. He could not say that she looked frightened; that was too strong a word; but her shining eyes were wide with bewilderment, and in each cheek burned a spot of crimson evidently not rouge. She approached him eagerly, hand outstretched with the informality of an old friend.

"Oh!" she cried, with what he fancied was relief in her tone, "how nice to see you! I've got such a lot to talk to you about!"

She faltered in the midst of the last sentence, as though disconcerted by the fixed gaze of the maid's eyes, somehow at variance with her smiling mouth. Neither she nor Geoffrey had any idea as to how much English the woman understood, but both detected a quick narrowing of the lids not altogether friendly.

"Mademoiselle has the key I gave her?" inquired the woman with smooth solicitude.

"Certainly, Jeanne, it is in my bag."

"And if you should come in late, mademoiselle, you will be careful not to make a noise?" pursued the other with perfect suavity. "It is so easy for madame to be disturbed."

"I'll be very quiet," returned the girl. "And I shan't be at all late."

Rather quickly she preceded Geoffrey through the door, and as he reached her side he thought that the colour staining her cheeks burned a still brighter hue, but she said nothing till the cage of the lift was sinking to the ground floor. Then suddenly she let herself go with a burst of confidence, though her voice remained lowered.

"Oh! how thankful I am to get away!" she cried, with a half-ashamed laugh. "That flat is getting horribly on my nerves. Silly, isn't it?" she added, with an appeal for tolerance.

"What's the matter?" he demanded anxiously. "Anything gone wrong?"

She hesitated, biting her lip.

"Yes and no. I don't know what to say. Mostly it's just a—a feeling. . . . What happened a few minutes ago, for instance. Did you see a man talking to Jeanne as you came up?"

"Yes, Mme. Bender's chauffeur, I fancy. They were having some sort of shindy."

"So that's who it was! I wondered. You see, I heard nearly the whole of the dispute, I couldn't help it. It was quite right, of course, for Jeanne to refuse to let him see Mme. Bender, but—well, she was abusively rude to him from the beginning, and I somehow felt he had a real grievance. Odd for him to be dismissed without any reason, don't you think? Not a bit like my cousin to do that. I can't understand it."

It flashed into Geoffrey's mind that in all probability the dismissal had come from the maid herself, in which case Mme. Bender knew nothing about it, but he shook his head in silence. After all, it was only supposition, founded on a knowledge of the autocratic ways of old and trusted servants.

"Oh, well"—and Catherine sighed as though trying to throw off an irksome load. "Why bother? I came out to enjoy myself."

"Right! Then first of all, where shall we go? A lively restaurant with music, or a quiet one?"

"Oh, a quiet one! You see I want to tell you about something rather dreadful which happened just before I arrived. That and other things. The fact is, it's all decidedly worse here than I thought."

"In what way?" he demanded quickly.

While they were abreast of the concierge's domain she made no reply, but as soon as she was seated in the car she described the incident which two nights ago had thrown the household into confusion.

"Good God!" he cried, seriously shocked. "So it's as bad as that! I'd no idea."

"I'm afraid it is. But let's talk of cheerful topics for a bit. Later on I'll tell you everything."

They whirled along by the way of the Champs-Élysées to a typically French restaurant in one of the Grand Boulevards, where the food was noted for its excellence. Here, against the wall in an alcove with shaded lights, they pored together over a menu-sheet, while an elderly functionary with a bottle nose bent an attentive ear to catch their gastronomic wishes.

Catherine was to find that her new friend knew how to order a meal. The first sip of the amber, icy cocktail set the stamp of success upon the evening and by the time the *oeufs Bourgognaises* arrived, embedded in their incomparable sauce, she was prepared to pay him the tribute of a willing admiration. With the first real hunger she had felt since she reached Paris, she fell to in appreciative silence.

Meanwhile Geoffrey studied her as closely as he dared, almost chagrined to find her much lovelier than the picture he had carried about with him. American women were as smart as the French, he decided, with better figures, too, and a look of finer breeding. Also they knew not only what to put on but what to leave off, scorning to distract the eye with irrelevant detail.

How effective her plain parchment-coloured velvet was against the red plush of the seat! It defined her slender body delicately, while her tiny, black hat was so close-fitting as to appear almost indistinguishable from her hair. Round her throat lay a necklace of flat, plaited gold, toning subtly with her warm pallor, and she wore but one other ornament, a ruby ring with a big decorative setting, its single stone repeating the crimson which formed her present background.

For the moment the luminous eyes were veiled by the pensive sweep of her lashes. He longed, man-like, to rekindle the dancing flames in them, but found himself tongue-tied. Poor girl, he was afraid she had been going through a nasty time. Better leave her in peace till she was ready to speak.

At last she looked up, absently twisting her wine-glass between nervous fingers.

"Do you know why I wasn't met at the *gare* last night?" she asked.

"No. Wasn't the telegram delivered?"

"It wasn't that. There was another reason."

She glanced for a moment at the adjacent tables. The sole diners within earshot were a pair of pompous, middle-aged Frenchmen greedily intent on their meal.

"The truth is, those servants don't want me there, and thought they'd begin by making things uncomfortable for me. They're rude, they're overbearing, they act as if they hated me. In fact," she finished with a rueful laugh, "both Jeanne and Eduardo are doing their utmost to drive me away!"

CHAPTER EIGHT

So that was the situation!

"You're sure about this?" Geoffrey inquired seriously. "Oh, quite! At first I made excuses for them. They must, of course, have been fearfully upset over what had just occurred, and in no frame of mind for looking after a guest. But—well, I'm giving them almost no trouble, and yet it is perfectly plain they are determined to get rid of me."

"Why?" he asked, though fairly sure of the answer.

"Oh, you know what servants can be like when they've had the uninterrupted run of a place. They don't want anyone there who might possibly criticize their arrangements or pull them up."

She went on to relate the incident of the Empire bedroom, laughing when she came to the offensive comb and soap. Her companion, however, exclaimed in sharp annoyance:

"By Jove, what impertinence! They are behaving as though they owned the flat!"

"They really are. You can't think what liberties they are taking. Everything is neglected and dirty, curtains unwashed, silver not polished. Eduardo looks like a desperado; the cook, who's not at all a bad sort, is so impossibly slack she scarcely bothers to cook me enough to eat. I suppose that's why I'm so ravenous to-night," she added, laughing. "This cook," she went on, "is a priceless person. This afternoon I glanced into the kitchen—filthy, of course, the sink piled up with dishes. What do you think she was doing? Sitting on the table, smoking a cigarette, and lacing a pair of pale blue satin stays!"

He joined her in mirth over the picture she drew, but sobered directly and frowned with noticeable displeasure.

"Jeanne," she continued thoughtfully, "is, *au fond*, a really splendid character. I don't want to minimize her devotion to my cousin, whatever faults she may possess. She is without any doubt deeply attached to her, giving her every possible attention, so that is really all that matters."

"You're satisfied about that, are you?"

She glanced at him, surprised.

"Oh, absolutely! And Mme. Bender is fond of her—quite dependent, in fact. I don't know what she would do without her."

He was silent at this, but after a moment turned the conversation to the invalid herself.

"How did Mme. Bender strike you when you saw her to-day? What exactly do you feel about her condition?"

She drew a long breath.

"I don't quite know. After what I was told I was astonished to find her so little changed. She talked for the most part reasonably and seemed much as she was after the accident last year. I almost think that's the worst part," she added, "to sit and chat with her quietly all the time knowing what she has tried to do, what she may want to do again. I shiver when I think of it!"

He nodded understanding.

"Yet you tell me she describes the thing as an accident."

She assented.

"I would have believed her story, only how can one? You see Jeanne is probably right about it's being the cunning of the madwoman trying to put us off the scent. Besides, it was the second attempt. There are bars up now, to prevent her throwing herself from the window. One can't explain those away, can one? Oh, I'm afraid it's really serious."

He dug his cigarette into his coffee-cup, listening attentively while she went on to relate various small incidents to illustrate her meaning. One thing was clear—she ought to remove herself from so gloomy an atmosphere as soon as possible. He wondered if he dared tell her so.

"You believe, then, that your cousin may be likely to repeat the attempt on her life?" he asked when she had finished her recital.

"I'm afraid she may. I can't help being apprehensive about it. But it isn't only that that's bothering me. I've got a horrid feeling about it all, something I can't put into words." Here she paused, striving to express an almost intangible idea that had come to birth during the past twelve hours. "I keep thinking there's something I don't quite grasp in all this, that things are going on beneath the surface, if you understand me . . .?"

"What do you mean?" he demanded.

She extended her hands with a helpless gesture.

"Exactly. What do I mean? You see I don't know. It was Jeanne who put it into my head. She is so certain about the unfortunate influence of this friend of Mme. Bender's, the one I spoke to you about."

He looked up suddenly.

"You don't mean—?"

"Yes, Hermione Cushing."

"Miss Cushing!"

She watched his face, but could tell nothing from it.

"It seems that she was with Mme. Bender on both occasions, immediately before those suicidal attacks. There may be nothing in it, but I shan't feel easy till I've seen what she's like. In fact, I mean to call on her to-morrow." She stopped, then went on again: "That's another thing—to-day when I rang her up, Jeanne overheard me making the appointment, and was quite rude to me afterwards. It was exactly as though she suspected me of conniving with Miss Cushing to make trouble for her mistress. Funny, isn't it? She's rather like a fierce watch-dog where Germaine is concerned."

On his side Geoffrey was indulging in a brief battle with his usual scruples. When he spoke it was with a conscious effort at naturalness.

"By the way," he said, "I don't want to prejudice you, and I am pretty sure it's hardly worth mentioning—but a few weeks ago Miss Cushing came to see me about Mme. Bender."

"She came to see you?" echoed the girl in amazed eagerness.

So that was it! At last he was going to tell her what he had so studiously kept back.

"She complained bitterly about being prevented from seeing her friend. She said she could scarcely ever get a word alone with her, and sometimes was denied admittance altogether."

"Ah!" cried Catherine, "that bears out Jeanne's story!"

"There was something else, too, though I'm not sure I ought to speak of it. I must rely on you not to give me away. She displayed an extraordinary concern in the disposition of Mme. Bender's property, inquired if a will had been made, and seemed very worried as to whether or not she was in danger of losing a legacy she had reason to hope would come to her when Mme. Bender died. Don't for Heaven's sake," he hurriedly supplemented, seeing the girl's gesture of startled interest, "run away with any wrong ideas on the subject. I don't attach any importance to this myself, I assure you."

"But I'm not sure that I don't," murmured his companion, her eyes dark with excitement. "I can't help thinking—"

"Don't think," he cautioned lightly. "Not at least till you've seen Hermione. I gathered," he went on, "that a more or less open warfare was going on between the lady in question and this Jeanne. Each no doubt thinks the worst of the other. I daresay there's a considerable amount of jealousy mixed up in it, for which reason I decline to take it seriously."

She considered this doubtfully, and he could see that her brain was busy with speculation.

"Shall you stay on there?" he ventured after a pause. "Or is it going to be rather too disagreeable?"

"I shall stay for the present, anyhow," she replied slowly. "You see, whatever her mental state is, Mme. Bender seems so really happy to have me there. I couldn't hurt her by going away, not at once, that is. Later in the spring I am leaving for Italy, so it couldn't be for long in any case."

His face fell.

"Oh! So you don't mean to stay long in Paris?"

"Not this time. I'm thinking of joining some people who are in England now, but my plans will depend somewhat on their movements."

She was powdering her nose, so did not see the blank disappointment in his face, rather like the expression of a thirsty dog from whom a basin of water has been callously snatched away.

"But meantime," she remarked with determination, "I am going to do my best to find out what, if anything, is causing these fits of depression with my cousin. I can't help thinking there may be some definite, outside reason."

He shook his head disparagingly. The vagaries of a hopeless neurotic were pretty difficult to fathom. If the case proved to be actually mental there was little chance of improvement, but he said nothing and gave his attention to the bill just presented to him.

The evening being still young, Catherine gladly agreed to his suggestion of a cinema, in her heart unwilling to return at once to the solitude of the gloomy apartment. Accordingly they presently found themselves seated in the warm darkness of a palatial building where shifting streamers of light played like the Aurora Borealis and an orchestra *en masse* rose as from the sea, shining pure gold against a violet curtain. In an instant they had entered a realm of fantasy.

"How extraordinarily good the music is!" whispered the girl in amazed delight.

He told her that each member of the orchestra was a *premier prix de Conservatoire*, the conductor a well-known figure in Paris.

As he spoke there was a hush, and the first violin, an elegant youth with sleek hair swept off his forehead, stepped forward with an air and raised his bow. Simultaneously the curtain parted, and a pair of Spanish dancers moved on to the stage. The man, bullet-headed and lithe, wore trousers of white cloth ornamented in silver, while his narrow body was tightly encased in a silver-braided jacket. His partner, sumptuous in snowy lace, stiffened at the hips Goya fashion, was draped in a magnificent mantilla, pendant above her glossy black coiffure from a towering comb of red coral. Against the black velvet back-drop the two figures poised, sheer, flashing white, and there were only four accents of carmine—the woman's comb, her immense earrings, her lips, and the heels of her shoes.

Then the music began, slow, deliriously exquisite, with a heavy sweetness, like the perfume of honeysuckle under a midnight sky. Catherine drew in her breath ecstatically.

"That heavenly tune! I've heard it before. . . . Oh, of course, it's the Albeniz Tango that Kriesler plays! It is too, too lovely!"

In a spell of enchantment she watched the swaying pair, while the violin with steady rhythm dripped notes that were like globules of clear amber. Never, afterwards, was she to forget the sensuous rapture of those moments. Always whenever she heard the Albeniz Tango, no matter in what surroundings, she had but to shut her eyes to feel about her the enveloping darkness, see the opening heart of brilliant light in which moved the dancers. There was something else she was to recall, though at the time she was only dimly aware of it. That was the right hand of Geoffrey Macadam as it rested on the arm of the seat dividing her from him, brown, muscular, a little over-large for his slight, wiry build. . . .

It was nearing half-past twelve when they reached the shadowy chestnuts of the Avenue Henri Martin. The neighbourhood was deserted, the buildings had a blind look with all the massive doors closed for the night.

"*Cordon, s'il vous plait!*" shouted Geoffrey, his voice ringing hollow against the black expanse of wood.

After a short delay a ghostly click sounded and one of the doors swung heavily ajar. Catherine stepped within the entrance and held out her hand, but her companion after a slight hesitation followed her in.

"I think I'd like to see you actually into the apartment, if you don't mind," he said. "You may have trouble with the key."

Their steps echoed across the paved way to the foyer, where a dim light shone in a suspended glass cage. Silently the *ascenseur* crept up to the *entresol.*

"I say, there's something odd about this lock. It's a good thing I didn't leave you to wrestle with it alone," remarked Geoffrey a moment later, after several fruitless attempts to open the door.

He struck a match and examined the key, an ordinary Yale one. There seemed nothing wrong with it.

"Let me have a go," suggested Catherine, taking it from him.

It appeared to fit, even to turn, but nothing happened.

"Curious, that. Here, give it to me again."

However, though he pushed and tugged and manipulated, the door refused to budge. Minutes went by with no result. At length, red in the face with effort and chagrin, he straightened up and shrugged his shoulders.

"No doubt about it," he declared shortly. "Someone has drawn the bolt. Damned careless—if you'll forgive the language. I suppose we'll have to ring."

"Oh, don't! I'm so afraid of waking Mme. Bender."

"There's nothing else to do! She won't hear, though, as it probably sounds in the kitchen."

He pressed his finger to the button and they waited expectantly. Within was unbroken silence.

"They must be sleeping very soundly. Try again."

There was a second interval of prolonged waiting. Far away, at the back of the apartment, sounded a faint, persistent ringing.

"Who sleeps on this floor?" Geoffrey inquired, frowning.

"Only Eduardo and Jeanne. The cook moved to-day up to the *sixième*."

"Well, either those two can't hear or they won't. Anyhow, you can't spend the night out here. I'm going to let go with the knocker;" and before she could protest he had laid hold of the wrought-iron handle and hammered resoundingly.

Somewhere in the interior a door opened and a padded footfall approached, barely audible. Someone was at last astir. Yet even now there was a long delay. The steps paused, retreated, and then, exchanging questioning glances, Catherine and Geoffrey fancied they caught the murmur of whispering voices, sibilant and cautious. Finally, after protracted silence, there fell on their ears the stealthy grate of a bolt withdrawn.

The next instant the door cracked open, and silhouetted against a rectangle of light the stocky figure of the Portuguese appeared, clad in an overcoat buttoned to the chin. From beneath bristling hair his small, animal-like eyes glowered at them suspiciously.

"Oh—it's you, miss," he mumbled with a touch of insolent surprise. "I took it you were in hours ago."

It was a flimsy pretext to cover his own thoughtlessness, or so it seemed to Catherine. Her eyes flashed at his rude tone, but she made no reply. Her escort, on the contrary, accosted the butler in a peremptory manner.

"Another time, please be sure before you put the bolt on. It's only by chance that mademoiselle hasn't had to wait out here a quarter of an hour by herself."

The man said nothing, but as he stared impudently first at the speaker, then at Catherine, his lips curled in an unmistakable sneer. Geoffrey's blood boiled at the unuttered insinuation, and even the girl, without understanding its import, felt indignation rise within her.

"You needn't wait, Eduardo," she coldly informed him. "I'll put out the lights."

Without replying he shuffled off, hitching his coat collar higher around his thick bull neck.

"See here, I don't care for that fellow's manner," whispered Geoffrey as he took her hand. "Are you sure you don't mind—"

"Oh, I'm not a bit upset over him," she returned scornfully. "You see, though, that I didn't exaggerate about the deterioration in him. It's as if the veneer had come off. Never mind—good night, and thank you for a marvellous evening."

For a second he retained her slender hand, reluctant to let it go. However, his expression remained studiously matter of fact, betraying no hint of his inward feelings.

"Let me know if that brute gives you any trouble," he said at parting. "I shall hope to see you again soon, at all events."

Glancing at his watch on the way down, he found it was just after one o'clock. That meant they had spent half an hour outside that infernal door. His wrath rose anew as he recalled the insolence of the butler, whom he would have liked to throttle.

"*Cordon!*"

The concierge had gone to sleep in the interval, and no wonder.

"*Cordon!*" he called more loudly.

An irate voice, heavy with sleep, issued from within the loge.

"Who are you, going out at this hour? What are you up to, *diable!* coming in with a woman and remaining with her all this time? I'll have you to know this is not the way to conduct yourself in a respectable house. Do you take this for a *maison de rendezvous?*"

Geoffrey's anger shot up like a flame.

"Hold your foul tongue, you filthy camel, and open that door before I lay hands on you!" he shouted, furious with rage.

More abusive wrangling followed, epithets in choice argot hurled on both sides. Not for the first time did Geoffrey rejoice in his command of Gallic profanity. Finally, with a last imprecation, the unseen porter pulled the cord and the door swung open.

Stupid to lose one's temper with a concierge. It was like beating one's head against a wall. Still it was impossible not to be infuriated by the man's insinuations. Rain was falling, but he did not feel the drops as with rapid strides he crossed to the car and started the engine.

"The swine!" he muttered as the Citroën purred along wet streets towards the Seine. "So he, too, had that idea in his putrid mind! I shouldn't have got so wild if it had been another sort of girl. But Catherine!"

Already in his thoughts he was calling her by her first name.

Alone in the hall, Catherine stood for a moment, her palm still tingling with the recent hard pressure. Circumstances had combined to rouse in her a fluttering emotion—uncertainty as to why she had been shut out, the interval on the dim landing with its faint suggestion of intimate *rapprochement*, and last, the butler's peculiarly offensive manner. Her heart beat with strong strokes.

Why, indeed, had Eduardo stared at them like that? There had been something insulting about it. If only Germaine could realize what his behaviour was like now, how quickly she would dismiss him! Not that she was likely to find out.

She tiptoed towards her distant room. Then as she switched on the light in the passage, she spied, at the top of the staircase before mentioned, a limp, dark object. Picking it up, she discovered it to be a man's glove.

A glove—but of an unfamiliar sort, made of black, stuffy fabric. Who on earth wore things like that? She stared at it curiously. Somewhere, not long ago, she had seen a man with gloves resembling this, but for the moment she could not say who it was. Certainly no one she knew. There was something rather horrid about it. With slight distaste she replaced it where it had lain before.

As she did this she noticed, a little lower down the stairs, a small heap of acrid cigar ashes, and nearby the muddy imprint of a square-toed boot, plainly marked on the pale grey carpet.

Her eyes narrowed in thought. Eduardo, she had remarked only to-day, wore pointed, rather foppish shoes, ill-according his thick, prize-fighter frame. Who, then, had been here this evening? The person, whoever it was, had been to the apartment in her absence, most likely using the private door.

With a shake of the head she gave it up. And then, all at once, she remembered the vulgar-genteel lounger who last evening had stared at her so curiously in the street below, and later had gone away with Jeanne. Yes, he had certainly worn gloves like the specimen lying there on the floor. She recalled in a flash the prim nastily-decent look of them, as she had passed him on the pavement.

"So Jeanne has a lover," she concluded with a touch of amused wonder. "But what a lover!"

Somehow the creature had suggested an undertaker.

CHAPTER NINE

HERMIONE Cushing inhabited a small apartment high up in the rue de la Bienfaisance, on the edge of the quarter known as that of Europe. It is for the most part a typically French neighbourhood, which explains why long ago Miss Cushing chose it, experience having taught her that in the sections of Paris given over to Americans one pays through the nose for everything, from rents to cabbages. In short, Miss Cushing was canny, knowing how to make ten centimes do the work of fifty.

She had lived here for twenty years, and everyone knew her. Moreover, in spite of petty bickerings, she was in excellent repute with the concierge and tradespeople, and for practical purposes one need say no more. She possessed, indeed, certain attributes revered by the French. She was *une dame sérieuse*, spent not a sou on display, and was well connected into the bargain. Did one not frequently see the imposing motors of la Baronne de Grèves and the Princess Guiccioli ranged in front of the entrance, positive proof that the Faubourg St. Germain had toiled up four flights of stairs to pay its respect to the singer? The fact spoke for itself.

None of this was known to Catherine, but her eye noted the respect in the concierge's mien when she spoke the name of Cushing.

"*Au cinquième, a gauche mademoiselle,*" instructed the woman promptly, and came forth like a mole out of a burrow to point the way, adding the further direction, "*C'est le deuxième escalier, en face.*"

There were two staircases, it seemed, one wide and grand, the other narrow and dingy. It was the latter, at the back of the small court, which led to the singer's abode.

The upward journey was steep, the day unexpectedly mild. Catherine took the first three flights in a rush, so that at the turn of the fourth she was obliged to pause before a window and take breath before finishing the climb. Gazing out on the mansard roofs and blackened chimney-pots, she took stock of her recent impressions and prepared herself for the coming interview, which for some reason made her slightly nervous.

The morning's experiences had been disturbing. The hour she had spent with Mme. Bender had failed to clear up the uncertainty in her mind, and she had gained nothing except a strengthened conviction that her cousin was frightened about something. How or why, she could not say. Again and again she had sought to probe the mystery of that quick, recurring gleam of positive terror in the grey eyes, but she had come away without reaching any satisfactory conclusion. Was the poor creature's fear merely a symptom of disordered intelligence, or had it some positive, external cause? That, as she had said to Geoffrey Macadam last night, was what she was anxious to ascertain.

Following her visit to the ill woman had come a disagreeable shock. Jeanne, not without a trace of malice, had informed her that the concierge's wife had sent a message to say she wished to hold converse with the young American lady staying with Mme. Bender. Catherine could not guess what she wanted, but on descending for a walk her ignorance was brusquely removed. The feminine half of the *ménage* which held sway over the tenants' lives accosted her with sour disapproval, and chid her severely for the fault she had committed in allowing her escort to accompany her upstairs after the house was shut for the night. Apparently it was a heinous offence against propriety. No *jeune fille bien élevée* would dream of doing *une chose pareille*, and while mademoiselle's youth and professed ignorance of national customs might excuse her this once, no similar escapade could possibly be tolerated. She would give the house a bad name.

Catherine had stared in stupefaction. At first the veiled implications had escaped her, for though she was no fool she had always regarded her motives as above reproach. However, the pinched face with its evil leer forced her to see that in this quarter at least she was an object of suspicion.

The revelation infuriated her. It seemed to her that not only her own decency was attacked, but that of all her countrywomen as well, and in the heat of the moment it was difficult to hold her tongue and refrain from telling the old harpy what she thought of her. She could still picture the woman's twisted smile as she withdrew into her lair, still feel the blood tingling in her own cheeks as bit by bit the full infamy of the suggestion sank into her mind. At last out of the flames of her wrath had risen the determination never again, if she could avoid it, to encounter the guardians of the loge. There was a way out which she meant to take.

Accordingly, at lunch-time, she had asked Jeanne for a latch-key to the private door, only to be met with a chill refusal. There was but one key, it seemed, which the maid and butler were in the habit of using. However, Catherine was undaunted. Her antagonism was roused by this and similar rebuffs, and she knew by now that Jeanne's autocratic ways must be met with equal firmness.

"Never mind," she had returned intrepidly; "if you won't give me the key, I shall have a spare one made."

She had won her point, though against a grudging displeasure only too apparent. The key now lay in her bag, giving her a sense of independence and triumph. Let the concierge do her damnedest, her gun was spiked.

How little could she guess the *rôle* this same key was to play in future events, or to what extent it was to shape her entire destiny! Thus lightly do we forge the links in the chain which will bind us prisoners, arrange the noose to encircle our unconscious necks. But for that insignificant shape of metal reposing beneath her powder-puff, handkerchief and lipstick—but the matter can wait. In peaceful ignorance she ascended to the top floor, and thinking only of the person she was about to meet, rang a jangling bell at the left-hand door.

The summons was answered by a gaunt grenadier of a servant in a starched apron and brown knitted jersey, too short in the sleeves. Behind steel-rimmed spectacles a pair of searching eyes regarded her with mingled goodness and severity, while a deep voice bade her enter. Simultaneously she was aware of a piano, close at hand, played in a florid and sketchy manner.

"Mademoiselle," announced the stalwart domestic, throwing open the door of the small salon, "here is the young lady you are expecting." Whereupon, without ceremony she pushed Catherine forward with a brawny hand. *"Entrez, mademoiselle,"* she commanded, and stalked away.

The music ceased. Miss Cushing rose from the tiny stool which she had completely obliterated with her bulk and billowed forward with a swishing of skirts. Catherine perceived that she was blonde, middle-aged, and of a shape and movement which made her think forcibly of a whale plunging in mid-seas.

"Ma chère Mademoiselle West," cried a voice, tempestuous with welcome. "Come in, come in! You find me busy arranging a programme with the help of some dear friends, but you won't mind, I'm sure, if I go on and finish. Let me present you to the Baronne de Grèves and Madame Strakosch."

Two plain-featured, elderly ladies in sombre black nodded ceremoniously from a sofa at the end of the room. Both wore old fashioned head-gear and soft, high, buttoned boots such as old women affect. One held an ear-trumpet glued to her ear; the other, wizened and with quick, hawk-like gestures, darted little sharp but not unkindly glances at the newcomer.

"This dear child," explained the singer, detaining Catherine's hand in her cushioned palm, "is a young cousin of poor dear Harry Bender's. She is staying now with my darling Germaine—*dont je vous ai parlé cet instant.*"

This clause she shouted down the ear-trumpet, and as a sign that it had registered the two ladies turned and gazed at Catherine with various nods of understanding.

"*Et comment va madame votre cousine?*" inquired the deaf lady in a sepulchral baritone, shifting the instrument to receive the girl's reply.

Catherine telephoned the opinion that her relative was far from well and extremely nervous, whereupon both listeners murmured, "*Neurasthènique.* Ah-h-h!" and exchanged glances of solemn meaning.

"*Vous voyez?*" demanded Miss Cushing with a dramatic sweep of her arm. "*C'est comme je vous ai dit,*"—and forthwith she returned to her seat at the piano.

Catherine thought she had never seen anyone who so completely filled the room as did Miss Cushing. She trembled for the insecure easel in her path, and eyed nervously a tottering vase of furry palm which stood precariously upon a fragile stand. Yet the singer was not shapeless. On the contrary, her vast bulk curved in at the waist and out again at the hips after the fashion of an enormous hour-glass, a resemblance heightened by her costume. She was dressed in black taffeta with tiny ruffles, a wide skirt and a bolero jacket, from the arm holes of which bulged white muslin sleeves covering arms as large in girth as Catherine's body. Her feet, in shabby bronze pumps, were by contrast quite ridiculously small, and her face, unlined and pink like a baby's, rested upon a series of chins undulating into well-cushioned shoulders. Her eyes were the faint blue of a winter sky, and her scanty, neutral hair was arranged anyhow in a twist, from which vagrant wisps strayed and clung to the creases of her neck.

"And now, *chères amies*, I shall give you the Sibelius. No one in France understands Sibelius as I do. I am without doubt his chief interpreter here."

Herewith she began a slap-dash prelude and proceeded to vocalize, in a voice piercingly thin, uncertain as to registers and now and then grazing from the key. Catherine set her teeth. The other listeners preserved expressionless faces, and it seemed to her she alone was marvelling at the temerity and verdant hope which could prompt an artist to appear in public with so vanished an equipment. She had yet to learn what Paris can stand in the way of music.

To distract her thoughts from the embarrassing performance, she let her eyes stray round the little drab salon, taking account of its fussy detail. Everything which could be draped was draped, from the upright piano to the shelves in the corners, and all the drapes had bobbles on them, while in some cases they were rucked into puffs between anchoring ornaments of silver and Dresden china. The chairs in particular arrested her attention, since she had never seen any like them before. Endowed with gilt cabriole legs, they were like little squat sofas, too wide for one, yet not wide enough for two. They were in fact precisely right for their owner, for whose use they might have been specially designed.

Everywhere were mementoes, signed photographs and faded knots of flowers under glass, while the room abounded in likenesses of the singer, of every possible description. Over the mantel hung a full-length portrait of Miss Cushing as *Marguerite*, with pendant braids and a daisy between her fingers; on the easel was a chalk drawing of the lady in the dress of the nineties; from the walnut commode beamed a marble bust, the head thrown back with artless coquetry, butterflies poised on the plump shoulders. Never, reflected Catherine, had the original not been endowed with a generous amplitude of form. Had she at any remote period possessed the semblance of a voice?

"And now, what about a little du Parc? One must give them something French."

Wheeling on the stool, the performer began thumbing over a pile of tattered sheet-music.

"Hah!" she exclaimed distractedly, *"ou se trouve cette chanson là?"*—then impatiently elevating her voice, she shouted towards the kitchen, *"Yvonne! Yvonne! Venez m'aider!"* The servant appeared, a woollen stocking on one hand, a coarse darning-needle in the other.

"Mademoiselle?"

"Find me that du Parc song—you know the one I mean," and she thrust the jumble of music into the unwilling arms. Yvonne shook her head with wooden disapproval. "Mademoiselle should not attempt the du Parc to-day," she advised severely. "Mademoiselle must not forget she had *moules marinières* for *déjeuner*. Better try something lower."

"Oh, well, then, find me another," returned her mistress petulantly. "Reynaldo Hahn, or Debussy. It doesn't much matter."

Muttering darkly, Yvonne departed, and through the open door Catherine, inwardly convulsed, could see her seated in the kitchen, going solemnly through the pile with grunts and sniffs of disparagement. Meanwhile Miss Cushing, unruffled, launched full steam upon the elaborate "Les Filles de Cadiz," swooping and curveting like a spirited Percheron.

The audition was over. The elderly couple, after discussing practical matters of *affiches* and subscription tickets, rose and made a ceremonious departure. Catherine was alone with her hostess.

"*Enfin!*" cried Miss Cushing with a gusty sigh. "Now, my child, we can talk. Only we must have tea. Yvonne! *Du thé, tout de suite! Je suis epuisée, moi—complètement finie!*"—and throwing her weight upon the creaking sofa she pressed her hand to the region of her heart.

For a second she remained thus, eyes closed, with an air of exhaustion. Then she roused herself and fixed upon her guest a gaze of intensity.

"Tell me at once, dear Miss West, just what your impression is of that unfortunate household. Don't leave anything out. It may be important."

Was this melodrama or farce? Catherine could not decide. However, sure that Hermione Cushing was ignorant of the recent crisis, she set out to enlighten her, watching closely to observe the effect of her news. She saw the pink face turn pale, the blue eyes start with unmistakable horror, while one hand trembled forward as though to ward off a blow.

"*La pauvre petite! Elle a fait ça?*" whispered the singer in an awed tone. "But no—it is not true! It can't be true!" she protested vehemently.

"I assure you it is," Catherine declared.

"*Mon Dieu! mon Dieu!* Then if it is so—if she did try to take her life"—she paused impressively, then bent forward to hiss in Catherine's ear—"then you may take my word for it, it was that demon who drove her to it! I have said that she would. That fiend of a Jeanne!"

"*Jeanne?*" repeated the girl, hardly able to believe her ears.

For a moment she was speechless over the arrant absurdity. Was Miss Cushing serious?

"I knew it, I knew it," her hostess murmured, half to herself. "It is what I have been expecting. Oh! that such a tyranny can continue, unchecked, in an age like this! It is infamous, it is—"

"Tyranny?" echoed Catherine again, then thinking it time to play her trump card, made an earnest bid for attention. "Forgive me, Miss Cushing," she began seriously. "But there is something I feel you ought to know. You see, Jeanne declares that after you left the other afternoon Mme. Bender was terribly depressed. She thinks it was something you said to her which threw her into that morbid state and made her—made her—" It was difficult to complete the sentence.

She was unprepared for the phenomenon which greeted her statement. The huge body swelled, appeared on the point of bursting. The round face turned a turkey-red hue.

"That creature said such a thing?" she gasped in a stifled voice. *"Impossible! Menteuse! Menteuse!"*

For half a minute she trembled on the verge of apoplexy, while the girl looked on in positive alarm.

Yvonne strode into the room, bearing on a tray the tiniest glass Catherine had ever seen filled with cognac.

"Drink this, mademoiselle, and calm yourself!" she commanded brusquely, and thrust the glass to her mistress's lips.

The artist swallowed, coughed and recovered her balance.

"Yvonne!"—and she stretched forth a detaining hand. "Did you hear that infamy? That devil, Jeanne, is saying that I—I—am responsible for Mme. Bender's trying to take her life!"

"Ah! Incroyable!"

The staid Yvonne scowled from one face to the other, muttering such expressions as *"folle!" "C'est un peu trop, ça!"* and *"C'est le comble!"* Finally, casting her arms with an irate gesture, she withdrew with a last, *"Elle est méchante, cette femme là,"* hurled into space.

"Listen," cried Miss Cushing, "now you shall hear the truth! On Tuesday afternoon my poor Germaine was almost happy. She was rejoiced over the thought of your coming. I said to myself that there was really going to be an improvement, now she would not be left alone to mope and brood. She kissed me and said, 'My darling Lili'—that is her name for me—'promise you will come again, very soon. You put new life into me.'—So! You see?"

"And you saw no sign of any delusions?"

"Delusions, indeed! I may say I have never seen anything of the sort. With me she has always been—well, not normal; that is a strong word; but absolutely sane. Why, the other day she was so much her usual self that I actually ventured to advise her upon a matter I had felt I ought to mention for some time past. I mean, of course,"—here she paused and moistened her lips—"the question of drawing up her will."

Catherine experienced a slight shock.

"Oh!" she exclaimed a little blankly. "So you spoke of that?"

"I thought it my duty," replied her hostess firmly. "You see, Catherine—I may call you that, *n'est-ce pas?*—Germaine has never made her will. It is a business she is unwilling to face. In consequence, if the poor darling were to pass away suddenly all Harry's entire fortune would go—who knows where? To the State, perhaps. It is appalling to think of such waste!"

Catherine sat quite still, struggling with the confusion of her thoughts.

"But surely Mme. Bender has heirs?" she suggested at last.

"Not one. Amazing, isn't it? But surely you must have been told that?"

Catherine shook her head.

"I know almost nothing about her before she married Cousin Harry."

"You didn't know, then, that it was I who introduced Harry to Germaine Dieulefit when she and I were studying together for the Opéra?"

"Dieulefit? What an odd name!"

"Yes, most unusual. There are no others, the family is extinct. Her mother was a singer, coloratura, and illegitimate—probably the child of some minor royalty and an Italian peasant. No one knew. Old Jerome Dieulefit was a wine-grower from the south, the last of a bourgeois line. So you see there is no one to whom this money can go, by law, unless Germaine leaves a will. In her present state of health it is madness not to think of such things."

Catherine fingered her gloves.

"Have you any idea who would benefit if she did make a will?" she asked presently.

Miss Cushing grew suddenly warm. She seized a worn copy of *Ouvre tes Yeux Bleus* and fanned herself vigorously.

"Not the slightest," she declared a little consciously. "All I can say is that there is a certain string of pearls, quite valuable, which she has promised to leave to me. I helped her choose them. 'Lili,' she said at the time, 'one day these will be yours, so be sure you approve of them!' Always she referred to them as Lili's pearls. She seldom wore then, only sometimes the copy she had made. The pearls themselves are insured for three million francs."

Three million francs! Catherine glanced about her. All the small evidences of gentility struggling against poverty which had been apparent to her since she entered the tiny flat took on a new meaning. Three million francs would represent security and dignity in old age to this woman who was striving against difficult odds to gain a decent livelihood. No wonder Hermione was worried lest her friend should die without putting her bequest into legal form.

Suddenly she thought of the Bender apartment, given over to servants. One of the latter was a stranger of whose morals she knew nothing. Eduardo himself was behaving so abominably he all but invited suspicion, and last night there had been some outside person, possibly the little man she had seen with Jeanne, prowling about the place.

"By the way, where does Mme. Bender keep her pearls?" she inquired casually. "I hope they're well locked up."

"Ah, yes, they, at least, are perfectly safe. She keeps them with all her most valuable jewels, at the bank in the Place Vendôme."

An indefinable qualm shot through the listener. What precisely did Miss Cushing mean by saying that the pearls *at least* were safe?

CHAPTER TEN

A MOMENT later Catherine was listening to a jumbled discourse, as full of irrelevant detail as the room about her. She could not take her eyes from the overblown spinster, who, having contrived in some astonishing manner to tuck one foot beneath her, was imbibing countless cups of tea as though to provide her system with the moisture which constantly suffused her pale eyes and occasionally spilled over the edge of her scanty lashes.

Unless she had remarkable histrionic powers, which Catherine was inclined to doubt, she was certainly much moved; yet, watching her, the girl was not convinced that all this easy emotion did not cover a grasping nature and a singular lack of tact. In short, she was not at all sure that Jeanne was entirely wrong in assuming that Miss Cushing had somehow or other precipitated those violent fits of depression which had so nearly ended in their victim's death. Yet she was even more sure that Miss Cushing had meant no harm, and was quite unaware that any blame could attach itself to her actions. Her own account of things, told with a ring of sincerity, bore this out.

Apparently Hermione had been in Germany at the time that Mme. Bender returned from America. It was only last October that she first called to see her old friend, on which occasion she was refused admittance on the plea that the poor lady was too ill to receive visitors. The same thing happened several times, not only to herself, but to other callers as well.

"Although there is no one here but me who was ever at all intimate with Germaine. She had so few close friends, you know: only myself and the Comtesse de Bréart, and the comtesse is in *Afrique*, shooting lions."

At last she felt there was something wrong about these refusals. Afraid lest the invalid might not be receiving proper care and suspecting that her messages were not delivered, she resolved to be put off no longer.

"What did you do?" asked Catherine curiously.

"I informed Jeanne that I intended to see madame, whether she liked it or not, and when she tried to keep me out I simply put my full weight against hers and forced my way into the room!"

Catherine could not repress a gasp of admiration. The picture of the redoubtable maid overborne on the threshold of her fortress by sheer avoirdupois was almost too much for her gravity.

"*Figurez-vous*," continued the singer, her eyes widening to circles of swimming earnestness. "*Figurez-vous* the shock I received when at last I beheld my *pauvre amie*, so terribly shattered, only a ghost of the woman I had known! Never shall I forget the look in her eyes. It was like some frightened bird caught in a snare."

So she had noticed that, too! Catherine felt more and more mystified. She watched her hostess dab at her tears with a sodden handkerchief and pause long enough to swallow another cup of tea.

"Forgive me, my dear, for being so stupid. You see, I am very fond of Germaine. *Elle a toujours été si gentille pour moi!*" The tears dripped down.

"Was she glad to see you?" inquired Catherine, mainly to stem the tide of emotion.

"Glad! Her joy was pathetic. Why had I not come before? Why, at least, had I not written? She had been so alone, was beginning to think that no one cared whether she lived or died. You see how it was? That woman Jeanne had never told her of my visits, never delivered a message or a flower!"

"But are you sure of this?" demanded the girl incredulously.

A scornful shrug answered her question.

"She swore, naturally, that she always informed her mistress, but that Mme. Bender's mind was so affected that she promptly forgot what was told her."

"And you think that may not be true?"

Miss Cushing made an indignant gesture which nearly capsized the teapot.

"Lies—lies, every word of it! Nothing will make me alter my opinion. She simply wants to keep me and everyone else away from that poor ill creature."

This on the face of it struck Catherine as manifestly absurd.

"But why? What possible reason could she have?" she objected argumentatively.

"There you have me. What reason can there be?" Miss Cushing stared helplessly in front of her. "She is, of course, frightfully jealous; one has always known that; she resents anyone having the least claim on her mistress's affections. Still, I can't help thinking there is more in it than jealousy. Sometimes I believe"—and she brought her face close to Catherine's before whispering mysteriously—"that she is afraid for strangers to see what is going on in that apartment!"

"Going on?" repeated the girl rather startled. "What do you mean?"

"Why, my dear, isn't it pretty evident that those servants are fleecing poor Germaine at every turn? Cutting down expenses and putting the difference in their pockets?"

Catherine was silent, recalling her own reception and the efforts, still continuing, to dislodge her. There might be something in it, though to suspect the hitherto upright Jeanne of such conduct was against all her previous conceptions of the latter's character.

"It's true," she admitted, "they are not the least anxious to have me there."

"Naturally not!" cried her hostess in triumph. "That clever Jeanne doesn't want you looking on while she is busy feathering her nest!"

The identical phrase Jeanne herself had employed in regard to Miss Cushing! The listener bit her lip.

"But how can she do this? I don't quite see—"

"Where are your eyes? Think for a moment. Until recently there were six servants kept. What has become of them? What has become of the chauffeur?"

"Oh, he has been dismissed. I happen to know about that," put in Catherine.

"Then you may take it from me it was Jeanne who dismissed him, for Germaine knows no more of it than the babe unborn. It was Jeanne who got rid of the housekeeper and maids and replaced the cook with that slattern of a Berthe, who is asleep or gallivanting two-thirds of the time. Oh, it's quite clear what she's up to! She is taking the usual weekly cheque for the housekeeping, and keeping most of it for herself."

Disagreeable though it was, the theory was certainly plausible.

"And Mme. Bender doesn't suspect?"

"Ah, she is too trusting and too utterly absorbed in herself to give the matter a thought. Besides, she never was good at money matters. But Jeanne is afraid that you or I might open her eyes to the truth. Tell me—has she left you alone, really alone, with her mistress for a single moment?"

Catherine was forced to admit she had not.

"*Eh bien—vous voyez?* She doesn't trust you. She is afraid also that you will discover what I have discovered—that all this talk about madame's insanity is untrue. That will give you something to think about," she added, nodding vigorously.

However, on this point Catherine was unconvinced. It was unfortunately so easy to see why Miss Cushing wanted to believe her friend sane, since evidently she was hoping to obtain a will in her own favour.

"Don't you think," she contented herself with saying, "it would be much better for Mme. Bender if she could be persuaded to go out?"

Her hostess raised a plump hand excitedly.

"Ah, now you shall hear something!" she cried. "I, too, knew that it was bad for her to remain always a prisoner, in that tiny room with scarcely any air—"

"Why does she use that room?" interrupted the girl curiously. "I've been wondering."

"It is simply one of the poor dear's peculiar notions. She grew up in a convent, and all her girlhood was accustomed to a little bedroom like a cell. Since Harry's death she has gone back to the time before she met him. *Voilà tout!* She told me so herself. . . . But to continue . . ."

It seemed she had been cooped up there for months, dreading the daylight, shrinking from the idea of strange faces. No wonder she was as white as a sheet of paper and trembling from weakness. At last, in January, by dint of great diplomacy and opposed every step of the way, Hermione had persuaded her to go for a drive. The car was brought round from the garage where presumably it was standing idle, the invalid was assisted downstairs.

"I went with her, my dear, so I can describe what happened. When we were out in the avenue she was astonished to find the chestnuts bare. You see, she had lost all count of time. Everything went well until she caught sight of the car, then suddenly I saw her tremble and turn the colour of chalk. Can you guess why?"

Catherine could not.

"Nor could I, at first. Then I saw that it was newly done up. It had been pale beige before, but now it was black outside and in—paint, upholstery, all. *Chic, mais un peu funeste.* Jeanne's idea, for it had been left to her. Now I want to tell you something strange. I had already noticed, on several occasions, that Germaine, since Harry's death, has had a horror of black. I dare not even wear a black dress when I go there. Not that she admits it—she is far too sensitive about showing her peculiarities—but I know what I am saying is true. Well, to return. All during that drive the poor thing sat huddled in her sable coat, shaking like a leaf, her eyes staring ahead of her. When we got her home again, she tottered to her room and fell across the bed in a dead faint! That was three months ago. Since then the very mention of going out throws her into a panic. Nothing will induce her to stir foot outside the apartment."

Catherine listened in distress. She had often heard how almost impossible it is to uproot the fixed ideas of a neurasthenic.

"You can see," went on Miss Cushing shrewdly, "how that incident played into Jeanne's hand. She blamed me for what had happened, and has redoubled her efforts to prevent my visits. Oh, she's a deep one! Believe me or not, she is wholly determined to keep Germaine under her thumb."

"You don't mean to suggest," ventured the girl in helpless amazement, "that she had the car painted black on purpose to keep Mme. Bender from using it?"

"That, my dear, is exactly what I do believe. Everything points to it."

The idea seemed ludicrously improbable. Catherine concluded that her companion was a woman of incurably romantic mind. Moreover, she remembered what Geoffrey Macadam had said last night about the warfare between Miss Cushing and Jeanne, and the likelihood of there being a good deal of reciprocal jealousy mixed up in it. Perhaps, indeed, the pot was taking a venomous delight in denouncing the kettle's complexion.

Her thoughts were interrupted by the appearance of Yvonne at the door.

"You will not forget, mademoiselle, that you have an appointment with the modiste," she announced in her deep voice. "It is almost six o'clock."

"Mon Dieu! Is it so late?" cried the singer, starting up. "I must go at once. Catherine, my dear, perhaps you would care to come along with me? My milliner lives only a step from here, and you may be glad to know of someone who will do up things cheaply. Oddly enough," she added confidentially, "it was this same Jeanne who first told me about her, almost ten years ago!"

Although Catherine had little faith that her own ideas of hats would coincide with Miss Cushing's, she agreed, since there was no reason why she should go home just yet. Accordingly, a few minutes later she followed her hostess down the narrow stairs, it being manifestly impossible to walk abreast of her. The spinster had arrayed her vast form in a coat composed of two quite different kinds of fur, suggesting that it had been fashioned from separate garments donated by wealthy friends—as was indeed the case. This she wore with an indescribable air of elegance, while her step was light, even jaunty. She might have been a debutante, sallying forth, sure of conquests.

Skirting the rear of the Gare St. Lazare, they arrived at the rue d'Amsterdam, then half-way between the rue de Londres and the Place de Clichy they turned into a sombre court and ascended a staircase at the back. At the first floor, before a door bearing the single name *"Honorine,"* blazoned in faded gilt, they paused and rang.

A little apprentice in a black apron admitted them to a square room, whose windows overlooked the court. In the centre was a table heaped with felt hoods of various colours, straw shapes, bits of velvet and ribbon. At a smaller table between the windows two young girls sat, making hats. They glanced at the newcomers without interest, going on with their work.

"If the ladies wouldn't mind waiting a moment," the apprentice said, "madame is busy with a client."

"Client!" murmured the younger of the two assistants with malicious drollery, "that is a new name for monsieur!"

Her companion caught up a huge pair of shears and snipped off the brim she was shaping.

"Such ardour, coming in the afternoon," she returned, giggling with secret enjoyment. "She's a lucky woman, if you want my opinion!"

"You've said it, at her time of life! It's a mystery to me how she's caught an admirer, a serious one, too. All these years living across the way, and all of a sudden he makes up his mind to marry her. I believe she must have put something in his coffee."

"Beer, you mean!"

They giggled again, secretly savouring their morsel of gossip.

While Miss Cushing rustled the pages of a fashion magazine, Catherine found herself idly listening to the two chatterers, who continued in undertones, probably ignorant that their audience understood French.

"Of course, you forget he's handled her affairs. That makes me wonder if she's saved up more than one thinks she has. Anyhow she doesn't throw it about."

"Well, all I say is, there's hope for all."

The inner door opened and the milliner appeared, following a small man in black, wearing, with disregard of manners, his wide-brimmed felt hat. Catherine saw a drab and tired-looking woman in the forties, who at another time would have appeared worn and spiritless with hard work. Now, however, in spite of her parchment skin and untidy hair, there was a twist to her mouth denoting gratified vanity, a general look of conscious pride. Catherine had seen that expression before and knew what it meant.

The man's face was hidden, but something oddly familiar in his stiff back caused her to gaze after him with sudden interest. Impossible that she could know by sight this insignificant Frenchman, and yet—

In the doorway he stopped, speaking in a low voice and with a hard, guttural accent—Belgian or Alsatian, she could not tell which. At the same time he flicked across his palm a pair of ugly, black fabric gloves.

Pair? No, strangely enough there was but a single glove. Catherine eyed it, fascinated. How odd to carry one glove! Odder still that it should so closely resemble the one she had picked up the evening before in Mme. Bender's apartment. However, it could be no more than coincidence.

"*Alors, demain soir,*" said the owner of the glove impassively.

"*Entendu,*" murmured the modiste, closing the door upon him.

Miss Cushing billowed into the other room, where Catherine could hear her haggling over the price of an ancient hat which the milliner gently declared was not worth the trouble of re-making.

Instead of accompanying her, Catherine moved to the window and stood looking down into the court. Almost at once she saw Honorine's visitor emerge, cross the flags to a door opposite, and fumble in his pocket for a key. Then, just before entering, he turned and looked up in her direction, the fading daylight revealing his features.

She saw an unwholesomely pallid skin, a small, bristling moustache, and eyes pale reddish in hue, staring upward with cold, unwinking fixity.

A queer sensation shot through her. She had seen him again—the pavement lounger, Jeanne's friend, the midnight caller who had dropped his glove on the stairs!

Who on earth was the man?

CHAPTER ELEVEN

She did not know why she should attach so much importance to the incident just related, nor why, during the next few days, she should keep seeing in her mind's eye the white, dull skin and pale, staring eyes of the little man in the rue d'Amsterdam. Again and again the vision recurred to her, always with a sense of distrust and vague repulsion, akin to the antipathy with which one regards certain specimens of the saurian kingdom.

As a matter of fact she was now acquainted with his name and occupation, for on the way out from the milliner's she had read upon his door the words, *"A. Blom, Notaire."* A *notaire* was probably a humble sort of lawyer, which offered a reasonable explanation for the man's connection with Jeanne. In France upper-class servants invariably have their legal advisers who help them with the investment of their savings. Jeanne, the soul of thrift, was undoubtedly putting aside every available sou against her old age, so that it was quite natural for her to consult an expert on the subject of stocks and bonds.

As Catherine turned this over in her mind a sudden thought struck her. Very likely Eduardo put the bolt on the door the other night to prevent her walking in and finding the *notaire* there. Then as the visitor had gone out by the private entrance the precaution was forgotten till the knocker woke the sleeping occupants.

Her position in the household was now less positively unpleasant, and while she felt that she was still regarded as a thorn in the flesh, she fancied the servants had accepted her presence as inevitable and were making the best of things. She even noticed an improvement in their attitude towards her. Eduardo was not actually insolent, and Jeanne, though distant, was for the most part as suave as in former days. Occasionally she betrayed a slight gleam of resentment, but for this the girl was ready to make allowances.

"Poor, warped creature!" she mused, full of compassion. "It's not that she dislikes me personally. It's only that she doesn't want to share her mistress's affection with anyone. What a starved life she must have lived, to be so completely centred on one object!"

It did, indeed, seem that the woman had but a single passion, her devoted attachment to Mme. Bender. Impossible not to admire the indefatigable care with which she surrounded her charge, her quickness to forestall the invalid's slightest wish. Steadfastly she refused Catherine's offers of assistance, and remained hour after hour on duty, scarcely ever quitting the apartment. If in the evening she slipped out for an hour, Eduardo took up his post in the converted dressing-room adjoining Mme. Bender's bed-chamber, and remained there until she returned.

Daily Catherine spent an hour or two with her cousin, trying to cheer her and at the same time to study her condition, but after a week she was as far as ever from coming to any definite conclusion. She was chiefly struck by the invalid's total lack of confidence in herself, her unwillingness to affirm anything positively, cunningly waiting to take her cue from the opinions of those about her. It suggested that she was distressingly aware of blank patches in her memory, which she was anxious to conceal.

Mme. Bender's spirits varied startlingly, passing from a childish, hectic gaiety to periods of moodiness impossible to lighten. At times she chattered volubly, jumping from topic to topic with utter inconsequence; then again she would sit for hours without opening her lips. It was on the latter occasions that Catherine noticed the look of terror before mentioned, but every effort to fathom the cause of it met with failure. All she succeeded in rousing was a hint of something very like suspicion towards herself.

Another thing puzzled the girl. This was neither more nor less the extreme readiness of Mme. Bender to agree with her maid on every subject, complaisance carried to the point where it seemed as though she were actually trying to curry favour in Jeanne's eyes. Absurd, of course! Yet so it appeared when again and again the weak personality bolstered itself up by leaning upon the strong one. Sometimes Catherine told herself that if Jeanne had declared black to be white her mistress would have hastened to say that it was so. Reluctantly she began to see that there were some grounds for Miss Cushing's view of affairs, and that for good or for bad her cousin was, to an alarming extent, under the maid's influence.

"I suppose it's only to be expected in the circumstances," she reflected. "So long as there's no harm in it, one oughtn't to care."

On the latter point she could not quite make up her mind. She continued to hold a high opinion of Jeanne, but as the days went by little doubts crept across her mental sky like clouds, each leaving its shadow beneath. Perfect as the woman showed herself in her devotion to the invalid, in other respects she was not so flawless. It became more and more evident that the establishment was badly run, that the maid did not trouble in the least what happened outside the patient's own room. The second week passed, and the sheets on Catherine's bed had not been changed. The windows wanted cleaning, not only in her bedroom but all over the apartment. The food served to her was carelessly cooked and all but insufficient. This neglect in a rich woman's dwelling was inexcusable. In spite of herself, Catherine could not help thinking of the singer's declaration that Jeanne was pinching and saving in order to put money into her own pocket. It must be so, for what other reason could there be for so niggardly an economy? Petty pilfering, for which one must not use too harsh a term, yet for all that it was distasteful to find the quality prompting it linked in the same character with motives of sterling excellence.

Meanwhile she was enjoying Paris. She presented introductions, made many acquaintances, and went about shopping and visiting picture-galleries to her heart's content. Each day brought a fresh invitation, so that soon she was caught up in a gay and active life. More and more often she saw Geoffrey Macadam, and it was somehow gratifying to note the frequence with which he sought her society, yet, although she was getting to know him extremely well, he continued to preserve towards her an unbroken attitude of matter-of-factness, as impersonal as that of a brother. Sometimes the feminine part of her was piqued by this unexciting behaviour, but presently she came to regard him as one of those beings preordained for bachelordom, and having settled this to her satisfaction felt even more than before that she could confide in him with freedom. Undoubtedly there was something solid and worth while about him which counted higher than the facile attractions of the other men she had met, and though he seldom paid her a compliment and had never once tried to hold her hand, she began to look forward eagerly to her meetings with him, sure of mental stimulation and sympathetic accord.

Existence flowed on, outwardly serene, yet there was a sub-current to affairs which rendered Catherine ill at ease. Was she imagining things, or was it perhaps true that Jeanne, under cover of her unremitting labours, was conducting some secret game for her own advancement? She could not be sure.

Take the single instance of Mme. Bender's car. Not once had she set eyes upon it, although her cousin appeared to assume that it was always at her disposal. What had become of it? No effort, she was sure, was being made to engage another chauffeur. Naturally she did not broach the subject to Jeanne, for at all cost she was anxious to avoid friction. At best her presence here was merely tolerated, and to stir up latent antagonism against herself would make life unbearable.

For the same reason she kept silent when, with a shock of surprise, she found that several of the best rooms in the apartment were under lock and key. Why was this so? Lying in bed at night she puzzled over the circumstance, unable to come to any conclusion. With one exception she had no desire beyond that of curiosity to penetrate the closed portions of the flat. Their contents did not concern her, but it was true she would have liked to go into the picture-gallery on the ground floor. Here were hung all the best of Harry Bender's collection, which included many interesting examples of the modern French school—a number of the Barbizon group, a couple of Claude Monets, a fine Cézanne, and three or four Renoirs. In particular she recalled with a thrill of pleasure a small still-life of apples and pears, executed by Manet during his sojourn at Boulogne—a gem of a painting, highly treasured by her dead cousin.

Several times she was on the point of asking Jeanne for the key, but always something—instinct or premonition—held her back. In the end an incident occurred to render the request unnecessary.

Returning home one afternoon, she saw in the street outside the private entrance a luxurious Rolls-Royce standing by the kerb. For a moment she wondered if someone were calling upon Mme. Bender, but that could hardly be, for there was no sign of a chauffeur. Then she noticed that the car was black, inside as well as out, and the knowledge flashed on her that it was her hostess' own. What was it doing here, and who was going to drive it?

As she fumbled for her key the question was answered. Eduardo came hurriedly out carrying a long cylindrical parcel wrapped in brown paper, took one startled look at her, and headed straight for the driver's seat.

So the car was being used, but only for the servants' convenience! The knowledge angered her, but hardly had she taken it in when she saw in front of her the door of the gallery standing wide open.

What luck! At once she stepped inside, then stood looking round her with blank disappointment.

Every painting was shrouded in ghostly muslin, not an inch of frame visible. Chairs and canapés, too, wore covers of linen, while even the carpet—a valuable Aubusson, if she remembered rightly—was hidden by an enormous dust-sheet.

"What a shame!" she murmured aloud.

She would have liked to remove the wrappers, but most of the pictures hung too high for her reach. The little Manet, though—that she might manage, for she remembered its position, lower down, at the end of the room.

"That's it, I'm sure," she thought, identifying a small rectangular shape. "No harm in having a peep at it—" and she loosened the muslin bag.

A cry of dismay escaped her. The gold frame, robbed of its precious canvas, stared her in the face.

What an odd thing—to part with the picture and leave the frame behind! She had never heard of such a thing. She stared at the open space, while in her brain a disagreeable suspicion began to take form.

Quickly she made the round of the other paintings, feeling the canvases through the material. There were several missing, she could not say which. Very strange, this. . . .

Next, her heart beating fast, she tugged at the enveloping linen upon the furniture, only to meet with a fresh shock. Every scrap of the eighteenth-century tapestry, fit for a museum, had been removed, leaving the coarse lining. Last she turned over a corner of the dust-sheet underfoot. As she expected, there was nothing between it and the perfectly laid parquet.

She remained rooted to the spot, while the blood sang in her ears. Who, she asked herself grimly, was responsible for these depredations? For that they were depredations she could not doubt. The artful concealment told its own story. Carpet and tapestries alone represented many thousands of francs, while the missing pictures might run into millions. Had they been secretly abstracted and sold?

A step ran lightly down the stairs outside. A pause, then in the doorway Jeanne appeared, a bunch of keys in her hand. Her brown eyes shot a rapid glance from Catherine to the muslin bag upon the floor and back again. In their hard gaze the girl caught the same expression she had seen in the mirror nearly three weeks ago—something alien, hostile. Now she fancied there was another emotion in them. Was it fear?

"Mademoiselle is searching for something?" inquired the crisp voice, edged with irony.

Catherine braced herself.

"Yes, Jeanne, I was looking for the little Manet. What has become of it?"

The maid raised her brows regretfully.

"Ah, the little Manet! It is sad, is it not? Monsieur parted with it, only a few weeks before his death. No wonder you are astonished to find it gone."

Incredulity swept over the girl. Cousin Harry part with the pearl of his collection? She could not possibly believe it. She still recalled the pride with which he had shown it to her four years ago. She kept her gaze rivetted to the composed face opposite.

"Why did monsieur let the painting go without the frame? It is most extraordinary."

A shrug answered her, indifferent, chill.

"Who knows? A whim, perhaps. I believe I heard them say that the picture was bought by some gentleman from South America. No doubt he paid a large price; but why he did not take away the frame I have no idea."

"There are other pictures gone, also the carpet and the tapestry from the furniture. Were those sold as well?"

"At the same time, I imagine, but as I was away on my holiday I know nothing about them. We sailed immediately afterwards for America, and when we returned, madame and I, the room was as you see it now."

"But madame? Has she never mentioned them to you?"

"Ah, poor madame? She does not occupy herself with these affairs. I doubt if she even remembers they were sold. I never dare speak of things which make her think of monsieur, as you well know!" She bestowed a cursory glance round the walls, then turned to Catherine with an air of polite dismissal. "And now, mademoiselle, if you have quite finished, I will lock up the room. It is safer, is it not?"

A plausible answer, which it was impossible to refute; yet as Catherine heard the key turn in the door instinct warned her that every glibly-uttered word was a lie. The servants themselves had disposed of those paintings, were probably planning the sale of others. She had wondered just now what the butler was carrying in that oddly-shaped parcel. Of course, it was a rolled-up canvas!

Her knees trembled as she walked up the stairs.

CHAPTER TWELVE

For the next few days Catherine was tormented by her suspicion. In justice she could not give it a stronger name, though from the first she was instinctively certain of the servants' guilt. Certain—but cold reason told her the thing would be difficult to prove. To breathe a word to the invalid might shatter the very foundations of her being, and, except for Mme. Bender, there was no one at all likely to be acquainted with the facts. Hermione could not help, since at the time Jeanne declared the pictures to have been sold she had been absent from Paris. Indeed, it was probable that for the past year no outside person had entered the gallery.

After the upsetting discovery she shut herself in the salon and painstakingly examined its contents. For some time she could find nothing missing, though she fancied the vitrines contained rather less than their former store of *bibelots*; but at last she gave a gasp of triumph. A blue enamelled patch-box and a miniature set with pearls, both of which she had admired the day after her arrival, had disappeared. The final shred of doubt was brushed away.

She burned now to explore the locked bedrooms, but that meant demanding the keys.

What ought she to do? The question haunted her. Useless to assure herself that dishonesty was one thing, unkindness to an ill woman another, that she could put her finger on no instance of neglect or lack of consideration towards Germaine. The ugly fact stared her in the face that her cousin, helpless and ignorant of harm, was being hourly ministered to by an unscrupulous thief. Nor was this all. Over and above the tangle of moral values one idea stood out clear. *If Jeanne could lie about one thing, she could lie about another.* The thought was alarming, though she did not draw any direct conclusion from it.

She resolved to consult Geoffrey. After all, he was not only a real friend, but he and his father were Mme. Bender's solicitors, so that no one could be better able to advise her. She was going to see him on Sunday, having been invited to his flat to meet his sister, up from Fontainebleau for the day. If she could get a moment alone with him, she would tell him the whole affair.

Till then she was forced to go on as though nothing had happened, though to do so was increasingly difficult. Her sensitive eye detected a hard defiance in the servant's manner towards her, saw in their grudging politeness the mark of an armed neutrality. They distrusted her now, regarded her presence as a menace to their safety. Well, let them—they would not dare to go ahead with their systematic thieving. That, at least, was a consoling thought. . . .

All this time she was assuming that not only was Jeanne almost indispensable to Mme. Bender, but that her firm, managing hand exerted an influence for the invalid's good. Now, however, she was to receive a second shock which ship-wrecked all her previous beliefs.

About the middle of the week, after lunching at the Ritz with some American friends, she came back to find her cousin, in one of her moods of apathetic depression. Usually at this hour she was sitting up in the bergère, a rug about her knees, but to-day she was in bed, her face pinched and wan, with purple patches beneath her eyes, an ivory rosary held loosely between her emaciated fingers. In the grey dusk of the room she looked like some poor, fear-haunted ghost.

"Is it you, Catherine? Come in—I have been waiting for you."

The girl bent to kiss her, holding out the bowl of violets she had brought.

"Look, aren't they lovely and fresh? All along the Madeleine the flower-sellers' stalls are so marvellous, a blaze of colour. I do so wish you could see them."

"And you brought me these? My dear, I am touched!" Her eyes filled with tears.

"I'll put them here on the little table where you can smell them. It is warm to-day, such gorgeous sunshine, and the chestnuts are actually budding. Oh, Germaine dear, if only you could bring yourself to go outdoors, I can't help thinking it would do you good!"

She spoke impulsively, then was distressed to see the result of her words. The ill woman shut her eyes shudderingly, her features contracted with a spasm of pain.

"Ah, no! Not that!" she murmured in positive alarm. "It is impossible! You do not know what you are saying."

Hermione's story about the ill-fated motor drive flashed into Catherine's mind. Yet almost against her will she found herself saying persuasively:

"But, darling, it must be bad for you to stay shut up in this little room. It's unnatural to want to, you know!"

The shrinking gaze turned suspiciously on her, eyeing her with a sort of pained distrust.

"You too!" muttered the invalid. "First Lili, and now you . . . Jeanne was right. She is always right," and she shook her head with a hint of fatalism.

Catherine was mystified, both by the words themselves and by the air of hurt reproach which accompanied them; but before she could muster a reply the maid entered with a tray bearing tea and a little pot of chocolate for her mistress.

"I will pour out, Jeanne," cried the young girl, welcoming a diversion. "Put it here on the table."

The woman complied, removing the violets, upon which she cast a brief, contemptuous glance, then hung about, needlessly officious, settling Mme. Bender's pillows and arranging the cups and saucers. It seemed to Catherine that she was unwilling to leave her alone with the patient, but presently she straightened up and stood as though waiting for orders.

"You may leave us, Jeanne," suggested the invalid timidly. "Perhaps as it is a fine day you might care to go out for a little."

Somewhat to Catherine's surprise the woman assented.

"As madame wishes. Since mademoiselle is going to remain, I will take this opportunity to get a breath of air."

For a second her eyes rested full on Catherine's face, with a look which the recipient read as a mixture of speculation and defiance. Then she withdrew, and presently a brisk step along the passage outside told the two listeners she had departed.

Catherine felt more comfortable, and fancied her companion shared her feeling, but after a little while she was distressed to see that the cup of chocolate remained untasted, her cousin's eyes fixed blankly on the window, through whose white drawn curtains showed faintly the two iron bars Jeanne had spoken about. She asked herself what the poor woman thought about those brutal reminders of her past folly, and if the sight of them preyed upon her mind. She had never mentioned them, but there they were, staring her in the face, proof, even if she had forgotten the episode, that she was not to be trusted.

"You are very quiet to-day, Germaine," remarked Catherine lightly. "Is anything troubling you?"

A tremulous sigh answered her. The white hand pressed itself against the tormented eyes as though to shut out disturbing fancies.

"I don't know . . . I don't know," murmured the sad voice with a touch of irritability. "Everything is so confused. My memory, you know. Things go from me, and I never can tell what has happened and what I—I have imagined. It frightens me. I don't know what to believe. . . ."

Catherine felt a wave of intense pity sweep over her. She would have given much to be able to help the poor, brooding creature, but what could one do or say to reassure her?

"Your chocolate is getting cold. Let me give you some more," she gently urged. "As for forgetting things, if I were you I shouldn't give it a thought! Memory is so very much a matter of health."

"Ah, you only say that to comfort me. I know—I know it is far more serious than you think. There are things I could tell you of, dreadful things, ghastly things, things like nightmares! Ah! If you knew only half that goes on here—" and she touched her forehead with a distraught gesture. "Sometimes I—but no," checking herself quickly, "I do wrong to speak of them. I am forgetting again. Jeanne says I am not to mention them to anyone, or else . . ." She stopped once more, setting her lips together with a look of frightened secrecy.

Things like nightmares! Here at last was a reference to the delusions both Jeanne and the doctor had mentioned. It was the first time Germaine had spoken of them, but the repressed terror in her manner showed the acuteness of her mental suffering.

"I don't know what you are talking about, Germaine," declared Catherine stoutly. "But I'm sure it is all due to disordered nerves. Remember the shock you have had."

"You mean my accident?" The thin hands quivered spasmodically. "Ah, if I could only believe it was due to that! But no—what I speak of began much later. Oh, a great deal later! That is what terrifies me so."

Catherine caught the fluttering hands in hers with a firm pressure.

"Nonsense, dear! Everything is all right. But since you are so worried, why not let us call in another doctor? Someone who specializes in nervous cases. Mightn't it be a good idea?"

At once she realized her mistake. With a violent movement the invalid recoiled from her, hiding her face in the pillows.

"Ah, not that, not that!" she whispered in an agonized appeal. "Ah, Catherine, if you love me, never call in a specialist! I implore you!"

There was nothing to do but soothe and coax her back into a quiet state. At last she lay back with closed eyes, seeing which Catherine gave up the attempt to make conversation and let her rest, thankful that the panic of the moment was over.

The fading light was all but gone. Catherine sat on, busy with her thoughts, believing that her cousin had fallen into a doze, although in the shadow of the bed-curtains it was difficult to tell. There was no sound save the faint ticking of the little tortoiseshell clock on the dressing-table, and the occasional honk of a motor-horn from the avenue.

Presently one of the draperies close to her side stirred slightly. She glanced at it, thinking the movement came from a breeze through the window, but no, the other curtains hung limp and still. The vibration continued, then a tiny, pricking noise reached her ears. What could it be? She sat motionless, holding her breath and watching fixedly descried a small, dark form creeping stealthily up the white fringe of the material from the floor. Surely she herself must be imagining things!

She stared harder. Good Heavens, it was a mouse!

Up, up it moved in jerks, its jewelled eyes glistening, its long tail slipping behind like a line of dark thread. It must have ventured forth in search of a meal, attracted by the cake-crumbs. But how bold, when there were people about! The thought came to the girl that it was treading familiar ground.

Fascinated, she stayed her impulse to shake it off, lest the sudden movement might alarm the sleeping woman. Now it had reached the surface of the bed, and with twinkling feet, halting and cocking its ears to listen, it proceeded confidently across the supine figure. Still Catherine did nothing. Into her mind had come the scrap of unintelligible conversation she had caught that first morning between the doctor and Jeanne. She heard again the deep voice saying. *"Vous êtes sûre qu'il n'y a pas de souris là bas?"*

Was Germaine asleep? Noiselessly bending forward, she stole a glance at the shadowed face. To her amazement she saw that the eyes were wide open, glued with horror and loathing to the darting form, while upon the forehead great drops of sweat stood out.

Catherine sprang to her feet, jostling the tea-table. The mouse vanished like a streak of light.

"Why, Germaine! Did you see? A mouse was actually running over your bed! Don't be frightened, it's gone now."

She ran to the wall-button and switched on the lights.

"What an impudent creature!" she exclaimed, laughing. "Were you afraid?"

Then to her utter dismay she saw the poor invalid sitting bolt upright, tears streaming down her checks, hands clasped.

"Catherine! Catherine! You saw it, too? It was real? Oh, my God, my God! And I thought it was my fancy!"

As long as she lived Catherine never forgot the anguished relief of the outcry, wrung from the Frenchwoman's very soul.

CHAPTER THIRTEEN

THE next moment she was on her knees beside the bed, her arms round the trembling figure.

"But of course it was real!" she declared vigorously. "I tell you I watched it climb up the hangings and didn't dare to speak for fear of waking you. There, it's quite gone. We'll set a trap and catch it. I promise you won't see it again!"

The unnerved woman clung to her, weeping hysterically.

"It always comes—again and again. I have told her, but she can't, she won't believe me. At last I've become afraid to say anything, because—because it is so plain what she thinks!"

Understanding flooded the dark places of Catherine's mind. This, then, was one of Germaine's delusions—mice running unchecked about her bed, while her poor bewildered brain strove to deny the evidence of her senses! What incredible negligence did it reveal, what wilful refusal to face facts? Or was there some much worse explanation?

For a second it seemed as though a curtain had been lifted, giving a glimpse of a monstrous scheme to cast doubt upon the invalid's sanity. Here was a single instance of it; there might be others. What if an organized attempt was going on to overthrow the insecure balance of this poor woman's reason?

Instantly common sense pulled her round. The idea was too utterly fantastic. Carelessness, yes, and inconceivable stupidity, but surely nothing more grave.

Still, the known facts were bad enough, and must be dealt with at once. While she fetched smelling-salts and eau-de-Cologne, chattering lightly and treating the whole affair as a joke, her mind was busy planning a surprise-attack on the offender now due to return. High time someone took matters in hand, but at the thought of facing Jeanne she inwardly trembled.

Presently she contrived without being noticed to lift the bed-valance and peer at the floor beneath. What met her eye filled her with righteous anger. Now she was no longer afraid.

Ten minutes later a hurried step approached, and the familiar figure stood in the door.

"Madame is comfortable? She has not required anything?"

The invalid summoned a tremulous smile.

"No, no, Jeanne! I have not needed you," she hastened to declare.

The maid's nostrils dilated, sniffing the eau-de-Cologne. Then she went back into the dressing-room to remove her wraps. Not heeding the imploring hand stretched out to stop her, Catherine walked straight into the adjoining room and closed the door.

"Jeanne," she said abruptly, "there are mice in madame's room. Something must be done about it at once."

The woman wheeled round in the act of taking off her hat. Her eyes glared with sudden annoyance.

"Mice?" she repeated shortly. "Impossible! Madame has been telling you that story."

"Not at all," retorted Catherine. "I myself have just seen a mouse crawling across madame's bed. There is no doubt about it."

For several seconds the two regarded each other fixedly. Then with a face hard as iron Jeanne turned deliberately and hung her coat upon a peg. She was silent so long that Catherine began to think she was not going to reply. Once more she started to remove her round, dark hat; then, changing her mind, left it on her head. When at last she spoke it was with great restraint.

"Mademoiselle will pardon me if I find it difficult to believe her. In all the years I have lived in this apartment I have never set eyes on a mouse."

"I'm sorry you think I'm lying," returned the girl with asperity. "In any case I must insist on your setting a trap in a place which I will show you. Madame is being terrified half out of her senses."

The woman darted a glance at her full of hatred and scorn. If she was intimidated, she showed no sign of it.

"*Jamais!*" Catherine heard her mutter under her breath. "*Jamais!* I cannot think what you mean to insinuate."

"Simply this, Jeanne. Quite obviously that room in there has not been properly cleaned for weeks, months even. I want you to come now and look under the bed. There has been something sticky there, and the mice have gnawed the carpet bare in patches."

The sallow face swelled till the eyes were reduced to pin-points. On the cheek-bones areas of mottled red appeared.

"Come, please, and let me show you what I mean," said Catherine, holding open the door.

After a brief hesitation, still wearing her hat, the woman obeyed, stooped to examine the spot Catherine indicated, and straightened up, her features set in a mutinous mask.

"I see nothing beyond a few drops of spilled medicine. Madame herself knows whose fault it is that no one but me is allowed to do her room. I slave from morning to night; when I go to bed, I am often too tired to sleep. I am a human being, not a machine! No other person would do for madame what I do; but if my efforts are not appreciated, if I am to be criticized and called to account over trifles, it is time to give up. It is plain that mademoiselle came here for the purpose of setting her cousin against me!"

"Nothing of the sort, Jeanne. I only want you to remove whatever it is that is attracting mice. That is all."

If Catherine spoke mildly, it was to spare Germaine, whose white face was quivering with agitated distress. Nothing could be gained by contradicting the maid, though what the valance concealed was not spilled medicine, but particles of food. She had even detected the odour of cheese. . . .

An hour later Catherine sat in the study, trying to think calmly. Difficult as it was to conceive of a well-trained servant leaving scraps of food upon the floor, it was equally incredible that the thing could have been done purposely. What was one to believe? One thing alone was certain, She had completely lost faith in Jeanne, whom she now regarded as a bad, if not dangerous, influence for Germaine. Devoted she might be, but for all that she was undermining the invalid's confidence in herself, fostering, whether by ignorance or design, the poor creature's fear of encroaching insanity. As things were, it was worse than hopeless to attempt to nurse the patient back to health.

"Somehow or other she must be got rid of!" she told herself, still shaken by indignation. "Perhaps this business will open the way. A thief; and incompetent into the bargain!"

She could not help feeling a little exultant over the recent scene. After this Jeanne must either mend her ways or go. She hoped it would be the latter.

However, she had much to learn, as the evening was to prove.

Amid the staid magnificence of the *salle à manger* she ate her solitary meal. Speculatively she looked round at the three fine pictures on the walls, at the tall, gold candelabra which once had adorned a palace. More objects easily convertible into money. Were the servants she now thought of as rogues merely waiting for her visit to be over before laying hands on these treasures? Well, they would wait in vain. It was her fixed intention to foil them at that or any other game they might be playing.

All at once her thoughts veered to the little notaire, A. Blom. What if he were in league with this pair, aiding them in disposing of their plunder? His visit here that night three weeks ago might have been to cast his appraising eye over things and possibly to take something off with him. Jeanne's secret conferences with the man took on a new meaning. She wondered if there were any way of finding out the truth.

It was usual on the evenings she spent at home for Jeanne to call her when Mme. Bender was ready for bed, so that she could go in to say good night. However, the hour passed and there was no summons. This did not astonish her, for the feeling between Jeanne and herself was naturally strained; but when ten o'clock struck and nothing had happened she put down her book and went toward her cousin's bedroom. The door was shut, but from the other side came sounds of tempestuous weeping.

She halted, full of consternation, thinking the strangled sobs came from Germaine, but a moment's listening informed her that it was Jeanne herself who was indulging in the violent outburst. Somehow she had not expected this. A second later words reached her, stormy with protest.

"No, madame, it is useless! All is finished, all, all! I swear to you I am going away, at once; I shall pack tonight and leave quite early in the morning. Nothing can stop me. Eduardo, too, will go. Madame will be left absolutely alone, to face the doctors, the nurses, the strange enemies who will swoop down upon her. I have done my utmost, I; but if madame distrusts me, then my time with her is over. I have my future to think of. I cannot support plotting and scheming behind my back by those who have their own ends to serve!"

Catherine held her breath, appalled by the hurricane of tears and recriminations. Through the outcries she caught a despairing whimper which cut her to the heart.

"Jeanne, dear Jeanne, you must not say such things! Have I ever doubted you? It is cruel to torture me like this!"

The feeble protest was drowned in a renewed burst of weeping.

"Cruel? It is madame who is cruel! She accuses me of neglect, me who have given fifteen years of my life to her service! It is too much! How could I know this one thing was true, when every day madame sees and hears what is not there? Even now I cannot altogether believe. No, I see it plainly. I am no longer wanted, and am to be cast aside like an old shoe. Enough! I go to-morrow, to give place to some persons for whom madame will be only a mental case. But if when I am no longer here it is thought wise to shut madame up in an asylum—"

"Jeanne, you cannot, you must not leave me! Listen to me, I implore you to listen!"

"I will not hear madame! I go to my brother in the Vosges to take the long rest I have been needing this twelve-month. Then madame will realize what I have done for her, how I have protected her. She will know, she will know!"

Unable to bear more, Catherine burst into the room. "Jeanne—what is the meaning of this?" she demanded in a stern whisper.

Quick as lightning the woman turned upon her, one finger outstretched in venomous accusation. She still wore her hat, while her face was swollen and streaked with tears.

"There!" she cried hoarsely. "Behold one who calls herself your friend! Why is she here if not to profit by madame's weakness? Does madame flatter herself for one moment that this young American has come across the ocean for love of a bed-ridden woman? Ask her what she hopes to get for her pains! Ask her if she is not waiting for madame to die and leave her a fortune!"

The shameless attack deprived the girl of speech. She could only stare while the stream of abuse flowed on.

"Madame's friends!" went on the voice with bitter scorn. "Who are they? I know of none but Mademoiselle Cushing and Mademoiselle West—paupers both! Why do they come here, why does the fat singer urge madame to make her will? Madame is indeed insane if she cannot see into the hearts of these creatures. Always this talk of the will, this fear that madame will die and leave these people penniless! Tell me—have I ever hoped that madame would leave me a single sou? Am I taking away with me more than I brought here? No, a thousand times no! Madame is turning away the one being who has tried to stand between her and these grasping—"

"Stop! Look, Jeanne, what you have done!"

The form on the bed had collapsed. Mme. Bender had fainted.

Instantly a miracle happened. Jeanne, her entire bearing transformed, every sign of hysteria vanished, cast a single appraising glance at the dead-white face of her mistress, then going to a little medicine-cupboard took out a bottle and measured a few drops of liquid into a glass.

Catherine watched the brisk, business-like movements with amazement, saw her raise the limp body, murmuring, *"Buvez-ceci, madame!"* in a tone of complete control.

Parenthetically she noticed that the bottle was labelled "Digitalis."

In another second Mme. Bender's eyelids fluttered open and a trembling sigh escaped her lips. With a grunt of satisfaction Jeanne turned to face the spell-bound girl.

"And now, mademoiselle," she said in an even voice, "perhaps you had better leave madame with me."

CHAPTER FOURTEEN

"BUT you aren't actually afraid of anything, are you? You don't think Mme. Bender is any the worse for what you've just told me?"

Geoffrey was trying hard to read Catherine's thoughts. Was she keeping something back? He fancied she was more deeply troubled than she was willing to admit, but he could not quite get at the cause of her anxiety.

It was late Sunday afternoon; the air was soft with the first full tide of spring, and half the Latin Quarter thronged the pavements, or lingered at little tables in front of the cafés, sipping aperitifs. Everywhere were flower-sellers laden with tulips and daffodils, while on the street corners venders of balloons exhibited their huge soaring bunches of multi-coloured grapes. The whole presented an effect of pageantry and that outpouring of the holiday spirit which Paris knows so perfectly how to achieve.

Catherine and Geoffrey, having quitted the rue d'Assas, had sauntered aimlessly across the space beside the Café des Lilas, ancient haunt of long-haired poets, and turned into the narrow avenue of flowering chestnuts which leads like the neck of a bottle to the Luxembourg Gardens. Now that they were alone, the girl had hastened to pour out the story of the past week, her pent-up feelings finding relief in the recital. Yet that her companion, in spite of his evident sympathy, did not take the situation as seriously as she did, was plain from the question he asked at the end.

She bit her lip, and considered for several seconds before framing a reply.

"I don't know what to say. On the surface things are going on much as usual. Mme. Bender was prostrated for two days, exactly as long as that woman kept to her word about leaving, but the minute Jeanne gave in and said she would stay my cousin revived again. Now she's just as she was before."

"Do you think this maid actually meant to go?"

"Not for a moment! I'm sure it was only a bluff on her part, but it was a most effective one. She's got her mistress now exactly where she wants her, more than ever under her thumb. Oh, I was blind not to see it before! Hermione was right. It's terrifying to think that any human being can be so completely dominated by another."

He let his eyes dwell on the straight parallels of chestnuts stretching ahead before speaking.

"I wonder if there's any use trying to persuade her to go into a nursing-home? It seems to me she would be better off with expert care."

"Of course! I have thought so from the beginning. But it is very difficult, as the doctor pointed out to me when I spoke to him. She has got some morbid dread of being put under restraint, and if one overruled her there's no telling what might happen. That, I begin to see, is at the root of her fear about losing Jeanne, who probably keeps her frightened with tales of French asylums."

"So she believes Jeanne alone is standing between her and a sanatorium?"

"Exactly. I tell you that creature is fiendishly clever! Whether because of egotism and jealousy or from some other motive, she has made Germaine think no one but herself is capable of a disinterested devotion. Everyone else is an enemy—even I."

Her cheeks flushed, there were tears in her eyes. He could see how deeply she was hurt.

"That's absurd!" he exclaimed hotly.

"Absurd or not, it's true! I can't bear to speak of it. You see, ever since that afternoon I have noticed a change in Germaine towards me. There's a barrier between us, she isn't frank any more, and I know only too well it's because of those vile accusations Jeanne made against me. She thinks—oh, it's too shameful!—that I am staying there simply for what I hope to get out of her."

"Can't you make her see how false all this is?"

"How can I? If I protest against the insinuations, the fact of doing so amounts practically to an admission. It's not as though she said anything openly, it's only a sort of subtle reproach in her manner. No, there's nothing I can do."

"Except," he suggested, "to leave there altogether."

She turned for a moment in his direction, then shook her head.

"I can't do that," she answered firmly. "I'd like to, but I daren't."

"Why?" he demanded. "It's not as though you could help matters by staying. What can you do?"

"Someone must be there," she replied obstinately, "if only to keep an eye on those servants. She's so utterly alone! Why, she even refuses now to see Hermione—another result of Jeanne's work. If I go away, she'll be completely cut off from the world."

He nodded thoughtfully.

"I see your point," he said. "But, after all, you can't be with her long. What about your visit to Italy?"

"That's off. I've written to the Hardwickes to say I'm not joining them after all. Too bad, but it can't be helped."

He stopped stock-still in astonishment.

"Is there any real need to sacrifice yourself like this?"

"I don't know. I hope it may do some good! Anyhow I feel I must see things straightened out for Germaine before I go away. Perhaps you think I'm foolish, but I believe you would do the same in my place."

He said no more. Secretly he was exulting over the knowledge that he was not going to lose her in a few weeks' time. The future suddenly held out rosy hopes.

In silence they passed through the big iron gates into the gardens. Ahead of them stretched the grey palace of the Luxembourg, and in the amphitheater before it the round basin of water shimmered in the sun, white-wringed boats dying across its bosom, and the fountain lifting a plume of diamond spray. Tiny children, dressed like gay dolls, darted about with hoops and balls, street urchins in black aprons chattered clamorously, rusty crows of old women huddled on the seats above which the stone queens of France gazed down in a majestic circle.

Close to the statue of Marguerite de Valois they found a seat and resumed their conversation.

"Now as to this thieving business," said Geoffrey, offering his companion a cigarette. "I don't say you are wrong, but it's possible Mr. Bender did dispose of certain things before he died. It strikes me that for those servants to sell anything as conspicuous as a Manet would be taking a frightful risk."

"Would it?" she retorted. "I'm not so sure. If I had not happened along, who would have been the wiser?"

He was forced to admit the logic of this.

"I daresay they are rogues," he said reflectively. "The moment you spoke of their cutting down the household expenses I had my suspicions. You say no one comes to the flat?"

"Not a soul, except that horrid little man I told you about. I suppose he is Jeanne's lawyer, but I am not satisfied about him somehow. I can't help thinking he is mixed up in this, though I can't guess how. Do you know, I actually went and had a hat copied at Honorine's, merely to try to find out about him; but although I've been to her place several times, I have not seen him again."

Geoffrey continued his own train of thought.

"Of course, the paintings would fetch large sums, even if sold through a *receleur*," he remarked.

"A *receleur*? What's that?"

"A receiver of stolen goods. Naturally such sales could not be conducted through legitimate channels."

She made an excited gesture.

"The little *notaire*!" she cried. "Perhaps that's what he is—a receiver of stolen goods. Had you thought of that?"

"By Jove, you may be right! That's a thundering good suggestion. I wonder if we can find out?"

He pondered the idea, bending forward and examining the pebbles underfoot with close attention. Presently without looking at her he spoke again:

"When you said just now that you wanted to stay there to keep an eye on the servants, had you anything in mind beyond the fact that they may be dishonest?"

She started slightly, shifting her gaze from the impertinent profile of the sculptured queen to the leafy avenue stretching out behind them.

"Nothing definite," she answered reluctantly. "After all, stealing is bad enough. No, I don't know that there's anything else."

He studied the tip of his cigarette.

"Yet you are nervous about something. Am I right?" How observant he was! She had tried to conceal her secret from him, but he had guessed it in spite of her.

"It's only an instinctive feeling," she admitted guiltily. "I can't define it. Do you think me frightfully stupid?" The confession brought relief. Since Wednesday she had battled with a nameless dread, vague yet sufficiently strong to account for her letter to the Hardwickes. She had been haunted by the consciousness of impending disaster, the more to be feared because of its obscurity—something which would require all her wits to circumvent.

Instead of replying he asked another question:

"Do you happen to know if this maid is trying to induce her mistress to make a will?"

"It's odd you should speak of that," she answered, surprised. "As a matter of fact, she has not done anything of the sort. It was the very point she made to prove to Germaine she had no mercenary motives. She brought it out like a trump card."

"Ah!" he exclaimed in satisfaction, "that's good!"

"Why?" she demanded, puzzled.

"Why? Simply that if what she declares is true, then there can be no actual danger threatening your cousin. You see what I mean?"

"Not quite."

"I'll make it plainer. Unless we can show that this woman is trying to secure a will in her favour, then it is clear she has everything to lose and nothing to gain by her mistress's death. In short, it is to her own interests to take the best possible care of Mme. Bender, knowing that she can profit so long as the latter lives, but no longer."

"Of course!" she cried. "How dense I must seem!"

A load of anxiety slipped from her heart. Why had she overlooked this utterly reasonable point of view? She understood now something of the nature of her recent apprehension.

"In fact," he continued, "I'll go so far as to say that the surer we are that the maid and the butler are fleecing their mistress, the better guarantee we have for her personal safety. Not that the thefts can be allowed to go on. We must do all we can to find proof and send the servants packing. It may be hard, though, since we can't look for any assistance from Mme. Bender herself."

"She won't believe anything wrong of Jeanne, nor does one dare ask her about the pictures, as any reference to Cousin Harry upsets her terribly. Besides, she does not think for herself any more, she only expresses Jeanne's opinions."

"Well, we must do our best without her. There's another matter, too, I should like to mention now we're on the subject. While I was in Havre the maid came to the office to obtain a duplicate key to Mme. Bender's safety-deposit. I don't know if there was anything wrong about it, but you might just try to find out if your cousin has that key in her possession."

Her eyes dilated with fresh suspicion.

"The safety-deposit? That's where Germaine's pearls are kept, in fact most of her jewellery; Hermione told me so. Oh! do you suppose Jeanne has designs in that direction?"

He laughed.

"Even if she has, you needn't worry. Banks are pretty careful."

"Just the same, I don't like the look of it. Poor Hermione! She's dreadfully in the dumps. That's another thing Jeanne is responsible for. She has succeeded in cutting Mme. Bender off from her one remaining friend. . . . Heavens! is it almost seven o'clock? I must fly!"

"I'll drop you, if I may. I am going over to the other side anyhow," he lied cheerfully.

"If you're quite sure," she agreed doubtfully.

His pulses leaped as he fancied he caught a gleam of pleasure in her eyes. Was it faintly possible that she, too, was glad to delay the moment of separation?

At the corner of the Boulevard they got into an open taxi, and in another moment were racing towards the river, the soft breeze in their faces. Catherine looked happier now. Colour stained her cheeks a delicate rose, and her eyes had lost the fear-ridden look so noticeable a little while ago. Geoffrey studied her with appreciation, delighting in the trim lines of her grey homespun coat and skirt, her tiny, close-fitting hat and the slender fineness of her hand's and feet.

"Did you like my sister?" he inquired abruptly.

She started at the suddenness of the question.

"Oh, tremendously! She's rather like you, don't you think?" she added naively, then blushed a deeper red.

"I wanted you two to meet," he said slowly, then was silent because of the thought in his mind. "I hope," he went on, "that you'll go and see her at Fontainebleau when she asks you, as she's sure to do. You'll like my brother-in-law—he's an etcher. Odd chap, but a decent sort."

"I'd love to go," she said hesitatingly. "Perhaps a little later. Just now I hate leaving Germaine."

"What rubbish! You can't stay tied to her for the rest of your life!"

She laughed at his impatient tone.

"I know you think I'm over-scrupulous. Never mind—I've a plan in my head which may help to straighten things out. Don't ask me what it is yet—it mayn't succeed," and she smiled at him tantalizingly.

At the Cours la Reine they were caught in a traffic block. It was dusk now, and the river on the one hand, the Place de la Concorde on the other glittered with a million stars. Suddenly Catherine gave a smothered cry.

"Look!" she whispered, grasping her companion's arm. "There is Eduardo, driving Mme. Bender's car. And do you see the man with him? It's the creature from the rue d'Amsterdam I have been talking about!"

Following her eyes, Geoffrey spied a jet-black Rolls, upon whose front seat slouched the Portuguese, his sullen face lit by an adjacent street lamp. The features of the man beside him were hidden by a wide-brimmed hat, but as the taxi crept forward a few yards they could be seen in profile.

Geoffrey uttered an astonished exclamation.

"By Jove, I know the fellow! At least I've seen him. . . ."

"Where? Who is he?" demanded the girl eagerly.

He thought hard, then shook his head, chagrined.

"That's the worst of it. I'm hanged if I know!" he admitted.

CHAPTER FIFTEEN

ALL THAT evening Geoffrey cudgelled his brain to recall how and where he had come across the butler's companion. There might be no special point in remembering, yet, on the other hand, if Catherine's suggestion were correct any facts concerning the *notaire* might prove useful. However, try as he would, he could not bring back the circumstances of the chance encounter, and went to bed thoroughly exasperated.

Next morning at the very moment of setting foot in the outer office the thing flashed on him. Why, it was here, in this room! The man had been standing by the table, stolid and a little furtive, apparently waiting for an appointment. He had looked up suddenly, and his unwholesome pallor, together with his red-rimmed eyes, one of them marked by a curious blemish, had photographed themselves on the onlooker's memory.

As soon as Geoffrey had run through his letters he called one of the under-clerks, a youngster named Ballou, into his private office.

"Guy," he said, "do you happen to know of a *notaire* called A. Blom, living at 359, rue d'Amsterdam?"

The clerk, a dapper French stripling justly proud of his good command of English, gave the question careful consideration.

"Blom?" he repeated, his black eyes sharply alert. "No, sir, I think not. A *notaire*, you say?"—and his tone expressed conscious superiority. "I don't often come across any of that lot, sir."

"He was here on business about a couple of months ago—a small chap, pasty-faced, with something queer about one of his eyes. I'd like to find out what he wanted."

Again the young man reflected, passing a long hand over his sleek, brilliantined hair.

"I will inquire, sir. One of the others may know."

"Do so, Guy, and let me hear the result."

Ten minutes later the youth returned to report failure.

"No one has heard of the person, sir. Of course, there's Mr. Howard, who's ill. Shall I get in touch with him?"

"You needn't trouble to do that. Instead, I want you to go to the rue d'Amsterdam—here's the address—and see what you can find out from the concierge. This much I will tell you: I have reason to believe Blom to be mixed up in the disposal of some stolen works of art. But don't let any hint of this leak out."

"Right, sir—you may depend on me," and with an air of enjoyment Ballou departed on his mission.

Geoffrey resumed his work, but between him and the dull routine of deeds and titles floated a delicate, troubled face. He could not forget the look in Catherine's eyes yesterday, nor the conviction forced upon him that she was living in the grip of constant if indefinable dread. Something must be done to set her mind at rest, and this move regarding Blom was the one immediate thing which occurred to him.

As for Mme. Bender herself, frankly he was not greatly concerned.

"It's a pretty rotten business," he said as, lighting a cigarette, he gave himself up to reflection. "She seems completely in that maid's power, and yet for the life of me I can't see any reason for alarm. The point is, there's no motive. . . . To allow the poor creature to die would be simply killing the goose that lays the golden egg—a folly that precious pair of servants are much too clever to commit! No, they'll play the game for all it's worth, knowing that once their mistress is dead they'll get nothing further, beyond a small legacy, which in any case is bound to come to them. . . . I can see, though, why they were furious when Catherine descended upon them. They don't want any watchful eye checking their movements. I'd give a good deal to have a look at Mme. Bender's pass-book, by the way. I'll wager that tells a story."

If the poor lady got either better or worse the position would right itself. In the former event she would be able to look after herself, in the latter his firm could assume authority. It was in this intermediate state that she presented such a problem and surely before long she would tend definitely one way or the other.

No, it was Catherine herself whose situation troubled him. He chafed at the thought of her living in proximity to a victim of mental illness, subjected to annoyances she had no power to check. He would have given much to put an end to it, but he could think of but one possible solution the risk of which he was frightened to take.

No, although he now knew he meant with all his soul to marry her if she would have him, he dared not put his chances to the test. Not till he felt more sure of her. Up till now he was miserably certain she did not care for him—at least not in the right way. Instinct warned him she would take a lot of winning. . . .

It was just before lunch-time that young Ballou re-entered the office with an important air, and laid his bowler hat and a pair of particularly smart new gloves upon the desk. His black eyes glistened with mystery.

"Well, Guy—any luck?"

"A little, sir." The youngster cleared his throat nonchalantly. "Not much, I admit. I've been gossiping with the concierge in the rue d'Amsterdam, and I flatter myself there's not much I can't tell you about this person, Adolph Blom. I posed as a *notaire* myself, in search of a bureau, and as such it was natural to want to know something about my professional rival."

"Excellent. What did you find out?"

"Well, sir, I'm sorry to say the concierge gives this fellow a most unassailable character. Nothing shady about him. It seems he is an Alsatian, who has lived for years at the same address, pays his rent regularly, numbers several of the *locataires* as his clients, and is universally regarded as a shrewd man of affairs. A little mean, perhaps, but that is not held against him. He is quiet, spends little on pleasure, and once a year takes a holiday of two weeks, always in Alsace, and invariably in August, like other people. A hard-working, reliable chap."

Geoffrey raised his brows in disappointment. Whatever questionable there might be about the *notaire*, it evidently did not appear on the surface.

"However," continued Guy, referring to a *dossier*, "this year he departed from his custom, and in February took an additional holiday, this time going South. From something he dropped on his return the concierge thinks he went to Bordeaux."

"Bordeaux!"

The name suggested nothing except that the town was a port from which many boats departed. It might offer a suitable point, well removed from Paris, from which to conduct nefarious operations.

"I also inquired into his private life, but I don't suppose that will interest you. Blom, it seems, is a bachelor, something over forty. Until quite recently he had a mistress, some young woman employed in a *usine*, but soon after this visit to the South he broke with her, and began paying serious attentions to a woman who lives across the court—a milliner named Mme. Baron. Husband killed in the war. Runs a business under the title of Honorine. She's a client of Blom, who probably knows all about her affairs. The concierge thinks she must have saved considerable money, or else our friend would not find her attractive, for she's middle-aged and not much to look at."

Geoffrey pondered this bit of information, then shook his head slowly.

"Thanks, Guy. You've done a thorough job of it, and if you didn't come across anything suspicious it's not your fault. There was only a faint chance."

But the clerk was in no hurry to depart. He picked up his hat, flicked an imaginary bit of dust from it, and coming a step closer, fixed his eyes on his employer's face.

"One thing more, sir," he remarked confidentially. "While I was in the loge the man we were discussing looked in to collect his letters, and although I kept well behind the door I had a good view of him. And, sir, I knew him at once."

"You did?" exclaimed Geoffrey, startled. "Who is he, then?"

"Ah, that's the question! You were right, he came to this office about two to three months ago. I saw him myself, and handed him on to Mr. Howard. I can't recall what it was he wanted, but the name he gave wasn't Blom. I can swear to that. It was something altogether different."

Here was a new development. The thing had a definitely suspicious look. . . .

"You are sure of this?"

"Oh, absolutely, sir. As a matter of fact, I noticed him at the time rather particularly, because I had seen him once before."

"Where?"

"At the archives bureau, sir. You remember that job I was doing in January? Well, I ran across him then, searching through some records. I thought he looked like a white rat nosing about among the files."

Geoffrey pushed back his chair.

"Guy," he said, "get on at once to Mr. Howard's apartment, and see if he's well enough to come to the telephone. I must just question him about this."

While the call was put through he paced the room impatiently. In the past few minutes the *notaire* had suddenly assumed a definite importance, although in what way it was impossible to tell. However, it was quite likely he would soon know something from Howard, who was their oldest clerk, a steady-going Essex man, and a walking repository of stored information. Howard never forgot anything, nor for that matter divulged anything without reasonable justification.

After a short delay Guy returned, his face regretful.

"No good, sir—that avenue's blocked. Mr. Howard is very ill, in fact, out of his head. It's a bad case of pleurisy."

CHAPTER SIXTEEN

ON TUESDAY evening Catherine dined with Miss Cushing with the idea of discussing a project formed in her mind. Since events had shown her how hopeless it was to get rid of Jeanne by ordinary means, she had concentrated on a plan which at first glance appeared impossible—namely, that of persuading the maid to go away of her own accord. If this could be accomplished, even for a short period, Germaine might become gradually accustomed to an altered regime, so that when a definite break came she could bear it with equanimity.

"For Jeanne has got to go," she declared to herself with passionate vehemence. "Thief or not, she's undermining the poor thing's vitality to a terrifying extent. The more Germaine clings to her, the more dangerous the situation becomes."

She had, in fact, begun to regard the maid as an insuperable barrier to her cousin's improvement—she hoped the only one, though that was an optimistic thought. Still if Mme. Bender could be given a chance to believe in her own sanity, who could say what wonders might not be achieved? She would have to be provided with competent nurses, and against these she would fight tooth and nail, but Catherine trusted to her own persuasiveness to overcome the unreasoning prejudice. After all, was the latter not due to Jeanne's insidious suggestions? Once the childish creature realized that she need not be removed from her home, she would probably cease to regard a professional nurse as an enemy.

Everything therefore depended on getting Jeanne away for a holiday. If she herself wished it, her mistress would raise no objection; but could she be induced to consider such a proposal? Catherine, after hours of thought, believed she had solved the problem.

However, she doubted if by herself she could accomplish her purpose. She was young and inexperienced, her word might carry little weight. She must have Hermione's support.

She outlined her idea with earnestness, seated opposite the singer in the tiny *salle à manger*, and resolutely keeping her gaze from gravitating towards the large photograph of her hostess which displayed the latter's ripe charms in the classic draperies of *Thaïs*, ready primed for seduction.

"You see, Jeanne is so clever that she has undoubtedly pulled the wool over that doctor's eyes. He may not be willing to believe anything against her. Will you back me up in what I am going to tell him?"

"*Mais certainement, ma chère—de grand coeur!*" replied the artist emotionally. "*C'est une bonne idée!*"

With moist eyes and utter self-forgetfulness she was drinking many little glasses of Burgundy, under the influence of which her depressed spirits were rising by rapid degrees. In the beginning she had been steeped in misery, and had donned an emblematic costume, nothing less than the gown of voluminous net in which she had many times died a lingering death as *La Dame aux Camélias*; but now she had so far forgotten her intended *rôle* as to allow the angel sleeves to dip into the *soupe à l'oignon*, so that they left little trails of grease and cheese across the table-cloth.

"But *naturellement* I will come with you," she cried, delighted at the prospect of outwitting her hated rival. "I scarcely know this man— *comment s'appelle-t-il?*—but he has undoubtedly heard of me. We will go at once, when we have finished dinner. I have eaten nothing for days, owing to my unhappiness, and Yvonne insists that I am in need *d'être nourrie!*"

Whereupon she did justice to the excellent *ragoût de veau*, following it with several helpings of *haricots verts*, a *crême renversée*, and two cups of black coffee, managing so successfully to fortify herself that she was in danger of lapsing into lengthy reminiscences of her opera days if Catherine had not reminded her to change into street attire before it was too late for their venture.

At nine o'clock they sallied forth in a taxi to a quiet street leading out of the Avenue de la Grande Armée, and soon afterwards were ushered into Dr. Girard's reception-room, ghastly with modern Francois Premier chairs and snowy marble groups set upon pedestals.

Catherine had barely time to collect her thoughts when the pompous figure of the physician appeared in the doorway. Bowing ceremoniously, he gazed at his visitors through thick convex lenses, meanwhile fingering his black, spade-shaped beard with a tentative hand.

"And what can I do for these ladies?" he inquired in his booming voice.

Hermione made the necessary introductions, then embarked with tumultuous dignity upon a narrative so jumbled and incoherent that presently Catherine was obliged to take pity on the poor man's bewilderment and explain matters herself. She described simply and forcibly all that had come under her observation during the past weeks, emphasizing her belief that Jeanne's influence on Mme. Bender was distinctly bad. The Frenchman listened with growing astonishment, and when she reached the mouse episode gave vent to an exclamation of shocked incredulity.

"*Est-ce possible? Est-ce possible?*" he murmured, wiping his glasses with a hand that trembled.

Catherine assured him it was.

"But, mademoiselle—you saw this animal, with your own eyes?"

"Not only that, monsieur, but I found traces of food under the bed, left—I believe purposely—to provide an attraction."

"*Mon Dieu!*"

He rose, pacing the floor, his brow heavily corrugated. Both women watched him eagerly.

"But this alters everything! It puts the whole case in a different light!"

"I hoped you would see that," cried Catherine earnestly. "Mind, I may be wrong about her doing this intentionally; it is possible she is only very careless; but the result is the same. Mme. Bender has been encouraged to think that she is suffering from delusions."

He scarcely heard her, snapping his fingers impatiently. After a moment he subsided into his chair, deep in thought.

"Since you tell me this, mademoiselle," he said at last, "I am forced to admit that my knowledge of the poor lady's hallucinations is founded chiefly on hearsay. There are indications to show that she is in a state of profound melancholia, but beyond that I can affirm little with exactitude. I now see that I have been disgracefully misled. I have looked upon this maid as a capable nurse, but if I had faintly suspected that she was falsifying her reports I should long ago have insisted on a trained attendant. It is mainly because madame herself so violently objected—"

"Ah, that is the difficulty!" interrupted the girl, and straightway described what had happened when Jeanne threatened to depart. "You see from this, monsieur, how useless it is to expect madame to send the woman away. She is completely under her thumb. That is why we want your assistance."

She waited till the good man had roused himself sufficiently to give her full attention.

"Yes, mademoiselle? I am listening. What do you suggest?"

"It seemed to us," began Catherine tactfully, "that if you could use your authority to order this Jeanne to take a rest—say that she was overtaxing herself and becoming unnerved—she would have to agree to go away. That would give us our chance. Once the woman is out of the house we could easily find an excuse to prevent her return, and meanwhile we might persuade my cousin to go into the country, where with new surroundings and expert care she could build up her strength again. Doesn't it seem a feasible plan?"

He nodded with slow approval.

"Excellent, mademoiselle! Excellent! The chief obstacle will be the patient herself, but if we can over-rule her objections—"

"We can do nothing without you, monsieur. Neither Jeanne nor madame would listen to us."

It was a wise move. The doctor was not immune to flattery.

"I see! Precisely! Well, then, I promise to do my utmost. I will warn this woman to-morrow that she is on the verge of a *crise* of nerves, order her to take a month's rest, and *voilà!* the affair will soon right itself—or at least we shall hope so!"

With an impulse of glad relief Catherine sprang up and seized his big hands in hers.

"Oh, that is good of you!" she exclaimed gratefully. "If you only knew what a load you have taken off my mind!"

"It is nothing, mademoiselle, nothing!" replied Girard, not unmoved by this appreciation. "It is I who should thank you for shedding light on a most troublesome case—not, however, the first in my experience," he added jealously.

"For I can assure you, mesdemoiselles, I have seen some strange things in my practice!"

When the two were outside on the pavement Catherine breathed a sigh of relief.

"Well, that's accomplished!" she cried with satisfaction. "We've opened his eyes a bit, which is something. Poor man, I felt rather sorry for him. He is now in a state where he doesn't know what to think."

"He is not the only one," replied Hermione with an ominous shudder. The exhilarating effect of the Burgundy having worn off, she was becoming mysterious and pessimistic.

"Why do you say that?" asked Catherine, slightly annoyed.

The singer shrugged her vast shoulders.

"Jeanne. She is a deep one. I warn you, Catherine, we have not got the best of her yet, any more than we have got to the bottom of her devilment. You'll see!" and she shook her head with a gesture Cassandra might have envied.

It was stupid to be cast down by any pronouncement so irrational. So Catherine told herself several hours later, when, unable to sleep, her mind tiresomely harped upon what she scornfully called the gipsy's warning. Hermione was always dramatic; she invariably read mysteries into things. It was simply her temperament, unchecked by common sense.

"And yet Jeanne is deep," she reflected apprehensively. "If she suspects this plan of ours she'll find some way of outwitting us. Oh! How I distrust the woman! It's her cleverness that frightens me."

The hall clock struck twelve, half-past, then one, and still she was wide awake. At last just as consciousness was beginning to film over a stealthy sound in the passage outside roused her again to alert attention. She sat up in bed and listened.

Footsteps, muffled by *pantoufles*, were descending the stairs to the lower floor. She strained her ears, but after some time had elapsed the person or persons had not returned. With a feeling of puzzled uneasiness she slid out of bed, put on dressing-gown and slippers, and went quietly out.

From the downstairs hall, in which a light showed, voices reached her. She tried hard to catch what they were saying, but could make out nothing beyond an angry whispered wrangling.

Curiosity got the better of caution. She crept stealthily down a step at a time until, crouching at the turn, she was able to peer through the balustrade into the illumined space.

What she saw made her gasp.

Against the closed door of the picture gallery Eduardo was stationed, with his foot braced in an attitude of defiance. Jeanne was ranged beside him, a dark coat thrown over her night-gown, her eyes hard and sullen, while confronting the pair stood the meanly built figure of a man, quivering with rage. One glance at the latter's black, broad-brimmed hat was enough. It hid the features of A. Blom.

What on earth was he doing here at this hour?

His manner frightened the watcher. Charged with malevolent animosity, it hinted at something arrogant and at the same time implacable. She held her breath, terrified lest he should turn and discover her, even while realizing that his fury was entirely concentrated on the two guarding the door. Guttural words reached her, but there was so much argot as to render their meaning unintelligible.

Catherine stared, fascinated. The Alsatian was no match for Eduardo, who could have throttled him with one powerful fist, yet for some reason the butler's bravado seemed a hollow sham, while the gleam in his small eyes was distinctly nervous. Only Jeanne remained calm, glancing from one face to the other with a cold calculation.

The whispering stopped, there was a pause during which nothing was heard save stertorous breathing. Then the *notaire* spoke between his teeth:

"Enough! Give me the key. I am going to see for myself," he commanded brutally.

"No! I refuse. It's not your affair," retorted Eduardo.

"*Hein!* Not my affair? Then listen: I will tell you something!"—and putting his lips close to the Portuguese's ear the speaker hissed a few words venomously.

Some of the butler's assurance wilted away. He wavered uncertainly, looking towards Jeanne in doubtful question. The latter considered for a moment, then with a shrug and a jerk of the head moved aside.

"Very well," she agreed indifferently, "let him have his way."

With slow reluctance the Portuguese drew a key from his pocket and inserted it in the lock. The next instant the *notaire* had pushed him away, and with a muttered expletive had vanished into the gallery, switching on the light within. The others followed with less confident steps.

Silence ensued, broken only by hoarse exclamations of rage. Evidently Blom had made some discovery not to his liking, doubtless in connection with the missing pictures. Yet what could it mean? Catherine's belief that the three were working in conjunction with each other was suddenly shaken.

If the listener had hoped to learn something conclusive, she was doomed to disappointment. The door was softly closed, and the voices, which had resumed their angry conference, sank into inaudibility. Still she remained, rooted to the spot, and shivering more from tension than cold, for the apartment was warm and close.

An endless time passed before the trio re-issued into the hall. They were no longer quarrelling, and Eduardo was obviously cowed, but Jeanne's features remained an enigma.

Without speaking, the *notaire* moved towards the street door and opened it. A damp breeze swept in, ruffling the tails of his ill-fitting coat. He turned and addressed his companions distinctly, with the air of laying down the law.

"Remember, this is the last time. Play that trick again, and you will find yourselves in the soup!"

In the glare of the overhead lustre his face showed pale like a fish-belly, his eyes horridly repellent. Catherine shuddered.

"Now mind what I say. I am the master here—I," he repeated, striking his meagre chest.

He was gone, swallowed up in the darkness. The door shut upon him.

Eduardo and Jeanne exchanged questioning glances. Then the woman's lips tightened with a mutinous expression.

"We shall see," she muttered briefly. "Put out the light. . . ."

Once more they disappeared into the gallery, while Catherine seized the chance to escape unobserved. Safe in her room, she sank upon the bed and waited with pounding heart till she heard the two servants come up the stairs and separate in the passage outside. Only when all was quiet again did her strained muscles relax and her pulse resume its normal beat.

CHAPTER SEVENTEEN

WHEN Berthe sauntered in with the breakfast-tray Catherine was already partially dressed. "Mademoiselle is up early," declared the massive blonde with engaging candour.

She herself looked half asleep, her hair untouched by the comb.

"Ah, well, what it is to be energetic," she sighed with a luxurious yawn and, craning her neck towards the mirror, examined a pimple on her chin. "As for me, I could have slept all day. My young man took me to the Pastry-cooks' Ball in Montmartre. I have not danced so much since *Mi-Carême*, and my feet are so swollen I can't get on my shoes. I daresay mademoiselle is fond of dancing?"

"Very," replied Catherine, pouring her coffee.

Difficult as it was to resent Berthe's placid familiarity, she was in no mood to encourage it this morning. However, the cook meandered on undisturbed.

"You are right. Enjoy yourself while you are young, I say, for when you are old, what man will look at you? That is what I am always preaching to Jeanne, but she—bah!—is all for being serious, and would die rather than spend a sou on a good dress. She will not even wear the beautiful clothes madame gives her, but sells them to the wardrobe dealers. Such stupidity! She might at least keep an occasional one for herself and make a decent appearance." She paused, then added with a change of tone: "By the by, that is a nice frock mademoiselle had sent home the other day—the green and silver. It looks as though it had come from one of the Grandes Couturières. If mademoiselle tires of it, she might care to sell it to me."

In spite of her preoccupation Catherine could not repress a smile at the thought of Berthe's buxom form compressed into her slender garments.

"Certainly, Berthe—but I intend to wear it for a long time."

"She's a sober one and no mistake, that Jeanne," continued Berthe, resuming her former theme. "Slave, slave, from morning till night, never a thought of pleasure. No doubt there will be a fine seat for her in heaven one day, but as for me, it is not of the hereafter I'm thinking! Nor Eduardo either, let me tell you,"—and she winked broadly.

"He likes his bit of fun, though he has to be sly about it. It is she who wears the trousers in that *ménage*, and she keeps a tight rein on him, poor man!"

Impatient though she was to be rid of the chatterer, Catherine gleaned something from the random remarks. Whatever manoeuvres Jeanne might be engaged in, she kept them well hidden from other eyes. Even to Berthe she was a model of rectitude.

As soon as she was alone she finished her breakfast hurriedly and went along to the study, passing no one on the way. Then, with the door closed and keeping her voice low, she rang up the Macadam office and asked to speak to Geoffrey. A second later the familiar accents answered her.

"Geoffrey—it's I, Catherine. I want to see you at once. No, I can't tell you what it's about, but it's important. Are you very busy?"

"Of course not. But you sound upset. Is anything wrong?"

"I don't know. That's why I must see you. I'll be with you in half an hour."

As she was about to ring off, her ear caught a faint but distinct click. Several times before she had heard that noise, which sounded like another receiver being replaced, but up till the present moment she had paid little attention to it. Now the idea came to her that some person might be listening-in to her conversation, perhaps close at hand.

Was there a second instrument in the apartment? She had never seen one, but she felt certain that formerly at least there must have been an extension, probably in her cousin's bedroom. She walked back to her own quarters, filled with a fresh apprehension. If someone had taken the trouble to listen, that meant that her movements were regarded with suspicion. Only how could she make sure?

As she passed the corner bedroom, until recently Mme. Bender's own, the door opened and Jeanne came out. Something in her face told the girl that her surmise was correct. Thank goodness she had said nothing definite, for she was sure the woman had overheard every word. The maid must have seen her go into the study, and had hastened to eavesdrop, as no doubt she had done on other occasions.

Returning after putting on her coat and hat, she tried the bedroom door, to find it locked. Yes, she was right. There was surely another telephone in there. In future she must not forget the fact.

Much as she now dreaded the moments spent with her cousin, she nerved herself to go and say good morning, partly to keep up the illusion that nothing was altered between them, and partly to make the inquiry about the safety-deposit key, a matter she felt must not be neglected. Now that she was going to report to Geoffrey, she wanted to tell him as much as possible.

Mme. Bender was alone, propped against pillows, her face shadowed by the white bed-curtains. After a single timid glance of reproach she averted her eyes so pointedly that Catherine, cut to the heart, found it hard to proceed. Yet in pursuance of her policy she ignored the tacit rebuff, making her usual inquiries as cheerfully as she could.

Presently she broached the difficult subject.

"By the way, Germaine," she ventured, "Mr. Macadam wanted me to find out if the bank had sent you the key you asked for. Did it reach you safely?"

She was met by an uncomprehending stare.

"Key?" faltered the poor woman in a puzzled tone.

"Yes—don't you remember? It was some weeks ago, I think. You lost the key to your safety-deposit, and had a duplicate made."

There was no mistaking the blankness of the bewildered gaze.

"Did I? I—I don't know. I can't seem to recall. I—perhaps you are right. . . ."

The muddled brain was making an effort to capture an elusive memory. Catherine took pity on its confusion.

"Why not ask Jeanne? She will know," she suggested casually. At the same time she was perfectly sure that this was the first time Germaine had heard the matter mentioned.

"Jeanne—yes. That is a good idea," assented the invalid with obvious reluctance. "I will speak to her. She—"

But at that moment the ever-watchful maid appeared in the doorway. Without a glance at Catherine she went at once to the chest of drawers and, picking up a tortoiseshell box, rattled it crossly.

"*Le voilà, madame!*" she exclaimed in annoyance. "What is all this fuss about? Have you so soon forgotten the trouble you put me to, turning out everything to search for that wretched key? You mislaid it, and sent me to get another made. There! You see?"—and she produced the small object, tied with pink tape, and dangled it accusingly before the fascinated eyes of her mistress. "It came by special messenger from the bank. Is it possible you have no recollection of it?"

Mme. Bender gazed as though hypnotized.

"How stupid I am," she apologized weakly. "Of course—it all comes back to me."

But the maid was not content. Shaking her head as one might at a tiresome child, she spoke with exasperated patience.

"Really it is too much!" she scolded. "You would forget your head, if it were not fastened to your shoulders! And you try to tell me your memory is improving!"

Replacing the box with a shrug, she went out, leaving the patient overcome with shame.

Indignation swept over Catherine. Jeanne might or might not be telling the truth—it was impossible to say—but the manner in which she had put the poor woman in the wrong called only for condemnation. While she was wondering what she could say to relieve matters, she caught a sudden piteous expression in her cousin's eyes, which could have but one interpretation. It was the craving for affection.

For a second she hesitated, then with a swift impulse ran to the bedside and put her arms round the emaciated figure. For a second she fancied the embrace was faintly returned. Then she felt herself pushed away, and before she could ask the reason was dismayed utterly to find that Mme. Bender had burst into a flood of tears. There was no word of reproach, no explanation, but none was needed. That silent, miserable weeping told her plainly that any advance of hers was unwelcome. For once she was almost relieved when Jeanne reappeared and with a single glance took in the situation.

"Leave madame to me," she said with her quick air of authority. "I am afraid, mademoiselle, you can do little for her."

The significant emphasis on the pronoun left nothing to the imagination. Catherine flushed and departed, a last glimpse of the room showing her the maid at the weeper's side, ministering to her with prompt efficiency. Even as she tingled with resentment, the girl heard Germaine's emotion subside under the influence of the cajoling voice, and told herself that Jeanne had done her work well. The unfortunate woman was firm in the belief that no one really cared for her except this single, humble companion.

Half an hour later in the office of Macadam Senior she sat facing the solicitors, father and son. Something severely sceptical in the older man's bearing intimidated her, but, thrusting her fears aside, she set forth in as few words as possible the event of the night before.

"It is perfectly evident there is something afoot between those three," she finished, her voice trembling a little from nervousness. "But what it is, or how it may affect Mme. Bender, I haven't an idea. What do you make of it all?"

The senior partner, who had listened gravely, leaned back in his swivelled chair and thrust out his lower lip. He glanced at his son and drummed on the desk beside him.

"Would you mind repeating word for word, Miss West, exactly what you heard these people say?" he requested after a pause.

She did so.

"I could catch very little. Most of the time they were whispering."

"And your impression was that this fellow, who appears to be their man of business, was put out with them over something, and that the dispute in some way related to the picture-gallery?"

"I was sure of that much. When the man was leaving he said, 'Mind, this is the last time. Do this sort of thing again, and you will find yourself in the soup. Remember, I am the master here.'"

"That looks as though he had got wind of their tampering with the paintings, and was warning them not to continue."

"Or else," put in Geoffrey, "he had arranged that they were to dispose of certain things together, and had just discovered the servants were going ahead on their own."

His father waved him aside.

"So far we can't be sure that the woman was lying when she said that Bender sold the paintings himself. It is possible he did so."

Catherine agreed doubtfully.

"You must realize, Miss West," he went on, "that your own prejudice against these people does not constitute evidence of guilt. Before we can establish any case we shall have to get track of those missing pictures, discover the dates and circumstances of the sales, and so on. We can't arrest the servants on suspicion. Exactly what paintings have disappeared?"

"The Manet is the only one I am sure about. Three more are gone, but I can't say what they were. Then there is the Aubusson carpet, and all the tapestries off the furniture."

Macadam made notes on a pad, then sat silent with wrinkled brow. The girl's spirits sank as she watched him. Less imaginative than his son, he presented a familiar type of dry and hard lawyer, impeccably just, but difficult to impress. Her recital had left him so little moved that she began to wonder if she herself were not attaching undue importance to what had happened. Only the knowledge that Geoffrey did not discount her suspicions saved her from utter despondency.

"Do you think you can trace the pictures?" she inquired.

Macadam cleared his throat.

"I trust we can. We must get to work at once. If your cousin sold them, we may hope for quick results; otherwise the purchasers will not readily come forward, of that you may be sure. I take it you have not mentioned the affair to Mme. Bender herself?"

"No," confessed the girl, more than ever ill at ease. "Besides, I doubt if she knows anything about them."

"Still, unless her mind is entirely gone, she can't be wholly unaware of anything so important as the disposal of a Manet."

Catherine looked at Geoffrey.

"She refuses to trust her memory," she said. "I had the most complete proof of that fact only this morning,"—and she went on to describe what had happened about the key. "I'm convinced she remembered nothing herself, but she was quite ready to accept Jeanne's word for it."

The old man glanced at his son in sharp inquiry.

"I asked Miss West to find out about the key the bank sent Mme. Bender. I admit I haven't felt comfortable about it."

"And you could swear that your relative had never heard of this matter?" demanded the solicitor.

"I can't swear anything. I can only tell you my belief. That is the great trouble," she added distractedly, "one can't be absolutely sure of anything!"

Macadam looked annoyed, rubbing his unruly hair the wrong way. Finally he spoke:

"The position is this, Miss West. Unless Mme. Bender is certified as mentally incompetent, which I understand is not the case, then we have no authority to act for her. We cannot check her expenditures, nor enter her apartment to make any sort of investigation. As things are we can only hold a watching brief—not, I admit, a very satisfactory method of solving the difficulty."

"I was afraid you'd say that," replied Catherine despairingly. "And yet—this man, Blom. Can't one get hold of him and find out what he's up to?"

"As a matter of fact, Catherine," Geoffrey put in, "I have been making some inquiries about him. I was only waiting for a chance to tell you."

"You don't mean it! What have you found out?" asked the girl eagerly.

"Nothing that's the least use, I fear," Geoffrey answered regretfully. "He appears to be a decent, hard-working fellow of unimpeachable reputation, though naturally that's not final. We may yet discover something."

"How?"

"Why, by employing a private agent to shadow him. It could be done."

Macadam senior tapped the arm of his chair. Who did the boy think was going to defray the expense? Not the firm, certainly. Geoffrey had no difficulty in interpreting the disparaging silence.

"If it were proved that this person was defrauding her," he said calmly, "Mme. Bender would be only too glad to bear the cost of an investigation."

Macadam raised his brows, but said nothing. There was an awkward pause during which Catherine rose.

"Anyhow," she said desperately, "something must be done to get that woman away. I am already pulling wires to remove her, but if my plan doesn't succeed we must try something else."

"You?" inquired Geoffrey, with sudden interest. "What have you been doing?"

"I've seen the doctor and have got him on our side. He's going to insist on Jeanne's taking a rest."

Admiration shone in the younger man's eyes.

"I say, that was clever of you!"

She blushed, less at his open praise than because of the shrewd look directed at her from beneath the old man's bushy brows.

"Miss Cushing went with me. She feels about it just as I do."

Macadam turned on her suddenly.

"Miss Cushing is in this?" he asked a little sharply. "Miss Cushing, the singing-teacher?"

She was disconcerted by the abruptness of the question, feeling vaguely that she had suddenly weakened her case, though she did not know why.

"Yes. She is an old friend of my cousin's."

She said good-bye hastily, relieved to find herself in the corridor with Geoffrey beside her.

"Your father makes me feel not only a fool but a mischief-maker!" she confided with a half-laugh. "Am I really being stupid about all this?"

"Good God, no!"

He looked at her with concern. Although she had told her story with the utmost composure, it was easy to see that she was unnerved by last night's experience.

"You mustn't mind him," he said quickly. "That manner of his is purely superficial. He means to take things in hand, never fear; but what is more to the point, I intend to have Blom shadowed. If there's anything queer about him, we'll run it to earth."

"But you can't do that," she objected, recalling the elder man's meaning silence.

"Of course I can. We'll discuss details later. Meanwhile, keep in mind what I said yesterday, that as long as these rogues are profiting by your cousin's condition she can't possibly come to serious harm. I say—what about lunching with me on Sunday? By that time I may have something to report."

She assented with a grateful look. It was comforting to know that she could rely upon his help, that he took a really personal interest in her difficulties. The memory of his shy and steady grey eyes dwelt with her reassuringly as the descending lift hid him from sight.

Outside the American Express a woman passed her with rapid, nervous steps, and vanished into the building she had just quitted. With a start Catherine turned to look after the disappearing figure.

It was Jeanne herself.

CHAPTER EIGHTEEN

His nerves still vibrating in response to the look he had just received, Geoffrey turned back for a moment to speak to his father. He found the old man running through some papers with an abstracted air, suggesting that his attention was already given to other matters.

"These Amalgamated Iron shares," he remarked, "I think I've found the reason for their depreciation. It's due to—"

"Never mind that now, father. I want to know your real opinion of this Bender affair."

"Oh, that!"—Macadam removed his glasses and rubbed the bridge of his nose exasperatedly. "When you've lived as long as I have and listened to as many stories of this kind, you won't attach too great importance to them."

"What do you mean by that?" demanded Geoffrey hotly.

"Oh, only that this girl has worked herself into a state where she is ready to believe anything. It's a mistake her being there at all. She ought to go home."

His son reddened with fury.

"I suppose you grasped why she was staying," he retorted with sarcasm. "She is unselfishly trying to protect her cousin from—"

"From what?" inquired the other calmly. "You don't know. Neither does she. Well, it's my opinion she's assuming far too much. Possibly the servants are stealing; how many would remain honest in the circumstances? If it's true, we'll put a stop to it. But I don't see any reason to believe anything more against them, beyond the fact that they've antagonized her. They are not mistreating or neglecting their mistress in any way. On Miss West's own statement, Mme. Bender is perfectly content with things as they are."

He returned to his desk, impervious to the indignant gaze fixed upon him. The strained silence was still continuing when Henri, the old Frenchman employed to receive clients, tapped on the door and entered.

"A woman to see you, monsieur. She gives her name as Laborie."

"Laborie!" repeated Macadam in surprise. "That, I believe, is the person who is causing all this fuss,"—and he exchanged glances with his son.

"Shall I stay?" inquired the latter, irritation giving way to curiosity.

"No, leave me to deal with her." He jerked his head towards the door. "Show her in."

Denied the satisfaction of hearing what the maid had come about, Geoffrey departed through the inner door. Left alone, the senior partner leaned back in his seat and was polishing his glasses with a grey silk handkerchief when Henri ushered Jeanne into the room.

"*Bonjour, monsieur!* I crave a thousand pardons for disturbing you. It is extremely kind of you to see me."

Macadam nodded curtly and made a gesture towards a chair.

"Sit down. What is it this time?" he demanded briefly.

"Oh, thank you, monsieur!"

With a manner respectful but not cringing, Jeanne Laborie brought forward one of the straight mahogany chairs and placed it a couple of yards away from the solicitor, then sitting down stiffly on the edge of it she fingered her bag with nervous hesitation. She was decently dressed in black, well-brushed and neatly put on. She might have been the wife of some superior tradesman. From beneath the brim of her hard felt hat her brown eyes looked out of her sallow face, direct, unflinching, yet with something of appeal in them.

"Monsieur, I have come on a rather delicate matter. The truth is, I desire to ask your help, though I am well aware you will think it extraordinary. I should not have troubled you if there had been anyone else who could possibly be of assistance."

She moistened her lips. Her entire manner, reasonable, restrained, conveyed the impression that she was embarking upon a painful undertaking solely because of a sense of duty.

"Go on. I am listening."

"Monsieur, I think you know something of the state of Mme. Bender's health. You are aware, perhaps, that she is subject to fits of depression, during which she has made attempts on her life."

"Suicide!" exclaimed Macadam, raising his brows. "I didn't know it was as bad as that."

"Unfortunately it is, monsieur. I may venture to say that if she had been in the care of any person less understanding than myself she would not be alive to-day. You may remember that I have looked after madame for fifteen years?"

The old man nodded. What was the woman getting at? He could not even faintly guess, but her manner of addressing him, making no obvious bid for favour, commanded his grudging respect.

She continued in a low voice:

"Monsieur, a little more than a month ago, just after the second of these suicidal attacks, and at a time when the household was in great confusion, a young lady, an American, suddenly arrived upon the scene. I believe she is some distant connection of Monsieur Bender's. I really do not know who she is. I had seen her before in Boston. She called repeatedly at the hospital and, if you will not misunderstand me, sought to ingratiate herself with madame when the poor lady was in a state even weaker than at present. Madame is soft-hearted. When this almost unknown young relative begged to be permitted to visit her in Paris she had not the power to refuse—or at least that is how I interpret it. Possibly I am wrong; but surely to invite a guest at such a time was not the act of a responsible person."

The old lawyer knit his brows non-committally, and the speaker proceeded with still greater hesitation.

"I was afraid it was a mistake for this young lady to remain in the apartment with madame in so precarious a condition. I did my best to dissuade her from staying, but without success. She overrode all my objections, and there she has been ever since. . . . Monsieur, I wish to tell you that her presence has had a most distressing effect upon madame. Really at times I have not known what to do. She upsets the strict discipline it is necessary to maintain, excites the patient, and has even set herself to weaken madame's confidence in me. In that respect she has happily failed; but all the same she has caused several severe crises. Last week, following a distressing scene, I was obliged to sit up the entire night with madame, and only this morning another terrible time occurred. I found my lady in violent hysterics, so uncontrolled that I had great difficulty in calming her. I have left her now in charge of the cook, for if she were unguarded I could not answer for the consequences. There was the look in her eye which warned me she was planning some fresh attempt to kill herself, only waiting for the opportunity. I must not be absent long, but I was so frightened I felt I must come at once and speak to you on the matter."

She cast a glance at the clock fixed in the panel opposite, then continued more rapidly:

"Monsieur, I appeal to you. This young lady, Mademoiselle West, is known to your son. Cannot you or he induce her to go away and leave madame in peace before anything irrevocable happens? I assure you it is of the gravest importance."

Macadam levelled a stern regard at her and swung his glasses to and fro by their slender chain.

"Why," he demanded, "do you think Mademoiselle West has this disturbing effect upon your mistress?"

She shrugged her shoulders.

"I would rather monsieur did not ask me that question. You see, I may be prejudiced, and do not want to make unjust accusations. However, it has been clear to me from the outset that mademoiselle has designs of her own. She is hoping that madame will make a will in her favour, in which respect she is not alone. She is close friends with another lady who cherishes similar expectations. There has been correspondence between these two before Mademoiselle West left America, and I am convinced in my own mind that they have arranged things together, to become joint heirs to madame's estate."

Her declaration met with a stern frown.

"Are you aware of what you are saying?" the solicitor shot at her brusquely.

Jeanne bowed her head.

"I realize I do wrong to hint at such a thing. But," she went on, speaking in measured, distinct tones, "right or wrong, madame herself suspects their intentions. She has told me so. It is for that reason that she is so distressed in their company. She does not wish to offend either of them by asking them to keep away, but she has at last implored me to forbid them to see her!"

The old man's eyes were like steel.

"Is that true?"

Here Jeanne betrayed her first hint of emotion. She clasped her hands rigidly together, raised her chin and looked him squarely in the eyes. Her voice, when she spoke, shook with a vibrant tremor.

"As God is my witness, monsieur, that is the absolute truth!" she said.

The words had a ring of sincerity. Macadam deliberated, looking away from her.

"Who is this other friend you mention?" he asked presently.

"There is no reason why I should not tell you, monsieur. It is Mademoiselle Cushing, the singer."

Macadam rose.

"I will look into the matter," he said laconically. "I'll see what can be done. Mind, I do not promise anything."

With this she had to be content, but that she was not disappointed was shown by a sudden gleam in her intent eyes.

"Thank you, monsieur! I am glad you have not mistaken my meaning. Naturally, since I have laboured so long, organizing madame's whole establishment with the sole idea of nursing her back to health, I do not like to see my efforts go for nothing. If this Mademoiselle West persists in going against the doctor's orders and causing trouble, I cannot hold myself responsible for what may happen."

He watched her go out with her dependable and unobtrusive air, then stood fingering his chin reflectively.

"By George," he muttered to himself, "I've always known if one waited a bit one would hear the other side."

He considered himself an excellent judge of character, not easily fooled. This woman had struck him as decent and straightforward, strongly biased, perhaps, but that was only natural. Of course he had purposely avoided sounding her on the missing articles, the mention of which matter could only serve to rouse her antipathy still further against Miss West, or, if she were indeed guilty, put her on her guard. No, he was too old a hand to commit that indiscretion. . . . Last night's affair looked queer, but there were various possible explanations. On her own admission Miss West had understood little of what had been said. Her accusations were decidedly vague.

"Jealousy on both sides, I'd be willing to take my oath," he concluded with a contemptuous snort. "There's usually jealousy where women are concerned."

After careful cogitation he drew a sheet of paper towards him and composed a letter in his own stiff angular hand. This he sealed and addressed, then turned it face downward on the blotter, just as his son appeared in the doorway.

"Well?" inquired Geoffrey shortly, "what did she want?"

Briefly the old man gave an account of the interview. The listener swore irritably.

"What unmitigated brass! You saw she was lying, of course?"

"I wouldn't go so far as to say that. There may be truth on both sides."

"On both—! You can't mean to tell me that after one look at Miss West you could believe this abominable story?"

The old man raised a restraining hand.

"You mean about her having designs on Mme. Bender's money? I didn't say I believed it. But have you ever known a business of this kind cropping up where the person involved was penniless? I thought not. There would be no point in it."

His son regarded him in cold fury.

"What exactly are you getting at?" he demanded.

"Nothing whatever, except that I'm fairly well convinced we are wasting valuable time. Take my advice: put your energies into persuading this girl to leave and find another place to live. I presume she's not without means?"

"I don't know. I haven't asked her," returned the younger man with contempt.

"Anyhow, she's only complicating matters by staying where she isn't wanted. That will do, now. Send Parkin to me. I shall get him to look through Harry Bender's papers in case there is any record of a picture-transaction. No use starting an inquiry till that point is cleared up."

Curbing his wrath, Geoffrey did his father's bidding, then called the French clerk, Ballou, to his own office.

"Guy," he said, "yesterday you mentioned a young girl who had a connection with that *notaire* you were inquiring about. Do you know where she worked, and if one can get hold of her?"

"The young person in the *usine*?" replied Guy promptly, "Oh, yes, sir. The concierge told me she was employed in a manufactory for artificial flowers, near the Place Clichy. I daresay I could find the place and the girl, too, if you want me to try."

"Thank you, Guy, it will be wiser to put someone else on the job. I'm glad you remembered about it, though."

As soon as he was alone he searched in the telephone directory for a number, rang it up himself, and a few minutes later took a taxi to an address in the rue Blanche. Here he entered the dingy bureau of a private agent already known to him in connection with one or two affairs, a man he had found both trustworthy and acute.

A solemn, thin Frenchman rose at his approach. He had round, pensive black eyes, a lantern-jawed countenance, and a scrawny neck enclosed in a wide standing collar, the gold stud of which protruded above a rusty black cravat.

"Monsieur Macadam? I am happy to see you, monsieur. Be seated, please. What can I do for you?"

As concisely as possible Geoffrey made his business known, and while he spoke the Frenchman's melancholy gaze ran this way and that, exploring the corners of the little room where dusty files were heaped upon the floor. Once or twice he coughed behind his bony hand, but beyond an occasional question in a lugubrious tone he remained silent.

"You see, although this man I refer to may be perfectly honest, I am not satisfied that he's all he appears to be. If he's mixed up in any nefarious proceedings, no matter what their nature, I must find it out."

"You desire me to look into his record, monsieur?"

"Yes, and follow him if necessary. Here is the information I have obtained, addresses and so on. Do what you can."

"You say this young woman is a discarded mistress?" remarked the agent sadly. "That would seem to provide our best mode of attack. Artificial flowers . . . I know the place—Achille Benet is the name. I will arrange to get in touch with the person and see what can be learned from her. No doubt I can persuade her to accompany me to a cinema or a Palais de Danse."

He uttered the suggestion in much the same tone he would have employed in proposing a tour of the Montmartre Cemetery. However, knowing his man, Geoffrey did not despair, and departed with an easier feeling than he had had for some hours. He still felt indignant towards his father for his insensitive attitude, yet was forced to admit that if he himself had had less knowledge of Catherine he might have adopted the same view.

All at once he recalled that his father was ignorant of Blom's visit to the office under an assumed name.

"By Jove!" he exclaimed, in annoyance. "What a fool I was not to have told him that! If only poor Howard hadn't chosen this precise moment to be laid up! I wonder how he is, by the way?"

Reproaching himself for not having inquired since yesterday, he hurried to the nearest public telephone and rang up the old clerk's home, only to learn that Mr. Howard was still very ill. His lungs were badly congested, though he was putting up a brave fight.

"Nothing to be hoped for in that quarter for days," reflected Geoffrey with exasperation.

Mixed with his genuine concern over the news was the thought that if the old man should die the knowledge he sought would pass beyond his reach.

CHAPTER NINETEEN

CATHERINE'S first feeling was one of relief that Jeanne had not seen her leaving the Macadam offices. Next she asked herself what errand had brought the woman to consult the solicitors—for there could be no doubt as to her destination. The look of concentration on the tight-lipped face suggested fresh mischief afoot.

Then her thoughts turned to Mme. Bender, and her eyes filled with tears over the memory of the recent scene. Never in her life had she felt so helpless to combat injustice. Her cousin's mind was poisoned against her, yet she could do nothing to put things right.

Worse, the talk with the old Scotchman had clearly shown her the weakness of her position. Thanks to his uncompromising logic she realized to what extent her suspicion against the servants rested upon isolated incidents, each capable of a dual construction. She began to wonder if she had magnified trifles till they pointed to conclusions wholly false.

Even Mr. Macadam's promise to investigate the question of theft gave her little comfort, for during the long and tedious inquiry Jeanne would remain firmly entrenched, working her will upon her mistress's susceptible imagination.

"What can I do? It's now almost impossible for me to stay there. Soon it may be quite so, if Jeanne persists. She'll end by driving me away."

It was true. Her self-appointed guardianship was being thrust aside; Germaine herself did not desire her presence. It would certainly be more dignified to withdraw. Her income was sufficient to enable her to live comfortably in some small hotel, where she would be free from indignities.

"Yet God knows it's not my own pleasure I'm considering!" she argued sincerely.

It was terribly difficult to help a person who did not want to be helped.

Pride drew her in one direction, conscientious scruples another, but now the latter's voice was obscured by doubt. Suppose she was altogether wrong about Jeanne? The mouse incident, even last night's scene, might have no guilty significance. The woman had been in her post for fifteen years, implicitly trusted long before Mme. Bender's judgment became impaired. Hysterical and crabbed she might be, but as yet there was no positive proof against her.

Thinking all this over, she wandered along the Avenue de l'Opéra and sat for some time in the little garden of the Palais Royale. The fountain plashed, pigeons strutted about, occasionally a lounger looked at her, but she noticed nothing. Unable to bear the thought of going back to the apartment, she decided to lunch out; but although there were several friends she knew would be glad to welcome her, she was averse to company. She must be alone to wrestle with her problem.

At last she made up her mind on one point, driven thither all but against her will. She would spend the afternoon looking at hotels and *pensions*, not with the idea of definitely engaging a room, but in order to have a place ready to go to if during the next day or two she decided to leave. In her little book were a number of recommended addresses. She would take them in turn.

This settled, she glanced at her watch, and saw with surprise that it was past her usual hour of *déjeuner*. She was tired, too, possibly because of her inward struggle. Then she recalled a tiny restaurant close at hand in the rue d'Argenteuil, a simple, homely *auberge*, where the cooking was excellent. In five minutes she had reached it, chosen a table against the wall, and was studying the big purple-scrawled sheet of the menu.

It was late and only a few tables were occupied, mostly by quiet-looking men she imagined to be journalists. The cook, an immense man with a snowy apron round his Gargantuan paunch, crisp curly hair and sparkling black eyes, approached with a friendly welcome and with his hands upon his hips offered advice on the subject of dishes.

"If mademoiselle would care to try the *plat de jour*," he suggested, pointing a fat red finger at the menu, "I can specially recommend it. Veal with mushrooms and little peas. Also the Chateaubriand garnished is good to-day. With it I should like to serve some *pommes soufflées*."

She chose the Chateaubriand which when it appeared was appetizing in its bed of fresh watercress and flanked by mounds of potatoes fried to a feathery lightness that she realized suddenly how hungry she was. She followed the course by spinach, piping hot and foaming up brilliant emerald green in a red copper pannikin, finishing the repast by a *tarte de la maison*. When at length she lit a cigarette and leaned back with a cup of coffee before her, she felt inclined to take a more cheerful view of things, letting her taut mind relax and drift where it would.

On the seat near by lay a paper *feuilleton* in a gaudy cover, left there by some departed luncher. She picked it up idly, then seeing that it was a collection of four or five short stories of de Maupassant, opened it at a tale entitled *Le Diable* and began to read. In a few seconds she was engrossed, fascinated.

It was a story of a peasant who hires an old woman of the village to remain beside his dying mother while he gets his hay in from the fields. The mercenary crone, paid for the entire job, becomes exasperated by the poor creature's slowness in dying and, loath to waste time over her, resolves to hasten the event by strategy. She describes with gruesome details what she declares to be a common experience with sufferers about to breathe their last, affirming that at the crucial moment the devil appears to them with horns and a pitchfork. Then, when she had worked the patient up to a suitable state of terror, she hides in a cupboard and steps forth suddenly, armed with a huge fork and wearing a three-legged saucepan on her head. The ruse succeeds, the peasant's mother drops dead of shock.

"Good God!"

The booklet fell from her hand, she sat quite still staring ahead of her at the opposite wall. One by one the tables had been cleared, she was the last customer to remain. The big chef untied his apron, struggled into a short, tight-fitting jacket which, when buttoned, strained across his abdomen like a bursting pod, stuck a small Trilby hat jauntily upon his head and a cigar in his mouth, then sallied forth for a stroll, pausing near Catherine to bid her a courteous adieu. She scarcely saw him or the questioning glances cast at her by the waiters.

All she could think of was the curious parallel between the tale just read and what was going on in her cousin's home. She had seen only too well the power of suggestion at work on the credulous victim. What if Germaine, left alone with the woman whose word she implicitly believed, should succumb to a like fate? In her present condition, how easy to administer a fright sufficient to kill her? The idea paralysed her with horror. . . .

At last she came to, as from a dreadful dream. What was she telling herself? Jeanne could not, by the remotest stretch of the imagination, wish her mistress to die. Geoffrey had pointed that out to her plainly. No, the more mercenary her motives, the more reason she must have for keeping Mme. Bender alive. All this had been thrashed out before to her entire satisfaction. With a shiver she shook herself free from the stupid obsession, motioned to the *garçon*, and paid her bill. She must not give way to these absurd fancies.

Yet oddly enough in those few minutes all her recent decisions had reversed themselves. She would go and look at hotels, since it was a way of killing time till evening, but she was resolutely determined not to abandon the field to Jeanne. However innocent the latter's intentions might be, her influence represented a force capable of being used with evil result. No, even if things were made still more difficult for her, she would stick it out, at least till something occurred to alter the position.

"If anything should happen," she whispered, "I should never forgive myself!"

Besides, she was forgetting the doctor's promise. Even now he might have seen Jeanne and persuaded her to go away. What an enormous relief if that were so!

Entering the apartment at six o'clock, she heard Dr. Girard's deep voice in the distance, and reflected with thanksgiving that the good man had not disappointed her. At the turn of the hall she stood trying to catch what he was saying, but although she listened hard she could make out nothing. Presently the front door closed.

Had he been successful? A thrill of anticipation shot through her as she told herself she would soon know the result.

On the table in the entrance hall several letter were awaiting her, one bearing an English stamp and writing she recognized as Claire Hardwicke's. Going into the study, she curled herself up in the big chair and was speedily engrossed in her correspondence.

Claire was upbraiding her for her deflection. What was all this nonsense about a sense of responsibility towards Mme. Bender? The latter was little more than a stranger, and till recently had got on very well indeed without her supervision. Florence would be lovely in May. Jim meant to buy a little cheap car and they were going to tour about among the adjacent villages, working their way south.

The picture was an alluring one. Catherine put down the closely written pages and gave herself up to dreams of what she was going to miss. Then she realized that she was not quite so regretful as she had expected to be. Was it because Paris held someone whose companionship had grown steadily more agreeable than she cared to admit? She blushed at the thought. Geoffrey Macadam had never given her a single look which she could construe in terms other than those of impersonal friendship. Possibly he was beginning to regard her as a bit of a nuisance, what with her continued worries, real or imagined. He was wonderfully good about it all, but really she was making a great deal of trouble for him. . . .

Padded footsteps, probably those of Eduardo, passed by the door, lingered a moment, then receded again. She listened mechanically, but thought little of the circumstance till, on issuing from the study, she spied on the table a solitary white envelope, addressed to herself. That was odd—there was no post at this hour, nor had she heard the concierge's customary knock. She wondered still more when she saw in the corner of the printed heading of Macadam and Langtree. The round yet crabbed writing was unfamiliar. Glancing quickly at the signature, she learned that the communication was from the senior solicitor.

So the old man had lost no time in writing to her! She felt a sudden qualm of misgiving.

In the seclusion of her own room she ran through the contents twice. Tactfully worded, it gave no hint that its author had anything other than her own interests at heart, yet the meaning was plain. When she had finished the second reading, she drew a deep breath and sat rigidly regarding the sheet with a smile that was lightly grim.

Here was an unexpected turn of events, not a pleasant one, either. Sensibly, convincingly and in no uncertain terms, Mr. Macadam was urging her to go away. What was this he said about unintentionally promoting discord? The phrase puzzled her. Then all at once she understood! Jeanne had been to him with her own version of things. This letter was composed after his talk with her.

Catherine tingled with sudden anger, then gave a little laugh at the irony of the affair.

"It really is rather funny! Here am I working hard to oust her, while she is equally determined to oust me. Mr. Macadam is the referee, and at the present stage of the game he's inclined to take her side. Which of us is going to win?"

She picked up the envelope and fingered it curiously. The flap had come open with surprising readiness, and now she noticed that the gum on it was slightly moist. Did that mean that it had been secretly opened? If so, that fact would explain why the letter had not been with the others when she came in. Eduardo understood English. No doubt he and Jeanne had been anxious to find out how matters stood. Once more she recalled her telephone conversation of the morning, and her impression that someone was listening. Wheels within wheels. . . . What was it all about?

"Yet they can't have any suspicion that I was spying on them last night. Why all this scheming to get rid of me? What have I done to make them afraid?"

For that they were afraid of her she had now little doubt. They must be apprehensive about those missing pictures, dreading lest she bring an accusation against them. She could think of no other reason for their actions.

Pondering this she changed slowly into another frock, still annoyed and a little resentful over the old lawyer's attitude towards her, and was in the act of brushing her hair before the glass when a tap on the door jarred on her reflections. In answer to her *"Entrez!"* Jeanne came in.

"Pardon, mademoiselle, si je vous derange . . ."

The maid's manner was quietly respectful. She paused a second in the doorway, then crossing, laid a package wrapped in white paper upon the bed.

"The laundry has just brought mademoiselle's linen. Perhaps mademoiselle will glance through the list to see that everything has been returned."

"Thank you, Jeanne."

Putting down the brush, Catherine undid the parcel and ran over the neat pile of clothing inside it—a *combinaison* and a *crêpe de Chine* nightgown, both beautifully pleated, a lace bodice, a sheaf of handkerchiefs. As she examined the articles she was uncomfortably aware of the woman's lingering gaze. There was a tentative quality about it as though the owner had something on her mind.

"Do you want anything, Jeanne?"

"Only this, mademoiselle. I trust you were not wounded by what occurred this morning. I am afraid it is the sort of thing one has to be prepared for. Madame is apt to be like that," she added with an air faintly conciliatory.

"You need not bother, Jeanne, I quite understand," replied the girl evenly, masking her surprise.

Still the maid was not satisfied. She hung about, smoothing the creases from the bed-cover and folding up the paper in which the laundry had come.

"Madame takes notions into her head, and while they last it is wisest not to cross her. Does mademoiselle grasp my meaning?"

Catherine faced her squarely. "What exactly is it you wish to say, Jeanne? You may as well be frank about it."

"Well, mademoiselle, I have been thinking it might be safer if you did not attempt to see madame for a little. No doubt madame's dislike of you will pass in time, but while it continues is it best to annoy her?"

She finished with a significant glance which brought the blood into Catherine's cheeks. Still one could not afford to get angry, thinking which, the girl replied with composure: "You may be right. At all events I shall not force myself upon madame."

"Ah, I see that you understand, mademoiselle! Naturally it is painful for me to mention this, but after all it cannot inconvenience you long, since in all probability your stay is nearly at an end. No doubt you will soon be proceeding with your tour?"

So it was this the woman wanted to find out! Not a word of what Girard must surely have said to her half an hour ago, only the scarcely veiled suggestion that the visitor was to take her departure.

Rapidly it dawned on Catherine that here was the turning-point. She must decide once and for all whether she was to stick to her guns or leave her cousin to this jealous guardian who brooked no interference with her rule. Was she making a foolish mistake? Perhaps she was wrong to meddle in things which did not concern her. If so, now was the moment to withdraw.

For a moment Catherine wavered, meanwhile putting her *lingerie* into a drawer, laying the crisp pleats in place with fingers which shook. Then as she straightened up she caught sight in the mirror of Jeanne's close-set brown eyes watching her every movement with an attention all too acute. In a flash her spirit rose to arms. Turning, she met the steadfast gaze with a fixed determination to fight the affair to a finish.

"I am not going to Italy, Jeanne," she declared shortly. "In fact, I do not intend to leave for some time. I shall not trouble madame, but I expect to remain in this apartment perhaps for months."

She saw the ragged brows shoot up, the nostrils widen with displeasure. A brief pause ensued while, like two fencers, the two eyed each other, wary and watchful. When the delayed reply came it was uttered in a tone of studied indifference, cold and calm.

"Ah? Ça m'étonne . . . Bien—c'est entendu, alors—"

That was all. The door closed, leaving Catherine with racing pulses, her heart pounding hard.

CHAPTER TWENTY

MEANTIME in the rue Auber investigations were going on with commendable thoroughness. Macadam himself telephoned to various well-known picture dealers to inquire first the approximate price a still-life of Manet was likely to fetch in the market, and second, whether at any recent time a Manet belonging to Harry Belmont Bender had passed through their hands. To the former question he received definite figures, quoted from sales, while the answer to the latter was an unequivocal negative. One of the dealers expressed surprise to learn that the painting had changed hands.

"Monsieur Bender made a number of deals through me," he said. "In 1924 I sold a Renoir for him and got an excellent price for it. At the time he asked me to value his collection, including the Manet you speak of, and it was my impression that nothing was further from his thoughts than to part with it. As a matter of fact I made him an offer, which he refused."

The dealer went on to say that if M. Bender's widow had disposed of the picture she must have done so with extraordinary secrecy, for when a work of so great importance changed owners all the world of art connoisseurs got to know about it. As to the possibility of its having left the country, it was rare nowadays that such a thing could happen without being found out. The port authorities were exceedingly strict.

Occasionally some canvas slipped through, but each year it became increasingly difficult.

Macadam hung up the receiver and scratched his ear thoughtfully. It began to look as though there were something in the American girl's story after all, though he must not jump at conclusions. He had yet to hear the junior clerk's report following his perusal of certain files, and there remained the study of his late client's pass-book, about which he had written to the bank. If any sum sufficiently large had been deposited during the weeks preceding Bender's death, it would tell a different tale. However, for the present there was nothing more to be done.

He had no suspicion of the fact that his son was pursuing another line of inquiry, and if he had been aware of it would have censured him severely for quixotic conduct. However, the mysterious Blom was not altogether absent from his thoughts was proved by a remark he made to Geoffrey the following day.

"This notary fellow," he observed ruminatingly. "Thinking things over, it occurs to me there may be a fairly plausible explanation for his behaviour the other night."

"What's that?" inquired the young man sharply.

"Why, blackmail. He may have something on those servants which he's using to force them to pay up. Have you thought of that?"

Geoffrey's eyes gleamed.

"Then you admit they are thieves," he replied shrewdly.

"I'm admitting nothing yet. I only say it's a possible solution." Whereupon he detailed for his son's benefit the result of his conversations with the dealers.

Geoffrey listened with interest.

"Good!" he exclaimed. "I confess that's what I expected. If you knew Cath—Miss West as well as I do, you'd know she's not a girl to be easily deceived."

"Be that as it may, we are still a long way from proving our case, and till we do so we can't make any arrests. It's a ticklish business prosecuting servants when their own employer regards them as perfect. We may not be thanked for our pains."

Alone Geoffrey rejected the blackmail suggestion, holding firmly to his belief that Blom, engineering the thefts, had called his confederates to account for exceeding instructions. He had little doubt that the crafty Alsatian was under cover of his profession a secret *receleur*, and that the visit to Bordeaux was for the purpose of getting the stolen canvasses out of France.

Not till Saturday, however, did he hear from the inquiry agent, and meanwhile, though he was in frequent communication with Catherine, there was nothing to tell her. As soon as Bernard's message reached him he hurried to the rue Blanche, hoping for news.

"I have made the young person's acquaintance, monsieur," his funereal friend informed him. "At first she was inclined to be off-hand and suspicious, but I have persuaded her to come out with me to a café to-morrow evening, and if things go well I may obtain some information from her."

"How does she appear to regard Blom?" Geoffrey asked.

"Ah, that is difficult to say. But while she does not strike one as a young woman of deep feelings, I fancy she is a little vindictive. If so, she may lead us to the truth."

On a sudden inspiration Geoffrey made a suggestion, to which the agent agreed.

"If you like, monsieur. There can be no harm in it. But mind, I do not promise anything startling."

"Ten-thirty, then," replied Geoffrey, and departed, tingling with anticipation.

Sunday broke warm and cloudless, a dazzling April day. The Bender salon, after the brilliance of outdoors, struck Geoffrey as more than ever depressing, but the girl who rose to greet him appeared the very incarnation of spring. She had put on a frock of *crêpe de Chine* the colour of young leaves, while her oval face was framed by a small felt hat also delicate green. Round her throat lay the necklace of plaited gold which suited her so well, and her suede gloves matched in tone her slender lizard-skin pumps. The faint fragrance of her garments went to Geoffrey's head like champagne as he took her hand and gazed in unrestrained admiration.

"How ripping you look!" he exclaimed.

It was the first open compliment he had paid her. The blood swept in a wave to her cheeks.

For a second she caught something in his eyes which unsettled her previous conception of him. There was a self-conscious pause, during which they eyed one another awkwardly.

"I thought we'd lunch in town at Ledoyen, then drive out into the country."

"Splendid! I was hoping you'd say that. I am longing to get out of Paris."

In taking her coat to put it over his arm his hand brushed hers. The momentary contact sent an electric shock through him.

"I say," he remarked, conscious of inner perturbation, "must you get back early? Because I'm going to suggest making a day of it and dining out as well."

Her eyes shone.

"Oh! you don't know how I should love it! I only meant to come back and write letters, a most dull proceeding. Let me run and tell Berthe not to expect me in,"—and she vanished on her errand.

She returned directly to say that the cook was enchanted, for now she could have the entire evening off.

"And Mme. Bender? Have you seen anything of her?"

Her face clouded.

"Not for days. There is no good forcing myself on her while she feels towards me as she does. Jeanne has advised me to keep away from her, but I shouldn't try to go into her room in any case now. I'm afraid there's nothing I can do."

He preserved a significant silence, but once they were seated in the car he spoke to her with quiet decision.

"Listen to me, Catherine. I am not at all happy about you. I wish you could be persuaded to leave that place."

She turned reproachful eyes on him.

"*Et tu, Brute!*" she murmured lightly, though with a catch in her voice. "Why me, too?"

"Wait. I have something to show you."

He was a little curious, but said nothing as the car slid into the Avenue Kléber and headed for the Étoile. In the Champs-Élysées he halted before a flower-shop and, leaving his companion for a moment, returned with a large cluster of lilies of the valley, crisply fresh in their frame of satiny green leaves.

"They go with your frock," he remarked shortly, laying the offering in her lap.

Something had happened to Geoffrey. It was like the preliminary melting of ice after a long winter.

He was aware of it when they entered the restaurant half-hidden by flowering chestnuts and made their way to the corner table he had reserved. The sun pouring into the glass-lined room shone no warmer than the glow within him, while the whole festive scene with its popping of corks, subdued chatter and tables garnished with spring blossoms formed a fitting background for his mood.

On a day like this every goose was a swan. The very waiters looked the best fellows in the world, to whom you might confide your heart's secrets with perfect safety. Every woman present was a miracle of exquisite smartness, every paste brooch flashed like diamonds of the purest water. Best of all not a male eye failed to note Catherine as she passed serene in her little green frock and with that look of fresh naturalness doubly dear to an Englishman's heart. A moment worth living for, to be recalled long afterwards with a thrill of pride.

"Now, what were you about to tell me?" Geoffrey asked as soon as they had ordered lunch.

He watched her fingers busy themselves, unfastening the glittering brooch on her shoulder in order to transfer the lilies of the valley to its keeping. Then when she had enshrined the nosegay in the V of her frock and surveyed the result with satisfaction, she opened her lizard-skin bag and took out an envelope.

"What do you think of this?" she asked. "Read it."

She saw his eyebrows go up in astonishment as he recognized the crabbed writing, and an expression of annoyance settle over his face when he had run through the letter's contents.

"The old devil!" he exclaimed softly. "What's the meaning of this? He never told me he'd written to you."

"It was sent off almost immediately," she said with composure. "Soon after he had talked with Jeanne, I think."

He looked quickly towards her.

"How did you know she came to see him?"

"I passed her in the street outside. She didn't see me."

She could tell that he was not only ruffled but embarrassed. For a moment he avoided her eye.

"Please don't pay the least attention to this," he said constrainedly. "I hardly know what to say."

"I'm not angry," she answered, "though I was a bit at first. He makes me feel he doesn't believe a word I said. Not only does he imply that I'm a fool for meddling in what doesn't concern me, but that I may be doing my cousin actual harm."

"Rubbish!" he muttered, impatiently.

"It's not rubbish. There's a certain amount of truth in what he says—at the moment. She would be upset if I insisted on seeing her, only I am convinced that's only temporary. Things can't go on like this. I'm only biding my time."

"God knows I hope we shall soon know something definite about these thefts," he remarked after a pause.

"Do you believe we shall?"

"I don't know. We've established the fact that the Manet hasn't passed through any dealer's hands, which is something."

"That's good!" she cried eagerly. "Oh! I hope we are not trying to hound down innocent people."

"Don't bother your head about that. I'm as sure as you are they have a good deal on their consciences."

She took back the letter and glanced at it.

"Another thing—you see what he says about finding some older, more experienced woman to look after Mme. Bender. Surely he must know that she has no relations?"

He frowned over this information.

"You are certain there is no one?"

"Hermione declares that Germaine has absolutely no family, and she ought to know. Since I have been at the apartment I have not seen or heard of anyone connected with her. I have never known anyone so completely isolated."

"That does make things extremely difficult," he observed thoughtfully. "Do you know, I don't believe I'd grasped that fact before. By the way, what was Mme. Bender's maiden name?"

She told him, and he repeated it with a curious inflection. "Dieulefit? Never heard it before. Most uncommon."

"Very. Hermione says the line is extinct."

He pondered the matter for a little, then drawing a note-book from his pocket scribbled the single word *"Dieulefit"* on an empty page. She watched him with interest but said nothing, though she noticed that his forehead was still knit with speculation.

The *sole Mornay* arriving, they attacked it with relish, nor until it was a thing of the past did they recur to any serious topic. Then Geoffrey asked if the doctor had yet settled the matter of Jeanne's holiday.

"He came yesterday, but so far Jeanne has said nothing. Still, one is bound to know before long."

It was nearly three o'clock when they again sought the out-of-doors to spin through the Bois, across the gardens of St. Cloud, and penetrate into the open reaches beyond. Larks sang high in the heavens where vague cloudlets drifted like puffs of smoke across an expanse of aquamarine. The whole warm sweet air breathed the fragrance of flowering trees, whose pink, white and yellow bouquets dotted the landscape. Catherine sighed in utter contentment. April at its loveliest, a well-run car, a companion who all at once had become something rather more interesting than a brother—what more could one ask? Hard to believe that the past week had been spent in a turgid tangle of doubts and fears. At the moment all life was bathed in the same soft sunshine which spread its radiance over the low-lying hills.

At five o'clock they stopped at a place unknown to her, but familiar to Paris pleasure-seekers. An ancient farmhouse nestled beside a narrow stream spanned by an enclosed bridge where in bad weather one might eat under cover. Now a score of motorists in gay attire sat under orange umbrellas at tables with orange cloths, along the side of the brook, whose edges glowed with thickly planted spring flowers, vivid blue and yellow. Gardens like those in a picture-book spread on each side, and a little distance away an outlet from the stream chattered over a rockery to fall into a pool.

Tea in an orange tea-pot, crisp toast, home-made *confiture*, and butter smoothly-moulded into little brown crocks! It was good that the air had given them fresh appetites to do justice to the feast.

When they had lit cigarettes, Catherine suddenly remembered a matter she wished to discuss.

"Geoffrey," she said. "About this agent you are employing. You understand, of course, that I must insist on paying for him. I can, you know. I don't want you to think—"

He reddened a little.

"Must we speak of that? I wish you wouldn't."

"Well then, I won't. But before we go any further, you must promise to let me know how much it comes to, otherwise I shall make it unpleasant for you!"

Seeing her determination, he nodded briefly.

"Well then, I promise. Now let's talk about something else."

But for a moment both were silent, while the look which passed between them left Catherine a little breathless. Why was Geoffrey so different to-day? She began to wonder if she knew him so well, after all.

They dined late at a small restaurant in the rue Jacob where the food was good, and although Catherine protested that she could not possibly be hungry again, the sight of the oysters Geoffrey ordered and the young duck with delicate *petits pois* made her change her mind.

"Oh dear!" she sighed, "when I'm with you I do nothing but eat!"

"You need to," he assured her lightly. "I'm sure that when you are at home you are half-starved!"

It was true that, lovely as she looked to-day, she had grown a bit thinner since their first meeting, while he noticed a faint shadow beneath her eyes which disturbed him, suggesting as it did a constant state of apprehension. Not blind to the absurdity of his action, he heaped her plate high with *fraises de bois* and piled thick cream upon them till she was obliged to stay his hand.

"I'm not a Strasbourg goose, you know!" she reminded him, laughing.

When with her coffee before her she leaned back in her corner and lazily took out her powder-puff, he studied her carefully.

"Tired?"

She shook her head.

"No—only blissfully content. I can't bear to think that to-day is over."

"It isn't," he returned, glancing at his watch. "There is something else I want you to do this evening."

"What is it?" she inquired languidly.

She fancied there was a slight air of secrecy about him as he paid the bill and left a ten-franc note on the saucer. Then with his characteristic caution he answered her question.

"Nothing much. Wait and see. But I hope it may prove worth while."

CHAPTER TWENTY-ONE

IT WAS almost ten o'clock, but according to Geoffrey it was yet too early for what he planned to do. Catherine asked no further questions and possessed her soul in patience as they drove slowly about for half an hour, along the *quais*, up to the Bois and back, and around the Cité and the Ile St. Louis. The night was perfect. The twin truncated towers of Notre Dame stood out in bold relief against a starlit sky; the river, swiftly flowing between its inky parapets, was studded with gems of light. One after another they passed the stately Palais de Justice, the Hotel Dieu, and the tall house where Abelard introduced the classics into the head of Heloise and love into her heart.

At last Geoffrey re-crossed the river, and threading the garishly lighted Boul' Mich', teeming with humanity, turned into the Boulevard Montparnasse. Here, a few hundred yards to the right, he parked his car at the tail end of a long queue of motors drawn up before a small building, the lower walls of which were painted in the crudest possible version of the Futurist style. Catherine looked at it with surprise. The name, "Tattenham Corner," roughly inscribed over the door, told her that it was a night-haunt then much in vogue, but which she had not visited and had heard her companion mention with contempt. Why he had brought her here she could not guess.

A blare of strident jazz music greeted them together with a hot rush of foetid air, heavily laden with scent, stale smoke and the odour of perspiring bodies. Shrill laughter and the babel of many tongues rose above unvibrant saxophones, and as they lifted a grimy curtain hung over a doorway and looked in upon the single cramped and crowded room, they had a confused impression of seething, jostling couples, hugged in tight embraces and swaying, cheek to cheek, upon a dance-floor little larger than a hearth-rug. Hell let loose was all Catherine could think of. Amusing but loathsome! Instinctively she drew closer to Geoffrey, who put out a strong arm to shield her from the horde of boisterous students who surged in behind them, shoving their way to the fore by brute force.

No one paid the least attention to them, and it was with difficulty that Geoffrey attracted the notice of the one frowsy waiter who plied his way among the jammed tables, executing orders and making change with an air of stolid indifference. Finally the man approached, wiped his hands on a dirty apron, and listened with dull eyes while Geoffrey said a few words to him in French. After a second he nodded, cast a glance over the room, and undertook to pilot them towards the far end, where they managed to squeeze their way to the only vacant places, fortunately against the wall.

"We shall have to order something," Geoffrey said, "but I warn you it will be bad."

Whereupon he commanded a *fine*, while Catherine chose an orange-ade, thinking it would be comparatively harmless. However, she was wrong. The drink, in a smudged tumbler, arrived, poisonous red in colour, syrupy and strangely chemical to taste. The *garçon* slopped it over on the table and made an ineffectual effort to mop it up with a filthy swab, his attention busy in other quarters.

What a place! Yet half the clients were of the leisured class, jaded but immaculately attired men, with women severely exquisite in the smartest of hats and the newest of ornaments. Why did they come here to stew in this stifling atmosphere, be served with nauseous drinks, and sit pressed like sardines against the unwashed bodies of midinettes, models and cocottes of the lowest type? It was a question only Paris can answer. They did not appear to be extracting any enjoyment from the experiment.

The music stopped, the dancers wormed their way to their seats. A thin girl with a chalked face, mouth like a vermilion scar, and hair plastered in dagger-points against her cheeks, threw herself into the chair opposite with a loud laugh and a wriggle of her snake-like figure. Her escort leered on her with a thick-lipped grimace, wiped the sweat from his forehead, and hammered loudly upon the table.

"Ent she sweet?" he carolled jocosely. "A walk-eeng down zhe street—I ask you confidont-zhallee, ent she sweet?" and he tweaked his lady's ear, to be rewarded by a smack on the jaw.

In the comparative lull the curtain swayed, and an ancient dame, familiar to Montparnassians, stood like an image peering into the smoky interior. On her sparse grey hairs perched a man's hat ornamented with a tiny bedraggled feather, while a soiled muffler was tied about her neck. Her toothless mouth was sunken between nose and withered chin, her bleared eyes ran slowly round with a knowing smile.

"*A'Ami du Peuple—A'Ami du Peuple,*" she piped in a monotonous sing-song, making it into a little tune.

No one noticed her, and presently she vanished, elbowed on her way by the waiter. She was promptly replaced by a little girl in a shawl, bare-headed, feet in ragged *pantoufles*, who carried a tray filled with bunches of flowers, one of which she extended in a grubby hand towards first one reveller, then another.

"*Des violets—des muguets—touts frais—messieurs, mesdames, des violets, des muguets. . . .*"

Then she, too, gave way before a jerk of the *garçon*'s head and departed without disposing of a single posy, but undaunted, calmly philosophical.

Geoffrey bent his head towards Catherine.

"I want you to notice the couple beside you," he whispered, his lips barely moving. "Watch the girl particularly and try to catch what she's saying. She is the person I brought you here to see."

She looked at him with amazed inquiry, then turned her head and surveyed her neighbour, whom till now she had scarcely noticed.

What she saw was a little wren-like creature of about twenty, jauntily arrayed in a bright blue jacket and skirt with a red-spotted neckerchief knotted round her throat and a hat like an aviator's helmet worn so as to display a fringe of hennaed hair. Her perfectly round blue eyes had a babyish stare amidst black-beaded lashes raying out like the petals of a flower, her nose tilted up, and there was a circular patch of crimson painted upon each cheek, giving her the look of one of those naive, slightly grotesque dolls seen in French shops. In a high, chirping falsetto she was chattering with an air familiar and inconsequent to a companion more than twice her age, a sober, hollow-eyed man, just now regarding her attentively while his bony fingers fumbled in a yellow packet of Maryland cigarettes.

"Who is she?" murmured Catherine, returning to Geoffrey in complete mystification.

"Never mind who she is. Listen."

She obeyed wonderingly. For a few minutes she caught nothing of interest, only a childish description of some escapade at *Mi-Carême*, punctuated with argot and laughter. At the end of it the young person drained her glass, set it down with a smack of the lips, and gazed at her escort blandly, eyelashes in full play. At once the middle-aged man beat solemnly upon the marble with a coin till the waiter looked his way.

"*Encore un porto pour mademoiselle,*" he called, abstracting a note from a battered pocket-book.

Not until the full glass was brought did he speak, and though his tone was low, Catherine heard every syllable.

"And that was the last time you saw this Monsieur Blom?" he asked purringly.

Monsieur Blom!—Catherine repressed a start.

"Did you hear?" she whispered to Geoffrey.

He nodded and signed to her to continue listening. The girl at her side had risen to the bait like a hungry trout.

"*Comment c'etait la dernière fois?*" she retorted shrilly. "*Ta mère accouchait un singe, alors!*" she added with rude raillery, and sipped her port.

"No," she continued more seriously. "I saw him lots of times after that. It wasn't till a month after that Bordeaux visit that I told him he could go to the devil, nasty little toad! As if I was going to play second fiddle to that bag of bones. There are too many chances for a girl like me, I can tell you." She sniffed contemptuously and ran a wetted thumb over her pencilled brows.

"I don't know where his eyes were," murmured her companion flatteringly, "to prefer this Madame Baron to you. Old, isn't she?"

"Is she old?" chirped the damsel rhetorically. "Older than God, and a skin like an ostrich! Eyes—my word! They're sharper than yours are, I'll wager. They see where she's got her savings hidden, Rich she must be, although you'd never guess it to look at her! That's all he really cares about—money. He'd sell his soul to the devil for ten thousand francs!"

"But he must do pretty well, what with one thing and another," suggested the other persuasively. "Shouldn't you say so?"

"Oh, I daresay. He's no spender, though. He was precious mean where I was concerned."

"Ever hear him mention any pictures?"

There was a blank stare.

"Pictures? Never—unless you count some postcards he showed me once—filthy little beast!"—and with a grimace she produced her lipstick and applied it freely, studying her reflection in a small mirror.

"But what took him to Bordeaux? Have you any idea of his business there?"

"Bah! He never told me his affairs. Never talked much at any time—just sat drinking his beer and staring like this with his spotted eyes. *Sacré!* It used to get on my nerves!"

"Secretive sort of man, was he?"

"Man! He's not a man at all, he's an animal, a crawling reptile, who has no knowledge of life. Mind you, he's not French."

The all but untranslatable phrase, *"qui n'a pas de savoir vivre"* was indescribably ludicrous, coming from these childish lips with an air of arrogant authority.

So this little piece of painted femininity had known the *notaire* on the most intimate terms, might perhaps be acquainted with his secrets. Was she going to divulge anything important? Catherine listened eagerly.

"Did you ever hear him mention a client of his by the name of Jeanne Laborie?" pursued the agent smoothly, always with the manner of one not particularly concerned.

"Laborie? Never. Who is she? Friend of yours?"

"Only a lady's maid, working at a place in the Avenue Henri Martin."

She repeated the name of the street musingly.

"He had a man friend in the Avenue Henri Martin. Drove a big car, a Rolls-Royce. One Sunday we went for a drive with him, all the way to Chartres—had dinner at a hotel, and the friend stood us a bottle of champagne. It was just before Blom went away. I remember it, because I ruined my new skirt getting champagne on it, and the stingy little brute wouldn't pay to have it re-pleated."

"What was the friend like? A Frenchman?"

"No—Italian, or maybe Spanish. I don't know which, but he could speak French well enough. Oh, he was quite *chic*, the friend. I could have had a good time with him, but I didn't get a chance. I was a bit tight after dinner, and slept all the way home. He and Blom sat in front and talked."

"What about?"

"How should I know? Didn't I say I was asleep?" She gave him a push. "I only woke up to hear the Spaniard, or whatever he was, telling Blom the name of a hotel."

"Ah! Can you remember what hotel it was?"

"No, of course I can't. I wasn't interested. But—well, now you speak of it, I believe I do know. It was the Hôtel des Négociants. Yes, that was it."

"In Paris?"

She shook her head indifferently.

"Perhaps. I haven't an idea. Anyhow, as he went away the next day, it may have been in Bordeaux."

"Did he write to you from Bordeaux?"

"Not a line! But he was like that. I might have died for all he bothered."

She sighed, but did not appear deeply affected. The agent continued to probe skilfully into her shallow little brain, but although the girl seemed quite willing to talk, there was no further information to be gained. However, just as Catherine was beginning to feel disappointed, she caught something which held her interest with a sort of fascination.

"No, I'm not sorry he's gone," observed the little creature callously. "I'm glad. I feel I can breathe again. I tell you, there was something about that little man I didn't half like. So cold, so calculating—always planning, always thinking about something, I never knew what. He would sit and sit. . . . Say we were in a café, a gay place like this. He used to forget all about me, just sit and stare without blinking. If I spoke to him he didn't answer, but kept his spotted eyes fixed on me with a sort of stillness, like . . ."

She broke off, wrapped in thought. Then with a laugh oddly nervous she went on again:

"I'll tell you what it was like. Once in the packing-room at our place I found a huge spider in the middle of a web. Such a wicked devil—oh, a monster! It didn't move, just stayed still and watched me. I screamed! You may laugh, but it was terrifying. There were flies tangled in the web, they couldn't get away. I felt if he looked at me much longer I wouldn't be able to get away either. You see? Well then, that is how I used to feel about Blom. He made me think of that spider, just sitting quiet in the midst of its web, waiting—and waiting. I wanted to shriek and run, and then it was as though my legs were tied together. Ah! It was frightful. If that Honorine can stand it, it's more than I could!"

Her high-pitched voice trailed away, and she remained with round eyes staring at space, while one coarse little hand plucked at the scarf about her neck. At last she shook herself free from the disagreeable memory.

"Here, this is no good!" she cried brusquely, jumping to her feet. "What did you bring me here for, a funeral? Let's dance. . . ."

When the space beside her was vacant Catherine drew a deep breath and turned to Geoffrey.

"Could you hear?" she asked, her eyes blazing.

He nodded with vexation.

"Total failure. The girl knows nothing against Blom."

"Perhaps," replied Catherine shaking her head. "But all the same she's terrified of him. Did you notice her face when she spoke about the spider? She positively shuddered! She's right, too, Geoffrey. There is something rather horrible about that little man. He gives me exactly that feeling of repugnance and—well, terror. I am quite, quite sure he is up to something evil."

"Catherine, what a romantic imagination! Hermione Cushing couldn't do better. I must take you home quickly, or you'll be seeing spiders in your sleep!"

She laughed, crest-fallen.

"Am I such a fool? I wonder . . . Tell me, what did you gather from all this?"

"Very little, except the fact that Blom is evidently marrying the widow for her money. Moreover, the suddenness with which he began to pay court to her suggests that he wanted financial help in a hurry, for some definite purpose."

It had, in fact, occurred to him that perhaps the *notaire* intended to set up as a picture-dealer in some other country, probably America, in which case he would need capital for the enterprise. He could even be buying the pictures from Jeanne and Eduardo, meaning to pay for them with his future wife's savings. If this were true, the visit to Bordeaux, a seaport, no doubt had a connection with his plans, since he would most likely consider it safer to remove the paintings away from Paris, preparatory to smuggling them out of France. Here at last was a clue for Bernard to work on.

"Come along, let's get out," he said, reaching for Catherine's coat. "This air is unbearable."

In the fresh night outside the clamour they had left behind seemed as unreal as a drunken dream.

"My poor lilies-of-the-valley!" exclaimed Catherine, touching the fading flowers at her breast.

"You must be wilted too. Do you realize I've dragged you about with me for eleven long hours?"

"Eleven hours! It has gone like a flash."

Twenty minutes later, inside the dark hall of the apartment, she held out her hand to bid him good night.

"Not just yet," he whispered, "Listen . . ."

Out of the spring night floated the strains of a violin, piercingly sweet. She held her breath, her eyes lit with reminiscence.

"Is it—? It is! The Albeniz Tango again! How wonderful it sounds, coming out of nowhere, like music from another world!"

They looked at each other, and suddenly under the influence of the darkness and the wooing notes the air became charged with electricity. Before she knew what had happened his arms were around her, his lips upon hers.

Strength ebbed away, she gave herself up to moments of exquisite rapture, during which time stood still. Under her fingers she felt his arm muscles tighten, while the odour of his warm skin and hair, so close to her nostrils, swept her away with subtle intoxication.

Seconds passed while they clung thus hungrily together. Then with a gasp Catherine pushed him from her.

"Don't! You mustn't!" she murmured, frightened. "I—I didn't want you to do that!"

"Didn't you?" he demanded, holding her hands fast in his. "I don't believe it!"

Her face burned. They were still so near each other that she could hear the pounding of his heart.

"Why?" he insisted urgently. "Catherine, I mean this—with my whole soul. Don't tell me you don't care too. Since that day in the train I've thought of nothing but you. I've never felt like this about any woman. I want you to marry me as soon as possible. Will you?"

The force of his tone took away her breath. She retreated a step, eyes wide and dark, trying desperately to think clearly.

He loved her, then! After all these weeks of calm, unemotional behaviour, he was begging her to marry him! She could hardly believe her senses.

"Oh, Geoffrey," she managed to answer in a shaking voice. "I—I don't know. You see, for a whole year I was engaged to a man I didn't love, and I swore never to make such a ghastly mistake again. I almost think I daren't be engaged at all, but that some day, when I'm quite sure, I'll marry someone all at once, before I can change my mind!" She finished with a wavering laugh.

"I'm not asking you to be engaged," he muttered, smiling a little.

"But marriage is so irrevocable, isn't it? I mean I've got to think things over . . . All the same, I did love—that." Her breast rose. "Only, because I loved it I must be all the more cautious and not be carried away. It mayn't be the real thing, and until I'm quite sure I mustn't let you kiss me again."

"Very well, then," he said briefly. "But it will be hard-going—now."

"Perhaps it will be hard for me, too," she answered with shining eyes. "But I must stick to it, for I know I'm right."

He was gone. She heard his car start, then with fluttering pulses groped her way towards the staircase.

Yes, she was right. Until she could determine the depth of this new emotion she dared not repeat the embrace which had robbed her of all reasoning power. Yet, oh, how terribly she longed to do so! She clung to the newel post, weak with the memory of physical ecstasy.

Round her was heavy stillness, broken only by the ticking of the hall clock. Then, out of the enveloping gloom, her ear detected a faint, distant sound which rose and fell spasmodically. She raised her head and listened.

It came from the court side of the apartment, a stifled piteous sobbing, heart-rending to hear. Could it be Germaine, and if so, was she alone? At this hour, too, past midnight?

Without stopping to think she crept quietly along the passages to her cousin's room.

CHAPTER TWENTY-TWO

OUTSIDE Germaine's door she stood, wondering what she ought to do. The sobbing continued softly, as though the hidden weeper were afraid of being overheard. It had a piteous sound which went to the girl's heart and at the same time vaguely alarmed her. Where was Jeanne? Then she noticed that the dressing-room door was ajar. Cautiously she pushed it open and stole a glance inside.

The room was empty, the cover of the couch-bed smoothly drawn up. So much she could make out in the dimness, and drew her conclusions accordingly. Jeanne had gone out—perhaps to meet Blom. For once the invalid was left unguarded.

Not without a tremor of nervousness, she took her courage in both hands and went into Mme. Bender's room.

But where was the occupant? The sobs had ceased. Two candles against the wall burned with a wavering light, casting black shadows across the disarranged but empty bed. The air was hot and stuffy.

All at once a movement caught her eye, and above the edge of the armchair showed a pallid face, tear-streaked, hair in disorder, eyes gazing fixedly.

"Germaine!" whispered the girl in consternation, mystified at the sight.

Then she realized that Mme. Bender was crouched on the floor before the crucifix, in an attitude of prayer.

It was a long second before she saw recognition come into the frightened eyes and the lips move stiffly, whispering her name.

"It's you—it's you—it's you . . ." murmured the invalid over and over, clutching the bed-curtain with a shaking hand. "At first I thought . . ."

"But of course it's me," said Catherine soothingly. "I heard you and came to see what was wrong."

She watched anxiously for any sign of recoil, but could detect none. Still puzzled, but with a feeling of relief, she put her arm about the older woman's shoulders protectingly.

"But you will catch cold, dear. You must let me get you into bed again," and she reached for the white *peignoir* lying on the chair and wrapped it round the unresisting frame.

"No, no, I am not cold. It is very hot in here—too hot. I could not sleep," whispered Mme. Bender vaguely, her eyes fixed like those of a somnambulist. "Sometimes the sedative does not work. I think it is because I have taken it so often."

She allowed herself to be led back to bed, and with complete docility let Catherine arrange the pillows and remove the stifling eiderdown. The window was closed, there was not a breath of fresh air. No wonder the poor creature could not rest.

"But where is Jeanne?" the girl could not help asking, as she lowered the upper sash a little and poured some water into a glass which she held to the patient's dry lips.

Germaine regarded her as though in a dream.

"Jeanne? I don't know . . . she went out, I think, an hour, two hours ago. Ah," she added quickly, "you must not tell her I was awake! It will only distress her. Poor Jeanne—she does so much for me, and I am so selfish. No one in the world cares for me as she does. I know that only too well," she muttered with curious insistence.

Catherine did not oppose her. She sat on the edge of the bed, stroking the trembling hand which she was glad to notice did not withdraw from her clasp. Then, seeing that the candles, still alight, were only a few inches removed from the draperies of the bed, she got up and extinguished them. The acrid smoke from the burning wicks filled her nostrils.

"Why did you light the candles, dear?" she asked, as she turned on the lamp. "You know, I don't think it is quite safe to do that."

The grey eyes avoided hers with a look of guilt.

"I was praying," whispered the invalid childishly. "I was so unhappy, lying here . . . I couldn't bear it any longer. I thought if I lit the candles and prayed I might get some relief from the pain here,"—and she touched her heart, while a spasm of suffering crossed her features.

"But why are you unhappy, Germaine? Won't you try to tell me?" begged the girl, afraid to speak the words.

"Because—because I am so alone. Who would not feel as I do, with no one to care for me except Jeanne? Ah—if you knew! I am lonely, I am desolate—I have not a single friend. I would be happier if I were so poor that I had not a sou to call my own, for then I should perhaps have someone to love me!"

It was the old story. Jeanne had distilled the poisonous suggestion into the poor credulous mind until there was no removing it. It was almost unbelievably cruel.

"Germaine," said Catherine firmly yet with an attempt at lightness, "all that is sheer nonsense. Listen to me, dear. Every one has friends— rich people as well as poor ones. It is Jeanne who has made you think this absurd thing—and is it possible you don't realize why?"

The wan face expressed nothing but bewilderment.

"Jeanne? I don't understand. Why should she?"

"Simply because she is jealous. She hates the thought of any other person sharing your affection. It has been plain to me from the beginning. I don't blame her, but it is so. She is jealous of anyone who might come between you and her. Can't you see that?"

She spoke with strong conviction, determined to drive home something she did not herself wholly believe any longer. She saw a light of wonderment come into her cousin's eyes.

"But can this possibly be true?" faltered the poor woman in amazement.

"I'm sure of it. Think for a moment. Who are your friends? Tell me their names."

The strained gaze wavered.

"Not many," muttered the invalid after a moment. "Some are dead. There was, of course, Madeleine de Bréart . . ."

"The Comtesse de Bréart is in Africa, with her husband. She has been gone for many months. Surely you know that."

But it was plain that Germaine did not know.

"A number of people have called to inquire about you, but you were not considered well enough to see them. They left cards and sometimes flowers. There was the Baronne de Grèves and Madame Strakosch." She mentioned the names at random, shamelessly, bent only upon uprooting the fixed idea which was causing so much mischief.

Incredulous joy flamed up in the starved eyes.

"They came? You mean this? And I never knew! Or if I did I have forgotten it," she added, pushing her hair off her forehead with a confused gesture.

"Of course! You see?" cried the young girl triumphantly. "Now you must never get such ideas into your head again." She waited a moment, then, growing bolder, continued: "And then there is Hermione. You forget her. She cares for you very deeply, more, perhaps, than anyone."

A shadow hovered over the sensitive face.

"Lili . . . do you think she does?"

"I swear it. For that matter, how is it possible you can doubt her devotion, after all these years, with nothing to go upon except the angry words of a servant?"

As she said this she shook inwardly, afraid that she had gone too far. However, the abashed expression on her companion's features assured her she was right to take a firm line.

"You must not reproach me," murmured the Frenchwoman, fidgeting. "She—she did urge me to make my will, you know."

"And why not?" interrupted Catherine quickly. "She meant no harm. Everyone makes a will. Even I, with my tiny bit of property, made my will soon after my father died. It is the only sensible thing to do." Here she paused to allow the common sense of this to sink into Germaine's mind. "You cannot realize how hurt Hermione is when you refuse to see her. To be shut out like this by the one friend of her girlhood—surely you must know how terribly it has wounded her feelings. You really owe her an apology!"

"But—but—"

It was easy to read the meaning of Mme. Bender's embarrassed hesitation. Half-convinced now that she had made a mistake, the poor woman was in terror of displeasing Jeanne by admitting it. She was far too weak to make any sort of stand by herself.

"Never mind that now," said Catherine gently. "I don't say this to upset you, only to make you understand things better. As for making your will, it is a matter only you can decide. No one wants to bother you about it. All we think of—Jeanne, Hermione, I—is to get you well again."

The shaking hand picked at the sheet mechanically.

"I ought to do it—I know I ought," whispered Mme. Bender indistinctly, as if arguing with herself. "Only feeling as I do about myself I dare not. My memory . . . Ah, what was that?" She started, trembling afresh. "Did you hear a noise?"

Listening, Catherine caught the sound of a door closing. It was Jeanne come back. Simultaneously the invalid's eyes dilated with nervous dread.

"Go-go!" she urged, pushing the girl away with both hands. "She must not find you here. Quick, I beg of you! I shall pretend to be asleep."

Catherine sprang up, put out the lamp, and slipped into the passage, shutting the door behind her. She was not a moment too soon, for barely had she time to step inside the neighbouring bathroom when she heard the maid's brisk steps approach and enter the room she had just quitted. She waited till all was silent, then made her way back in the darkness to her own side of the apartment.

The past quarter of an hour had cheered her enormously, proving as it had how amenable Germaine was to the influence of any vigorous mind. How readily she had responded to the suggestion of Jeanne's jealousy! A very little more and all that unhappy distrust in her soul could be melted away. Wonders might be achieved if only one had a free hand.

She took off her hat and began to unfasten the cuffs of her frock. Then, glancing down, she saw that the lilies of the valley which had been pinned into the front were gone. A little pang shot through her. Where could she have dropped them? They had been in place a little while ago, for she recalled their fragrance during the moments when she had leaned against the post at the top of the stairs. That meant they had fallen off either in the passage or in Germaine's room.

Suddenly oppressed, she retraced her steps cautiously all the way to the distant bedroom, feeling the carpet every inch of the way. No, the flowers were not there. She had certainly lost them in her cousin's room, where they would remain till the maid discovered them, silent evidence of her presence there.

Would the incident lead to further trouble? It had been only too plain just now that Germaine was afraid of what Jeanne would say if she knew. Well, the damage was done now, there was no help for it. One must simply hope for the best.

In bed at last, with weary body but alert mind, she saw the day's events pass before her in a series of vivid pictures. The brilliant restaurant of Ledoyen, the April countryside, moonlight on the dark quais, the lurid interior of Tattenham Corner . . .

Those round staring eyes of the Montmartre grisette! What a note of fascinated loathing there had been in the piping voice when it described the huge spider, watchful in its web! Almost as though the girl herself were the hapless fly entangled in those paralysing meshes. . . . Geoffrey was right, all the same. One must not let one's fancy be governed by such absurdities!

Candles . . . too close to Mme. Bender's bed. They were dangerous. One flicker of a draught, and the draperies might be set on fire. All that must be changed. Never mind, tonight's conversation was a distinct step forward. A little more scheming, reasonable luck, and Jeanne with her bad influence and slack ways would be gone forever. . . .

Meanwhile a warm thought flooded her consciousness. Geoffrey loved her, wanted her! Just now it mattered little what her own feelings were. Enough that she had been held in strong arms and kissed as all her life she had longed to be kissed . . .

She fell asleep, the Albeniz Tango pulsing rhythmically in her inner ear. Peace, oblivion, and not one disturbing hint of what the following day was to bring forth. . . .

CHAPTER TWENTY-THREE

SHE felt strangely sick and queer, her head going round.

What was wrong with her? She had slept till ten, rung for her coffee and drunk it before she had noticed anything amiss. Then, after reading her letters—one a note from Geoffrey's sister, Elspeth Baxter, inviting her to spend a week with her at Fontainebleau—she had risen lazily to dress, only to discover an unexpected faintness combined with racking pains in her stomach.

Oh, well, it could not be serious. Yesterday she had eaten and drunk rather unwisely. Her thoughts flew to the poisonous, over-sweet concoction, falsely called orangeade, which she had imbibed at Tattenham Corner. Foolish to drink the stuff, only she had been so thirsty.

"I'll take a starvation cure to-day," she told herself, plying her hairbrush vigorously.

What about her lost flowers? Had Jeanne found them? If so she would instantly jump at the idea of collusion and perhaps make trouble. How annoying, at this crucial time!

Elspeth's invitation. . . . How much she longed to accept it! She knew that Geoffrey would spend as much time as possible out there, and she thrilled at the prospect of rambles in the forest with him these warm, sunny days. If only she dared to go! But she must not think of it while things hung in the balance. Perhaps later on, with affairs satisfactorily settled—but they couldn't be for some time yet. She did not even know what had come of the doctor's interview with Jeanne.

She rose to go into the bathroom, then had to steady herself with a hand on the nearest chair. A wave of giddiness overtook her, thick beads of perspiration broke out all over her body.

Really, it was too stupid! Why, yesterday she had felt more than usually fit!

"I can't, I won't be ill!" she declared angrily, making a second movement to pick up her bath-towel. "I'll dress and go out into the fresh air. All this is nonsense!"

The next moment she had collapsed across the bed, panting for breath and doubled up with pain like the stab of a knife. She tried to rise, but gave up in despair.

There she lay, uncovered in her thin *crêpe de Chine* night-dress, helpless and weak as a baby, for what must have been twenty minutes, before she could summon strength to ring the bell. All but unconscious, she wondered dimly what could possibly be the cause of the alarming attack. Her skin burned, her mouth felt parched, while her body seemed strangely swollen. Appendicitis occurred to her. Never in her life had she given it a thought, but now all at once the disease seemed a dreadful reality.

She was too miserable when the door opened to feel surprised that it was Jeanne and not Berthe who answered the call. She could not even raise her head as she lay huddled and racked with agony, and was barely able to articulate.

"Jeanne—I am feeling dreadfully ill. I can't imagine what it is." She succumbed again, speechless with a terrific fit of cramp.

"Ah, ah, mademoiselle! Vous êtes bien souffrante!"

The voice came from far away. At the same time practised hands lifted her capably, placed her between the sheets, while dimly she heard something about a possible chill and the advisability of summoning the doctor. Then she was once more alone.

Whatever this was, it was no joking matter. She was shivering from head to foot, her teeth chattered like castanets, and for a little time it seemed as though she would lose consciousness.

Presently Jeanne returned with a hot-water bottle which she placed at her icy feet.

"Eduardo is telephoning to Dr. Girard," she said. "I am afraid to give you any medicine, as I do not know what is wrong. Where are the pains?"

Catherine tried to show her. It was an unwelcome turn of events which had brought this woman to minister to her needs. She would far rather have had Berthe, but there was no help for it.

"In the stomach, is it? Ah!" There was a grunt and a faint shrug. "Ah, well, that looks bad, but perhaps it is nothing serious!"

Through half-closed eyes Catherine saw the maid straighten up and survey her with an appraising frown.

"A hot drink will do you no harm, and may bring some relief. Lie quite still, and I will prepare you a *tisane*." She departed briskly on her errand.

At least, thought Catherine, the doctor will soon be here. Then in a momentary cessation of pain she recalled an additional reason for wanting to see him. She could now find out if he had settled matters satisfactorily. What a blessing if Jeanne had given in!

Ten minutes passed, then the maid returned to hold a steaming cup to her lips. She took a sip of the hot liquid only to cough and choke with a qualm of renewed nausea.

"What bitter stuff!" she murmured in disgust.

"Bitter? But no! It is simply *tilleul*. Sure mademoiselle has tasted it many times?"

"Never."

She forced herself to drink, then fell back exhausted.

"That is better. Now rest, it will do you good."

For a brief interval it seemed that Jeanne was right. A sort of numbness ensued during which she drifted into a half-doze. Then she was roused anew by horrible sickness and suffering worse than before. Mentally she resolved not to touch *tilleul* again . . .

"Fancy," remarked Jeanne, busily tidying the room. "We have been wondering why Dr. Girard failed to come yesterday. Now we learn that he has met with an accident—slipped on the parquet, and torn some ligaments in his leg. Poor man, he will not be able to go out for several days. However he is sending his assistant to see you."

What bad luck! Nothing seemed to go smoothly. In the midst of her anguish the girl found time to question the complacent ring she detected in Jeanne's voice. Did it mean that Girard had been stupid enough to betray some hint of their scheme?

So violent were the paroxysms now that she scarcely knew when Jeanne left her, nor was she able to speak to Berthe, who presently appeared, round-eyed and awed, to offer suggestions of brandy and mustard-plasters. She shook her head and with set teeth waited for the doctor, wondering if he would hurry her off to a hospital for an immediate operation. Even the thought of an anaesthetic was welcome in her present torture.

It was midday when the door opened to admit a plump, serious-looking young man, ushered in by Jeanne. He glanced at the patient's white face, removed his gloves with deliberation, then turning his back on the bed engaged in a whispered colloquy with the maid. Catherine could not catch what they said, nor did she care, but she was aware of a brusque hardness in the assistant's manner which would have roused antagonism if she had been less ill.

At length, as though satisfied, he motioned Jeanne outside, closed the door, and proceeded to make a brief examination, muttering to himself with an air of displeasure. Finally he sat down close to the bedside and leaned forward, solemnly confidential.

"And now, mademoiselle," he began with a sort of accusing disapproval, "I want you to tell me precisely what it is you have taken, and how much."

"Taken?" echoed Catherine in amazement. "I don't understand."

"Yes, certainly," he persisted. "I want to know what drug you have taken. Do not be afraid. I will not give you away."

She stared at him mystified. What was the man driving at?

"But I haven't taken anything. What do you mean?"

He uttered an abrupt exclamation, jerking his plump shoulders. She could not think why he seemed so annoyed with her.

"Mademoiselle, I beg of you, don't attempt to deceive me! It is most foolish. If I am to help you, you must play fair with me. Now, once again—what medicine, what drug did you take last night? I insist upon knowing."

Weak though she was, she felt bewilderment succumb to irritation, and roused herself to a more emphatic denial.

"I tell you, nothing whatever. I drank some rather horrid orange-ade at a café last night, and I had two cocktails, one at lunch and one at dinner. But I haven't taken any medicine, and I felt all right till after breakfast this morning."

"And that is all, absolutely all?"

"Certainly. Why should I want to deceive you?"

By the half-veiled scorn in his eyes she could see that he only partly believed what she had said. An explosive sigh escaped him as he fixed his full eyes on the wall over her head, muttering to himself:

"Ces jeunes filles—tellement stupides, tellement ignorantes!"

Catching the indistinct words, she was stirred to a vague resentment. A flush mounted to her cheeks, but she forebore to argue.

"Eh bien! If you are determined to keep silent, I must do what I can without your help."

"I'm sorry you think I'm lying," she said bluntly, "and I wish you would say what is in your mind. You believe I've taken a drug. Is it possible"—she hesitated, frowning incredulously—"is it possible you think I have been trying to kill myself?"

"Kill?" He gave vent to a short, ironic laugh which grated on her ear.

"No, mademoiselle, not that. Assuredly not! But if one tampers with dangerous medicines, no matter for what purpose, one runs the risk of committing suicide!"

She gave up trying to understand, and mastered her growing indignation. What a disagreeable young man! Then the idea occurred to her, only to be rejected, that perhaps he had got hold of this notion from his talk with Jeanne. There had been something odd in Jeanne's manner, only how could the woman have any opinion one way or the other? There was no point in it.

He began to ask a great many questions, some of them intimate ones, the bearing of which she could dimly surmise. She answered him frankly enough, but with an inward sense of embarrassment. Then, as the consultation went on she saw his expression change, grow less cocksure, and finally take altogether another phase. He rubbed his chin thoughtfully, and still looking at her with searching eyes, led the inquiry in another direction.

"Enfin, mademoiselle, let us hear what you had to eat yesterday. Everything, please. Don't leave out a single article of food."

Thinking back carefully, she enumerated the items of the various menus. When she came to last night's dinner he gave an exclamation of triumph.

"Oysters!" he cried. "The end of April! You have been poisoned by the oysters, there is little doubt of it. The trouble is gastric."

She did not know why all at once he should appear both relieved and mollified. His brow cleared and he looked at her in quite a different way.

"Well, mademoiselle, first of all I must prescribe for you a large dose of an unpleasant remedy. I will give directions to have it prepared for you at once, with orange juice."

He mentioned the name—*huile de ricine*. That was merely castor oil. She nodded, quite ready to believe that it was the oysters which had caused the mischief. As for the trouble being gastric, it had never entered her head that it could be anything else.

"I will call again this evening. Meantime you are to keep warm and eat nothing until the middle of the afternoon, when you may have a cup of tea. You English like your five o'clock, is it not?" he added, heavily jocose.

She smiled at him wanly. After all, he meant no harm.

Yet, thinking it over after he had gone she was again affronted by his disbelief and the severe cross-examination he had put her through. She was still dwelling upon these things when Berthe entered with the castor oil, and she could not help noticing that in the friendly cook's eyes she was an object of interest and curiosity. Why should Berthe look at her like that? A moment later, while the door was temporarily ajar, she caught a scrap of whispered conversation, which explained it even while it increased her mystification.

"*Mais non! Tu crois?*" She heard Berthe gasp in astonishment.

"*Humph! J'en suis sûre,*" retorted Jeanne's voice, contemptuously emphatic.

Whatever it was the maid was so sure about, it seemed certain, after all, that the doctor had taken his original cue from her.

After this she dozed from exhaustion, but at seven o'clock when the physician reappeared she was still in so much pain that it was necessary to administer an injection of morphia.

CHAPTER TWENTY-FOUR

THE suffering passed, but she was distressingly ill for three whole days, during which she was ably cared for by Jeanne, who proved an efficient nurse. Berthe, too, bestirred herself to prepare the simple dishes ordered by the doctor, and hung about, much concerned as to the patient's progress. From her Catherine learned that Geoffrey had telephoned several times daily, a fact which brought solace even while she felt too weak to see him.

Also he had sent flowers—more lilies-of-the-valley and great bunches of golden daffodils, filling the room with colour. She lay feasting her eyes on them, now and then slipping the accompanying notes from beneath her pillow to read again his ardent messages.

The fourth afternoon Dr. Girard himself arrived, hobbling with a stick. He had been fully informed of her alarming symptoms, which he agreed were those of acute ptomaine poisoning, occasioned by the oysters eaten on Sunday evening. Oysters at this season were a bit of a risk. She might think herself fortunate to have got off so lightly.

"But fortunate or not, mademoiselle," he added with pompous kindliness, "you have had a bad time which has left you extremely weak. You must go slow, and as soon as possible get away from Paris into the country, for a change of air."

She stared at him in slight annoyance. This was not the right tack at all—for her to go away. It was the last thing she had thought of.

"But I'd rather not leave Paris just now," she said. "And I shall be all right in a few days."

"Not so soon as you think," he contradicted with a shake of his head. "I should really like to insist on your getting out of town. It is what you need to put you on your feet."

Why was he so determined? In spite of his amiable face suspicion assailed her that Jeanne had been getting at him. This might mean a fresh manoeuvre on her part.

"Tell me, doctor," she said, looking him straight in the eye, "has anyone suggested this to you?"

He wavered a little.

"Well, yes, I admit it. Someone has, only yesterday."

Ah! She knew it! What an exasperating irony!

"Does it occur to you that this person is being rather officious on my behalf?" she inquired sarcastically.

"I would hesitate to call it that," replied the old man in a conciliatory tone. "As a matter of fact, it was a young man, who appears to take a very warm interest in your welfare."

So! It was not Jeanne but Geoffrey who had stolen a march on her. She was relieved, yet could not repress a rueful smile at the doctor's insinuating repetition of the words, *"Un jeune monsieur, tres distingué—un Anglais—"* What a reversal of the situation! Here she had lain, praying for Girard to order the maid away, and now it was herself he was virtually commanding to go!

"But, monsieur, have you forgotten our conversation last Friday?" she asked, ready to cry with disappointment.

"Ah, no, mademoiselle, assuredly not! I had meant to speak of it this afternoon. I broached the subject to the person in question the last time I was here, and I am happy to report that I met with almost no opposition. The affair is arranged most satisfactorily."

"Arranged?" she exclaimed, electrified with astonishment. "You mean she is willing to go?"

"But certainly—quite willing, even pleased at the prospect. She desires only a little time to make her plans. She was to write to her brother to prepare him for her visit and make sure he has room for her. That is all. You can put your mind at rest."

Catherine sank back, overcome by the unexpected good news. How simple it all was! If only she had known, she might have spared herself endless anxiety. She began to laugh softly, while tears of weakness came into her eyes. She wiped them away hurriedly, aware that Girard was watching her with concern.

"There, mademoiselle, you see? It is you who are unnerved now. Your friend the Englishman was right, you must get away from this atmosphere for a little in order to recover your strength. Yes, the woman was most reasonable. She only stipulates that madame should be gradually accustomed to her leaving, and that she should not be left entirely alone with a strange nurse during her absence. In short, she wishes that you yourself should be here while she is away."

"I?" echoed Catherine, hardly able to believe her ears.

Either Jeanne had experienced a change of heart, or else her own suspicions were hopelessly false. It was difficult to take it in.

"Yes, you, mademoiselle. As she says, Mme. Bender is attached to you and will be less likely to feel the change if you are with her. It is for that very reason that I urge you to get your own holiday first, so you will be perfectly strong and equal to the responsibility."

She looked at him searchingly, wondering if he knew what a clever method he had hit upon for gaining her consent. His heavy features gave no hint of duplicity, showing merely complacence at his management of the situation.

"*Eh bien!* We may regard the matter as settled. Naturally you must stay in bed for a few days longer, while we watch the diet and give you a tonic to put some strength into you. Towards the end of the week we might think of getting you to the country. What do you say to Fontaine-bleau?" he added, with a look of arch cunning.

She was silent. Much as she wanted to go to Fontainebleau the idea that wires were being pulled to make her do so was distasteful. Moreover, Jeanne's complete veering round provided food for conjecture. Not once had the woman mentioned the flowers she must surely have discovered in Mme. Bender's room, or hinted at the possibility of a reconciliation. True, all this week she had been extraordinarily assiduous and kind, a gesture one might construe as a desire to bury the hatchet.

Catherine pondered the matter, languidly puzzled.

"Perhaps she has some reason for wanting to placate me," she reflected. "Or is it that I've been mistaken about her all along?"

At the moment she felt thoroughly confused.

Still her main purpose was accomplished. Soon Germaine would be under competent care, free from adverse influence. A month was not long, to be sure, but before it was over one might reasonably hope to find means to prevent Jeanne's return to power. Eduardo, too, must be dealt with, but alone he presented no formidable difficulties.

A knock sounded and Berthe's voice was heard saying that a gentle-man had called. Might he be permitted to come in?

For the first time in days Catherine's heart leaped with glad expect-ancy, while a flush crept into her cheeks.

"One minute, Berthe. Fetch me my mirror and powder-puff, please."

Vanity had revived—a healthy sign. Hastily, with Berthe's aid, she made herself presentable, smoothing the dark mass of her hair and rebraiding the twin, short pigtails which fell over her shoulders. The thinness of her face shocked her. She had not looked in a glass since early Monday morning.

"*Un peu de parfum, n'est-ce pas?*" whispered her attendant with the air of a sympathetic conspirator.

She assented, laughing, and the thick finger of Berthe planted a spot of scent behind each of her ears.

When Geoffrey entered he found her propped up against pillows, her eyes shining in their wells of dark shadow. He took her hand in his warm clasp and stood looking down on her with intensity.

"Catherine—my dear! What is the meaning of this?"

She shook her head with a grimace.

"Oysters, I suppose. Anyhow, that's what they tell me."

"It's my fault. I was a fool to suggest the damned things in this weather. I ought to be kicked!"

"What rubbish! Besides, I'm well now. In a few days I shall be up."

"In a few days," he retorted grimly, "I mean to have you out of this. Whether you like it or not, you're going to leave this place."

Her eyes opened wide with amazement.

"Aren't you a bit premature with your airs of authority?" she demanded with severity. "For that matter, what do you mean by plotting with the doctor behind my back?"

He looked slightly abashed.

"Maybe I'd no right to," he muttered doggedly. "But someone has got to take you in hand. It was bad enough knowing you were ill, but much worse to think of you at the mercy of these slovenly servants. I very nearly had the American Hospital at Neuilly send an ambulance to fetch you away."

"You needn't have bothered. I've had nothing to complain of, except feeling absolutely rotten."

He sat down, still retaining her hand, which she could not bring herself to withdraw. She was battling with a sudden absurd desire to cling to him and weep upon his shoulder; instead of which she assumed a bantering smile and tried to turn the conversation away from her illness.

"Elspeth wrote you," he said presently. "What are you going to do about it?"

"Oh, that! I haven't felt up to making plans."

"You needn't make plans. Decide now when you think you can go, and I'll send her a telegram."

His new assurance astonished her. Had those brief moments on Sunday night been to him like the tiger's first taste of blood? The idea amused her, at the same time causing a faint thrill. Clearly it was impossible for them to resume their former friendly relations.

Yet his very urgency roused in her a perverse desire to object.

"I'm not sure I want to go just yet, Geoffrey. You see the unexpected has happened. Jeanne has consented to take a holiday."

"The devil she has!" His thick brows shot up in rueful consternation. "By George, that alters things, doesn't it? I mean if she's really a bad hat, would she be willing to walk out and give us a free hand at investigation? Either she's extremely sure of herself, or else . . ."

Their eyes met guiltily.

"I know," replied Catherine, nodding. "I've been thinking that, too. Perhaps we—or rather I—have been misjudging her all along. It makes me feel so ashamed. Oh, Geoffrey, do you think me an utter lunatic to have stirred up this hornet's nest?"

"Your suspicions were quite natural."

"Yes, they were, weren't they?" she whispered. "However innocent she may be in the main, her conduct has been open to reproach in many ways. In any case I am positive about one point—her really bad effect on Mme. Bender. That is what actually matters."

He agreed heartily, not thinking it necessary to tell her that, judging by his own talk with Dr. Girard, the latter's opinion of the maid was not seriously shaken. It was just as well, according to the doctor, to supplant Jeanne, or at least to supplement her services by professional ones, but on the whole she seemed to him a devoted, obstinate servant, a person of one idea, unwilling to admit herself in error, as the unfortunate mouse episode proved. She had been on a long, severe strain at a time of life when a woman's nerves are apt to prove uncertain; moreover, quite possibly she had a touch of the *type hystérique* in her make-up, which would account for many peculiarities. This was his pronouncement, uttered sanely, without rancour. He struck Geoffrey as an intelligent and well-meaning man, kindly disposed towards Catherine, but withal anxious to be just.

Coming out of a brief reverie, Geoffrey again attacked the subject of Elspeth's invitation.

"If, as you say, Jeanne means to get off as soon as she hears from her brother, then obviously you ought to lose no time over your own visit. What about Saturday? Do you think you'll be well enough by then?"

She remained quite still for a few moments, her brows knit over troubled eyes which avoided his gaze.

"I don't like being hurried into a thing," she murmured presently, trying to take a light tone.

"My dear!" he laughed, but was plainly annoyed. "Don't you realize you've been deucedly ill, and that the doctor says it's most important for you to have a change?"

She gave him a scornful look.

"I realize he said that before he'd seen me at all," she retorted. "Besides, I always pick up with amazing speed. No, that doesn't mean anything," she added, as he spread her thin, olive-tinted hand out on his palm and traced the bones with a significant finger. "I can gain that back in a fortnight. Anyhow, I don't intend to go, so that's that," she finished, her chin stubborn.

"Why?"

She resented the fashion in which the question was shot at her. How could she put into words the rather preposterous idea which was wandering about in her brain, seeking confirmation? Already she had exposed herself to sufficient ridicule.

"The same old reasons, I suppose," she admitted reluctantly. "I don't want to leave Germaine till Jeanne is away."

He exclaimed in exasperation, giving her hand a squeeze which made her wince.

"Catherine, you're impossible! Can't you see it will be only for such a short time that it can't make any difference to anyone? That you'll come home feeling strong and able to cope with things? I've no patience with you. You deserve a smacking."

"Who's going to inflict it?" she laughed at him.

He hesitated, eyeing her sternly.

"I am. I made up my mind what I should do if you took up this unreasonable stand. I'm going to resort to pressure."

She could not be sure whether he were joking or serious.

"That sounds like a threat," she said lightly.

"It is. Here's the situation in a nutshell. The doctor has definitely ordered you to go away from Paris. If you refuse, I shall simply send a cablegram to your family in Boston and tell them the whole story."

She stared at him, drawing in her breath.

"You don't mean that. You couldn't do it."

"Why not?"

"For one thing," she said, laughing, "you don't know their address."

He smiled confidently.

"I have already got your brother-in-law's cable address, which shows how much you know about it. I intend to send a night-letter outlining the position."

He meant it, that was plain. In a flash she foresaw the appalling row which would ensue when Barbara and John learned what was going on here, realizing that her own silence on the subject would make a bad matter worse. Barbara could not compel her to return to America, but she could stir up a deal of trouble. The prospect frightened her.

Geoffrey saw her eyes smoulder with indignation, but he did not give in an inch.

"Think it over," he said calmly. "I'll give you till to-morrow morning, but no longer."

Without rhyme or reason a quick change came over her face. Her mouth softened into a smile wholly disarming, her eyes shone at him through a mist as she answered with a catch in her voice.

"Very well. I'll go. Tell Elspeth, if you like, to expect me on Saturday."

"Good girl!"

The abrupt capitulation took the wind out of his sails. With a laugh he bent his head and kissed the hand he held, outside and in.

"But mind, it's only because you're being so horrid to me," she warned him reproachfully. "And remember I haven't promised anything about— you know what."

With a deep breath he relinquished the imprisoned hand.

"I understand."

Now she had made the decision her brain was working feverishly.

"I must put certain things right before I go. Germaine will have to make it up with Hermione, so there will be someone to keep an eye on Jeanne. I think I can manage that though. Will you ask her to come and see me?"

"Miss Cushing? Certainly, if you think it a good idea."

Why did he hesitate in that embarrassed manner? Had she said anything wrong?

"Don't, if you'd rather not. I'll drop her a line."

"No, no. I'll telephone her. I was only thinking that in your present wobbly state she might prove slightly overpowering."

He was a bad liar, and consequently became disturbingly self-conscious when her eyes rested on him thoughtfully. Had she guessed that he was feeling more than a little queer about Hermione?

It was nothing serious, of course, but all the same an incident had occurred that very afternoon to sow doubts in his mind regarding the singer and set him once more struggling against a crop of peculiar surmises.

CHAPTER TWENTY-FIVE

GEOFFREY earnestly hoped his stupidity about Miss Cushing had passed unnoticed. Seriously concerned over Catherine, his one idea was to get her quickly and safely into his sister's care, a project easily jeopardized if one introduced her to fresh worries.

Besides, the information recently obtained might prove of no importance, though he had to admit it had given him a jar.

Two hours ago he had had his first talk with the senior clerk since the latter's illness, and questioning him about Blom's visit to the office had received a somewhat startling reply.

"I recall the fellow," the old man had said at once. "Renier was the name he gave, and he came on a rather delicate mission, respecting one of our clients—in fact Mme. Belmont Bender. He wanted to know if this lady had executed a will."

"Why should he wish to know that?" Geoffrey had demanded, suspiciously.

"He was acting on behalf of another lady, who, as she is a personal friend of Mme. Bender's, felt a natural hesitancy in approaching us on the matter. It seems this individual has hopes of inheriting something substantial in the event of Madame's decease, and was anxious to learn if the bequest had been put into legal form. Renier also inquired the terms of Mr. Bender's own will, and as the request appeared a harmless one I informed him that Mr. Bender had left the whole of his property unconditionally to his widow. That was all."

Geoffrey's mind had leaped to the conclusion that Jeanne, fearing her mistress had stolen a march on her, had taken this roundabout means of learning the truth.

"I suppose you don't know who the client was?" he asked.

"Oh, but I do. It seems she is an American lady by the name of Cushing."

Hermione! Geoffrey had sprung from his chair, all his previous ideas in confusion.

"Yes, Miss Cushing, the singer. I heard her once, at the Salle Erard—a large woman, with a wreath of rosebuds on her hair. No kind of voice, but I believe she has an influential connection. . . ."

Feeling as though he had doubled on his own tracks, Geoffrey had departed, chagrined and mortified. The revelation that the mysterious Blom was acting for Hermione shocked him curiously. Was it possible that under cover of pretended hatred the singer was in collusion with Mme. Bender's servants? For a wild moment he asked himself if Miss Cushing herself was concerned in the thefts, using Blom as a go-between. It was a monstrous thought.

Going over the circumstances he felt it could not be true. The singer bore a blameless character, and moreover had herself asked him frankly about this will some time ago. In any case as a *femme du monde* she would not be likely to employ a common *notaire*. Then, too, it was she who had first dropped hints of the servants' possible dishonesty, a proceeding manifestly absurd if she was in league with them towards a mercenary end.

The only other explanation was that Blom was representing Jeanne, and had substituted Miss Cushing's name to hide his client's identity.

Ah, that must be it! The maid was plotting to establish herself as her mistress's legatee!

Ambitious, yes—but it was not the first time such a thing had been done. Possibly Jeanne's protestations were so much dust in the eyes of onlookers, while she played a devious game to obtain her object. To alienate the poor woman from her friends by doubts cast upon their disinterestedness, to work upon her affections by subtle degrees—did it not all point in one certain direction?

This was what he had feared in the beginning, only Catherine's statement had put him off the track. Now he was filled with a new uneasiness, which was relieved only when he recalled the fact that Jeanne was undoubtedly profiting by her mistress's present condition. Yes, he had overlooked that point. There was as yet no talk of a will, and whatever the maid's secret intentions might be she was pocketing all she could lay hands on. He breathed again.

Still—Miss Cushing! Her name stuck in his mind like a burr. Perhaps she did have an obscure connection with Blom, who, innocent of thieving, might be acting in a quite different capacity from the one first suspected.

"By Jove!" he exclaimed in annoyance. "If that is so the man may be trying to protect Mme. Bender instead of de-frauding her, in which case I have sent Bernard off on a goose-chase!"

For, although he had not mentioned it to Catherine, he had just instructed the agent to go to Bordeaux, with the idea of making inquiries into the *notaire*'s visit in that city three months ago. It now began to look as though the mission might lead to nothing.

However, in the main, events were shaping towards the desired end. With Jeanne away, there would be an opportunity for searching the apartment and ascertaining the exact state of affairs. Meanwhile, they would probably be able to frame a definite charge against the two servants and remove them from their posts. Altogether things looked promising.

When he opened the door of his own flat, his father called out to him from the library.

"Come in for a moment, Geoffrey. I've something which may interest you."

Sunlight gilded the book-lined walls, a wood fire burned on the hearth, and a pot of blue hyacinths bore witness to a visit from Elspeth. Macadam Senior, seated in a worn leather chair, was turning over a sheaf of papers, his glasses perched on the tip of his nose.

"It's this Bender business again. I've got hold of Harry Bender's pass-book and all the details I can assemble regarding his movements prior to his death. There's no record of a picture-sale, nor any unidentified deposit large enough to correspond with one. If he did dispose of those paintings, he must have received cash, which he failed to pay in to his account."

"He never sold them," declared Geoffrey shortly.

"Not so fast. You may be right, but one mustn't jump to conclusions. Suppose, for example, Bender wanted to make a payment in some quarter in such a way that it could not be traced? In the event, let us say, of such a thing as an entanglement with a woman?"

"Did you ever hear of any entanglement?" demanded his son bluntly.

"I admit not, but my ignorance proves nothing. Mind, I only state a possibility."

Geoffrey lit a cigarette and threw the match into the fire.

"I don't believe he would have parted with the Manet. He would have found the money in some other way."

His father made no comment.

"Well, then, I've had a talk with Ellsworth, the manager of Mme. Bender's bank, to find out if any use has been made of that duplicate key. It was used, only a few days later, by the maid herself."

"The devil it was!" exclaimed the young man sharply.

"Yes—but everything was quite in order. It seems Ellsworth received a note from Mme Bender saying she wished to exchange her string of pearls, which she felt nervous about keeping in the apartment, for the copy then in the bank, and proposed sending her maid to attend to the matter."

"Stop a moment—you say the *copy* was kept at the bank? Surely that's a bit absurd?"

"She explained that. Apparently no one but herself was aware that the pearls in her possession were the genuine ones, as for safety's sake she had always pretended they were the copy. She had given up wearing them, because their lustre was suffering from her low state of health, but she wanted the imitations to keep up the deception."

"I see," replied Geoffrey rather blankly.

"Foreseeing the chance of a hoax, Ellsworth himself telephoned to Mme. Bender and was assured by her that the maid was completely to be trusted. The next day Laborie appeared, was conducted by one of the clerks into the vaults, made the exchange and went away. The clerk watched her closely and saw nothing amiss. The two strings were identical, the copy having a clasp of real diamonds set in platinum."

Geoffrey frowned incredulously.

"You say the manager spoke to Mme. Bender herself? He recognized her voice?"

"Certainly—he's known her for years."

"I suppose I ought to be satisfied, but it seems odd for all that," declared Geoffrey, moving about restlessly. For the life of him he could not reconcile Mme. Bender's action on this occasion with her recent helplessness. His eyes narrowed in thought. "See here," he said suddenly. "When Miss West asked about that key only last week, her cousin disclaimed all knowledge of it. At least she appeared not to recollect until the maid reminded her. Doesn't that strike you as queer?"

"And nothing was said about changing the necklace?"

"Not a word."

The elder man wiped his glasses upon a silk handkerchief, then rubbed the bridge of his nose exasperatedly.

"I give it up," he said briefly, adding after a moment:

"Either her memory is subject to lapses, or she was displaying a sort of cunning in keeping the matter dark. There's no accounting for the vagaries of neurasthenics."

Geoffrey was silent. A voice whispered to him that these were the pearls Hermione Cushing considered as hers by right, at least when her friend should die. She had assured him they were safe in the bank.

"Where that woman can't be tempted by them," had been her exact words.

For the second time misgivings assailed him. Was the story about the copy a true one? Suppose there was some fraud, with Miss Cushing at the back of it?

"Still, Ellsworth recognized Mme. Bender's voice, so she evidently approved of the transaction. That much is fairly certain, so why bother?"

At the same time he added to himself that it was a blessing Catherine knew nothing about it.

CHAPTER TWENTY-SIX

IT WAS evening. Elspeth was bidding her children good night, Clement Baxter, her husband, was rummaging in search of some etchings, in the adjacent studio. Four candles in silver candelabra flickered upon the bare waxed refectory table, their yellow flames casting deep wells of shadow. The curtains were yet undrawn, and through the long windows, square-paned and arched at the top, could be seen the walled garden, fresh and still in the gathering dusk. At the back stood a row of lime-trees with clusters of snowy blossom, whose fragrance stole into the room, penetratingly sweet.

Catherine gave a deep sigh, and nestled further back into the pale cushioned *bergère*. It was with a little start that she discovered Geoffrey beside her, holding out his cigarette-case.

"Not too tired, I hope?" he inquired in an undertone.

She shook her head, smiling.

"Only blissfully comatose. I don't want to move so much as a finger. It is heavenly just being here."

She glanced about the agreeable room with appreciation. Every-thing about it pleased her. The colours, the space, the very perfection with which the pictures were hung brought balm to her troubled spirit, so that she felt content to lie without thinking and drink in the beauty and tranquillity.

"You're not sorry you came, then?"

"Sorry?" She shook her head. "I'm glad. It's good to be away from—all that."

He hung about anxiously.

"And the drive here wasn't too much for you? It's been a bit of a day for anyone just out of bed."

"I'm all right. I expect to have ten full hours' sleep to-night. That's what an idiot requires, isn't it?" she added, laughing.

She was still very pale, but her attitude showed that her nerves were beginning to relax. To-morrow he meant to keep her outdoors as much as possible so that the air might bring her colour back.

"That's right, Philomène—put the coffee on the hearth. Madame will be here in a moment."

The maid set the coffee, foaming in a copper pot, upon a tripod close to the log fire. The tray, bearing majolica cups of blue, green and orange, she placed on an oak stool, then she moved away to close the curtains. When her back was turned Geoffrey laid his brown hand lightly upon Catherine's white one, where it rested listlessly on the arm of the chair. She let it remain for a second, feeling her own tingle with the warmth of his touch, then as Elspeth's step approached she drew it gently away.

"Coffee, you two?"

Elspeth bent over the hearth and lifted the copper pot. Her bronze head shone in the firelight, her blue frock made a pleasant splash of colour. She had the fresh complexion of her brother as well as his heavy brows, slightly modified, and her grey eyes, honest and candid, held a sparkle of humour.

"Not for me, thanks," replied Catherine. "I've been sleeping rather badly for the first time in my life, and I don't want anything to spoil the marvellous rest I mean to have." Elspeth surveyed her critically as she handed a cup to her brother.

"Then you'd better have a cup of my *tilleul*. See, I've got some here. I always take it after dinner. It's supposed to be soothing for the nerves."

As she spoke she took up a little teapot from the tray and held it poised above a cup. Catherine shook her head.

"*Tilleul*? Oh, no, if you don't mind, I won't take any. I've only tasted it once—last Monday when I was feeling so rotten—and I'm afraid I rather hated it."

"Did you? I think it's good stuff."

"It seemed to me bitter and—queer," explained Catherine apologetically.

Her hostess looked surprised.

"Bitter? It couldn't have been *tilleul*, then. Why, it's only lime-flowers, you know. We make our own. Can't you smell the lime now, from the trees in the garden?"

Catherine hesitated. The taste of the drink Jeanne had given her came disagreeably before her, mingled with memories of racking pain. She could not associate it with the honeyed odour of the blossoms outside.

"Let me try some of yours," she said. "It may seem different now."

She took the cup of pale amber liquid, upon whose surface floated a few tiny petals. A pleasant aroma rose as she sipped.

"Why—it's delicious!" she exclaimed, astonished.

"I think so. Anyhow, it won't keep you awake."

Catherine drank it slowly, then leaned back among the cushions, slightly puzzled. This concoction seemed totally unlike the other. She could almost swear it was not the same thing at all. Had her illness made such a difference? It was true that on the wretched morning in question nothing had tasted as it should. Even her coffee had not been quite as usual, though she had supposed the berries to have been scorched. . . .

Oh, well, that was all over. Nothing mattered now. She was very tired, more so then she wished Geoffrey to know, and the thought of bed was pleasant to her.

The past few days had been rather nerve-racking. She had had the task of re-establishing Mme. Bender and Hermione upon terms of friendship, at the same time avoiding friction with Jeanne, so that she now felt as though she had been steering a frail barque between Scylla and Charybdis. Jeanne, she was forced to admit, had proved unexpectedly amenable, but the strain had proved severe up till the moment of departure.

Jeanne! She still marvelled at the improvement in her. Why, the woman had actually offered to pack her bags, had smiled on her from the doorway this afternoon and called out, "Bon voyage, mademoiselle! Soignez-vous bien!" with the utmost good-nature. A wave of shamed compunction swept over the girl as she thought of what she planned to do on her return to the apartment. If her late enemy even faintly guessed her intentions she could not have borne herself with such cheerful composure.

Meantime it was delightful to lie here in the candlelight, to listen to the conversation without taking an active part in it, and watch drowsily the three people in the glow of the fire—Elspeth cool and steady-eyed, Clement Baxter sandy and thin, sucking an old briar and recounting droll incidents of Paris life in a drawling voice, and Geoffrey at her elbow, his face shadowed but turned, she knew, towards her own with a steadiness which soothed her vanity and made her feel as a cat does when its fur is stroked by a firm hand. She was wrapped in a sense of extraordinary peace.

In the morning she was roused by the twitter of children and the voice of their nurse trying vainly to keep them silent. It was not yet time for her breakfast to arrive, but she was rested and refreshed, all the faculties which last evening had lain dormant now vividly alert.

All at once she began to think over her recent illness and to wonder about it. Strange that she had slept peacefully the night before, that nothing had happened till after she had got up. Did that mean the poison from the oysters took all that time to make itself felt, or was it that . . . Oh, of course, it couldn't have been the coffee! How impossible! And yet, there certainly had been a bitter tang about it, which curiously enough had some quality in common with the hot drink she had taken later on. Or was she imagining things?

Her mind went back to the young doctor's insistent questions, his accusing manner, and again it occurred to her that perhaps Jeanne had purposely given him a wrong idea.

But why on earth should she do such a thing? Why should she want him to believe what was not true, that is, unless—

Suddenly it struck her that there was a possible reason. Jeanne might conceivably have taken this attitude if she herself was aware of the real cause of the attack, and was eager to put the doctor off the scent. It sounded wild, but was it altogether out of the range of possibility?

Arrested by this new view of the case, she set herself to recall in detail everything which had occurred on Monday morning, from the time she waked up. Berthe, she remembered, had been very late, had the look of having hurried into her clothes. At the time she had even wondered that the woman had been up in time to make the coffee. Perhaps, for that matter, Berthe had not made it. It might have been Jeanne.

A shiver ran through her. Yes, the pains had come on a little while after she had drunk the coffee, and had increased in violence following the cup of supposed *tilleul*—which since last night she knew was either not *tilleul* at all, or else had some strong substance mingled with it to alter its flavour. Could all this mean that Jeanne had deliberately introduced something into the two cups of liquid with the purpose of making her ill? Not poison—no, the doctor had laughed at the suggestion. Medicine, a drug of some sort. . . .

She shook herself angrily. "What absolute nonsense! What a fool I am to invent such an improbable story!"

Granting it were true, she could not imagine any motive for such an act. Easy to call it pure malevolence, but people did not go about doing things like that for the fun of it.

She pondered deeply, feeling her heart beat as it had done so many times since the attack, whenever she became a little agitated. Slowly and uneasily the conviction stole upon her that she was a pawn in a game, moved about against her will and made to do things she had had no intention of doing. Was it possible that in coming away she had simply been following out a course of action designed by Jeanne herself? Was her illness a preliminary step towards it?

She saw again how the way had been smoothed, her objections removed one by one. Jeanne's good nature and reasonableness, the armistice between her and Hermione, the whole new air of complaisance which had transformed the household during the last few days—oh, surely it was too good to be true! In fact, during the entire week the maid's attitude towards her had been altered, beginning with—when exactly did it begin?—yes, *from the time when she had found the flowers in Mme. Bender's room.*

She became so nervous that it was all she could do to keep from springing out of bed.

"Yes, I am sure of it! She wanted to get me away from Germaine. She's afraid of me, that's what it is! She knows I have made it up with the poor thing, and she's terrified of the consequences. Is that because she thinks I may expose her? Or because Germaine may get too fond of me? Is it jealousy again?"

It must be partly that, she concluded. Yet it could mean only a petty triumph to the schemer, a small result for so much plotting. A week—there was comfort in the thought. Nothing was likely to go far wrong in so short a time. Besides, Hermione would be there daily, glad to watch over her friend. Not much would escape her suspicious eye.

Her *petit déjeuner* arrived, deliciously appetizing, with a plate of huge strawberries and a little jug of cream. Philomène, a genial soul, beamed upon her.

"*Mademoiselle a une meilleure mine ce matin,*" she declared, eyeing Catherine with interest, adding that the air at Fontainebleau was very bracing and would bring her an appetite. Madame had sent a message to say mademoiselle was to rest as long as she liked, that no one expected her to appear before *déjeuner*. Perhaps she would care to lie in a deck-chair in the garden. The sun was beautiful now, the birds singing.

However, Catherine did not want to rest. The idea had come to her that she would feel more comfortable if she could telephone through to Paris and inquire after Mme. Bender, just to see that everything was as it should be. Foolish, perhaps, but there could be no harm in making sure.

As soon as she had bathed and put on a pale grey jumper-suit with a band of green about the hips—a dress she somehow felt Geoffrey would like—she slipped into the living-room to negotiate a trunk-call, feeling just a trifle guilty, and glad that the room was deserted.

"*Elysée zéro deux dix. . . .*"

She was lucky in not having to wait long for the connection. In only a few minutes the bell summoned her, and picking up the receiver she heard a man's gruff voice saying, "*Allô, allô!*" It was Eduardo.

"Eduardo, this is Miss West speaking. I wanted to know how madame is this morning. Can you tell me?"

She caught an indistinct mumble, then there was silence. He had departed, no doubt to fetch Jeanne. She pressed the receiver to her ear in slight suspense, waiting. Presently a faint, gentle voice spoke over the wire:

"*Allô, allô . . . qui est là?*"

Catherine started so that she nearly dropped the receiver. *The voice which addressed her was Germaine's.*

CHAPTER TWENTY-SEVEN

GERMAINE at the telephone? But this was impossible! Yet it was unmistakably her voice. Confused ideas rushed headlong upon her, instinctive attempts to supply an explanation for the phenomenon. At the same time she was so paralysed from shock that speech deserted her, and she could only gasp, clutching the receiver in a hard grip. When the pause had become noticeable, the voice at the other end of the line spoke again, this time with impatience:

"Allô! C'est de la part de qui? Est-ce que c'est Mademouselle West qui parle?"

Mademouselle West! A second shock neutralized the first, leaving her weak. So it was not Germaine at all, but Jeanne herself. Jeanne—but with a tone, an accent indistinguishable from those of her mistress! What an amazing similarity! Never before had Catherine noticed it, but then never till now had she spoken to the woman over the telephone. People's voices played strange tricks over the wire. . . .

All this passed rapidly through her brain as she forced herself to reply calmly:

"Yes, yes, Jeanne. I only want to know if madame passed a good night, and is feeling well this morning?"

The answer came promptly, with reassuring emphasis: "But certainly, mademoiselle, everything is going marvellously well! Madame is quite cheerful, and looking forward to seeing Mademoiselle Cushing this afternoon. You need have no concern for her."

Replacing the instrument, Catherine sank on the nearest chair. What a turn that deceptive voice had given her! She had been totally unprepared for it, simply because she had never before spoken to Jeanne over the telephone. She could not get over the startling illusion.

Growing calmer, she recalled that this was not the first time she had noticed a similarity between a maid's voice and that of her mistress. Indeed, she knew that the conscious or unconscious aping of an employer's speech is a fairly familiar phenomenon. That in this case it was unintentional she felt almost sure, for why should Jeanne want to deceive her?

A step in the doorway made her jump with a nervous start. Geoffrey, fresh in grey flannels, stood before her. "What's this—up already? Why—is anything wrong?" She sprang up, smiling at him.

"Of course not! I've been telephoning to inquire about Mme. Bender, that's all."

His keen eyes searched her face.

"You look as though you had seen a ghost."

Laughing apologetically, she explained what had happened.

"The most amazing likeness—inflection, tone, everything. I could have sworn it was Germaine."

He stared at her hard as though puzzled.

"By Jove!" he exclaimed under his breath, and then again, "By Jove!"—in a manner betokening a sudden revelation.

"Is anything wrong about it?" she inquired curiously.

He shook his head.

"No, only it struck me as queer."

She was unconvinced, but said no more till they had wandered out into the garden and seated themselves on a bench beneath the lime-trees. Then, seeing that he was distrait, his brow furrowed in perplexity, she attacked him boldly.

"Geoffrey, you can't fool me. What is it you've got in your mind?"

"Nothing important—I swear it. Hardly worth mentioning."

"What a bad liar you are! You ought not to be a lawyer if you can't hide your feelings better than that."

He laughed.

"Are you praising or condemning me?"

"Never mind which. I'm determined to know what you are thinking."

"Catherine, you're incorrigible! If I don't tell you everything, it's because you are so quick to worry over trifles."

"I shall worry ten times more over this trifle if I don't know what it is."

Seeing that she was in earnest, he gave in reluctantly and in a few words related what he had learned about Jeanne and the bank manager.

"I should not have given it much thought if you hadn't mentioned this trick about the voices. Now I am naturally asking myself if Ellsworth didn't mistake Jeanne's voice for Mme. Bender's."

She leaped up with a feverish light in her eyes.

"You say she took the pearls away with her?"

"Calmly, my dear! Only the copy. The actual necklace is in the bank now."

She quivered with excitement, her brain working rapidly.

"But don't you see? The whole affair is probably a fraud. I am quite sure Germaine has not spoken on the telephone for many months, and as for the note supposed to have come from her, couldn't it have been a forgery? By the way, was it written by hand, or typewritten and simply signed?"

"I'm ashamed to say I didn't inquire, but I will do so."

It was a searching question. To copy or trace a mere signature presented fewer difficulties than forging an entire letter, yet both he and his father had overlooked the point. He wondered if the note was still on file, as well as the one in which Mme. Bender had applied for the new key.

"Still, if all the woman did was to take out a string of imitation pearls—"

She turned on him with withering scorn.

"You poor innocent! Have you ever seen a really good copy of an actual pearl necklace? You couldn't tell it was imitation. I couldn't. Only an expert would know the difference, and a bank clerk is no expert. No, the more I think of it the surer I am that Jeanne put the copy into the box and took away the real ones!"

No good trying to smooth down her ruffled feathers. He could only stand abashed by her ruthless argument.

"She's stolen them, Geoffrey—I know she has! Even now they are probably disposed of, one by one. Oh! to think what the wretched creature has been up to, while we've looked quietly on."

"We are not sure of this yet, you know," he reminded her. "Besides, it happened before you arrived in Paris, so you can't reproach yourself."

She seemed not to hear him, staring before her unseeingly.

A breeze stirred the lime trees, sifting a few petals down upon her dark hair where they rested like snowflakes. Gently he put both hands on her arms and pressed her down upon the seat.

"You may be right. I've a suspicion myself that there's been mischief going on. But as far as the pearls are concerned, we can do nothing without a statement from your cousin. We can't open her private box and examine its contents. Do you think we ought to tell her what we believe?"

She looked at him dumbly.

"I daren't risk it," she murmured after a pause. "The shock might kill her. Later, when Jeanne is away and we have got her into a more normal frame of mind, I might sound her on the subject."

"I thought you'd say that. It's a question of which is more important—Mme. Bender's recovery, or the loss of something she can well afford to part with."

She nodded, her face filled with painful doubt.

"Those were Hermione's pearls. What a blow it will mean to her!"

"Never mind Hermione," he retorted with slight impatience. "What we've got to be careful about now is to see that Mme. Bender does not execute some fantastic will, leaving her property to Jeanne."

Her eyes widened in alarm.

"Then you think that is what she is up to?"

"I do. I've come to believe that her pretending other people are after her mistress's money is merely a blind."

"But why—? I don't understand. She seems to be actually trying to prevent her from making her will."

"So she is—now. That is because she's afraid the money would go to someone else. But I am pretty certain she pictures herself ultimately as the fortunate legatee."

"Good heavens!" cried the girl, jumping up in fresh agitation. "Then I'd better hurry back at once!"

He laughed at her look of fright.

"It's not so bad as all that. Even if the will were drawn up it wouldn't be irrevocable, and besides I fancy Miss Cushing will act as a restraining influence while you are away."

"That is so," she admitted thoughtfully. "What a blessing I managed to make it up between them! No, I suppose there's no danger at the moment. For that matter, Jeanne's practically beaten, although she has used every possible weapon against me. Why, I almost believe she . . ."

She checked herself abruptly, on the verge of relating the notion which had just come to her regarding her illness. If Geoffrey believed it to be true he would certainly try to prevent her going back. His recent conquest over her will made her nervous of a second encounter.

Fortunately he did not notice her sudden pause.

"There's one thing we can do," he remarked. "We can submit those letters of Mme. Bender's to a handwriting expert, and determine if they're genuine. If they turn out to be forgeries, we can arrest Jeanne on the spot."

"Oh! I hadn't thought of that! What a marvellous idea!"

He was not feeling particularly brilliant. Here, obviously, was something he ought to have considered days ago.

"Of course it's possible the letters have been destroyed, but we'll hope for the best, I'll see to it the first thing to-morrow. Come along now," he said, pulling her to her feet. "We've a couple of hours before lunch. Let's take a drive through the forest. I've brought the car round."

They spent the rest of the morning exploring the leafy fastnesses, winding their way along cloistered roads, where immense trees interlaced overhead. Occasionally they came on patches of warm sand heaped with rugged boulders, amethyst in the shade, then plunged back again into the cool green depths of woodland, silent but for distant bird-calls. Once in a clearing they surprised a group of villagers in Sunday attire, dancing out-of-date steps to the thin strains of a few stringed instruments.

The tunes, simple and sugary, like all popular French music, reminded Catherine of an old musical-box, while the entire scene was singularly charming in its total absence of sophistication. Far through the forest sounded the tinkling notes, punctuated by singing and laughter.

It was a relief to Catherine that Geoffrey did not refer to the question he had put to her a little more than a week ago. Sometimes she fancied he was on the brink of doing so, but always the momentary tension passed with the words unspoken. She did not yet know her mind, and conscious of physical languor wanted simply to let herself drift, absorbing the beauty and peace of the spring day. There was ample time to decide, provided her companion's sentiments did not alter—and she was sure from the look in his eyes that there was little likelihood of that.

It was not until she was alone that evening that she permitted her thoughts to return to Mme. Bender. Then it was that she remembered the letter, written by her cousin in February, just before she planned to leave for Paris. Here was a genuine instance of the invalid's handwriting which might prove of value to the expert Geoffrey intended to consult. It was still in the back pocket of her bag. She read it over once again, then enclosed it in a note to Geoffrey who was leaving too early in the morning for her to see him.

As she made ready for bed she found herself wondering uneasily what was going on in her absence, and whether Jeanne was using the opportunity to press her impudent claims. What a leech she was! She was doing her utmost to suck her victim dry, always under cover of intense devotion. Nothing more detestable could be conceived. . . .

Yet was she alone in her infamous designs? Was there some guiding intelligence in the background, thinking for her, actuating her conduct? More than once this idea had occurred to her vaguely, yet except for the definite instances of theft, she could not think of any way in which the woman could have an associate other than the stupid Eduardo. The little *notaire* might be helping her to dispose of stolen objects, but did he play any other part? According to Geoffrey, the man bore an impeccable reputation.

Thinking this over, she stood by her window gazing out into the dark garden below. Along the wall the inky shapes of the lime-trees stirred and whispered together, while at the far corner, aloof from the rest, a small, malformed hornbeam stood remote. Its stunted trunk and branches like antennae seemed to her distorted fancy like a gigantic spider watchful in the centre of an invisible web. Almost she could imagine that the other trees were prisoners, spellbound in the evil power of this misshapen creature. . . .

"It didn't move—just stayed still and watched me . . . there were flies tangled in the web. . . ."

She could hear again the little *grisette*'s shrill voice uttering the words. Geoffrey had laughed at her, but she had never been able to get the haunting impression out of her mind. Even now, when a black cloud blotted out the moon, she could feel the presence of something coldly insensate and grasping, lying in wait to drain its captives' blood.

She swept the curtains together with a jerk. What a childish idea! Besides, there was no positive danger, could be none. She had thrashed the whole thing out to her satisfaction.

Yet the face she turned to the mirror was pale, the eyes dilated with speculative dread.

CHAPTER TWENTY-EIGHT

GEOFFREY lost no time in getting hold of Mme. Bender's notes, neither of which had been destroyed. The bank manager expressed some astonishment at being asked for the one in his possession, but produced it readily, remarking as he did so:

"Your father has already mentioned this matter to me, Mr. Macadam. Is it possible you think there's some hanky-panky about it?"

"I trust not. I will let you know what we find out."

"I observed the usual formalities. It's hard to see how there could be any fraud."

"It's no fault of yours if there was. But knowing something of Mme. Bender's state of health, it seems to us unlikely for her to have spoken on the telephone at any recent time."

The manager started slightly.

"I could swear it was her voice. You believe it may have been someone impersonating her?"

"I'm afraid so."

Ellsworth, a confident man with a smooth round face and pince-nez, looked decidedly perturbed. He fidgeted with a waistcoat button, letting his gaze stray round the room, then as though struck by a bright idea brought his plump hand down on the desk with a bang.

"Surely, my dear fellow, the simplest course to pursue is to ask Mme. Bender straight out whether she did or did not sanction the transaction."

"It's less easy than you think. First, we do not want to agitate her, and second, she happens to be in a state where, to put it crudely, one cannot rely upon her word as conclusive evidence."

The manager's pale eyebrows shot up.

"Dear me! You mean she is—" He stopped, touching his forehead significantly.

"At least her condition is such that we have to act without her knowledge or consent." Geoffrey spoke cautiously, as he examined the sheet of grey note-paper. "Typewritten." He murmured with disappointment. "Still, the signature is distinctive."

The sloping, spidery hand had the typical character of most French calligraphy. As soon as he was alone he compared it with the letter received from Catherine, only to find his unpractised eye unable to detect any differences. Enclosing the three specimens in an envelope, he despatched them in Henri's care to the expert, with a request for a speedy opinion.

On Wednesday he motored again to Fontainebleau, where he found Catherine much improved in strength and spirits. However, he had only a few minutes alone with her, and his ardour was damped by the feeling that she was far more interested in what he had to tell her than in himself. An evasive manner and a touch of unexpected shyness depressed him, causing him to wonder if she were trying to prepare him for a definite refusal. Had she thought things over and come to the conclusion that she could not love him? He was ready to swear at himself for fatuously expecting too much.

When he took his departure, it was Elspeth who followed him out to his car.

"Poor old boy," she murmured as he put his hand on the starter. "Aren't things going too well for you?"

"What in heaven's name do you mean?" he demanded, reddening savagely and brushing off her caressing touch.

She laughed with a touch of feminine malice.

"Never mind—it will do you good," she replied enigmatically. "You've had it all your own way far too long. She's worth a struggle, and I wish you luck. I can't say more, can I?"

So they all knew he had been captured at last! No wonder, the truth must be written all over him. Desire had laid hold of him so powerfully that he could scarcely eat or sleep, much less take an interest in anything which did not concern the object of his hopes. Life without Catherine—! It was a prospect of slow starvation.

So entirely engrossed was he by his personal problem that the letter received the following day from Bordeaux came as a distinct surprise. He had for the time being forgotten Bernard's mission, from which, in the light of his recent conclusions, he expected little result.

As he read his face altered. The agent had traced Blom to the Hôtel des Negociants, where he had apparently spent a few days early in February, afterwards moving on successively to several small towns in the district. The quest had been difficult owing to the fact that the *notaire* had in each case left no address, so that it was only by dint of many inquiries that his movements became known. In each of the towns visited he had passed several days, but it had been impossible to find out how he had filled in his time, except that he appeared to have examined into various local records of births, deaths and marriages—a pursuit legitimately compatible with his profession. So far Bernard had discovered nothing to connect the man with any nefarious dealings, or anything other than a rather aimless pottering about.

"Yet I am not satisfied," concluded the writer. "I am inclined to think that all this activity among the archives was intended to cover up his real business. If he carried any unframed canvases, he could easily have concealed them in his normal luggage, and my idea is that somewhere in this neighbourhood he has hidden them in a secret *cache*. I have one or two lines of inquiry to follow up, and will let you know if anything develops."

Geoffrey lit a cigarette and pondered the matter, reflecting that it seemed impossible to catch the *notaire* at anything shady. What could be farther removed from picture-thieving than this harmless poking into provincial archives? But for the two known facts testifying against him, one would be tempted to declare him a wholly spotless character. However, those facts stood out like black question marks, demanding an answer. The man had undoubtedly held a violent dispute over the contents of Mme. Bender's picture-gallery, and he had paid a visit to the Macadam office under an assumed name, inquiring into Mme. Bender's affairs. Plainly he was up to something he wished to keep secret.

"Decidedly a dark horse," concluded Geoffrey, with annoyance. "Indeed, we should never have known of his existence at all if Catherine had not seen him that first evening and later recognized him as the milliner's fiancé. Just accident—that's all. On the surface he seems nothing more than a money-grubbing notary, with a taste for records," and he recalled what Ballou had said about running across the Alsatian at the Bureau des Archives. How was it Guy had described him? *"I used to think he looked like a white rat nosing about among the files."*

Yes, this record-hunting was probably a blind, at least at Bordeaux. Moreover, for the second time Geoffrey was struck by the man's pursuit of the widow, Mme. Baron, immediately after his return. Honorine's reputed savings would furnish the wherewithal for his start in a new field.

"By Jove, I shouldn't wonder if we'd hit the trail at last. The servants are selling him those pictures, and he is planning to set himself up as a dealer. The thing to do now is to notify the police of Bordeaux, give them a description of Blom, and have all out-going boats carefully watched. I'll telegraph to Bernard at once."

It occurred to him that it might be wise to keep both Blom and the milliner under strict surveillance, but that matter could rest until Bernard's return.

Late Friday afternoon he was hard at work when the office factotum announced M. Bernard. Leaping up in astonishment, Geoffrey beheld the agent, adorned with a bowler hat green with age and a black muffler wrapped round his cavernous neck.

"So you've come back! Did you get my telegram?"

"Yes, monsieur. I informed the Bordeaux police, and will forward them a description of our friend, with a photograph, if obtainable. But I regret to state I have not been able to discover anything definite regarding the paintings. He has covered his tracks too well. All I could do was to warn the port authorities."

Geoffrey was conscious of disappointment.

"Yet you still hold the opinion that he means to take them out of the country?"

"I assume so, monsieur, but I confess there is little to support the theory. All my inquiries led me to was a series of records offices, one after the other. I have spent the past two days interviewing the archives officials in three small towns, trying to ascertain what object Blom had in mind. At last I found it, but I am afraid it will tell you little. It seems that the man was seeking particulars about a family apparently extinct in the district—people by the name of Dieulefit."

"Dieulefit!"

The young man jumped as though shot.

"You know the name, then?"

"Do I know it," cried the other excitedly. "Why, it's the family name of Mme. Bender herself. My God, Bernard, don't you see what it means? The fellow is searching for an heir to our client's estate!"

The solemn eyes regarded him with interest.

"Then you think he has not stolen the pictures at all?"

Geoffrey frowned in confusion.

"I can't say. No—yes. . . . At any rate, this business has nothing to do with theft. He's got something quite different up his sleeve. . . . I've got to think this out. I'll let you know if I shall need you further."

Indeed, it seemed doubtful whether the agent could supply the missing link in the chain, namely, Blom's reason for his investigations. There must be some strong motive to take a canny *bourgeois* on an extensive journey. The *notaire* was not likely to spend money without hope of an ample return. But in what way could he hope to profit?

Over a solitary meal at a restaurant Geoffrey argued the question out to a tentative conclusion, his legal knowledge providing him with a clue. He knew that when a person of property died intestate it was the custom to look about at once for the next of kin. If the search proved difficult, anyone furnishing information as to the missing heirs invariably received remuneration for his services, based on a percentage system. Where the fortune was a large one, the commission might run to a considerable sum, well worth scheming to obtain.

Undoubtedly, Blom, in his capacity of legal adviser to the Bender servants, was in a position to know certain useful facts. He could easily be aware of Mme. Bender's former name, of the probability of her dying intestate, and of the precarious state of her health. Armed with his knowledge, he might very naturally wish to locate some remote connections of the ill woman, in order to be first in the field to claim the said commission.

Now at last he began to see daylight. He understood Blom's anxiety to make sure whether a will had been executed, since if that were the case his hopes vanished automatically. Probably also he suspected Jeanne's private machinations, and had tried to put a stop to them by the threats Catherine had overheard, knowing they would foil his own scheme. It all fitted in with surprising ease.

Only one point remained obscure. Was Blom acting purely on speculation, or had some rumour of a possible heir reached his ears?

Suddenly Hermione Cushing flashed across his mind. As Mme. Bender's oldest friend, it was likely that no one better than she would be acquainted with the invalid's antecedents. Perhaps she had supplied Blom with the necessary facts, meaning to split the commission with him. Or else—and here was a totally new idea—she herself might have French blood in her veins, and unknown to anyone possess some shadowy claim she wished to substantiate. Was she by any remote chance connected with the family of Dieulefit? If so it would explain everything.

Determination seized him. Quitting the restaurant he jumped into a taxi, and in ten minutes was climbing the stairs to the singer's apartment, bent upon taking the owner unawares and subjecting her to a few blunt questions.

Decidedly brutal, that! His face burned at the thought. Yet he felt he must know once and for all what part Miss Cushing played in the affair, and he was shamelessly taking this course because he believed the lady could not withstand a frontal attack.

The door opening to his ring, he found himself confronting a spectacled grenadier who regarded him severely, a steel thimble on her roughened finger, and a chemise, of dimensions suitable for a baby elephant, draped over one arm.

"*Mademouselle est sortie,*" he was informed.

He did not know whether he was disappointed or relieved. Under the *bonne*'s righteous gaze he reluctantly gave his name, realizing that any hope of catching Miss Cushing unawares was now extinguished. The singer, hearing he had called, would be on her guard.

"Monsieur Macadam?" repeated the domestic, her visage softening.

Clearly she knew who he was. Indeed, there was probably little of her mistress's affairs she did not know. She warmed, becoming communicative. Mademoiselle was dining in the Faubourg St. Germain, after calling on her friend, Mme. Bender. If Monsieur cared to leave a message. . . . But Geoffrey was already half-way down the stairs.

He felt curiously at a loose end, his brain revolving the new information and burning to impart it to the person most likely to be interested. A glance at his watch told him it was barely nine o'clock. Why not drive to Fontainebleau and talk the thing over with Catherine? He could be there in little more than an hour.

His waiting taxi bore him swiftly to the garage where his car was kept, and presently he was speeding towards the Porte d'Italie, the wind whistling in his wake. In record time he alighted in the broad, quiet street outside his sister's dwelling, and a second later burst unceremoniously into a somnolent family group lounging before the wood fire.

Elspeth looked up with surprise.

"Geoff! You did give me a start. What's up?"

He cast a rapid look round the room.

"Where's Catherine?" he inquired shortly.

"Gone," she replied composedly.

His jaw dropped.

"Gone? Where? Why?"

"That's all. She left us, this evening. On the 10.45, to be exact. What's the excitement about?"

His eyes blazed at her.

"I don't understand you. She knew I was coming to fetch her to-morrow afternoon. Why this sudden change of plan?"

"Don't be silly. It was quite unexpected, of course. On the evening's post she had a letter from some friends of hers who are crossing to Dieppe to-night and arriving in Paris early to-morrow morning. They are only stopping over a couple of hours, and want to see her. She would go."

Still he stared at her, visibly annoyed.

"I can't make it out," he muttered, frowning. "You mean to say you let her go back there—alone?"

"Yes. Why not? We couldn't stop her, and she refused to let us ring you up."

"Do the servants expect her?"

"No; but it doesn't matter, does it?"

Then he realized that both listeners were eyeing him oddly and with a glint of amusement at his concern.

CHAPTER TWENTY-NINE

GEOFFREY remained with the Baxters only long enough to smoke a cigarette and swallow a whisky and soda. Even this he consented to do with an unwilling air, elbows on his knees and an expression moodily abstracted. Then with a curt good night he vanished into the darkness.

When the doors had closed his brother-in-law raised humorous eyebrows after his departing figure and rose with a stretch.

"What's his trouble?" he lazily inquired.

"Catherine, evidently. He's hurt because she ran off without letting him know."

"A rift in the lute, I fancy. Looked as though he had something on his mind he didn't want us to know."

"That's what I thought. Did you see how he almost bit my head off when I told him she had gone?"

Her husband nodded, yawning.

"Oh, well, he can see her to-morrow and put things right. My God, the agonies these lovers go through! I never pictured the old blighter losing his self-control like that, though,"—and he knocked his pipe against the side of the fireplace.

Meanwhile, with jaw set and a feeling of indignation seething in his breast, the object of these remarks was making full speed along the Paris road. Somehow Catherine's abrupt departure wounded him like a personal affront. Was she really so anxious to meet these precious friends of hers, or had she taken the sudden decision in order to avoid the drive back with him to-morrow? Unreasonably he inclined towards the latter opinion, recalling how reserved and standoffish she had been when he last saw her.

"Yet she liked me well enough two weeks ago," he argued resentfully. "No one could fool me on that subject."

Once again he smelled the fragrance of her skin mingling with the crushed lilies of the valley as she had pressed against him, felt the warmth of her lips upon his. Yes, for a moment at least the same sensation had surged up in them both, binding them together. Yet how little that physical *rapprochement* must have meant to her if she did not desire to repeat it! He felt strangely humiliated.

Oh, well, she had warned him not to expect too much. If he had been living in a fool's paradise, it was his own fault. Only he must know exactly how he stood with her and end this maddening suspense. He would ask her to dine with him to-morrow and have the whole thing out.

So absorbed was he in his sense of grievance that he had come to the Porte d'Italie before he thought of the girl at home in the hated apartment. She must have reached there half an hour ago. Was everything all right with her? He could not define the vague uneasiness which prompted him to cross the city and make straight for the Avenue Henri Martin.

A little later he stopped his car in the turning outside the Bender apartment, and peered up towards the darkened *entresol*. The fourth window along was Catherine's. His eyes could just detect a faint glow of light through the closed curtains, and a thin line of radiance along the edge. Watching he saw a shadow cross the window, pause an instant, then pass on.

She was there, safe and sound, so close to him, too, only a dozen yards away. Probably she was just about to get into bed, little dreaming who was beneath her window. He longed to throw a stone at the pane, but thought better of it as he realized the lateness of the hour. He struck a match and looked at his watch. A quarter past one. No, he must not disturb her now. When he raised his eyes again the glow was extinguished.

Geoffrey slept but little. His personal chagrin over Catherine's abrupt departure gave place after a time to uneasy conjectures over Adolph Blom's mysterious movements, and all during the night he devised first one theory then another, only to reject the lot. Finally, when it was almost time to rise, a new idea struck him, turning him cold all over. He leaped out of bed.

Why in God's name had he not thought of this before?

As soon as he heard the maid go into his father's room with coffee he followed to set before the older man his recent information. The senior partner groped for his glasses, put them on, and stared.

"Hunting for Dieulefit? Why the devil should a stranger do that?"

"In case of an heir, to collar the commission," replied Geoffrey. "What other reason can there be? The point that bothers me is, is he working alone, or in conjunction with another person?"

"What person do you suspect?"

"There are two possibilities. First the maid, and second"—he paused, then brought the name out resolutely—"Miss Cushing."

"Miss Cushing!"

His father set down his coffee-cup with a jerk.

"Well, what of it?" he remarked dryly. "It is not a criminal offence to make inquiries. At all events it is a waiting game."

Geoffrey paused before replying.

"Are you sure it is a waiting game?" he inquired pointedly. "Has it occurred to you that in all this there is one feature we have overlooked? I refer to Mme. Bender's attempts at suicide."

The old eyes narrowed.

"Exactly what do you mean?"

"What if the person to benefit by her decease is impatient for the event to happen? What if those reputed attempts weren't suicide at all but something much worse? Remember we have only the maid's statement for them."

"Good God!" The solicitor started, all but capsizing his breakfast tray. For the first time the Bender muddle had assumed a grave aspect. "But who would profit? Not these servants, that is unless—"

"Unless they are in collusion with the unknown heir. The *notaire* may be banking on a fat commission which he proposes to share with them."

"The commission on the Bender estate will amount to a pretty penny. . . . Geoffrey, this looks bad!"

"I thought you'd say that. What is our best move?"

The old man was making for the bathroom, but paused and thought for a moment.

"Get hold of that maid at once and put the fear of God into her. Telephone to her now and say that I want to see her at eleven o'clock. Don't rouse her suspicions—simply tell her to come. She daren't refuse. I'll soon put a stop to any nonsense. Once she knows we are on to her schemes she'll have to clear out."

The vagaries of the Paris telephone service are perhaps the worst in the world. After repeated attempts to establish a connection, Geoffrey was forced to admit failure.

"Can't be helped," grunted his father. "Well have another go at the office, and if there's still no reply I'll send Henri up there. I don't mean to delay this a single day."

A single day! Geoffrey reflected cynically that here they both were, roused at last over something which had happened fully two months ago. At the actual moment the woman they were crediting with villainous intentions was quietly planning to take a holiday. Did that mean someone was going to deputize in her place, or were there suspicions wholly unfounded?

Nothing seemed clear when at the rue Auber he again besieged the telephone, still without success. Finally an angry appeal to the chief operator elicited the information that the line he wanted was out of order.

He slammed down the receiver and rang the bell. After a long wait Ballou stuck his sleek head in at the door.

"Henri's out, sir—won't be long. By the way, if you're not too busy, there's something I wanted to tell you. You recall that *notaire* you were inquiring about?"

Geoffrey glanced at him sharply.

"What about him?"

"He's going to be married within the next few days. I was at the Mairie in the rue de Lisbonne yesterday, and I happened to see the announcement on the *affiche* board. He's marrying a widow."

"I knew that. She's a Madame Baron."

"Quite. But it was her other name—what you call in English her maiden name—which caught my eye. I can't remember it now, but it was rather odd, something beginning with a D."

When he had gone out Geoffrey sat for some minutes spellbound. An odd name, beginning with a D! But of course it was absurd, it couldn't be. And yet . . .

With a sudden movement he crammed his hat upon his head, left the building and hailed a taxi.

"The Mairie, rue de Lisbonne," he instructed the driver.

He might as well see for himself.

Five minutes later he alighted and strode into the paved courtyard of the Mairie. There, facing him, stood the announcement board, its surface covered by scribbled notices pinned into place and protected by wire netting. Here, according to French custom, the names of every prospective bride and bridegroom resident in the quarter were posted for two weeks previous to the legal ceremony, a formality corresponding to the English banns.

Rapidly his eye ran over the scraps of paper till he hit upon the one he sought. Here it was in crabbed script, for everyone to read:

"Adolph Gustav Blom, *notaire*, of 359, rue d'Amsterdam, and Marie Honorine Baron, *née* Dieulefit. . . ."

There was no mistake.

He had come through a long dark tunnel to find himself on the brink of a precipice.

For a moment he was completely staggered. Then he swore aloud, cursing his lack of imagination. Why in the name of all that was damnable had this possibility never occurred to him? Why had he not at once dreamed of questioning the identity of "Honorine," instead of passing her by as of no importance? She it was who provided the key to the whole mystery, she alone—and a single inquiry would have secured the desired information!

Now in a flash he saw the *notaire*'s game. Why, the man was not juggling for a paltry commission, he was marrying the heir to the Bender millions!

What a stroke of genius, superbly daring, amazingly simple! Blom had known the milliner for years, was intimately acquainted with her history, but had paid no attention to her till by accident he learned that her former name was identical with that of the wealthy invalid in the Quartier de l'Étoile. Secretly and systematically he had set out to prove that a tie of blood existed between the two women so widely separated by class and fortune; then, assured of the relationship, had with the same calculation severed his connection with his little *grisette* and begun paying his addresses in a new quarter, calmly certain that sooner or later the whole of Mme. Bender's property would pass into his control.

As the details rushed through Geoffrey's mind one supreme fact stood clear. Blom could not possibly intend to wait for his victim to die a natural death. Every day added to the uncertainty of his future wife's inheritance, since it needed but the stroke of a pen to ruin his scheme. Jeanne, with her diabolical cleverness, might postpone the making of a will for a time, but she could hardly be relied upon to circumvent it altogether. No, whatever occurred must not be long delayed, and must bear the stamp of accident or suicide. Perhaps at this very moment plans were maturing. The fact that Blom's marriage was scheduled to take place within a few days suggested an imminent *dénouement*.

On tenterhooks to acquaint his father with this latest turn of the wheel, Geoffrey arrived breathless at the office and flung open the door. Then he stopped on the threshold, aware that some unusual disturbance had taken hold of the place.

The entire force was gathered in the outer room, heads together, eyes intently studying the front page of the *Paris Midi*, fresh from the press. All looked up at his approach, while Ballou spoke in a tone of marked excitement.

"Mr. Macadam was asking for you, sir. Have you seen this?"—and he thrust the paper into Geoffrey s lands.

At that instant the senior solicitor appeared in the opposite doorway, his face an ashen tinge, his eyes narrowed to steel points.

"It's happened," he announced in a dry voice. "Accident or not, that poor woman is dead."

"*Dead?* You don't mean—"

"Just that. She was burned to death last night in her bed-room."

CHAPTER THIRTY

FATHER and son exchanged looks of mute horror. Through both minds rushed the same thought.

"Read what it says. There's not much."

Riveting his attention upon the page before him, Geoffrey forced himself to digest the scant particulars the journal had to offer. In emotionless brevity it stated the following:

"Mme. Henry Belmont Bender, of Numéro 44 Avenue Henri Martin, met death in the early hours of this morning as the result of a fire in her apartment. No facts are yet known as to how the conflagration started, or whether the victim's decease was due to heart failure or to suffocation from the fumes. The maid and butler made a valiant attempt to effect a rescue, themselves sustaining injuries. The fire department was speedily summoned and contrived to save the major portion of the building.”

For a second the words swam before his eyes. Then he made a seemingly trivial observation.

“This explains why I couldn’t get through on the telephone . . .

The clerks looked at him. No one could know that his thoughts had flown in a rush to Catherine, wondering why it was he had had no word from her. The clock was striking twelve. Had anything happened to her? Thank God, her room was on the opposite side of the flat. . . .

“I must go up there at once,” he muttered.

His father nodded grimly. For all his outward composure he was badly shaken. With a brusque gesture he drew the young man apart from the group, saying in a low voice:

“Find out everything you can and keep your eyes well open. I needn’t remind you how difficult it is going to be, that as far as we know the only persons to give evidence are the suspects themselves. If we could bring to light any suspicions of a motive—”

“Motive?” repeated Geoffrey, suddenly coming to from his brief stupor. “But there is a motive! Something stupendous!”

In a rapid undertone he made known his discovery. His father listened, struck dumb. Several seconds elapsed before he found his voice to gasp.

“An heir . . . marrying the heir! Good God, how blind we’ve been!”

He seemed paralysed, all at once ten years older. The effort with which he pulled himself together was painfully apparent.

“We’ve been fools, Geoffrey—utter, hopeless fools! We’ve stood by and allowed that wretched woman to be done to death, and even now there may not be a chance of bringing the scoundrels to justice! Do you realize that fact?”

“We can at least order a post-mortem.”

“And what will that prove if, as is probable, she died of heart failure? No, I am afraid even now they may slip through our fingers. . . . But do your best; get back as quickly as you can and let me know the result.”

Within a few minutes Geoffrey was speeding towards the footle, his consciousness harassed by two dominant emotions—futile self-accusation for his failure to avert a dreadful calamity, and a growing apprehension in regard to Catherine. Nothing serious could have happened to her, or there would have been some mention in the newspaper, yet it struck him again as strange that in all these hours he had received no message. In vain he told himself that it was only natural in the shock and confusion of the terrible happening, with the telephone out of commission into the bargain, for her not to have communicated with her friends. His solace lay in the knowledge that soon he would see her and, if she were willing, take her back again to Elspeth's home.

A knot of curious spectators clustered round the entrance to the apartment building, and as he hastened through the archway several pairs of eyes followed him with morbid interest. At the doorway of the *loge* the concierge's wife was discoursing with an air of ghoulish enjoyment to a handful of cronies, for the main part servants, hatless, and laden with string-bags of marketing. Seeing Geoffrey, she darted forward and seized his arm with a horny talon.

"Vous désirez, monsieur?" she demanded sharply, every line of her witch-like face avid with the righteous opportunity of showing her authority.

Impatiently he gave his name, the woman cringing away with a servile shrug to stand looking after him curiously.

Although from the avenue there was no sign of destruction, the damage was now only too apparent. The windows of the *entresol* and several on the floor immediately above were blackened and smashed to atoms, all visible woodwork charred to a crisp, while the three interior walls ran with rivulets of water, still dripping into pools on the stones below. The lift, however, was unharmed, and the larger part of the building appeared to be little injured.

Above, the broad mahogany doors gaped wide. The pale grey carpet was soaked through and plastered with muddy footprints, the walls on both sides sodden with moisture which had seeped through in streaks of discoloration. No actual indication of the fire showed, but the entire atmosphere was permeated with the acrid odour of burnt and drenched wood.

Geoffrey entered and glanced about. Not a soul was in sight, but from the salon came subdued voices, speaking with that curious deadness and restraint usual on such occasions. Reaching the open door, he perceived a small gathering composed entirely of men, some of them with an official aspect, the rest nondescripts whom he took to be representatives of the press. The first excitement had died away, the prevailing atmosphere now being that of tension and hesitancy.

Rapidly his eyes explored the rooms in search of Catherine, but she was not in sight. He was still staring about with a frown of perplexity when a police sergeant, trim and efficient-looking in his tight uniform, stepped forward with an interrogatory gesture:

"Monsieur?"

Briefly Geoffrey stated his business.

"There is a relative of the dead lady staying here, a young American. Can you tell me where she is?"

"An American lady, monsieur? I have not seen her. You think she had been here?"

"There is no doubt about it. I am anxious to find her."

Hie sergeant, a small man with sharp features and black, observant eyes, shook his head, his attention straying back towards the salon.

"You must be misinformed, monsieur. I understand there was no one in the apartment last night except the two servants. You had better inquire of them. There is the butler now,"—and he motioned towards the squat figure of Eduardo.

The Portuguese, his left arm in a sling and his shiny face daubed with smut, was speaking jerkily to one of the reporters, a grubby Frenchman who was busily engaged in taking notes. As he talked his bloodshot eyes glanced in Geoffrey's direction, then away without a sign of recognition. The young man took a step towards him, then hatred as a choking voice from behind uttered his name:

"Monsieur Macadam!"

Wheeling round, he beheld Hermione Cushing tottering towards him, officiously escorted by the concierge. The huge singer, garbed in voluminous black, surged forward and grasped his hands to steady herself. Her large moon-face was drained of colour, her lips quivered pathetically, while every inch of her immense body vibrated with emotion. Whatever his secret thoughts had been Geoffrey could feel nothing but pity for a grief so evidently sincere.

"You have just learned of the accident?" he whispered.

She nodded, closing her red-rimmed eyes. Then with a stupendous effort at control she opened them, fixing her watery gaze upon him.

"Twenty minutes ago. . . . Yvonne heard it in the fish-monger's. I cannot yet take it in. I was with her till seven last night. . . ."

For a second he feared she was going to swoon, and braced himself in anticipation. However, drawing a tremulous breath she drew herself up with commendable resolution and laid a shaking arm on his arm.

"Catherine—?" she murmured interrogatively. "She knows nothing of this, I suppose? Poor child, poor child! What a shock for her, too!"—and before he could disabuse her mind of error she moved away into the salon.

At her approach the group disintegrated, and for the first time Geoffrey caught sight of a still figure at the far end near the windows, huddled in a bergère covered with violet brocade. From a drab countenance, deeply lined, two dull eyes stared up, expressionless, apathetic.

They were the eyes of Jeanne.

The maid was wrapped in a dark dressing-gown buttoned to the chin. Her disordered hair clung in dank wisps to her forehead, her lips were set in a straight line. Immobile as an effigy, she sat with her feet in black *pantoufles*, and her arms, swathed in bandages, resting stiffly upon the wings of the chair. If she was aware of Geoffrey's presence she gave no sign, her opaque gaze passing him by and coming to rest upon the singer's face.

Moving quickly towards her, he bent over and spoke in an undertone.

"Jeanne, where is Mademoiselle West?"

She seemed not to hear him, and only when he had repeated the question insistently did she turn her head slowly in his direction.

"Mademoiselle West? But how should I know, monsieur?" she muttered in a lifeless voice. "I have been through too much to think of mademoiselle."

"But you must know where she is," he urged impatiently, trying to fix her attention. "Has she gone out?"

Her gaze wandered away. She appeared utterly absorbed in herself, with the indifference of nervous exhaustion. Again he was forced to repeat his words, this time with noticeable impatience.

"But I do not understand," she replied at last. "Surely monsieur is aware that I have not seen mademoiselle for a full week."

"Not seen her?"

The words leaped out. Had the woman turned silly? Irritation laid hold of him so that he longed to catch her by the shoulders and shake her. Several of the men behind him had drawn closer, listening with marked curiosity.

"But you must have seen her! How could you help it? She was here last night."

One of the bandaged bands made a slight gesture of protest, as much as to say that this was scarcely the moment for idle questions.

"You are mistaken, monsieur. It is this evening she is supposed to return. I should have thought you knew that."

His face reddened with anger. Leaning nearer, he spoke slowly and emphatically, as if to a stupid child.

"Listen to me, Jeanne! You know as well as I do that mademoiselle came home last night. The point is, where has she got to?"

For answer he received an uncomprehending shrug and a blank shake of the head. Either the maid could not or would not grasp his meaning. Alarm began to creep into his mind. Was it possible she had not seen

Catherine? He felt utterly at sea. Then as he rallied himself for a fresh attack, Hermione addressed him in astonishment, her black-gloved hand upon his sleeve.

"What is this you are saying? Catherine here last night?"

He opened his lips to explain, but before he could speak Eduardo, who had been listening, moving quietly to his side.

"Some mistake, Mr. Macadam," he mumbled. "Miss West did not come home. If you care to look, you'll see for yourself that her room has not been occupied."

Speechless with rage, Geoffrey returned the man's unflinching stare. In spite of the usual covert insolence in the butler's manner, his statement somehow carried conviction.

"Is this true what you are telling me?" demanded Geoffrey rudely.

"Quite, monsieur; if she had been here, we could not have failed to know it, could we?" came the supercilious retort.

Catherine not here!

The room reeled before his eyes.

CHAPTER THIRTY-ONE

For the moment every other consideration was submerged in the wave of staggering doubt which swept over him.

He stared hard into the Portuguese's bloodshot eyes, trying to read the thoughts that lurked behind, then shifted his scrutiny to Jeanne's sallow countenance. The two faces were like a blank wall. Neither servant treated his agitation seriously, or showed any particular concern. He saw the maid's eyes close with spent fatigue, as though to shut out wearisome discussion.

He became aware that the onlookers were eyeing him queerly, that Miss Cushing was gathering her forces to bombard him with questions. He strode out of the room, just managing to elude an American reporter who was sidling towards him, pad in hand.

Quickly he gained the corridor and make for the passage leading to Catherine's bedroom.

Although the court side of the apartment had been gutted by fire, the exterior portion was untouched. He reached the familiar chamber, threw open the door, and cast a searching glance round.

The bed was smooth beneath its *toile de Jouy* cover, the dressing-table bare save for a few stray bottles and scattered oddments. There was no sign of luggage, nor anything to indicate the girl's return. Opening the cupboard he descried Catherine's grey squirrel coat, an evening wrap, and several frocks, none of which he had seen her wear at Fontainebleau. Most of the hangers pendent from the steel rod were empty. Three or four pairs of shoes were ranged on the floor beneath, while upon the shelf lay a couple of felt hats beside an oval hat-box covered in flowered paper.

He stared blankly, his brain revolving possibilities.

If she had meant to spend the night elsewhere, she would certainly have told Elspeth her intention. Besides, what of the light he had seen in the window, the shadow on the blind? Only a few hours ago the feeling of her presence here had been an overwhelming reality.

As he looked about him a sickening fear crept into his mind. *She did come home.* Whatever Jeanne and Eduardo might declare to the contrary, she reached here at midnight. Inconceivable for her to have slept through the clamour and excitement. No one, unless heavily drugged, could have done so. Did this mean that for some reason she had removed her belongings and gone quietly away, unnoticed? Such an explanation was manifestly absurd!

Rapidly the suspicion grew upon him that something sinister lurked behind this. Terror clutched at his heart as he made his way back to the front, while the thought hammered in his brain that somewhere, close at hand, Catherine was concealed. He must find her without loss of a moment.

The sight of the police sergeant brought him to his senses. Drawing the man aside, he pinioned him by the arm, and poured forth an incoherent story. His auditor, stolidly inattentive, began at last to realize that the young Englishman was in earnest, whereupon he brought his eyes to bear upon him with a faintly incredulous smile.

"Young lady? Disappeared from here? No, no, monsieur, you must be dreaming! There was no young lady in the apartment, as I told you just now—only two servants, whom you have seen. Look—there is the cook, who slept on the top floor, and was roused by the fire-engines. She will confirm what I say."

He motioned towards Berthe, who now loomed on the scene, eyes swollen with weeping, her vacuous face full of self-importance. Geoffrey seized her arm.

"Have you seen anything of mademoiselle?" he demanded fiercely. "I know that she returned last night."

The china-blue eyes opened wide in amazement.

"But no, assuredly not, monsieur! What makes you say that? It is to-day, Saturday, that we expect her, but now, of course, she will not come!"

Geoffrey turned away with an exasperated cry.

"You see," remarked the sergeant in triumph, and glancing towards the astonished Berthe, raised his brows slightly.

"But I tell you I know what I'm saying. She has been spending the week at my sister's in Fontainebleau. I was there last evening, and she had just left by the 10.45 train!"

The sergeant drew a toothpick from his pocket and used it discreetly. The smile in his black eyes grew more pronounced.

"Perhaps, monsieur, your sister was having a game with you. No doubt the young lady was there all the time and did not wish you to know. Take my advice, make sure of this before you upset yourself."

Game? The childish suggestion offered a ray of hope. It was true that Elspeth, long ago, used to indulge in practical jokes. . . .

"I don't believe it for a moment," he rejoined shortly, "but I will put through a trunk call to find out."

Without pausing for a reply, he took a couple of strides towards the study, throwing wide the door. Instantly the sergeant bounded upon him.

"Not in there, I beg of you, monsieur! No one is allowed in that room!"

No need to ask why. In full view confronting him loomed a long shapeless farm shrouded in a sheet. The curtains were drawn, the room in semi-darkness, out of which the stark mass met the eye, placed on stretchers beneath the painting of the race-horse.

Geoffrey drew in his breath sharply.

At his elbow the sergeant spoke, pulling him back.

"In any case, this instrument has been put out of commission by the fire. I would try the one in the *loge* below."

Geoffrey waved hum aside.

"I want to know first what time the fire started. Can you tell me?"

"I understand the alarm was given in at one-thirty this morning."

One-thirty! It was a quarter of an hour earlier that he had stopped his car outside.

"And the cause?"

"Candles, before a prie-Dieu, monsieur, or that is the maid's opinion. The flames caught the bed-draperies. It is said that the poor lady was a bit touched here"—and he tapped his forehead significantly. "She was trapped. The fire spread in a ring, the body was found collapsed beneath the crucifix. The servants dragged her out and wrapped her in blankets, but—" He shrugged.

"She was badly burned?"

"Frightfully, monsieur. Recognizable, of course. If you would care to take a look . . ."

For a second he drew back a corner of the sheet, disclosing the grisly remains. Geoffrey cast a glance at the body, then averted his eyes. Devoutly he hoped that Catherine had been spared this sight. Tormented by indecision, he asked himself which course of action to follow first—telephone his sister, or go over the apartment on the chance of lighting upon some trace of the missing girl. He resolved upon the latter.

"Sergeant, I want you to accompany me while I make a thorough search of this floor and the one below. I must inspect everything—even the damaged portion."

The officer appeared somewhat surprised, then a gleam of intelligence showed in his face.

"Willingly, monsieur—but if you have the least fear of the young lady's having fallen a victim to the fire, let me set your mind at rest. I can assure you positively no other remains were found."

Geoffrey did not trouble to explain that so far it had not even remotely occurred to him that Catherine, too, had been burned to death. Such an idea was grotesquely unthinkable.

No, whatever had happened, he felt positive it was something quite different; but find her he must, without delay. Other investigations could wait.

The puzzled expression in the sergeant's eyes increased when his companion briefly requested him to fetch all the keys to the apartment.

"The butler will give them to you. I will wait for you here."

"But, monsieur, this seems somewhat irregular. I do not know by what authority—"

"Never mind the authority, he won't refuse. If he objects, tell him I intend to make a demand for a search-warrant."

Impressed at last, the man departed, to return a few minutes later with a bunch of keys which he handed to Geoffrey. Together the two set out on their tour of inspection, the sergeant in the rear, mystified and a trifle bored. What was this mad Englishman getting at? Surely he had a bee in his bonnet.

Beginning with the *rez de chaussée*, they explored everything— picture-gallery, billiard-room, small salon, guests' cloak-room, lavatory, cupboards—all empty and thick with dust. Apparently no one had entered them for months. Then proceeding to the *entresol* they inspected one after another a series of bedrooms, baths, housemaids' cupboards, linen-rooms, not overlooking a single hiding-place large enough to secrete a cat. The search revealed nothing whatever. The girl was simply not there, nor was there any indication of her return.

In spite of Geoffrey's previous conviction, doubts began to creep into his mind. Had the servants spoken the truth? He caught the little sergeant's eyes upon him sharp with inquiry.

"Have you thought to ask the concierge whether or not the lady passed the *loge*?"

"That would be useless, as mademoiselle came in by the private entrance."

"Ah, indeed! You are satisfied, however, that you were mistaken?"

Geoffrey shook his head. He was satisfied of nothing beyond the obvious fact that she was not here now. With each step of the way the problem had grown more momentous, his mind more seriously disturbed. For a second he had the wild feeling that he might indeed be going mad. . . .

They were standing now at the rear end of the passage leading past the ruined portion. In front the way was blocked by wreckage, the floor at their feet an irregular cavern barred across by blackened beams. Over heaps of charred debris and sodden plaster great holes gaped in walls and ceiling, the whole saturated with water. Of the dead woman's own room little was left, but through a jagged opening at the side one could see the bathroom, the bath itself intact in the midst of a litter of twisted pipes and shattered appliances. Ten hours ago the place must have been a roaring furnace. It spoke well for the fire department that they had managed to check the flames so quickly.

The sergeant pointed at a spot against the outer wall.

"There, monsieur, is where she was found. The bed was to the right, I'm told, but naturally nothing remains of it."

Geoffrey looked, but the sight told him nothing he wanted to know. Meanwhile precious minutes were slipping away.

"Sergeant," he said rapidly, but with caution, "I am now going to telephone to Fontainebleau, but if I obtain no news of Mademoiselle I intend to make a report at once to the Commissariat. However, I have one more question to ask. Has any person from outside been here to talk with either of these servants during the morning? I am particularly interested in a small blond man with a thin moustache and eyes which are not mates."

The sergeant considered, and shook his head.

"No, monsieur, I have seen no one of that description. The doctor of Mme. Bender has come, and one or two officials, but I am positive the servants have seen no one alone."

"Good. It is private interviews I wish to prevent. Can I look to you to keep an eye on things, report to me anything out of the ordinary, and if possible try to keep the butler from going out?"

"But, monsieur,"—in evident astonishment—"I have no right to restrain anyone's movements!"

"I can only beg you to do your best. I may tell this much, that very probably I shall have to place those two under arrest. Until that occurs they must not be allowed to suspect our intentions."

He had exploded a bombshell.

"Arrest! but this man and woman are regarded as heroes! They have risked their lives to—"

"Never mind that. Do as I say. It is of the utmost importance."

As be spoke he took a hundred-franc note from his pocket and thrust it into the sergeant's hand, then without further explanation retraced his steps by way of the uninjured passages to the front door. As he was going out the American reporter's eagle eye fastened itself upon him.

"Pardon me, Mr. Macadam, but could you oblige me with a few facts about the deceased? That woman in there is too dazed to say much, and I want to prepare my story."

"Not now," returned Geoffrey in desperation. "I have urgent business to attend to. Some other time."

"One moment, please! What about this American lady I heard you mention? Did you say her name is Miss West?"—and with undaunted persistence he linked his arm through the other's and followed him to the landing.

"Yes, Miss West, of Boston, a cousin of the late Mr. Bender. She has been visiting here, but I find she has gone away."

It seemed the wisest thing to say.

A moment later in the concierge's abode he assailed the difficulties of establishing a connection with Fontainebleau, and, fuming with impatience, waiting for what seemed an aeon of time. Finally to his relief he heard the sound of his sister's voice.

"Elspeth—this is Geoffrey. Tell me at once—were you joking or is it true that Catherine left you last night? No nonsense, I've got to know."

The reply came fraught with amazement.

"But of course she left. What on earth do you mean?"

His heart sank as he nerved himself to go on.

"Simply this: Mme. Bender is dead—burned to death in her room last night—and the servants swear they have not seen anything of Catherine."

"Not seen her? Impossible! Why, she must have reached there about midnight."

"Apparently she didn't. Is there any other place she might have gone? Any friend's house, or—"

"Certainly not! There must be some mistake. Geoffrey—this is too frightful! I'll take the next train up to Paris. I—"

He waited for no more. Staring him in the face was the concierge's big clock, the hands pointing to one. An hour gone, and nothing accomplished.

Instinct warned him not to lose sight of Jeanne and Eduardo, but whatever happened he must not delay his visit to the police, who should be informed at once of Catherine's disappearance. Unfortunately he could attend to only one thing at a time.

As he quitted the archway he saw at the corner of the street a man's figure in the act of diving into an open taxi-cab. A glance was enough. The heavy shoulders, the rakish angle of the hat, to say nothing of the injured arm, revealed the person of the butler. In short, one of his suspects was even now making off, probably on secret business.

Where was he going? Faced with a fresh dilemma, Geoffrey decided that the Commissariat must wait.

Luckily a second cab approached, unoccupied. He flung himself into it, pointing towards the Place du Trocadero and shouting. "You see that red taxi just ahead? A hundred francs if you keep it in sight!"

French chauffeurs are quick-witted. With a comprehending grunt the man jammed down the accelerator, and they were off, even as the quarry turned the corner of the Avenue Kléber heading towards the Étoile. Ten seconds more and they caught sight of it again, one of a score of swiftly moving cars.

Round the vast circle of the Arc de Triomphe sped the red taxi like a crimson streak, the other in hot pursuit. Along the Avenue Wagram, past the Place des Ternes, then with a lightning swerve into the Boulevard de Courcelles. So far no hitch. A glance told Geoffrey that the prey was still within sight, though a hundred yards ahead.

From the Place des Ternes to the Place de Clichy is a straight run, the thoroughfare altering its name midway and becoming the Boulevard des Batignolles. The way ahead was clear.

Pszt! Without warning came a grinding of brakes, and the cab stopped with such violence that Geoffrey was thrown off the seat, his head crashing against the glass. Then he saw what had happened. They had struck the mudguard of a large Mercedes incautiously rounding the entrance to a side-street.

Foreseeing the inevitable altercation, Geoffrey got out, paid the driver his hundred francs, and leaving the two infuriated Frenchmen to exchange volleys of profanity gazed up the boulevard. In the open space of the Place de Clichy he could just make out a spot of red negotiating a rapid right-turn to plunge down a narrow street.

No good continuing the chase, the butler was gone. Besides, Geoffrey knew beyond doubt his destination, for the street which had swallowed him up was the rue d'Amsterdam.

CHAPTER THIRTY-TWO

Within the next three minutes Geoffrey had found a telephone-booth and was in communication with his father, exasperated to find the old man not greatly impressed by Catherine's absence.

"Probably gone to stay with some friend," he suggested. "In which case it's likely she hasn't yet heard of this disaster."

"What, descend on people at twelve o'clock at night?"

"It has been done."

Geoffrey cast his mind over Catherine's acquaintances. Only two families did she know at all well, some Americans named Barton, in the rue Freycinet, and a young married couple, artists both, in the rue Léopold-Robert. He mentioned their names, giving the addresses.

"Get in touch with them at once and see if they have heard anything of her," he ordered briefly. "You'll have to send a message up to the O'Briens, as they are not on the telephone. I am going to see Bernard and get his help, but I would like you to meet me at two o'clock at the Commissariat. There are three divisions in the district—the one we want is in the Rue Mesnil."

"You think there's been foul play?"

"I am sure of it—but the important matter now is to find Catherine."

From the Place de Clichy to the rue Blanche is but a step. By great good luck the agent was in his office, and listened attentively to the story Geoffrey poured out. He ruminated a moment, then gave his opinion.

"I agree, monsieur, that in the light of this man Blom's approaching marriage last night's affair was deliberate murder. But your friend's failure to appear may be easily explained. I should think she would probably turn up during the day."

He coughed discreetly, as though he could if he wished disclose a vast amount of information regarding feminine vagaries.

"But I tell you I saw the light in her room last night! The servants may swear what they choose, I don't believe them. Something tells me they know where she is. My God, man, don't you see what that means?"

"Certainty, if they do know. But I am inclined to believe there is nothing in this beyond a change of plan on her part."

"However that may be, the Portuguese I mentioned is at this moment with Blom, at his office. I am sure of it. I want you to shadow him and find out what he has up his sleeve. Come at once, before he has time to get away."

The agent reached for his rusty hat. Geoffrey arranged to meet him at two-thirty in the foyer of the Hotel Claridge, and hailing a taxi drove quickly to the Commissariat. It was now half past one.

The narrow rue Mesnil leads out of the Place Victor Hugo, the small building of the Commissariat being situated at the farther end, its unimposing facade marked with a faded tricolour. Passing the *agent* on duty at the entrance, Geoffrey found his father waiting within, and eagerly inquired news.

"There's none, I'm afraid," Macadam made reluctant answer. "Neither of those families even knew she'd been out of Paris. But there may be other possibilities."

Geoffrey could see none. Badly shaken by the report, he motioned to his father to precede him up the wooden staircase to a door on which was written, *"Entrez Sans Frapper."*

Entering they found a bare room divided by a desk behind which lounged an employee diligently engaged in paring his nails with a pocket-knife. This individual listened vacantly to Geoffrey's urgent request to see the Chief, and after clicking his knife-blade into its warty case, blowing his nose thoroughly on a soiled handkerchief and staring the two Englishmen up and down in a wooden manner announced that it would be necessary for them to state their case first to the *Secretaire du Commissaire.*

They were caught in the toils of officialdom. Geoffrey ground his teeth as he watched the underling amble out and heard him in an adjoining room exchanging feeble jests with an unseen company for fully five minutes before there was any sign of activity. Eventually there emerged from the doorway a pink-faced official, dapperly-built, with hair freely plastered with pomade.

"Vous désirez, messieurs?"

Macadam made a concise statement in excellent French, while the secretary's eyes wandered dreamily this way and that, finally coming to rest on the speaker's waistcoat, which they appeared to find mildly interesting. In the end without betraying the slightest degree of concern or hurry, the man motioned languidly towards a couple of hard chairs against the wall, and remarked that if the Commissaire was not engaged he would perhaps hear the complaint himself.

Another maddening wait, and the two solicitors found themselves in a second office, facing a dry-as-dust little person with a stubble of grey beard and a pair of gold-rimmed spectacles. This was the Commissaire.

Bent over his desk steadily covering a sheet of foolscap with angular writing, he did not look up when the secretary retailed to him a garbled account of the visitors' mission, continuing for endless minutes to dip his fine pen into the ink-pot and pursue his labours unmoved by rumours of murder and arson. Long after Geoffrey's patience was frayed to breaking-point he pushed aside his document and cleared his throat.

"And now, messieurs, what is your business?" he calmly inquired.

No expression crossed his face till he caught the words, "double affair, relating to the death last night of Mme. Belmont Bender," when a gleam came into his eyes.

"Ah, the victim of the fire in the Avenue Henri Martin. But—double affair, you say? Kindly explain."

This time it was Geoffrey who set forth the circumstances and his suspicions of foul play. Several times the Commissaire indulged in a meditative shrug, and now and then raised a hand for the benefit of the secretary, who made a note in a little book.

At last the little chief removed his spectacles, rubbed his eyelids with a reflective finger, and summed up the case with bloodless precision.

"You wish to suggest, monsieur, first of all an affair of sequestration supplemented by undue influence, object pecuniary gain. As to the possibility of murder, from what you tell me there seems little actual evidence. Failing witnesses, the charge may be difficult to prove, unless, of course, the examination of the corpse reveals some trace of poison. That, naturally, remains to be seen. Since you have managed to hit upon a plausible motive for a crime, it will be my duty to order a post-mortem, though I understand you are not certain that this Mme.—what is the woman's name?—Mme. Baron, is a blood relation of the deceased. You only assume that she is. However, we will waive that point. The aggregate of circumstances will provide us sufficient excuse to go on."

He wiped his lenses carefully and set the spectacles again upon his nose.

"Now for the other matter, the supposed disappearance of Mademoiselle—how does she call herself?—ah yes, Mademoiselle West. It seems to me rather early, monsieur, to conclude that she is actually missing. Several solutions suggest themselves. On your own statement she was not on the best of terms with Mme. Bender's servants. Is it not possible that on her way home last night she felt a sudden reluctance to descend upon them unawares, and in consequence spent the night at an hotel? I am thinking also of your mention of the fact that she intended an early start in the morning, to meet her friends."

Geoffrey admitted this might have happened, but declared it to be unlikely. What, he demanded, was one to do about the light in mademoiselle's bedroom and the shadow on the Wind?

The Commissaire shook his head disparagingly.

"One cannot rely upon that as proof that she was there. The shadow may have been that of some other person."

"But at a quarter past one, monsieur! The alarm was given in at one-thirty. At the time I mention the servants must have been either asleep or occupied with the fire—if one is to believe what they say."

"True. You are sure it was a quarter past one?"

"Absolutely. I looked at my watch."

"Ah, well, that fact may be of value to us, particularly if it shows up any flaw in the servants' evidence. We shall see."

He rang a bell on the desk, the sluggish employee before mentioned appeared.

"Send Inspector Bazin to me," he commanded, and closing his eyes, lapsed into silence.

Presently a stalwart officer appeared in the doorway. His fresh, sun-burned colouring and small blond moustache suggested a Norman heritage; his pale blue eyes, stolid and honest, gazed forth from beneath a square forehead several shades lighter in tint than his cheeks. But for his alert air and more nervous movements he might have been a representative of the London Police Force. Geoffrey took an instant liking to him.

"This, messieurs, is one of my men to whom I am going to entrust your case. Kindly inform him of the details. He will look after you, I trust satisfactorily. Inspector, conduct these gentlemen to the waiting-room and hear what they have to say. I wish you good day, messieurs," and with a brief nod the Commissaire resumed his writing.

On the threshold the father and son separated, Macadam to return to the office and Geoffrey to go through his story once again to the inspector.

The past half-hour had been a nightmare. Not only had it consumed valuable time during which anything, everything might be happening, but the Commissaire's refusal to treat Catherine's disappearance as serious had seemed to him densely lacking in imagination. Now another ordeal faced him, one more official to try to impress.

However, Inspector Bazin proved human. He showed keen interest, asked many questions, and having written down every salient detail read it aloud briskly, beginning with the description of Catherine.

"American, United States. Age twenty-four. Slender, dark, height one metre sixty-three centimetres. Well dressed, beige coat trimmed with castor fur, small hat of pale green felt, gown to match. Luggage, one fairly large pigskin cue, initialed G.W., and one round patent leather hatbox, black. . . . Is these anything else, monsieur? Jewellery, for instance?"

Geoffrey thought for a moment.

"Only a ring, a ruby, oval-shaped, set in gold, and—but I am not sure about this—a flat gold necklace worn close round the throat."

"Should you say she had any large amount of money on her?"

"I don't know. I imagine not."

"Now, then, monsieur. At what time did she leave Fontainebleau?"

"Ten forty-five, which means she must have arrived at the Gare Fontainebleau-Avron at about eleven-fifty."

The inspector twisted the waxed ends of his moustache thoughtfully for a second, then spoke with decision.

"As I see it, monsieur, we have three distinct possibilities to consider. First, the young lady may have gone elsewhere of her own accord—either because on reaching the apartment she found herself bolted out, or for some other reason. In this event you will no doubt soon hear from her."

"We may as well rule that out," cut in Geoffrey shortly.

"Permit me to say, monsieur, that that is merely your present opinion. To be quite candid, you do not know that it is not the case. Well, then! My second surmise is that some fate may have overtaken her on the way, so that she never arrived home. I suppose I need not explain my meaning?"

Geoffrey's rigid face showed that he understood. Already his mind had flown to accounts of persons robbed, murdered and thrown from moving trains, as well as to those other familiar occurrences where the victims are taken to the lonely reaches of the Bois, and left there dead or in an unconscious state.

"Go on," he said briefly.

"In consideration of this second theory, I shall try at once to get in touch with the chauffeur who drove her from the Gare; also find out if any unidentified bodies of young women have been discovered in the vicinity of the city. *Bien!* Let us look at our third possibility, which I fear is not more pleasing than the last. You permit me, monsieur?" and he looked at Geoffrey with grave hesitancy. "I know what you are going to say. The servants themselves . . ."

"Exactly. If your assumption of their guilt is correct, and if the young lady chanced to surprise them in the act, they would naturally have to remove her for their own safety. In such a case it is as well to be prepared for the worst."

The listener's eyes were bleak. This was the identical thought which had tortured him since the moment he learned of the disappearance.

"I suppose we may obtain a warrant for their arrest on suspicion?" he forced himself to say.

To his astonishment the inspector shook his head.

"That, monsieur, is exactly what I do not wish to do. Examine the situation for a moment. Placed under restraint they will stick to their prepared statement, and we shall be obliged to institute a tedious investigation. Given a sufficient amount of rope, they are certain to betray themselves in some way. My idea is this: granting that it was mademoiselle's shadow you saw on the blind, whatever happened must have taken place between one-fifteen and one-thirty when the fire engines were summoned—a bare quarter of an hour. In so short a time they could not have taken her far. She must therefore be hidden about the premises or somewhere close at hand. In either case they dare not leave the body for long for fear of its being discovered, and will take the first opportunity of removing it."

A shudder passed over Geoffrey as he noticed the speaker used the word "body."

"What I propose to do is to surround the building with a cordon of police in plain clothes, so that if the suspects attempt to go out their movements will be watched. If our third surmise is the right one, then before many hours—probably to-night—one or the other of them will lead us to the missing lady."

"Remember they have an accomplice—the *notaire* in the rue d'Amsterdam. The butler was with him at noon today."

"That fact is suggestive. Give me the man's address, and I will see that he also is shadowed."

Geoffrey complied, and the inspector wrote it down.

"Am I to understand that you and your father are Mme. Bender's legal executors?"

Geoffrey nodded.

"That is very useful, as in your position of authority you can issue certain orders. My advice to you is to suggest that these servants remain in the apartment till the inquest is over. In all events they will be required to give evidence. On no account let them imagine that you suspect anything. As soon as I have set my plans in operation I shall question them and conduct a thorough search of the building, but in such a way as not to arouse needless alarm." He glanced at his watch. "It is now three o'clock. I will meet you at the apartment at a little before four. Meanwhile, monsieur, bear in mind that we have been adopting an extreme view of things, and that at any moment we may find our fears groundless."

Five minutes after this Geoffrey entered Claridge's Hotel and hastened through to the central lounge. At his approach a figure in rusty black, as conspicuous as a lone crow in a corn-field, rose from one of the little tables and came to meet him.

"Well?" cried the young man eagerly.

"I am afraid, monsieur, I have not much to report. Twenty minutes after I left you the Portuguese came out, then took a taxi back to his own neighbourhood. I trailed him all the way, but instead of returning at once to the apartment, he paid a call on a concierge, apparently a friend, several houses farther along the street. I made a point of dropping into the *loge* on the pretext of inquiring for an imaginary *locataire*, and found the two discussing the fire. I did not see anything that looked wrong."

Geoffrey considered the information, which meant nothing whatever to him. Although disappointed at the result of the agent's mission, he comforted himself with the reflection that if the butler had any designs he had not been able to carry them out.

"Did you do anything further?" he demanded.

"I hurried back to the *notaire*'s office, hoping to hit on something in that quarter. I saw him for a moment, representing myself as a life-insurance agent, and tried to get him to talk, but it was no good. He was preoccupied and, I think, a little suspicious—all but shut the door in my face. However, I found out this much—his marriage takes place at the Mairie on Tuesday next—just three days off."

Well timed, was the listener's inward comment. If Blom had married the milliner while Mme. Bender was alive there would have been considerable doubt as to whether the latter's fortune would ever come into his wife's possession; while if he postponed the wedding until Mme. Baron actually occupied the enviable position of heiress, she might easily throw him over, being then independent and able to pick and choose. . . .

"Is there anything more you wish me to do, monsieur?" queried Bernard when the silence had lengthened to minutes.

The young man roused himself from his reverie.

"Not at the moment, but I want you to hold yourself in readiness for the next day or so in case I need you," and in a few words he outlined the theories set forth by the police inspector.

The agent listened with solemn attention.

"Perhaps, you will allow me to do a little investigation on my own account. There is half an idea in my head . . . nothing may come of it of course. . . . Nevertheless," he added with an effort at cheerfulness similar in effect to the passing of a hearse, "let us not look too much on the dark side of things. Who knows but the young lady may have had some reason of her own for spending the night away? You tell me she was to meet some friends early this morning. In that case she might easily remain ignorant of the news for a considerable time, since few strangers read the *Paris Midi*. Even now she may be on her way home."

The same lingering hope was in Geoffrey's mind, though he was afraid to bank upon it. At any moment now the agony of the past few hours might dissolve like a hideous dream. He could hardly wait to get back to the Avenue Henri Martin to end his suspense.

He reached the scene of the fire, and the lift being above-floors, started to mount the broad stairway, too keyed up with expectancy to notice a dull shuffle of feet approaching from the *entresol*. However, rounding the turn he pulled up abruptly, flattening himself against the wall to avoid a descending cortege—nothing less than a company of stretcher-bearers, engaged in removing the body of the deceased.

So, he reflected, the Commissaire had lost no time in carrying out his intention. The remains would now be taken over by the Institut-Medico-Légiste, and the cause of death determined by post-mortem. That much at all events had been accomplished.

From the top step the dapper sergeant superintended the operation. Slowly the sheeted mass went on its way, the men manoeuvring the turns cautiously to avoid the balustrade. Geoffrey waited, hat in hand, till the party had crossed the lobby, then cleared the remaining steps at a bound. As he did so, Eduardo came out of the open doorway, started to speak to the police sergeant, then noting Geoffrey, checked himself.

The young man accosted him directly:

"Have you seen anything yet of Mademoiselle West?" he demanded.

The Portuguese looked coolly amazed.

"Certainly not, monsieur. Unless you yourself have communicated with her, I should doubt if she has heard the news."

Geoffrey's heart took a sickening plunge. Instinctively he put out a hand towards the lintel of the door to steady himself under this fresh blow. For a second his eyes and the hot brown ones of the butler met in an unwavering stare.

CHAPTER THIRTY-THREE

CATHERINE's letter from the Hardwickes came as a complete surprise. Jim had finished his work at the British Museum sooner than he had expected, and the English weather remaining persistently raw and cold he and Clare had decided to set off at once for Rome and Florence, travelling for economy's sake, via Newhaven-Dieppe. Crossing by the night boat they were due to reach Paris early Saturday morning, and as they would have only a short time between trains Catherine felt she must snatch this opportunity of seeing them. Hence her sudden decision to return to the city and sleep at the apartment in order to get an early start.

She was now almost fit again, nerves calmer and eyes bright with renewed energy. Yet up till two days ago she had felt languid and unequal to any effort, so much so that there was a physical excuse for her behaviour towards Geoffrey, much as she reproached herself for her apparent coldness. What had he thought of her? She knew he had been puzzled and disappointed, but she had been unable to pretend an emotion she did not feel. Now all that was changed. Perverse though it seemed, she longed to be alone with him, to touch him and respond to his advances, this time freely, with a full realization of all he meant to her.

Geoffrey! The vision of strength filled her mind all the way back in the train. To-morrow she would see him, atone for her tiresome conduct. It pleased her to know from Elspeth that he did not wear his heart on his sleeve, that neither the wealthy young woman in Passy nor the beautiful Irish girl who had tried to ensnare him during the past year had met with the slightest success. That he was beginning to be regarded as a hardened bachelor enhanced his value in her eyes and simultaneously flattered her own self-esteem.

To-morrow! It was not long to wait. She would meet the Hardwickes, and then, perhaps, lunch with him. Her heart swelled with excitement.

It was nearing midnight when she arrived at the Gare Fontaine-bleau-Avron, secured a taxi, and set off towards her own quarter. The night was mild and soft, with a gusty breeze that held a hint of moisture. A pale moon dodged among floating clouds lit by the glow of the city, the buildings to left and right cast masses of shadow, laced occasionally by a golden ribbon of light where a door stood open. She leaned back, drowsy and content.

What a relief to think things were all going smoothly! Did Jeanne faintly suspect that her power was almost at an end, that when she returned—if she did return—it would be to find herself displaced by capable nurses? Perhaps she did know what was in the air, and was taking this method of withdrawal, hoping to evade the police before her thefts were proven. In that case, Eduardo too would vanish. Only a few days now . . .

Triumphant reflections—yet it was with a slight feeling of dread that she approached the house. Possibly it would have been wiser to let Jeanne know she was coming tonight, but there had seemed no need, particularly as she planned to slip out early in the morning and get a cup of coffee on the way to the station.

With her key ready, she opened the side door, and directed the driver to set her bags in the hall. Then very quietly she crept up the stairs, listening at every step.

All serene, no reason to fear that anything had gone wrong in her absence. What a fool she had been to worry! She had made herself miserable for weeks past anticipating events not in the least likely to materialize. She must take herself in hand and stop making mountains out of molehills.

She had meant to go straight to bed, but now there was nothing to prevent her doing so she succumbed to the temptation to dally, and consumed considerable time in aimless trifles. She wrote a dozen post-cards of Fontainebleau to friends at home, added a long postscript to her letter to Barbara, and sat before the mirror dreaming of the past week and still pleasanter days to come. More than half an hour had gone by and still she had not bothered to finish unpacking. Boring task! She would leave it till next day.

Finally she opened the cupboard to put away her hat and coat, and as she did so her eye fell on the parcel containing the new hat Honorine had copied for her. Only once had she tried to wear it, on which occasion she had more or less given it up as a failure. Now she took it out of the bag and looked it over, frowning.

What was wrong with the thing? It was all but identical with the one she had just removed, pale green felt and the same model, chosen because it suited her particularly well. Yet the old one, getting shabby now, was still smart, while the copy somehow missed its aim. An experiment in economy which had ended in waste; but then she had ordered it purely as an excuse for trying to secure information about Adolph Blom, so she must not complain.

Humming a tune—it was the Albeniz tango, she recalled with tender reminiscence—she tried the hat on once more, setting it at a different angle and arranging her hair at the sides. A survey in the glass brought agreeable surprise. Why, it was not so bad, after all! Like this, the flat wing at the right hugging her cheek, it looked distinctly possible. The colour, anyhow, was admirable. Geoffrey liked her in green.

As the thought rose to her mind, a tide of red flooded her face, with the result that the hat became positively becoming. Ah, that was it! She had been pale before.

Taking her lipstick from her bag she touched her lips lightly, then stood back to note the improvement. As she did so her sleeve brushed the bag to the floor, and its contents spilled in every direction.

"Damn!" she muttered with annoyance, stooping to retrieve the fallen articles.

Were they all here? Latchkey, powder-compact, diary, cards for a private view of pictures, but no lipstick. She searched for several minutes, then gave it up. It must have rolled far away under some of the furniture. Never mind, she could find it easily in daylight.

As she straightened up she stood still and sniffed the air inquiringly. Some queer odour had crept into the room. What was it? It could not come from outside, for the window was tightly closed. She sniffed again with growing intentness. Smoke . . . something was burning. But where? Not, surely, in the apartment. It couldn't be, unless the careless Berthe had left the gas-stove in the kitchen alight with a saucepan upon it.

She opened the door and peered into the passage. Here the smell was distinctly noticeable, acrid, insistent. She went along softly towards the back of the apartment, came to the kitchen door and looked in. No, there was nothing wrong in this quarter. Yet the odour increased, carrying with it a pungent flavour of burning varnish. There was even a faint streaked haze in the air, hovering in her direction from the passage on the court side. At the same moment her ear detected the ominous crackle of flames.

Good heavens, the place was on fire! She could not be mistaken. . . .

Something must be done, she must rouse Jeanne, give the alarm. She quickened her pace towards the dressing-room, then, as she reached it, drew up abruptly, her heart in her mouth. There, just in front of her, she beheld the source of the conflagration. Smoke, thick, dark grey, oozed in ribbons from beneath her cousin's door, streamed through the keyhole and round the cracks at the side.

"Oh, my God!"

She choked suddenly as the fumes mounted in her nostrils.

Germaine's room was on fire. Did the poor creature know? She took drugs to make her sleep. The crackling grew, small popping explosions came from the other side of the door. She seized the knob and turned it, only to meet with an unexpected resistance. She pushed with all her strength, beat upon the panels, then gave up. Cold sweat broke out all over her. God in heaven, the door was locked!

Like lightning she darted into the adjoining room, straight to the couch in the corner, where in the tempered gloom she was just able to make out the dark mass of the maid's recumbent body, covered to the ears with a thick eiderdown. A smothered snore greeted her. She grasped the huddled shoulders violently, shouting:

"Jeanne, wake up! Madame's room is on fire. She will be killed."

Then she dashed to the inner door, tried it, pushed with might and main. To her horror this, too, was securely fastened, nor was there any sign of a key. What could it mean?

In desperation she turned back to the bed, amazed to see that for all her shakings the woman yonder was still wrapped in slumber. How was it possible? The small room was filled with smoke. With a ruthless hand she swept the covers to the floor, and as she did so a double clink of metal tinkled upon the floor. Yet throughout the sleeper had not stirred. There she lay in her stuffy nightgown, her head buried in the pillow. The idea shot into Catherine's mind that the maid herself was drugged. Once more she attacked her vehemently, screaming in her ear. At last a grunt came, the form moved in the darkness, protestingly, and a voice thick with sleep muttered:

"*Qu'est-ce qu'il y a donc? Qui me dérange?*" Then as the girl continued her merciless pounding, the eyes opened with a dull vacancy. "*Mademoiselle—? Qu'est-ce que vous faites ici? Vous êtes revenue, alors . . .!*"

Without replying, Catherine made a dive for the light, switched it on. The glare shone on the hazy room, revealing the pile of neat garments lying across a chair, the heap of bed-clothes on the floor, the stripped couch with its supine occupant.

"Get up, Jeanne! Don't you hear me? Madame's room is in flames and the door is locked! Quick—where is the key?"

"Flames? Impossible! What is all this fuss about?" Hysterical with despair, Catherine gazed at her helplessly. The situation was like some fantastic dream. Had the keen-witted Jeanne taken leave of her senses? Then all at once she caught a gleam in the brown eyes, and in a flash saw through the whole ruse. This stupidity was assumed—the woman was pretending! No other explanation was possible with the smoke pouring in through every crevice, the fire next door swelling to a roar. . . .

Suddenly she recalled the metallic clink of a moment ago. She looked down and spied a little distance apart, two keys lying where the cover had swept them from the bedside table. She swooped upon them, even as a hand from the bed shot downward like a bird of prey, striking her own in its descent.

No time to think. She was at the door now, fitting first one key then the other into the lock. The next instant there was a cataclysmic movement behind her, her arms were grasped and she felt herself powerfully dragged away.

"What are you doing? Are you mad?" a harsh voice grated in her ear.

Jeanne, every vestige of sleep or shamming gone, had clutched her in a grip of steel. Catherine fought like a tigress, her brain too distraught to grasp the significance of what was happening. All she knew was that a few feet away the helpless invalid was trapped in a furnace, while this idiot of a woman tried to prevent her going to the rescue.

Terror lent her super-normal strength. She wrenched herself free, turned the knob and threw open the door. A column of smoke billowed through the gap, and even as she recoiled before the suffocating fumes her starting eyes beheld like a vision in a nightmare a picture she was never to forget.

In the room beyond, lit by a red glare, she saw the bed wreathed in pennants of fire, galloping, racing to the ceiling. The carpet, scorched to a cinder, spouted with jets of orange, while through the blackened draperies gleamed upon the wall the silver crucifix, the candles beneath it melted to dripping streams of wax. On the floor between the bed and the chair, outstretched and motionless, by Mine. Bender, her night-dress just beginning to ignite. One glance at the still face revealed to Catherine the awful truth. Germaine was already dead. . . .

She screamed and took a step forward. Then an incredible thing happened. The door was driven back upon the seething holocaust, and she herself was pushed aside by an impact so violent as to knock the breath from her body. Through the choking atmosphere a voice was saying:

"Too late. . . . You are insane to go in there, mademoiselle. Do you wish to be burned alive?"

Then and only then did the truth rush upon her. The locked doors, the cool deliberation of Jeanne's speech!

Like a maniac she cast herself upon her assailant, who, with set face and shoulders squared, had braced herself against the closed door. Her heart-beats stifled her, she shrieked in a voice that was not her own the horrible suspicion now hardened into belief.

"Murderess—murderess! It is you who set fire to that room, you who planned this! You have killed her, locked her in so she couldn't escape! Open the door, beast that you are!"

Out of the saturnine face the dark eyes bored into hers with an expression of venomous hatred. Slowly a dark smile twisted the corners of the mouth.

"*En bien—et aprés?*" she caught the words, uttered in a curious undertone.

"Murderess! Murderess!"

Her voice made no sound. Her breath was exhausted, yet she continued to rain blows upon the rigid figure which hardly seemed to feel them. Jeanne's eyes, narrowed with bitter triumph, were fixed now, not upon herself but at a point just over her shoulder. Even in the anguish of the moment the girl noticed an attitude of expectancy, as though the woman were watching for something to occur.

It all took place within a few seconds. She suddenly became aware of a pounding noise, like that of a heavy knocker hammering upon a door. At the same instant she saw the woman's face alter, the eyes suddenly dilate with a look of terror. Then, behind her a board creaked, and instinctively she turned her head.

There, only a pace removed, stood the Portuguese, swarthy features livid, lips drawn back to disclose yellowed teeth. His right arm was uplifted, there was a glinting object in his hand, probably a heavy candle-stick. For a second he poised above her, and she knew from his transfixed gaze that he, too, was listening to that persistent clamour.

That was all she saw. The same instant a crashing blow fell upon her skull and she crumpled to the floor.

Even then she made one final supreme effort to raise herself, groped in a world suddenly grown black. Across her mental vision shot points of dazzling silver, like meteors threading a midnight sky. A roaring as of the sea filled her ears, then that, too, subsided, and consciousness ebbed away.

CHAPTER THIRTY-FOUR

NO WORDS can convey Geoffrey's agony of mind on receiving the butler's cool denial. In that moment every shred of delusion was swept away, leaving him face to face with a stark reality nothing could cloak or soften. Catherine was gone. Whether she had fallen victim to the rapacity of an unknown assailant, or was at this moment hidden away in some dark corner, silenced for ever by the mongrel confronting him, he was powerless to fathom; both suppositions were possible, both equally appalling.

As on a former occasion, a savage impulse seized him to drive his fingers into Eduardo's thick neck and throttle him. His desire must have showed in his face, for with a watchful look the man retreated a step. Noting the movement, Geoffrey took an iron grip of himself, recalling the part he had to play.

"Evidently," he remarked in even tones, "you did not take in what I said to you this morning. The fact is, Miss West left Fontainebleau last night, meaning to return here. Since that time she has not been seen."

What might have passed for a glimmer of interest showed in the small wary eyes.

"That's odd," he replied insolently. "I am sure I don't know what to say about it. We've not seen her, I promise you that," and he scratched his ear defiantly.

"In any case," continued Geoffrey, "I have thought best to report the matter to the Commissariat, and they are sending a man here presently to look into the matter. He will want to take a formal statement from you and Jeanne, in order to make certain she did not come home. Also the apartment has got to be searched."

"Quite so," replied the Portuguese imperturbably. "Jeanne has been put to bed. She's come over a bit queer after all this, but I daresay she is well enough to answer questions."

He turned to walk away, but Geoffrey stopped him.

"That is not all. You and Jeanne will naturally be required to give evidence at the inquest. Until that is over I wish you both to remain here, occupying the uninjured rooms. Your wages will be paid, and you will assist with the inventory and removal of Mme. Bender's effects."

The butler gave this a brief consideration.

"I understand," he agreed casually. "Anything more?"

"Not at the moment," answered Geoffrey.

He stood watching the thick-set figure move stolidly away towards the bend of the hall, satisfied that he had said nothing to rouse suspicion. Then he pushed open the salon doors and stepped inside.

Not a soul of all the mixed assembly now remained, only the trampled carpet and a litter of cigarette ashes, bearing evidence to the scene of the morning. From the left wall the mediaeval figures in the tapestry looked down upon him with placid indifference, while opposite, above the mantel-mirror, gay ladies and gallants made frivolous love in a sylvan paradise. A pall-like stillness pervaded the place.

Mechanically he moved towards the window and, pushing aside the curtains, stared into the street below. Then, with sudden interest he fixed his eyes on a roughly-clad labourer, at that moment hoisting a ladder against one of the chestnut trees. On the ground beside him lay a canvas bag of implements. An odd time of the year to clip the trees, reflected the watcher. Then it dawned on him that in all likelihood this inconspicuous workman was one of the persons employed to surround the house. If so, the inspector had been prompt.

A step sounded on the carpet behind him and, turning, he saw the little police sergeant approaching with a confidential air.

"About that matter, monsieur," whispered the Frenchman with a backward jerk of the head. "I regret to say I was not successful. No sooner was your back turned than the fellow put on his hat and—*pszt! Quel trace!*" He swept an expressive gesture.

"Never mind, it was just what I expected. I have made a report to the Commissariat, and they are going to take things in hand."

The black eyes widened with interest.

"*Ah, mon Dieu!* So you intend to make a charge?" he whispered.

Before Geoffrey could reply a loud knock shattered the silence, causing both men to jump. They reached the hall to find Eduardo in the act of admitting Inspector Bazin and two supernumeraries.

"Any news, monsieur?" inquired the officer expectantly.

"None. She has not come back."

The blond countenance expressed surprise.

"I confess that astonishes me. Well, then—we will proceed."

In a few words he despatched his men on their business of searching the premises, having first demanded the keys to the *cave*, which the butler promptly produced. His manner towards the Portuguese was affable, creating the impression of enlisting assistance.

"One never knows what to expect in these cases," he remarked to the party at large. "One is obliged to allow for the most unlikely possibilities. As a matter of fact," and here he addressed Eduardo directly, "although most of this search is a pure formality, I have an idea that the young lady did come home without anyone's knowing it and went away again soon afterwards. I suppose that has not occurred to you?"

Thus appealed to, the butler was forced to give some sort of reply, which he did in an unresponsive fashion.

"No," he said shortly. "But I have not thought about it."

"I see," assented the inspector, unmoved, and got out his note-book and pencil. "However, as the stairs from the *rez de chaussée* emerge close to her room, and your room is on the other side of the apartment, would it not be possible for her to come in without your hearing her? Did you, in fact, hear her on the evenings when, for example, she was out late?"

"Not as a rule."

"Ah!—and now what was your first intimation of last night's trouble?"

For a second the butler's glance flickered in the Englishman's direction. Was there something furtive about it, or had Geoffrey's imagination become over-acute?

"I waked up with the maid shaking me. She was screaming out that madame's room was on fire, that she had tried to put it out, but—"

"Never mind the maid's part. The time is what I want to know."

"Can't say exactly. Something after one."

"And on your way to your mistress's room did you hear any sort of noise?"

Eduardo hesitated, thought a moment, then to Geoffrey's surprise said, "A moment later I did."

In spite of himself the young man leaned forward eagerly, his eyes on the heavy face. The inspector went on calmly:

"Indeed! What did the noise seem to be?"

"There was no seem about it. Someone was beating on this door here, nearly breaking it in. I've told all that to M. l'agent here," he added, motioning towards the little officer. "It was a gentleman from the third floor who was crossing the court, saw the flames through the window, and came up to wake us. While the maid and I tried to get madame out he ran down the avenue and gave the alarm."

"Ah—so it was he who gave the alarm? I did not know that."

"Yes—first he had a go at the telephone, but the line was dead."

"Were the engines quick in getting here?"

"Quick enough, but the fire had made a fair headway. You see, the maid did not wake up till her own room was filled with smoke. She was up with Madame most of the previous night, and slept heavily in consequence."

"Precisely. Well, that is about all I wanted to know." The Inspector ran an alert eye over his notes, then added suddenly, "By the way, can you account for a light being seen in the young lady's room at a quarter-past one this morning? About the time you were attempting the rescue, I should say."

If this news came as a shock, not a muscle of the swarthy face betrayed the fact. Only the small eyes grew watchful, and it was almost half a minute before their owner answered indifferently.

"It's the first I've heard of it. Maybe one of the women went in the room early in the evening and left the light on."

"Ah, that seems possible. Still, if mademoiselle took it into her head to go quietly out just then, I take it there was a good chance of her doing so unobserved?"

"I daresay," returned the man, who was now looking a little puzzled. "A good deal might have happened about then without our knowing."

"Naturally. That will do, I think. And now if you will conduct us to the maid we will see if she has anything more to suggest."

For the first time a trace of hesitation appeared in the confident manner.

"I'll ask the doctor if you can see her," he muttered, making off to the left. "He is with her now."

Feeling sure that the fellow was anxious to have a private word with his associate, Geoffrey shot a questioning look at Bazin, but the latter did not heed him. Already he was striding after the Portuguese with long easy steps.

"That is all right, my man: I will speak to the doctor myself. Is this the room?"

They had reached the door at the corner, giving on the largest bedroom, indeed, the one formerly occupied by Mme. Bender. The butler's thick hand was already on the knob, but with a firmness not at all discourteous, the inspector pushed it aside.

"Allow me," he said, and the following instant he and Geoffrey stood within, while by the simplest manoeuvre Eduardo had been left alone in the passage. Geoffrey fancied he caught a contraction of annoyance in the murky brown eyes as they watched the door close.

The two men paused for a moment, their eyes accustoming themselves to the semi-twilight, for the curtains of apple-green damask were drawn across the windows, excluding every ray of sunlight. The wide, irregular chamber, furnished with a delicate magnificence, had a general look of abandonment and neglect. The panelled walls showed here and there a faded rectangular patch, where at some time a picture had hung; the dressing-table, formed of a beautiful Venetian console, was bare of ornaments, as was the painted eighteenth-century escritoire opposite. The thick neutral-toned carpet showed streaks of dust.

In an alcove stood a wide decorated Italian bed, with a table beside it on which was a telephone instrument and an open medical case. A black-clad, pompous figure straightened up to take a survey of the intruders through thick glasses.

"Ah, monsieur," murmured the doctor, coming forward as he recognized Geoffrey. "What a truly shocking affair! Who could have foreseen such an event? That poor woman there"—he motioned to the bed—"is completely prostrated! Would not give up, however, until I threatened her with hospital. She has spirit."

"Badly injured?" asked the Inspector.

"Not physically. Some painful burns about the hands and arms. It is her nervous system which is suffering most, and no wonder. I have given her a small injection of morphia, and presently she will get some sleep. You wish to speak to her?"

"Only to ask her a few questions. I shall not be long."

The good man nodded. Watching him closely, Geoffrey was confirmed in his former impression, that here was a well-meaning, somewhat old-fashioned muddler—just the sort of physician Jeanne would be likely to choose for her purpose, accurately sizing him up as a complaisant, unsuspecting tool.

"This will prove a severe blow to the poor Mademoiselle West," went on the doctor, preparing to depart. "I thank God that she was away when it happened."

Geoffrey did not attempt to undeceive him. He allowed the other to press his hand with kindly solemnity, then shutting the door upon him, turned towards the alcove with a taut feeling of expectancy, letting his eyes rest upon the still figure lying upon the bed.

There was little light in the shadowed recess, and for a moment he could not tell whether the woman's eyes were open or closed. All he could make out was the outline of her body beneath the satin coverlet, the dark streaks of disordered hair above the sallow forehead, and her two stiff, white-swathed arms. Intense loathing seized him. The apparent fact that she was suffering from nervous collapse stirred in him no compassion, since her very state argued an abominable scheme to extort sympathy and divert suspicion from herself. She had taken everyone else in, but she had no power over him. He told himself that whether or not she had had any hand in spiriting Catherine away, she had at any rate one crime upon her soul, and that a peculiarly cold-blooded, diabolical one.

The inspector had switched on a reading-lamp beside the bed, and its shaded rays fell now upon the drawn and pinched countenance, revealing the expression of dull apathy Geoffrey had noticed earlier in the day. It was impossible to guess the thoughts that lay behind that indifferent stare, or to tell whether or not its owner could be trapped into any damaging admission.

In a few words the inspector explained his business. The prostrate woman let her opaque eyes rest upon his face for a full minute, then slowly turned them upon Geoffrey, her ragged brows contracted with puzzled incredulity.

"But surely monsieur was not serious in what he said this morning?" she murmured. "Even now I cannot understand. You say that mademoiselle came here last night?"

"That is what we have got to find out," replied Bazin soothingly. "We cannot tell yet what has happened. You were asleep up till the time your room became filled with smoke?"

"Yes, monsieur, I woke up half-suffocated."

"And before that—was everything as usual?"

She drew a long breath.

"Not quite, monsieur. Madame had a caller, a lady, who remained with her till seven o'clock. This lady had always an exciting effect on madame, and when she had gone last night I had great difficulty in quieting the patient."

Geoffrey's thoughts flew to Miss Cushing.

"What did you do?" inquired the inspector.

"I massaged her for a quarter of an hour, and at nine o'clock administered the usual dose of veronal prescribed by the doctor. At half-past ten I looked in and found her just dropping off to sleep. Then I went to bed."

"Have you any idea as to how the fire started?"

There was a long pause. Geoffrey listened with strained attention for the reply.

"I have, monsieur," replied the maid slowly. "Indeed, after what I saw when I first opened the door there can be no doubt as to the cause. The curtains of the bed caught in the flame of the candles on the wall."

"Candles!"

"Yes, monsieur. Madame must have waked up, got out of bed, and lighted the candles before the *prie-dieu*. I saw plainly the streams of melted wax. . . ."

"But surely it was dangerous to have candles so close to the draperies?"

"Most dangerous. Indeed, when I discovered recently that madame had been burning her candles during the night I took them away, fearing she might do herself an injury."

Watching closely, Geoffrey saw the still face darken with a look of accusation.

"That is what I am asking myself, monsieur. It is evident that unknown to me madame had obtained others, as well as matches. Someone must have given them to her secretly. That person, whoever it was, is responsible for madame's death . . ."

The cold deliberation of this statement caused both listeners to stiffen. Here was something totally unexpected.

"But is it possible that anyone knowing madame's condition could have done so foolish a thing?"

There was the faintest perceptible shrug of the supine shoulders.

"Ah, monsieur, you do not know what I have had to fight against with those who refused to recognize madame's mental state, and set themselves to humour her whims. . . ."

"You mean to suggest that the caller yesterday brought candles with her and helped madame to hide them?"

Another pause, while Geoffrey hung breathless upon the next words, which came hesitatingly:

"Ah, no, monsieur, I cannot believe it was the friend I mentioned. She is a lady of a certain age, who though sometimes unfortunate in her speech would, I believe, know better than to commit such an indiscretion. No, monsieur, in my opinion it was someone else—someone younger and less responsible . . ."

"You mean?"

"The young lady you tell me is missing . . . Mademoiselle West . . ."

Geoffrey made an angry movement forward, the cool infamy of the suggestion acting on him like the prick of a spur. Catherine responsible for the victim's death! Even as his lips parted to voice a furious protest he caught a warning glance from the Frenchman's eye, and subsided, breathing hard.

"That statement implies a serious accusation," Bazin replied somewhat sternly. "You are aware of what you are saying?"

The lined face remained inscrutable.

"I do not think that mademoiselle realized the gravity of her action, consequently I accuse her of nothing but thoughtlessness. But if I am questioned in court as to the cause of my mistress's death . . ." She allowed her sentence to end in ominous silence, and with an air of exhaustion closed her eyes.

Geoffrey's fingers twitched, but the inspector proceeded, unperturbed.

"Listen to me," he said, referring to his notes. "If the young lady did reach the apartment last night, she must have done so shortly after midnight. Well, then—at a quarter-past one there was a light in her room."

The eyes opened abruptly. Geoffrey saw that their dullness had vanished, giving place to a sharp attention. For a tense moment they searched the speaker's face.

"*En effet!*" The words were muttered under her breath with a mixture of wonderment and cogitation. "Is it true what you are telling me?"

"It is an established fact. This gentleman here was outside in his car, saw the window lit up and a shadow across the blind. Then the light was put out."

With a jerk Jeanne turned her head and stared at the Englishman in silence. She seemed to be thinking deeply.

"*En effet!*" she repeated slowly, as though some new light began to break over her. "Now I see why you are asking me all these questions. So she was here! . . . One might almost suppose, monsieur, that she was hiding in her room waiting for a chance to steal away unobserved. . . ."

"Why unobserved? Have you anything in your mind?"

She did not answer at once, her dark eyes still narrowed with their look of concentrated thought. When she spoke it was with halting deliberation.

"It is difficult to say, monsieur. . . . But the idea has this moment occurred to me that perhaps—who knows?—mademoiselle discovered the fire before I was aware of it, realized that it was the consequence of her own folly and—you follow me, monsieur?—took herself off in order to avoid the result of an inquiry. Mind, I know nothing, I. But if the unfortunate young lady saw at a glance that it was impossible to save madame . . ."

Geoffrey never knew how the interview terminated, nor by what exercise of diplomacy Bazin managed to get him out of the bedroom without making a scene. All he recalled was that somehow or other he was outside in the passage, struggling to throw off a firm grasp which detained him by the shoulder. Through a red haze of anger he heard a voice saying:

"Gently, monsieur! There is nothing to be gained by violence. Do not speak now—follow me to the back of the apartment."

With an effort at control the young man allowed himself to be led along to the left and into an unused room, the door of which the inspector closed. Then his indignation burst its bonds.

"You heard what that devil said?" he cried in stifled accents. "You heard? She has had the audacity to assert that mademoiselle—"

He broke off, dimly aware of a change in his companion's manner. The blue eyes level with his held a shade of uncertainty, one rough hand upraised itself to twist the ends of the blond moustache.

"Monsieur," came the reply, hesitatingly and with a slight hint of embarrassment, "either that woman in there is exceedingly resourceful, or else—" he paused.

"Else what?"

"Or else she has hit upon what very possibly may be the true explanation of mademoiselle's absence."

Geoffrey's eyes blazed at him.

"My God! You don't mean to tell me you believe her story!"

"Monsieur, I do not believe anything till we have absolute proof that the young lady returned last night. Remember our first two theories. But if we find that she was here, then what we have just heard suggests the happiest way out of the difficulty."

"*Happiest?*"

"Naturally—for in that event she is at this moment perfectly safe, only dreading to come forward . . ."

Thunderstruck, Geoffrey stared at him, temporarily deprived of speech.

CHAPTER THIRTY-FIVE

GEOFFREY was still trying to master his outraged feelings when his companion turned his head towards the passage and lifted a warning hand.

"Let us not speak of this here, monsieur. We can discuss it all better at the Commissariat, if you will accompany me there." Whereupon he led the way briskly towards the front entrance, leaving the Englishman no choice but to bottle up his indignation as best he could and follow submissively.

As they passed the ruined passage one of the two subordinates came forward from his inspection of the debris and spoke a few words to his superior. The latter, in turn, addressed Geoffrey in an undertone, first glancing round to see that they were not overheard.

"It seems there are certain personal effects of the young lady in her bedroom. Our problem is to decide whether any of them were taken by her to Fontainebleau on her visit. Can you help us?"

Geoffrey considered, and shook his head.

"The best person to know about them is my sister, who I believe is in town this afternoon. Shall I try to get in touch with her and ask her to come here?"

"If you please, monsieur. You can telephone from the rue Mesnil."

Outside, a low-built grey car, strong and efficient-looking, was drawn up close to the kerb. Into it the inspector climbed, taking his place at the wheel, and motioning to Geoffrey to take the seat beside him. As they drove away the young man cast a backward glance at the building and touched his companion on the sleeve. In the window of the room occupied by the maid stood Eduardo, staring into the street below, his gaze directed, not upon the car, but at the blue-clad figure of the workman busy on one of the chestnut-trees.

"Is that one of your men?"

Bazin nodded.

"If you had taken the trouble to look out of the kitchen windows you would have seen a brick-mason, tinkering with the rear wall. Our friend seems interested. If he has anything on his conscience, he will not venture out while the daylight lasts. . . . You know, of course, that the deceased's body has been removed to the Palais de Justice? However, I took care not to allow the servants to guess our intention. They believe the body has been taken to a mortuary to await the usual inquest."

"I wonder if the post-mortem will reveal anything?" The inspector gave a disparaging shrug.

"Who knows? I warn you, monsieur, that they may find nothing worse than veronal. To employ actual poison would be running a serious risk."

"Unless the criminals reckoned on the body being too badly burned to discover anything," retorted Geoffrey. "I have an idea the intervention of that *locataire* came at an inopportune moment, and that the intention was to let the fire go on for another quarter of an hour before the alarm was given."

"Possibly. In any case we shall soon know what the Médecin Légiste has to say."

Geoffrey said nothing. His concern as to Mme. Bender's mode of death was completely overshadowed by anxiety regarding the missing girl, his feelings at the moment chaotic and contradictory. That the man beside him could have read in the maid's cool assertion anything other than a fabrication of lies so astounded him that his brain still recoiled from the shock. Catherine—Catherine, to have perpetrated so appalling a stupidity and, having done so, to flee from the consequences of her act without a word of warning to the occupants of the burning flat! The suggestion was so monstrous that his ire rose afresh against any being capable of according it serious consideration.

Still, the Inspector knew nothing of Catherine's character, nor for that matter of Jeanne's, and the theory in the abstract was plausible. No stranger could be expected to see in it a quick-witted schemer's ruse to cast her own weight of guilt on innocent shoulders. At the same time the very fact that the woman had dared to put forward this dastardly explanation argued an inner knowledge of her own safety in so doing. In other words she must know that the person she accused would not be able to contradict her.

At the door of the Commissariat the Inspector left Geoffrey to do his telephoning and went to inquire if any report had come in from the taxi-driver who presumably picked up the missing girl at the Gare Fontainebleau-Avron. Ten minutes later he returned to find the English-man pacing the floor.

"No news has come in," he announced. "But it is a little early to look for any. However, I have started a new line of inquiry which I hope may lead to results." He hesitated, glancing at the young man's haggard features. "In short, I want to find out if anyone answering to Mademoi-selle's description quitted Paris by a morning train."

Geoffrey's eyes flashed.

"If that is what you have in mind, I can assure you your efforts are wasted. Mademoiselle West is not trying to hide from us."

There was the ghost of a smile in the Frenchman's practical blue eyes.

"In any case, there is no harm in making sure," he replied amicably, and dropped the subject. "You have located your sister?"

"She is on her way to meet us at the apartment," Geoffrey informed him shortly.

The other's manner made him uncomfortable. It hinted at a secret belief that Catherine's disappearance was not only voluntary but had something of duplicity in it; that, indeed, the poor girl had some reason of her own for keeping out of the way. Nothing he could say would refute the unspoken charge, he could only chafe inwardly.

"Now, monsieur, I have another little matter to attend to on our way back. The deceased had a car. I obtained the address of the garage from the concierge, and I propose to give instructions that on no account is the car to be taken out."

Geoffrey looked at him quickly.

"You think the butler may want to use it?"

"Either he or the *notaire*, Blom—although I cannot say if the latter has a driving-licence. It is only a chance, but we may as well be on our guard."

As they drove rapidly round the Place Victor Hugo and into the Avenue Malakoff, Geoffrey acquainted his companion with the facts concerning the Portuguese's sortie that morning.

"It is certain that he held some sort of conference with Blom, though his subsequent movements appeared harmless enough. All he did was to pay a call on one of the concierges lower down the avenue."

Bazin listened attentively.

"The fact that he took the first opportunity to see his friend is certainly suggestive. I congratulate you, monsieur, on having had him watched. Ah, here we are!"

Turning into a narrow mews, he sounded his horn in front of a large garage. A youngish man with tousled hair and a face stroked with oil came out to meet them, wiping his hands on a piece of cotton-waste. To him the inspector stated his business.

"You understand? This car—a Rolls, is it not?—is in no circumstances to be allowed out of the garage. If anyone calls for it, you are to give a point-blank refusal and communicate at once with the Commissariat."

The proprietor nodded, but looked slightly surprised.

"Certainly, monsieur, I will carry out your instructions—when the car is returned."

"Returned! Do you mean it is not here?"

"No, monsieur. It was taken out two days ago. I understood it was going into the country for the week-end."

The occupants of the grey car exchanged startled glances, and Geoffrey swore under his breath.

"You are sure of this?"

"But yes, monsieur. I know the car you speak of well. For the past few months there has been no regular chauffeur, but it is sometimes used by a manservant—a Spaniard, I think he is. It was he who called for it on Thursday."

There was nothing to be done. As they backed out of the mews the Inspector's bland face was contracted with annoyance.

"This looks as though they had stolen a march on us," he muttered. "I don't like the look of it. I daresay I could find the car, but it might mean searching half the garages of Paris. On the whole I am afraid we must let it go."

This development deepened Geoffrey's conviction of a pre-arranged plan. It looked as though Eduardo, foreseeing the chance of things going wrong, had removed the Rolls to some locality where he was unknown, in order to facilitate a quick get-away.

Well, things had gone wrong, although perhaps the servants were as yet unaware of that fact. In the circumstances they would probably sit tight, knowing that any false move would jeopardize the stake for which they had played.

Catherine's absence was another matter, the most maddening feature of which was the complete uncertainty surrounding it. What if the servants were not involved? As Bazin had pointed out, there were other explanations. But for the tell-tale shadow on the blind Geoffrey would have been ready to picture the poor girl as the victim of robbery and murder, perpetrated either in the train, or in the taxi later on. Perhaps before the day was over her body would be found.

Elspeth came out of the *loge* to meet them, her fresh colour faded, her whole manner betraying anxiety.

"Have you heard from her?" she demanded, grasping her brother's arm.

He shook his head. She drew in a dismayed breath.

"If only I could make some suggestion! I have racked my brain. Could something have frightened her so that she was afraid to come here? She disliked the servants, you know."

"We are absolutely in the dark. All we know is that both the maid and butler deny having seen her. Come along, the police are waiting."

They overtook the Inspector at the lift, and a few seconds later the three were admitted to the apartment by the little sergeant, who was preparing to depart. The pair who had conducted the search came forward, the taller of the pair, a finely built Auvergnais, acting as spokesman.

"We have gone over the whole building from top to bottom, monsieur," he announced in a confidential tone, "not omitting the *cave* and the roof. Nothing has come to light barring a cabin-trunk in the box-room, marked with the lady's initials. We broke it open, but it is quite empty. There are only those few personal belongings we should like to get an opinion on."

The party made their way to the distant bedroom Catherine had occupied and, taking a key from his pocket, the Auvergnais unlocked the door.

The afternoon sun flooded the disordered room, revealing a heap of clothing on the bed, empty drawers pulled out to their farthest extent, and cupboard doors gaping wide. Motes danced in the bars of brilliant light which the yellow, *toile*-walls rendered the more dazzling.

"If madame will take a look at these?" suggested Bazin, motioning to the confused mass of apparel.

One by one Elspeth picked up and examined a frock of beige kasha, a tweed skirt and jumper to match, an old cardigan, an afternoon gown of parchment-coloured velvet and two evening-dresses. The onlookers watching tensely, saw her reject the lot, then turn to a smaller collection of underclothing, delicate garments of *crêpe de Chine*, some primrose yellow, some pale apricot.

"No," she said decidedly, "she had none of these with her. I am certain, because I helped her pack."

"And the toilet articles?"

There were not many of these, merely a few books, an almost empty powder-boat, and a small pot of cream for chapped hands. Again Elspeth shook her head, instinct telling her that here was the unimportant flotsam one leaves behind. Then she turned towards the open cupboard, where the squirrel coat hung lonely from the rod, let her eye wander over the shoes at the bottom and the two last winter's hats on the shelf.

"Do you recognize this, madame?"

It was the tall Auvergnais who addressed her, extending his broad palm, in the centre of which lay a tiny red cylinder.

"*Une tube à rouge*, madame—we found it lying against the wall under the bed."

Elspeth gave a sharp exclamation.

"Catherine's lipstick!" she cried, her eyes meeting Geoffrey's. "I saw her use it when she was changing her dress to go."

Geoffrey's hand shook as he reached for the lipstick and examined it. Crimson morocco, outlined in gold.

"I know it, too," he muttered. "I was with her the day she bought it, in the Trois Quartiers. . . ."

The three men were eyeing him eagerly. He repeated his remark in French, his manner betraying excitement.

"But are you sure it is the same?" inquired Bazin. "Sometimes ladies possess more than one of these things."

Elspeth took it again and removed the cap. The dark red composition within appeared scarcely used.

"I can't be absolutely positive," she faltered. "She may have had two alike. . . ."

Brother and sister continued to gaze as though fascinated. The little object seemed to both a silent witness of its owner's presence in the room: yet, as the inspector had suggested, it was not conclusive proof, since it was possible Catherine had owned an extra one of the same make. There was a moment of tantalizing suspense.

Once more exploring the room, Elspeth's eyes came to rest on the despoiled cupboard.

"What is in that?" she asked suddenly, indicating the flowered hat-box.

"*Encore un chapeau, madame. Je vous le montrerai—*" and the Auvergnais removed the carton, setting it upon the bed.

The next instant Elspeth uttered a cry.

"Geoff! Look, look!"

Inside the box, resting upon smooth layers of tissue-paper, was a small green felt hat. She snatched it forth tremblingly, turned it round on her hand.

"Don't you see? It's hers, the one she was wearing. Oh, there's not the least doubt of it! I can prove it to you. See here,"—and displaying the lining, she pointed to a black silk tag sewn inside, on which were embroidered the words "Jane-Mary, Boston."

Geoffrey stared transfixed. He, too, knew this hat, had noticed it on many occasions. The memory of its narrow brim hugging the oval cheek on one side and upturned on the other, brought a choking sensation to his throat. Instantly he turned to the inspector, his entire manner charged with electricity.

"Monsieur, we need look no longer, here is the proof! This is the hat mademoiselle wore when she left Fontainebleau!"

For a second there was no sound in the room save the quickened breathing of the startled hearers.

CHAPTER THIRTY-SIX

BAZIN was the first to break the silence, his eyes ablaze in his sunburned face.

"Madame there can be no mistake about this?"

"None whatever. I tell you this is the hat she was wearing when my husband put her into the train last night. It is one she brought from America."

"She was here, then. She came home and went away again soon afterwards, leaving nothing behind her but her hat and this." He indicated the lipstick. His tone was one of puzzled reflection. "Why her hat?"

"She could have worn another one," suggested Elspeth impatiently. "I do not know what other hats she has."

"Then let us say she changed her hat. But does that help us to a solution?"

On the contrary it deepened the mystery. Blank looks met the question, and it was some seconds before Elspeth spoke, with a trace of eagerness.

"If she took the trouble to put on a different hat, don't you see what it may mean? That for some reason she changed her mind about spending the night here, carried her bags down again just as they were, and went somewhere else."

"And the *tube à rouge*, madame?"

"That must have fallen out of her bag, and she did not bother to search for it."

"It suggests she was anxious to get away."

"Exactly my opinion," agreed Elspeth quickly. "Don't you see, Geoffrey? She must have gone of her own accord, else why should she take off one hat and put on another?"

Her brother continued to stare at the tell-tale head-gear. Its presence did not argue haste, but a certain deliberation, yet he was unconvinced.

"We don't know that she did do that. Besides, if all this is true, why don't we hear from her?" he objected stubbornly.

"But think, my dear—if she met those friends of hers this morning she may have spent the day sight-seeing with them, and even now may not know about Mme. Bender. Depend upon it, we'll soon have news."

"She knew I was going to drive out to Fontainebleau this afternoon and bring her back."

He glanced at his watch, the hands of which marked a quarter to five. By now he would have been on his way.

"It looks damned odd," he remarked stonily. "It must have taken some strong motive to make her quit the place with her luggage at past one in the morning."

"Ah, *ça!*" the inspector waved an expressive hand round the disarranged room. "I agree there must have been some unforeseen happening to account for so sudden a departure. Does madame know the explanation offered by the maid?" he inquired, sinking his voice.

"The maid? What does she think?" demanded Elspeth, searching the four faces.

Before Geoffrey had conquered his obvious reluctance to divulge what was so distasteful to him, the inspector threw open the door and scanned the passage in both directions. No one was in sight.

"Now then, monsieur," he said with a slight nod.

"It's simply this, if you must know: Jeanne suggests that perhaps Catherine found out about the fire and Mme. Bender's death before anyone else was aware of it, that she got into a panic and took herself off because"—here he hesitated painfully—"because she was terrified lest blame should attach to her."

His sister gasped in bewilderment.

"Blame! Why, what on earth—"

"You see, she insinuates that it was Catherine who supplied the poor woman with the candles which caused the fire."

"Oh!" She stifled a horrified cry. "Do you believe that?"

"Not for a moment," replied Geoffrey between set teeth. "It is not in the least like Catherine to do either one thing or the other."

There was an uncomfortable silence. He could see Elspeth grappling with this new idea, her eyes narrowed in thought.

"I wonder?" she whispered slowly. "Geoff—you don't know. She might have done it, in utter innocence. Remember, she did not believe Mme. Bender was insane. And supposing she did discover what was happening, mightn't she have been so overwhelmed by the shock that she lost her head completely? Her one idea may have been to rush away and hide, pretend she had not been here at all. One can't say how one would behave if faced with such a crisis."

He did not reply. Put into words, the thing sounded remarkably plausible. The inspector made a sign to show his agreement.

"Precisely, madame. One still does not altogether grasp the meaning of this"—and he indicated the hat—"but it is fairly clear to me that the young lady is well and safe, only does not wish her presence here last night to become known. It would not astonish me, monsieur, if before many hours you had some news of her. Probably she has gone to an hotel and will communicate with you later on. If she should care to assume total ignorance of this affair"—he paused with a tolerant shrug—"then the less said about our discoveries the better."

A steely light had come into the young man's eyes.

"Does it not occur to you," he said slowly, "that if what you suggest is the case, she may not turn up at all?"

His sister stared at him frowning, then exclaimed in sudden dismay:

"You don't mean she might . . . oh, no, Geoffrey! She wouldn't do anything so mad!"

"Why not? If she believed herself responsible for her cousin's death?"

Bazin's quick intelligence took in the implication.

"Ah, hardly, monsieur! It takes a great deal to bring one to suicide. No need to exaggerate matters at this stage of the game."

However, the horrible idea had taken hold of Geoffrey so that he could not throw it off. No one but himself knew to what extent Catherine had brooded over her relative's situation, and had striven to put it right. If, after all her planning and contriving, she had suddenly been faced with last night's horrible revelation, who could say what the result might be? All these apparently contradictory evidences of hasty departure might point to one dreadful conclusion. Yet, even as his distraught mind grappled with its new obsession, the vision of Jeanne's enigmatic eyes came before him, and he asked himself if, against his will, he were not being made the dupe of some cleverly conceived infamy. . . .

He watched the inspector place the lipstick in an envelope, seal it up and consign it to an inside pocket. Then, rousing himself, he inquired what arrangements had been made for guarding the apartment after nightfall.

"Ah, yes, monsieur! I shall have two of my men posted in the buildings at the back and side, and I myself intend to pass the night in the apartment directly opposite, across the avenue."

"May I share watches with you?"

"Willingly, monsieur. Shall we meet at the Commissariat at eight o'clock? That is to say, if nothing is heard from mademoiselle in the meantime."

"But you may hear, Geoffrey," put in Elspeth quickly. "I can't help thinking there is some foolish mistake about all this which may be cleared up at any moment. Those friends of hers she was to meet—she may be with them now, sight-seeing somewhere. Had you thought of that?"

There was nothing he had not considered, but in spite of all a leaden pall lay upon his heart, crushing out hope. A voice whispered that he would never hear from Catherine again.

They quitted the room, which was again locked behind them, and retraced their steps through the silent passage to the front entrance, where Elspeth and Geoffrey took leave of the police officers.

"Leave everything to me, monsieur," murmured Bazin reassuringly. "By this evening I hope to have something cheerful to report."

At the glass doors of the *loge* they came upon a familiar figure, no less a person than the office factotum, Henri, at that moment shuffling forward to meet them. His wrinkled face held a trace of unusual excitement.

"Ah, Monsieur Geoffrey, you have not gone! Here is a telegram just come for you at the rue Auber. Your father has sent it on."

Geoffrey snatched the blue paper, the seal of which had already been broken, glanced at the contents, then uttered a sharp cry.

"My God!" he exclaimed. "Elspeth, you were right! It's from Catherine!" and he thrust the flimsy slip into her hand.

She devoured it with eager eyes. Upon the form was scrawled the following words:

"Overcome by frightful news unable go out but will telephone you to-morrow and explain my absence do not trouble yourself all goes well with me Catherine."

The wave of relief that swept over Geoffrey engulfed all reason. Voiceless, he could only stare stupidly at the jumbled sentences, reading in them a reprieve from utter despair. Catherine was safe, he would soon see her again. The knowledge overwhelmed him.

Elspeth's hand on his arm brought him to his senses.

"Geoffrey! It's too marvellous! I can hardly believe it!"

There was an hysterical tremor in her voice. "Oh! to think nothing is wrong, after all!"

"Are you so astonished?" he demanded suspiciously. "A moment ago you were positive we should hear from her."

"I know I said that," she replied a little guiltily. "But—well, I wasn't so sure as I sounded. Uncertainty is so awful—one thinks of such appalling things."

He nodded. What use now to admit that since noon today he had been haunted by the fear that Catherine had met a violent death? As his strained nerves relaxed he felt a foolish desire to laugh, to shout aloud, and at the same time realized that he was extraordinarily tired. He had

had nothing to eat all day since his morning coffee, but the fact had altogether escaped his notice.

"Where is she now? Does she give an address?" Together they examined the form, but beyond the message it bore nothing beyond the hour when it was handed in—three o'clock—and the words. "Hôtel des Postes."

"That's queer," Geoffrey muttered. "Why doesn't she tell us where she is?"

"Too upset to think of it, I suppose. It's not really strange. I should say she went to some small hotel last night, one where there are no room-telephones, that she is simply prostrated by the shock, and only able to collect her thoughts sufficiently to realize we may be worried about her. She's got the concierge to send this wire."

"I daresay you're right." He continued to stare at the blue slip as though striving to force some additional information out of it. "Oh, well, the important thing is that she's found. Here's the inspector now."

He turned back to announce the welcome tidings, translating the telegram into French for the other's benefit. Bazin's blue eyes widened with relief.

"Well, well, monsieur! I felicitate you. The young lady has given you a bad quarter of an hour, but, *voilà!* the mystery is cleared up, as I hoped it would be."

"I am not so sure of that. I can't help feeling there is something odd behind it."

From the tactful avoidance of his eye it was plain that his opinion was shared by his two companions. During the uncomfortable pause which followed, the inspector studied the message and made a few notes in his book.

"I will look into this, monsieur, and see what I can find out, since you are no doubt still somewhat anxious, though, as mademoiselle promises to communicate with you tomorrow, you will not have long to remain in suspense. As for the other affair—" He left the sentence unfinished, and with one accord the three moved through the archway and into the street before resuming the conversation.

Geoffrey detected a note of uncertainty in the other's voice, and thought he could guess the reason. Bazin was thinking that since Catherine's disappearance had turned out a false alarm, the rest of their suspicions might prove equally groundless. He spoke decidedly:

"Whatever may be the truth about this," he said, motioning to the slip of paper, "nothing is altered in regard to what happened last night. We had ample reason for starting an investigation, and I should think it extremely likely those servants are going to be indicted for murdering their mistress. Meanwhile, they are still at liberty. You see what I mean?"

"Perfectly, monsieur. You need have no fear; I shall not abandon watch of the house. However, there is now no need for you to sacrifice your night's rest. You will do as you think best, naturally, but if you decide not to come this evening I shall proceed without you."

"One thing more: do you think we ought to let the servants know we have heard from mademoiselle?"

"I shall inform them now. Undoubtedly our best purpose is served by setting their minds at rest."

They separated, Bazin returning to carry out the intention just stated, the brother and sister setting out aimlessly in the direction of the Avenue Kléber, both wrapped in thought.

Now that Geoffrey had grown accustomed to the shock of joy, he found himself grappling with doubts and questions. The problem was only partly solved, his mind still in utter confusion. A mad impulse seized him to begin at once a tour of all the hotels in the district surrounding the Hôtel des Postes, but such a proceeding was manifestly stupid. It would be like hunting for a needle in a haystack. Presently he pulled himself together sufficiently to inquire of Elspeth where she wished to go.

"Home," she replied. "I would have stayed the night, but now there is no need to, is there?"

"I'll take you to the station," he murmured mechanically, and raised his hand to stop an approaching taxi.

A little later, seated beside his sister, he leaned forward with a moody expression, chin in hands.

"I am not satisfied about this," he declared morosely. "It has a deuced queer look. . . . It is not like Catherine to funk anything, yet that appears to be what she's done. I wish to God I could go and see her now. . . ."

Elspeth eyed him shrewdly and with kindly impatience.

"Geoff, Geoff! Why can't you wipe the whole thing out? If the poor child made some fearful mistake and doesn't want us to find out—"

"You keep harping on that!" he cried, as though stung. "How do you know she did? You have only the word of a woman who's proved herself a thief and a liar, and may be something far worse. There is only one fact we can be sure about, which is that Catherine came home and went away again."

She sighed tolerantly.

"At any rate, Geoff, Clement didn't take her disappearance very seriously, nor did father. Both of them thought there was some mistake about it, that she would turn up after a bit, and it seems they were right. Not that I blame you for getting frightened."

There was nothing to say. Perhaps it was true that his infatuation had played havoc with his common-sense.

"You're worn out," she said suddenly. "You look absolutely finished. Promise me you'll go straight home and get a bath and some dinner. You need both."

Following her glance, he saw for the first time the streaks of smut upon his hands, and realized that his collar was wilted.

"You will do as I say?" she urged.

"I suppose I may as well."

"Let me know what happens," she added as the taxi swerved into the open space before the Gare. "And whatever you do don't bother Catherine about this affair. Let her alone."

She waved her hand and was gone. He remained staring after her in a daze from which the driver's gruff voice presently roused him. Then he drew a deep breath, and with a sense of flatness and lethargy, got back into the taxi and gave his own address.

CHAPTER THIRTY-SEVEN

GEOFFREY'S father had read Catherine's message before sending it on, consequently at dinner there was little to discuss. The meal passed in strained silence, Geoffrey consuming food mechanically, while the other scanned with a gloomy frown the evening papers' accounts of the fire.

Through the open windows a breath of sun-drenched air stole in from across the Luxembourg Gardens; the tall candles flickering on the table filled the young man's mind with an uneasy suggestion, driving home the fact that while his worst fears were allayed, he was still restless and dissatisfied.

If only Catherine had told him where she was! For the life of him he could not regard the omission as accidental. At one moment he imagined sensitively that she shrank from seeing him for some personal reason, at another attributed her motive to a desire for concealment. The occasional probing glances directed at him by his father goaded him to irritability, for it was not difficult to read their cause.

The coffee arriving, Macadam pushed back his chair and thrust a cigar into his mouth at an irascible angle.

"Whatever Miss West's reasons may be for her behaviour," he pronounced gratingly, "she has given us a deuced deal of trouble and made us look a couple of fools as well. If you enjoy this sort of thing, it's more than I do."

The sarcasm flicked Geoffrey on the raw.

"We may as well reserve comment till we know the facts," he retorted curtly.

With a shrug the old man wadded the newspapers into a ball and strode from the room, reappearing for a moment to toss an envelope in his son's direction.

"There's your report about the handwriting. The notes were forgeries right enough—though much good it does to know it now! The next thing will be the discovery that the pearls are missing, so we can arrest that woman for theft, whether or not there's any foundation for a more serious charge."

It was with feelings bordering on complete indifference that Geoffrey read the enclosure. Indeed, so absorbed was he in his own contradictory emotions, he did not realize to what extent his father's ill temper was occasioned by a sense of failure in averting a calamity.

Much as he wished to ignore Jeanne's detestable theory, he could not deny that Catherine's present conduct was strange. The idea that a cloud of doubt might for ever hang over the past twenty-four hours was loathsome to him. Then the thought of her fearless eyes and frank honesty rushed before him as a reproach, and he tried resolutely to postpone all conjecture till to-morrow.

To-morrow—!

All at once, with a pang, he understood why he was so disturbed. Was he really going to see her? The vagueness of her message held something elusive, a quality summed up in a repetition of the phrase, "not like Catherine." That was it—it was not like her. What was it she had said?

Taking the telegram from his pocket, he studied it closely, once more trying to discover some hidden meaning.

"Overcome by frightful news unable to go out but will telephone you to-morrow to explain my absence do not trouble yourself all goes well with me . . ."

Awkwardly put, that. He wondered now why she had employed the expression, "do not trouble yourself." Much more natural to have said "Don't worry." The reflexive verb sounded oddly un-English. He pondered it, then passed on to the following sentence.

Suddenly he frowned, staring hard. Here was a combination of words he would not have expected an American to use. Surely the obvious thing to say was, "Don't worry, I'm all right."

"All goes well with me." He repeated the stilted form, annoyed and exasperated. What did it suggest? At first the significance escaped him, then in a flash he knew. Why—it was pure French construction! Of course! Its equivalent was the phrase *"tout va bien."*

For a few seconds he remained stupefied, his brain in confusion. Then out of chaos emerged an awful, crashing truth. This telegram was not composed by Catherine at all. It was the concoction of some foreigner—someone with an imperfect knowledge of English idioms. It bore two glaring marks of falsity.

The revelation stunned him. How had he been such an unmitigated ass? Catherine would not, could not, construct sentences like those, the thing was impossible.

His fatuous security tumbled about him like a house of cards. Catherine might or might not be alive, but instinct warned him that all hope of recovering her was lost unless immediate action were taken. His chair clattered to the parquet behind him as, leaping to his feet, he made a bolt for the door.

He was still cursing his blindness when, at the rue Mesnil, he met the inspector just setting forth for his night's vigil.

"So you are coming with me after all, monsieur? I promise you it may prove a boring affair. Why—has anything new occurred?" he ended in surprise as he took in the Englishman's distraught bearing.

"Look at this again!" cried Geoffrey, thrusting the telegram under his eyes. "It is worded in such a way that it could not possibly have been written by Mademoiselle West. I don't know how I was such a fool as not to spot it at once," and he hastily attempted to explain the two paradoxes contained in the message.

Bazin listened with an altered face.

"You are sure of this? The English language is a sealed book to me. Perhaps you had better compare that paper with the original, which I obtained an hour ago from the Hôtel des Postes," he added, producing a pencil-written form. "None of the employees could recall who handed it in, but you will probably know if it is in the young lady's hand."

Eagerly Geoffrey seized the form, only to see what at first glance appeared to be Catherine's writing. He stared nonplussed, then hunting through his pockets, found the note sent him several days ago from

Fontainebleau. Examining the two specimens, he decided that one was a creditable but faulty imitation of the other.

"They are not the same," he pronounced positively. "See, all her own o's are separated from the other letters, while in the telegram they are joined on. Besides, there is an angularity about this writing which is distinctively Continental."

Bazin's blue eyes had a hard brightness.

"I agree. They were never written by the same person." He fingered the slip with manifest excitement. "You are right, monsieur. This telegram is the work of someone anxious to put us off the scent, and for to-night, mind—since the deception would surely have been revealed when you failed to hear anything further."

"Then you think that whatever is planned will take place before morning?"

"I do. I was wiser than I knew when I arranged to have that house watched."

His face was grave as he got into the waiting car and motioned to Geoffrey to take the seat beside him. In another second they were circling the Place Victor Hugo.

"I have some more news for you, monsieur. I have now heard from the taxi-driver who brought mademoiselle home from the Gare. He declares that he set her down at the private entrance at about ten minutes past twelve last night, and as he is able to furnish a satisfactory account of himself for several hours afterwards, we can safely eliminate him from the inquiry. So far no other driver has come forward, which leads us to assume that while your friend arrived at the apartment, she did not leave again in the way that has been suggested."

As Geoffrey listened to this confirmation of his worst fears, dread lay like a leaden weight at the pit of his stomach.

"Furthermore, I have instituted a search at some thirty hotels in the rue de Rivoli district, and while there may still remain some small place we have overlooked, it begins to appear a useless quest."

"Who do you suppose sent the telegram? Was it Blom?"

"Not in person, certainly, for he has been under strict surveillance all the afternoon, and I have my man's word for the fact that he has gone nowhere, except across the court to his fiancée's apartment."

"He may have sent it by one of Honorine's work-girls."

"A risk, in case of embarrassing inquiries. Your name is sufficiently unusual to impress itself on a French person's memory. I am inclined to believe he employed a public messenger."

Geoffrey considered this.

"He would be bound to take some risk in order to telegraph at all, but from his point of view it would be a small one. Remember, he has not the slightest reason up till now to think that any of us is aware of his existence."

"Ah, in that case he may well consider himself safe. Certainly, if you had not had the good fortune to discover his connection with the affair, last night's happening would have been regarded as a tragic accident, with blame attaching to no one, least of all to him. As things stand, what with mademoiselle's disappearance and this deliberate attempt to make it appear a voluntary withdrawal, I now see that the situation looks distinctly serious."

Geoffrey forced himself to utter the question which was gnawing into him like a canker.

"You believe, then, that mademoiselle may be dead?"

The inspector bit his lip.

"It may be as well to accustom oneself to the idea, monsieur," he said in a low voice. "It seems extremely probable that she has been murdered because she is a dangerous witness, and that the criminals are merely waiting till a suitable moment to dispose of her body."

They had slowed down in turning off the Avenue Henri Martin. The rays of an arc-light shone full on the young man's face, revealing its ghastly pallor.

"I suppose we can doing nothing but watch?" he suggested, his tone deadened with repression.

"Not for to-night. If nothing occurs, then to-morrow we shall have to take definite action, but so long as a bare hope remains of the young lady's being alive we must tread warily."

Leading the way, he turned into a narrow passage squeezed between the rows of buildings, passed through a doorway and began to ascend a winding stair, lit by a dim wall-bracket.

"This is the rear entrance to the house we want, monsieur. It is better not to use the front way, for fear of being seen."

On the first floor he tapped upon a door, which was opened by a middle-aged *femme de chambre*.

"Will you kindly inform M. le Commandant that Inspector Bazin is here?"

The woman nodded.

"If you will come this way, messieurs, I will conduct you to the room monsieur has placed at your disposal."

Following her along a passage, they found themselves in a small study, the walls of which, above compactly filled bookshelves, were ornamented by a collection of arms arranged in a coruscating pattern—spears, poniards and scimitars of an interesting variety. Brown velvet curtains covered the window, while deep chairs and a sofa were grouped about a low table bearing smoking materials, among which were a narghileh and a Turkish chibouk.

When the servant withdrew, Bazin informed his companion that they were the guests of M. le Commandant Jules Heller, well known as an authority on modern warfare. Geoffrey recognized the name, one frequently seen signed to articles in *Le Gaulois* and similar journals. As he looked restlessly round at the weapon-hung walls a clock somewhere in the flat struck a single metallic *ping*. A glance at his watch told him it was half-past eight.

The door opened to admit their host, a small, bald-headed man, one-armed and with a glass eye. His spare body was attired in a velvet jacket, the lapel of which bore the tiny red ribbon of the *Légion d'Honneur*.

"Good evening, messieurs!" The Commandant bowed with exquisite courtesy, his lone eye beaming with welcome. "I trust this study is suitable for your purpose? It is near the corner and commands a view of both entrances opposite, although unfortunately the trees are in full leaf and may obstruct the vision."

The inspector declared the position excellent, adding that he trusted they were not causing inconvenience.

"Not in the least! I confess I would like nothing better than to share your watch, but alas, I am suffering from migraine, and my wife insists on an early retirement. However, I have given orders for refreshments to be brought you, and if you require anything further you have only to ring."

He seated himself, offered them liqueurs and cigars, and for a short time discoursed with a charm and fluency which, at another time, would have delighted both listeners. As matters were, it was a relief to Geoffrey's nerves when at the stroke of nine he rose to bid them good night. In the doorway he paused, his manner suddenly altering.

"That maid across the way," he remarked with serious thoughtfulness, "I have watched her going about her duties for eleven years—respectful, efficient, but, messieurs, hard—as hard as those,"—and he pointed a finger at the polished blades on the wall. "I know her accent; she is from the Vosges. The butler I cannot place, he is probably of no nationality, but I know what I am saying when I tell you that there is bad blood *chez lui*. If you wish to trap those two, messieurs, you will need to be like our friend the fly—all eyes, below, above and in the backs of your heads! *Bonsoir, messieurs—et bonne chance!*"

The door closed. The two men exchanged glances.

"He is right," muttered the inspector shortly.

He turned off the lights, then cautiously drew aside the curtains. The room was saved from complete darkness by the street lights and the silver radiance of the moon, just risen above the house-tops.

"Too much illumination. We must be careful not to show ourselves."

Yet it was a point in their favour that no one could possibly issue from either of the entrances over the way without being plainly seen. The avenue was quiet except for an occasional car whizzing past, but from all around came the staccato honking of motor-horns pitched in various keys. On a level with the eyes stretched the double row of chestnuts, their waxen blossoms stiffly upright like candles on a Christmas tree, while above the odour of warm asphalt and petrol rose the fragrance of the spring night, fresh and thrilling. To Geoffrey it was like a knife turned in a wound.

Opposite, the wide doors gaped open, with a thin blade of light from the loge lying athwart the pavement. On the *entresol* floor all was gloom save for a slender thread of radiance round the edge of the corner window.

A woman's figure, flamboyantly dressed and with a scarlet hat perched on her blond hair, emerged from the gates and stood looking up and down the street. As she turned her rouged face towards the light Geoffrey recognized Berthe. Presently she was joined by a coarse, thickset man, and the two went off arm-in-arm, discoursing volubly.

"The cook, setting out with her friend," whispered Bazin. "That is good; the others will feel freer."

Seating himself in the shadow of the curtains, he offered a packet of Marylands to his companion, masking the lighted match with his hands.

During an interminable interval the two puffed in silence. Ever and again Geoffrey's cigarette went out and had to be re-lit. His muscles twitched, his features in the tempered gloom showed blanched and drawn. He chafed helplessly at the tediousness of the vigil, haunted by the fear that while they sat here idle, elsewhere events might be moving forward with fatal rapidity.

The unseen clock struck ten. A groan escaped him. The night had barely begun!

A moment afterwards he stiffened and laid a hand on the inspector's arm.

On the narrow balcony of the corner room Eduardo had appeared, his squat shoulders silhouetted against the glow within. He stood with his right hand resting against the railing, and Geoffrey saw that the sling had been abandoned. Slowly, indifferently, it seemed, his bullet head turned, surveying the avenue in both directions, then, throwing back his chin, he stared up at the night sky. A cloud of pale smoke wafted out over the chestnuts from the cigarette between his lips.

For several minutes he remained thus, then withdrew, closing the casement. All was quiet once more, though the light inside the room was still visible.

Silence and another endless wait. Would nothing ever happen?

Then suddenly out of the soft night rose the thin notes of a violin. The tune, charged with poignant associations, clutched at Geoffrey's heart. It was the Albeniz Tango. . . .

He shut his eyes. Across velvet blackness swayed two white figures like glittering frost-flowers, accented here and there with spots that were crimson as drops of blood.

Then the vision melted kaleidoscopically into another, and he sensed around him a different darkness, with the odour of lilies of the valley filling his nostrils. He could all but feel the pliant body close against him and the pressure of those lips which for two weeks had been a constant memory. Acute anguish shot through him. His nails dug into his palms.

CHAPTER THIRTY-EIGHT

WHAT was this red glow round her, sending forth waves of pulsing heat? Was she still dreaming?

The night had been one long jumble of phantasmas, sucking her back like quicksands whenever she seemed on the point of waking. In most of them fire had figured, thick foggy smoke, pierced by flashes of murky flame. It must be a repetition of her fevered delusions, this furnace-like atmosphere which caused her head to throb and her parched throat to ache from dryness.

Incapable of analysing her impressions, she lay surveying the crimson haze through eyelids drooping of their own weight. Meanwhile, her languid brain recalled the visions sleep had conjured up to torment her, reviewing them one by one.

A waxen face—whose was it?—tear-stained and lit by tall white candles, which as she watched, grew, lengthening into rockets which shot off through space. Then another face, sallow and hard, with round, close-set eyes, which stared steadily at her with venomous hatred. Curiously enough, this face showed crossed and recrossed by an iron grille, as though it were seen through prison bars. Whenever she turned it was there, watching her, baleful and livid. She could not get away from it. Indeed, she had been possessed by the familiar nightmare of paralysis, feeling herself bound, unable to move. Finally in her dream she had made a sickening discovery. She was trapped in a huge web, legs and arms imprisoned by pitiless meshes, which cut into her when she turned and twisted to escape.

Next, periodically recurring, had been an impression surely culled from the *Arabian Nights* of her childhood. A crack in the ground at her feet had yawned wide, while out of it poured dun-coloured smoke, assuming to her fascinated eyes the form of a demon. Rapidly it swelled to gigantic size, its swart features horribly magnified, one upraised hand brandishing a cudgel with which to strike her. There was no eluding that certain doom. Inexorably the arm descended, she reeled with the shock of pain, and sank again into oblivion. . . .

Now the faces had vanished, leaving her to wander with leaden feet in a desert of dazzling sand. On every side stretched the hot waste, upon which the copper disc of a sun beat down through waves of quivering heat. The sand itself suffocated her, filling her eyes, her teeth, her throat with its clogging particles. She longed for water, with a thirst more devastating than any she had ever known. Water—water! Was there none in the world? She scanned the horizon in search of some spring where she could throw herself down and drink to repletion, but although a faint shimmer appeared in the distance, she knew she could never attain it, for at every step she sank into the yielding mass of sand.

Even now, though her head ached blindingly and she was conscious of a dire sickness in her stomach, every other sensation was dwarfed by appalling thirst. She could drink a well dry. The thought came to her that she was ill once more and had wakened early after a night of fever. The red light must be that of early morning.

Opening her eyes wide, she glanced curiously round, wonder growing to find her room so strangely altered. What was this thick material hanging beside her, cutting off the air? Why, it was a curtain—heavy, red damask. Her bed had no curtains. The windows, too, were covered in red, and so were the walls—crimson damask, all alike. With the light showing through the cracks the entire place had the look of being suffused in blood.

All at once it dawned on her that this was not her room at all, nor yet the one she had occupied at Fontainebleau. No, it was some new bed-chamber she had never seen before. In the hot glow she spied a walnut dressing-table, its oblong mirror touched by a shaft of sun, which by reflection threw a brilliant patch upon the opposite wall. There were chairs with red cushions, a stool, and a stand filled with books in yellow paper covers. On the stand stood a vase containing a bunch of dead anemones, withered and dried into the mere ghosts of flowers. The air between danced with sparkling motes.

Where was she then? Had she been here a long time, and had her memory gone?

Her baffled cogitations occupied but the fraction of a second. Almost immediately recollection rushed upon her, and in a vivid flash of horror she saw again the picture last witnessed with her waking eyes—Jeanne's dark face close to her own, Eduardo's swarthy, furious features, the glitter of the candle-stick in his lifted hand, and round her swirls of grey smoke.

She tried to scream, but there was a tight gag between her teeth; to spring up from the bed, only to find herself securely bound so that she could stir neither hand nor foot. All she could do was to struggle into a sitting posture, an achievement which tore her hair away from the material beneath with a sensation of pain. Turning she saw that she had been lying upon a folded bath-towel, on which were dark stains. That meant she had been wounded. This stickiness contracting her forehead and brows was blood, dried into a cake. How badly was she hurt? She could not loose her hands to explore the injury.

At a little distance lay her new green hat, crushed and blood-smeared. It came to her that it was probably due to that protective covering that she was alive at all, the felt having deadened the blow which struck her down. The hat had saved her—but for what? Yet surely someone would discover her, help would come soon.

Then, even as hope crossed her mind she noticed again the withered anemones, the dust thick upon the furniture, and grasped the fact that wherever she was, the room had not been entered for days, perhaps longer. No one was likely to look for her here. The place was unoccupied. . . .

Where was she? There was nothing to guide her. She might be near Mme. Bender's apartment, or miles away in some distant quarter of Paris. At least she was reasonably sure that this room was not one of the locked ones in her cousin's flat. These red damask walls spoke of an alien taste in decoration.

Terror gripped her, sweat burst from every pore and streamed down into her eyes. She felt she must not waste a minute, but make a desperate effort to free her hands, get the choking gag out of her mouth so that she could shout till someone heard her. For a short time she fought with might and main, but presently, forced by exhaustion to give up the attempt, fell back limp and panting. Not only were her wrists tied, but the bands, which seemed to be strips of linen, encircled her body layer after layer, up to her elbows. Similarly her legs were swathed in mummy-like wrappings, while the knot which fastened the gag was so well contrived that without the use of her fingers it was hopeless to think of removing it. The struggle had left her weak and dizzy. Nausea overcame her, the room swam before her in a red haze.

At last she mustered her faculties. Round her was unbroken stillness, and such sounds as came from out-of-doors were muffled and faint— only distant motor-horns, nothing to indicate whether she was in the neighbourhood she knew or another locality altogether. However, the street noises were so far away that she concluded the room must be at the rear of a building. Beyond this she could decide nothing at all. Who owned the place, why it was deserted, remained a mystery.

She must have been faint from loss of blood, for every now and then the scene clouded over and she was unable to concentrate. When, after one of these intervals of semi-stupor, fear roused her afresh, she noticed with a shock that the light, instead of increasing, was fading rapidly away. The glow was gone, swallowed up in a deepening twilight. Night was coming on. In a little while she would be in total darkness. She shuddered as with ague at the thought.

It was Saturday evening then. A swift calculation told her she must have been here about seventeen hours. What had happened about the fire? Germaine was dead. There could be no doubt of that. The memory of the still face lit by flickering flames came before her poignantly. Well then, the thing could not be hushed up, the news by now must be in the papers. Did Geoffrey know? Then she remembered that he had planned to drive to Fontainebleau soon after lunch, consequently if he did not hear what had happened before that time there would be nothing to stop him. Perhaps even now he was ignorant, asking himself why she had not telephoned to save him a useless journey. As likely as not he was feeling annoyed with her for her thoughtlessness. The Hardwickes, too—what had they thought when she failed to meet them this morning? They were on their way to Italy hours ago. In all Paris there was not one person who would miss her till it was too late.

Her brain recoiled from the obvious conclusion. Shivering in every benumbed muscle, she lay still and strove to pray. . . .

It was darker now. She could just make out the shapes of the furniture, with the pale rectangle of the mirror dimly visible. Alone, powerless to move or cry out, here she would have to lie like a rabbit in a snare and wait—how long? Perhaps till reason deserted her. As to her ultimate fate she harboured no delusions. Since last night she was a dangerous witness, and as such must be suppressed. Those murderers could not afford to let her live. To save their own skins they must do away with her completely before anyone could guess the truth.

How did one dispose of bodies? Safest and surest way—the Seine, that swift-flowing tide which yearly carried away a toll of victims! Or would they carry her to some remote corner of the Bois de Boulogne, or the Bois de Vincennes, there to leave her for the police to find? No, they would hardly attempt that. Drowning was so much simpler.

Thus she lay with cramped body and tortured brain, freezing and burning alternately, till a merciful coma engulfed her senses. Hours passed and she knew nothing.

What was this new sound penetrating her consciousness, calling her back persistently to reality? Music—a violin playing, not far away. She listened, straining her ears to catch the high, pure notes. Silvery and fine they soared, above a faint piano accompaniment, and with a measured rhythm she knew at once for that of the Albeniz Tango. Where had she heard it played like that, with that identical phrasing, and with the lilting *ritardando* just where she knew it would come?

Then she remembered.

Tears sprang to her eyes, her dry throat contracted as a voice whispered that this was probably the last time she would listen to music, and that never again would she feel the embrace of strong arms. At the same time another portion of her brain registered the knowledge that she was still within close range of the unseen violinist, consequently not far removed from her former dwelling.

Oh! If only she could make a noise, break a window, knock over a piece of furniture—anything! As the tango drifted on to its final cadence she began a renewed struggle, battling hard to shift her body towards the edge of the bed. It was worse than useless. She was far too weak, nor could she move her elbows to get sufficient leverage.

The playing continued. Now it was the *Caprice Viennois*, with its wooing double-thirds and its fantastic interlude, making her picture masked figures flitting along a dark alley, mysterious moths moon-lit under a sky dappled with inky clouds. Carnaval, a spring night, all the thrilling aspects of life which she was about to leave for ever. Then followed the César Franck sonata, graceful and delicate as a spray of apple-blossoms. The agony of it now seemed more than she could endure.

The recital ceased. How quiet it was! Only those distant staccato motor-horns, stabbing the stillness, reminding her that all around free and careless pleasure-seekers went their various ways, little dreaming what torment existed within this locked and airless room. For perhaps ten minutes she lay and listened to the pounding of her heart, thump after thump, quick, regular blows of a hammer. She counted the strokes mechanically, to keep from thinking.

Suddenly she stiffened as another noise reached her ears. Without warning a door was opened stealthily, and muffled footfalls approached. Instantly she sat up again, bathed in sweat. Someone had entered the flat, was coming softly and without hesitation towards her hiding-place. Before she could do more than brace her pinioned body against the wall, a key grated in the lock and the invisible intruder entered. In the dense darkness she caught the quick inhalation of a hurried breath, and for an instant thought that her heart would burst.

A hand fumbled along the wainscoting, as though feeling for a switch, then close by a man's voice whispered peremptorily:

"*Touche pas la lumière. J'apporte une bougie, moi . . .*"

At the same moment there was a scratch of a match, followed by a dazzling glare, and in the light of a candle-end sheltered by a broad palm, two dark figures emerged from obscurity. The smaller of them came near on tiptoe, bent down and peered into her face.

It was Jeanne. Behind her rose the shadowy mass of the Portuguese, his bloodshot eyes gleaming in the candlelight. Both servants wore coats and hats, and the woman carried a bundle under her arm. Her hands were bandaged.

For a second Catherine stared back at her with fascinated eyes. Again she tried to scream, her voice ending in a gurgle.

Eduardo spoke in an undertone:

"She has come to herself, then? That is good. Now! Be quick about it. Do you need any help?"

"No. Better keep watch at the outer door."

"Well, sharp work then. Here's the knife. . . ."

They were going to kill her outright! She cowered away with a suddenness which sent her toppling.

"None of that!" commanded the woman's voice sibilantly.

At the same time she felt herself rudely grasped and thrown upon her back. The sallow face leaned over her, the eyes boring into hers.

"You can hear, I suppose? Well, then, listen carefully. You are to obey me, everything I say—and if you make one sound you will find this between your ribs!"

At the word "this" a sharp point pressed into her side. The yellow light shone upon the polished blade of a long carving-knife, clutched in murderous fingers.

"*C'est entendu, n'est-ce pas?*"

Although the girl could make no sign, her jailer was apparently satisfied. She withdrew the weapon, bent over the prisoner's feet, and with a quick ripping noise severed the strips confining the helpless ankles. Next she dragged her body into an upright position, slid it to the edge of the bed so that the feet touched the floor, and unrolling the bundle, which proved to be Catherine's tweed coat, produced a package of medical gauze.

What was this for? The victim was not long in doubt. Even as she asked herself the question swift, expert fingers began to wrap her face and head in bandages, covering the gag and leaving nothing free save nose and eyes. She was swathed like a cocoon in surgical wrappings, fastened here and there with safety-pins. A dive behind her back, and with a spasm of unbearable pain she felt her hat thrust upon her head, pulled well down to hide the upper part of her face. For a second she swayed, the candle was blotted out, and she grazed the borders of unconsciousness.

When she recovered it was to hear the words brusquely uttered: "You are able to walk, I hope? Stand on your feet. . . ."

She was lifted bodily, an arm steadying her to prevent her falling. When the darkness cleared, she was aware that her coat had been thrown round her shoulders, dangling loose over her bound arms. The woman was saying with hard emphasis, driving home her meaning:

"You have got to walk as far as the car. You will be able to manage. Stay where you are—there is a chair beside you to lean against."

By the smoking flame of the candle, stuck on a chest of drawers, she could see the maid busy herself rapidly with the disordered bed, smoothing down the red damask cover and wadding the blood-stained towel and linen strips into a ball, which she placed in her coat pocket. Hardly had she finished when Eduardo reappeared in the doorway, his distorted shadow rising behind him.

"Ready? She can stand upright?" he whispered.

"With us to help her."

The ironic laugh accompanying the reply sent a chill down the girl's spine.

"Well, then"—impatiently—"what are you waiting for?"

Catherine, too, sensed an ominous pause which at first she did not understand. Then she felt her left hand grasped from underneath her coat and pulled as far as it would go towards the flaring candle, while the woman stooped over it, her breath audible through compressed nostrils. Simultaneously the Portuguese moved a step closer.

"Ah, that! It is a good stone, too. A pity to let it go."

Then Catherine knew that Jeanne was examining her ruby ring.

Another pause.

"Suppose I take it off her. He will never know. . . ."

"No, but the police will, when they fish her up. It's suicide, remember, not robbery. A little thing like that might make all the difference . . ."

A sigh, charged with baffled cupidity, then her hand was released.

When they fished her up! Now, with sickening certainty, she knew what her end was going to be.

With a strong smell of smouldering wick the candle was put out. She felt herself seized on both sides and hurried across a second room, along a tiled hall-way, and thence to a lighted landing where a lift waited. The door was shut behind them.

"Better leave the key in the lock," muttered Jeanne. "The old fool will think he left it there. Have you got the bags?"

"Here, beside you. Look sharp now—in with her."

She was pushed roughly into the lift while a bag and hat-box she recognized for her own were jammed alongside of her. Evidently no trace was to be left. Her captors followed, the metal doors closed with a click, and the cage sank, slowly, past three landings to the ground floor. As it came to rest, a final ray of hope shot through the speechless girl. It could not be very late. Perhaps the concierge might see her and question her identity. She must be on the alert to attract his attention.

Then, as if in answer to her unspoken thought, Jeanne bent towards her, hissing in her ear, "You have not forgotten what I showed you just now? One attempt to escape and you will feel it! I have it ready in my sleeve."

The following instant she was supported down a flight of shallow steps into a court, which had a tiny garden in the centre, bordered with hyacinths, pale in the moonlight. No one was in sight, but above, on the first floor, the casements were open, and through them issued laughter and the babble of clamorous voices. A party was in progress. Someone struck a few chords of a popular song on a piano and began to sing, only to be silenced by a feminine voice raised in mock annoyance, shrilling the words, *"Qui a versé la Benedictine sur ma broderie Perse? Cochon, va!"*

As she was led forward on tottering feet she glanced desperately towards the *loge*. Now she was abreast of the lighted window, through which she could see every detail of the room within—the stickily bright, machine-carved dresser, the blue cover on the table, the clock upon the wall, and beside it a lurid oleograph of Maréchal Foch. She was past it in a second, but not before her eager eye had taken in the rear view of two seated figures, one that of a little elderly man whose head was encircled by a half-hoop of steel terminating in head-phones pressed tightly against his ears. In that instant hope perished. The concierge, a devotee to the *sans fils*, was dead to the outer world, intent upon his evening's enjoyment.

Now they were in the street crossing the familiar avenue of chestnuts. As they set foot on the opposite pavement a man in evening dress brushed by them, casting a curious glance at Catherine's bandaged face. With all her strength she tried to move in his direction, only to find the grip on her arms tightened and to feel a sharp prod in her side. At the same time Jeanne's voice spoke soothingly, but loud enough for the passer to hear:

"Courage, madame! Only one little step farther. Lean on me."

Crushed by despair, the prisoner felt her legs give beneath her, but she was borne up strongly and propelled with haste to an adjacent turning, where in the shelter of overhanging trees stood an empty car. Almost before she could grasp what was happening, she found herself upon the deep seat inside, with Jeanne whispering in a tone of triumph:

"There, mademoiselle, that was neatly done, I think!"

A few seconds passed, while Eduardo placed the bag and hat-box on the floor at their feet and climbed into the driver's place. The engine started, but they did not move. Instead, in the darkness, Catherine felt rather than saw the two servants straining round to look behind them, their attitude full of alert expectancy.

From out the gloom rapid steps sounded, coming towards the car. The girl's heart gave a wild leap. Someone was approaching, a possible rescuer, perhaps. Oh! if only she could scream, or at least make some sign to attract attention! With a mad effort she threw herself forward, her head colliding with the glass in front. Immediately she was violently seized and thrust back again.

"Ah, you would, would you?" There was a smothered imprecation.

The next instant the door at her side was flung open and a man, out of breath from hurrying, got in. There was just sufficient light to discern a dead-white face close to hers beneath the brim of a wide hat, and two eyes fixed upon her with a cold, unwinking stare.

She shuddered with sudden nausea. They were the eyes of Adolph Blom.

Simultaneously the car lurched forward. They were off.

CHAPTER THIRTY-NINE

ELEVEN o'clock sounded.

The watchers at the Commandant's study window sat in almost unbroken silence, their eyes glued to the building across the way. In the window opposite a glow still showed, suggesting that at least one of the occupants of the flat was yet awake. The street noises had partially subsided in the lull between the dinner hour and midnight when the theatres close, and the real night life of the city begins.

Suddenly a peal from the telephone ripped the stillness in two. Geoffrey jumped, while the inspector reached his hand towards the instrument. Almost his first words showed that the call was for him.

"You have lost him? Where? How long ago?" Then a pause, followed by an exclamation of mingled annoyance and resignation. "*Zut!* Well, he is gone, now. No telling where he has got to by now."

He replaced the receiver, and in reply to his companion's glance whispered: "It is one of my men who has been covering the entrance to the *notaire*'s bureau. Half an hour ago Blom went out, got into the Métro at the Place Clichy, took a train and made two or three changes. At the Concorde he disappeared in the crowd, so all our vigilance is gone for nothing."

"Do you think he is up to anything in connection with this business?"

Bazin shrugged. "Who knows? The repeated *correspondance* looks as though he suspected he was being followed. If our conclusions are right, he is in a very nasty position. However, we can be very sure of one thing—he did not take any part in getting the young lady away last night. I have proved that he spent the entire evening up till two, at the apartment of Mme. Baron, who was giving a party; consequently, if anything was done, it was those people over there who managed it. That is why I am concentrating on the house itself, for in the extremely short time at their disposal they could not possibly have removed her any distance.

If the butler left the apartment at all, it must have been while the *locataire* from the third floor was out giving the alarm, for he was there when the man returned five or at most ten minutes later."

Geoffrey grasped his meaning. Alive or dead Catherine must at this moment be somewhere in the immediate vicinity. His harassed eyes explored the façade opposite, vainly striving to fathom the secret of her hiding-place.

"Ah, that is the question," remarked the inspector in answer to his unuttered query. "There is not an inch of those premises which has been overlooked. We have searched all the apartments and the servants' quarters above. There is no sign of her or of the bags she brought home."

"Yet she must be there!" muttered Geoffrey. "What about the space between the flooring? There is a gap where the fire burned through."

"I examined it myself."

"And the roof itself? Is it easy to get out on to it?"

"Simple enough, by means of the usual trap-door, but it, too, has been inspected."

Leaning forward, Geoffrey studied the parapet. It extended along a group of five houses, the line varying in height and shape, but continuous. After the fifth house came a break before a second group began.

"I wonder," he said suddenly, "if there are any vacant apartments in that row?"

"Not one. I am informed there has not been an apartment to let in any of those houses for three years."

A groan escaped Geoffrey. In spite of himself, it began to look as though they were on the wrong tack after all. Perhaps it was true that, distracted by grief and shock, Catherine had wandered off and found some means of leaving the city. Then the telegram recurred to him and he rejected the idea. Much as he longed to believe that it had come from her, the evidence against the supposition was overpowering. No, the message was patently false, and as obviously contrived to serve a definite purpose. Bazin must be right. The words *"but will telephone to-morrow"* surely meant that something was planned to take place before that time. Seven hours at most remained. Meanwhile the minutes were slipping away. . . .

His reflections were broken by a touch on his arm.

"Look!"

Following the direction of the pointing finger, he saw that the light opposite had been extinguished. What did it mean? Were the two over there going harmlessly to bed, or did they merely wish the outside world to believe they were doing so?

"They can't do anything without getting out first," muttered Geoffrey to himself.

"Exactly—and the house is well guarded. There are two others watching as well as ourselves."

Ten minutes passed, then Geoffrey knew that he could no longer support the maddening inaction.

"I am going out," he said abruptly. "Not far. If you want me, tie your handkerchief to the knob of the casement. I shall be able to see it."

"Very well, monsieur," assented his companion. "But use the back exit, and if you cross the street let it be farther along, out of range of those windows. For all we know they are watching to see if the coast is clear."

It took but a few seconds to descend the dimly lighted stairs and emerge into the side-street. With his hat low over his eyes and the collar of his Burberry well up, Geoffrey set out at a brisk pace to make a tour of the neighbourhood. Without stopping he inspected the darkened windows along the turning, then after a brief detour came back again, re-crossed the avenue lower down and, pursuing an idea that had come to him during the recent conversation, walked boldly into the loge of the house adjoining the corner one.

He was met by a yawning concierge who, by the look of him, was at that moment revolving in his mind the suitability of closing up for the night. Apologizing for the lateness of his call, Geoffrey inquired if any of the *locataires* wished to sublet his flat. He was answered by a supercilious negative. No, these apartments were seldom sublet; all the *locataires* were in residence now, and not one of them had any intention of leaving. Yes, he would take the gentleman's address, but there was nothing to be gained by it. Monsieur would do better to go to an agent.

"You say they are all here now?" persisted Geoffrey, undaunted by the man's arrogant manner.

"Certainly, monsieur—but it would be the same if they were not."

Geoffrey thanked him and departed, to repeat the questions in the house next door, where the result, framed with less discourtesy, was similar. Again in the fourth building he received a like response.

He was beginning to think there was nothing in his theory after all, but he did not mean to give up without trying the last of the five. He was in the act of entering the wide opening, through which issued sounds of laughter and high-pitched voices, when a man's figure detached itself from the shadow of the chestnuts and took a step towards him. To his amazement he heard his name called in an undertone:

"Monsieur Macadam! A word with you, please!"

The subdued voice was charged with excitement. Turning, Geoffrey made out the lugubrious features of Bernard, whom since midday he had entirely forgotten.

"You! What are you doing here?"

Instead of replying the agent stalked away under the shelter of the trees, where, after a glance round, Geoffrey followed him. In the darkness the man's cavernous eyes appeared mere sockets of gloom beneath the hard rim of his bowler hat.

"Monsieur! It is fortunate you have come! Who do you suppose at this moment is with the concierge in that *loge* you were about to enter?"

Geoffrey shook his head, his eyes fixed on the other's face.

"It is Adolph Blom. I have been watching this house, because it is the one to which the butler went this morning, and I have had an idea that that fact might mean something to us. A quarter of an hour ago I saw the *notaire* go in. He is with the concierge now, chatting as though he were an old friend."

Blom—here, in this neighbourhood!

"What do you think it indicates?" demanded Geoffrey quickly.

"I do not know. I glanced in the window and saw them tinkering with the *sans fils*, but I cannot believe it is merely a social call. It is my opinion he is waiting for someone, that the loge there is a rendezvous—but for what I cannot say. Perhaps . . ." He stopped and let his gaze wander slowly over the lighted doorway, but though the listener waited eagerly he did not complete the sentence.

Meanwhile the young man was cursing his stupidity for allowing this particular house to escape his calculations.

Surely he ought to have guessed that Eduardo's visit here to-day must have had some significance, yet because he could see nothing in it he had all but dismissed it from his mind. Hurriedly taking stock of the situation, he explained his own presence, pointing out the window a hundred yards along the street where till recently he had been stationed.

"The police inspector is there now. Stay here while I tell him what has happened. Only a little while ago Blom gave one of his men the slip, so that may lead us to some clue. We have been assuming that Mademoiselle West is hidden in the corner building, but now—" He hesitated, looking round.

"I understand, monsieur. I am asking myself the same question. I will remain on guard while Blom is here."

Three minutes later, panting from his dash up the stairs, Geoffrey opened the study door. A few yards away the red tip of a cigarette told him the inspector was still at his post.

"Well, monsieur?" came the expectant whisper.

"Blom!" burst out Geoffrey. "He's turned up in this street, in the *loge* of that last house there. It's the house the butler visited this morning. What do you make of it?"

Accustomed now to the gloom, he could see the inspector's glaring at him with incredulity. Then he caught a smothered expletive as the man leaped to his feet and fixed his gaze on the long line of the opposite roofs.

"*Sacré!* What fools we are! That house below there is the one we should be watching—not this! How did you find this out? You have seen the fellow?"

Geoffrey related briefly what had happened. As he listened intently, Bazin consulted the luminous dial of his watch, the glimmering hands of which pointed to twenty-five minutes past eleven.

"It is getting late, but that concierge yonder will not close up till his visitor has gone. If they have got mademoiselle hidden somewhere in that building—"

Even as he spoke they saw the fat old porter over the way amble forth and begin swinging the heavy doors together.

"You think she may be there—that they have carried her across the—"

The sentence died in his throat as he leaned suddenly out the window, staring intently at a man who came running toward them between the lines of chestnuts. The swiftly padding steps reached the pavement beneath, and at the same instant a hoarse voice called Geoffrey's name.

"Monsieur, come down again—not a moment to lose! I have just seen the Portuguese together with two women cross to the Square Lamartine and get into a car. I do not know, but I believe one of the woman may be your friend!"

The warning acted on the listeners like a galvanic shock. With a single impetus the two men sprang for the door, made a plunge down the broad stairway and breathlessly confronted the excited agent.

"A car? What sort of car? When?"

"It is a large black Rolls-Royce, standing in the Square. I watched the three of them come out of the house—a man and a woman leading an invalid lady between them, her face covered in bandages, so I could not see who she was. As they reached the car I thought I recognized the butler."

Geoffrey's blazing eyes met the inspector's.

"It is they! I'm sure of it! Quick—we'll follow them! Like hell!"—and not pausing for a reply he led the way at top speed round the corner into the turning where showed the lights of the inspector's car.

No time to consider how the pair whom they had believed safely confined in the flat opposite had emerged from another building two hundred yards farther along the street. Besides, there was but one way in which such a trick could have been managed—a passage over the roofs. The invalid lady must be Catherine, and at the thought Geoffrey's heart gave a great leap. She was alive still, but in imminent peril. At this moment she was being conveyed to her death, of that he felt horribly certain.

Within less than a minute Bazin was at the wheel with Geoffrey beside him and Bernard on the seat behind. Swiftly the car moved forward into the avenue, now empty as far as the eye could see. The Square Lamartine lay ahead of them on the right-hand side.

"It has not been more than a few minutes," the agent assured them. "If we are lucky we can catch them up. Here we are! Look sharp!"

They had entered the Square Lamartine, a secluded spot comprising a group of detached houses, each surrounded with its own patch of walled garden. Geoffrey leaned out, scanning the darkened roadway in every direction, then struck his knee with his clenched fist and swore aloud.

The entire place was deserted.

"My God, they've given us the slip!"

It was true. Short as the interval had been, the trio, car and all, had completely vanished.

CHAPTER FORTY

The chill of utter blackness descended. The inspector spoke first, glancing behind as he backed out into the avenue again.

"They cannot have more than a few minutes' start of us. The point is, in which direction have they gone?"

Before either of his companions could answer, a man-servant in livery entered the square, turning into it from the lower end of the street. Geoffrey called out to him.

"Have you seen anything of a black Rolls-Royce which was here a little while ago?"

The man stopped in the act of pushing open the nearest gate, and eyed the party with slight surprise.

"As a matter of fact, I did see such a car, monsieur," he returned civilly. "It was standing along there, empty, twenty minutes ago, and just now it passed me as I crossed the Avenue Victor Hugo."

"Which way was it heading?"

"Towards the Bois, monsieur."

The inspector gave a grunt.

"As I thought—the Porte Maillot," he muttered.

In another second they were out of the square and hastening towards the Bois, which they entered at the Large Henri Martin, at once turning to the right along the Allée des Fortifications. Not a word was uttered as they whizzed past the Pavillion Dauphine and the Porte of the same name, their three pairs of eyes riveted upon the gleaming roadway in front. A few minutes brought them to the Porte Maillot, where they were obliged to halt. As the *gabelou* handed them the ticket of exit Bazin fired a terse inquiry at him.

"A Rolls, monsieur? Black, you say?" The man thought for a moment, while the three men hung upon his reply. "Yes, a large black car came through not very long ago. Six or seven minutes, I should say. Three passengers and a chauffeur in ordinary clothes—a foreigner, I think. They were taking an ill lady to a hospital somewhere out there," and he jerked his head in the direction of Neuilly. "I fancy she's had an operation on her face, for she was covered in bandages. Is that the party you mean?"

"M. l'Inspecteur, it is they!" cried Bernard.

"Ah!" exclaimed Bazin. "We are on the right track so far," and driving down the accelerator, he plunged ahead into the broad Avenue de Neuilly.

At the second mention of bandages Geoffrey's heart missed a beat. Still, Catherine was undoubtedly alive, had managed to walk a couple of hundred yards to the car. He must not allow himself to dwell upon gruesome possibilities, but try to think that the covering of her face was merely an attempt at disguise. The whole business before them now was to overtake her before any further harm could be done, a proceeding which challenged to the utmost their powers of ingenuity and speed. The Commissariat car possessed a good engine, but with a six or seven minutes' handicap it seemed a hopeless matter to out-distance a Rolls, besides which at any moment the prey might elude them altogether by some unexpected turn. He voiced his fear to his companion.

Intent on the road in front, the inspector answered with a shake of the head.

"It is true they have a fair start of us, but that does not necessarily mean we shall not be able to catch them. Remember, they can as yet have no idea that they are being followed, consequently they will not risk a hold-up by excessive speed. They have several hours before them, ample time to cover a considerable distance and yet be back by morning."

"You think they intend to return, then?"

"But of course, monsieur! When they have accomplished their purpose. Unless I am totally misled, those servants mean to slip into the apartment by the private door before anyone is stirring—say at four or five o'clock."

"And their destination?"

"I am afraid there can be little doubt, monsieur. Some lonely point along the river."

Geoffrey controlled a shudder. It was what his own belief had told him, and with a sick mind he visualized those head-lines unfortunately so familiar in the daily press: "Body of Young Woman Found in the Seine. . . ."

"Have you any idea what spot they will choose?"

"Ah, that is difficult to say. They will scarcely venture anything too close to the city, but whatever place they have in mind they will make straight for it, you can depend upon that. From their point of view the sooner the thing is done the better for them. That is why I dare not risk telephoning ahead to have them stopped. It seems to me our wisest course to keep hot on their trail."

Geoffrey said no more. With gaze fixed on the vista stretching before him, he leaned forward, every muscle in his body rigid as steel. No sound reached him save the engine's hum and the tense, slightly asthmatic breathing of Bernard behind.

The Pont de Neuilly loomed in sight. They crossed it, then slowed down in doubt as to which way to take. A sleepy *sergent de ville* emerging into view, they shouted to him a question which after a stupid stare he managed to answer.

"A Rolls-Royce? I believe one passed five minutes or so ago, but I was talking to a motor-cyclist at the time, and did not notice. . . . Wait a moment, though. A large black car, going pretty fast? Yes, I recall it now. It was making in the direction of La Défense."

With a cry of triumph Bazin shot forward.

"I believe we are gaining a little," he commented. "At all events we have not gone astray."

They reached the monument to the Defence of Paris, inquired again with less certain results, and hesitatingly chose the road to Nanterre, from thence pressing on to Rueil. Here they met with further encouragement. A motorist changing a tyre informed them that he had seen a car corresponding to the Rolls' description only a few minutes before.

"Good! Then we are still right. Unless something turns up to upset our calculations, I propose going through Malmaison to Bougival and see what we hear when we reach there. I begin to have an idea. . . ."

Geoffrey looked at him eagerly, but he shut his mouth with a snap and kept it closed for another mile or so.

There were now short stretches of open country. The smell of pavements had yielded to the fragrance of fields, while an occasional flowering fruit-tree showed white in the moonlight. As they rushed past the Château at Malmaison, that tranquil dwelling filled to the brim with the intimate memories of the great Napoleon, Geoffrey recalled with a stab of pain how only three weeks ago he had set with Catherine in the garden and listened while somewhat shyly she had for the first time spoken to him of her broken engagement. He could see now the colour in her cheeks that was like a stain of claret, the liquid brightness welling up in her eyes, her delicate nervous fingers as she played with a stem of grass.

For the hundredth time he cursed his stupidity in not foreseeing the trap into which she had walked. If only the knowledge of Blom's intentions had come to him a day sooner! It seemed to him incredible that not until this very day had he grasped the monstrous truth, although the affair had been going on steadily under his eyes for over two months.

The agony of suspense continued. At Bougival they learned nothing fresh, so that it was only the inspector's instinct to guide them that they pushed on to St. Germain, hoping there to obtain tidings.

Soon they were within sight of the Château's gloomy mass, with the dim glow of Paris behind them and the dark hills of Montmorency cutting off the view. Below them the Seine wound like a serpent, its shining surface marked with splashes of golden light.

The town was almost deserted. In the principal boulevard a *sergent*, blinking in the glare of their head-lamps, considered their unvarying question with a stolid face. A Rolls? No, he had noticed no such car. He had been at this very spot for the past quarter of an hour.

The pursuers exchanged blank looks. The thought came to them that the Rolls must have taken a side-turning the other side of St. Germaine, in which case it was now miles away in another direction.

"Yet this is the direct route," muttered Bazin obstinately. "Unless I am totally misled, this is the road they would have taken."

What was to be done? Geoffrey began to think that perhaps they were wrong in assuming the river to be the objective. In any case the quarry had vanished. They had tracked the Rolls for many miles only to lose it now when another twenty minutes might have brought it in sight. Every second's delay lessened their chances.

With a hopeless feeling they prowled along the quiet streets of the town until they came to the outskirts, where they met face to face a belated market-wagon wending its way towards Paris with a load of vegetables for the Halle. The driver dozed in his seat, but the woman beside him, brawny and moustachioed, stared hard at them from beneath a battered hat.

Had she seen the car in question? She surveyed them coolly and spat into the dust. Yes—*diable!*—they had just encountered a car like that, scarcely half a kilometre back, going towards Aubergenville. The chauffeur had taken the middle of the road, pig that he was, and had nearly run over them. The horses had shied, she had had to take the reins herself to avoid a mishap. If monsieur would put on a little speed he might overtake the road-hogs—bad luck to them and theirs!

Before she had stopped speaking the Commissariat car had leaped ahead in the direction of Aubergenville. Again the faint glimmer of hope—yet Geoffrey was far from being convinced that their course was the right one. Somehow he feared that they were now trailing some other car. However, the inspector seemed satisfied.

"Listen, monsieur," he said, without removing his eyes from the road in front. "From Aubergenville there is a lonely stretch leading directly to the Seine. It is the first suitable spot this side of Paris, and I would have gone straight for it if that *sergent* had not confused me. I believe that our friends skirted St. Germain for fear of being identified later on. If, as I think, they are nearing their goal, they do not want to take chances, but their little detour may have lost time for them. If that is the case, we may catch sight of them at any moment."

Three kilometres farther along Geoffrey gave a sudden shout. Far ahead a tail-light was just visible, moving at high speed. Occasionally it vanished at the dip of a hill, only to reappear upon the approaching brow. Like this always the same distance in the rear, they went on for some minutes, Geoffrey upon the edge of the seat, his eyes straining to keep in view the faint point of light.

Before them swept the long road, straight as a length of ribbon, nothing to be seen except the recurrent gleam of the tail-light. They were going at a terrific rate now, and presently their efforts were rewarded by seeing a quarter of a mile in advance the dark shape of a car emerge from the surrounding shadow. A cry of triumph burst from three pairs of lips.

"Shall we overtake them?"

"That will depend on whether or not they suspect we are following them. Still, they must slacken when they come to the town."

A few straggling lights now appeared, marking the limits of Aubergenville. At the same moment they realized that the distance between the two cars was gradually diminishing. At last in a brilliant patch of moonlight they could plainly make out the swiftly-moving black body.

"Ah, good! Now if we are lucky we shall catch them!"

A few seconds of supreme tension, then to Geoffrey's dismay the car ahead, instead of slowing as they expected, put on a sudden spurt, and in another instant had completely disappeared.

"What does it mean? They have seen us?"

"I am afraid so. It looks as though they were trying to give us the slip."

One minute more brought them to the centre of the small town, but although they had wasted no time the black car was not to be seen. How in so short an interval it had contrived to disappear was a mystery; perhaps even now it was close at hand, concealed by one of the obscure turnings; but as far as the trackers were concerned it might have been leagues away. The empty market-place showed not a sign of life as they purred along its cobbled stones, the darkened buildings offered no assistance.

At last they came upon a solitary *sergent de ville*, sauntering languidly along the pavement. To him Bazin shouted the inevitable query, to be rewarded by the information that a Rolls-Royce had passed only a few moments ago, stopping long enough for the driver to inquire the road to Poissy.

"Poissy!"

The inspector's tone was furiously amazed, while his two companions reflected his sentiments. Were their conclusions entirely wrong?

"You are sure it was Poissy he asked for?"

"But absolutely, M. l'Inspecteur. I showed them which turning to take—the second along there,"—and he pointed ahead. "They set off at once in that direction, and must be well on their way by now."

"Eh bien!" the inspector muttered with a shrug.

There was nothing for it but to press on towards the turning indicated and trust to increased speed to bring them once more within sight of their prey. Soon they were shooting along the highway headed for Poissy, uncertain now as to the miscreants' intentions, and maddened by the minutes lost in the town.

"It's odd, that," fumed the inspector, watching the road between narrowed lids. "If they really mean to make for Poissy they have something different in mind from what I thought. I half believe they are playing a trick upon us, that they suspect we are after them and want to throw dust in our eyes. . . . Here! What is this ahead of us? Do you see those tyre tracks just in front?"

He had jammed on his brakes so suddenly that the other two were thrown out of their seats. In answer to his question Geoffrey sprang out and examined the roadway immediately before them. The fine white dust revealed an imprint of wide tyres curving first to the extreme right, then making a horseshoe bend till finally they went off, twin streaks, in the direction from which they had come.

"My God, you've hit it! These are recent tracks. They've doubled on their traces and gone back. We must have missed them by about a couple of minutes."

In a trice they had repeated the manoeuvre of the other car and were facing back towards the town.

"What a chance!" murmured Bazin excitedly, as Geoffrey flung himself back beside him. "If I had not suspected that ruse, we should have gone on without noticing. We shall have to look sharp now if we are to catch them. I could take a right-hand turning I know of and attempt to cut them off, but at this stage I dare not risk it. The river lies just down there, only a short distance,"—and he nodded his head towards the declining ground. "Another moment and we come to the lonely road I spoke of."

Already the car was rushing ahead like a rocket. Dusty hedges flashed past; as far as the eye could reach there was no impediment. Watching breathlessly, Geoffrey could discern no glimmer of a light, nor were his ears able to detect any sound save their own regular drumming on the hard surface of the road. If a tyre should go now—but no, one must not think of accidents. Every second brought them closer to the Seine, flowing silent at the bottom of the slope, far removed from habitation. Perhaps already the Rolls had reached it by some adjacent route. Certainly at this speed it seemed incredible not to overtake the car, if it had indeed come this way.

They dashed through the heart of a wooded expanse, out again into the open, then back into the shadow of a group of pine trees. Still no lights. Now in the distance appeared the thin line of poplars bordering the river. Three seconds more and they would be in sight of the banks. A horrible conviction assailed Geoffrey. They were too late. That parley in the streets at Aubergenville, brief though it had been, had dished their hopes. By now the villains were probably homeward bound, one passenger the less. . . .

"Look out! My God, don't you—"

The warning came an instant too late. Intent on the prospect in front, neither of the two men had seen the concealed lane on the right till they were full upon it. There was a confused vision of a whirling black monster on wheels hurling itself upon them, and before Bazin had had time to do more than swerve abruptly to the left a smashing blow struck them broadside, driving them with a terrific impact into the opposite hedge. The door beside Geoffrey was burst open and he was pitched headlong on to the ground. In the same moment sounded a mingling of curses, shouts, grinding of brakes and splintering of glass. Leaping to his feet, half-stunned, he beheld, three yards away, the dark mass of the Rolls they had been chasing poise tottering for a second, to crash over ponderously upon its side.

There was no time to wonder how this final *débâcle* had happened. Already Geoffrey's two companions had leaped out of their battered car and were standing beside him, uninjured save for small cuts. Bazin, his set face glistening with blood and sweat, grasped a revolver in one hand. The three men faced the prostrate Rolls in strained expectancy. All was silent. Did this mean that the occupants were stunned, dead perhaps? If any of them had been thrown out, the immense weight of the falling body must have crushed them utterly. Geoffrey's heart stood still. Catherine—inside that death-trap! Was this the end of it all?

During what seemed an infinite age he remained rooted to the spot staring with starting eyes at the tomb-like car, round which clouds of powdery dust still swirled. Then with a feeling of grotesque unreality he beheld two figures emerge, clambering out of the exposed windows— first the Portuguese, hatless, his swart features streaming with rivulets of blood, while the lobe of one ear dangled from a shred of skin; then Jeanne, her hair dragged back from a face of ghastly pallor, out of which her close-set eyes glared with a dreadful fixity. Hardly had she grasped the sill to hoist herself clear, when from behind came a man's hand shoving her aside and pawing the air in the manner of a drowning person. Then a dead-white face was thrust out of the aperture and a pair of pale, red-rimmed eyes surveyed the scene.

Events now followed one another so rapidly that it was impossible to sort them out. Eduardo, alighting on the ground cast a single glance at the group close to him and made a headlong dash towards the bottom of the slope. Instantly Bernard sprang upon him, there was a short tussle, the noise of a pistol-shot, then the agent was thrown to the earth, while the flying figure of the Portuguese sped onward. He had covered twenty yards when a second shot crashed, this time from the inspector's weapon, and the entire party saw the thick-set body reel, sway and collapse face downward in the middle of the road, a smoking revolver clutched in his hand. One, at least, of the scoundrels was accounted for.

"Attention! Ah, crapaud!"

Geoffrey wheeled at the inspector's sharp cry in time to see the mean figure of Blom backed against the Rolls' mudguard, pale eyes glittering in the moonlight, a revolver raised in the act of taking aim. A third resounding shot. Geoffrey felt a hot flame sear his shoulder as he flung himself upon his assailant, closing with him in a death-grip. In that moment he realized that his left arm was useless, broken above the elbow by his recent fall. Undeterred by the mishap he wound the fingers of his right hand round the lean throat, felt the twist of muscles as the imprisoned man bent double to free himself, displaying an unexpected force. A red haze blotted out everything. With a foot round the *notaire*'s leg he threw his victim to the ground, fell atop him, aware of nothing save a rapidly purpling face and a tongue beginning to protrude horribly . . .

A voice panted in his ear, "That will do beautifully, monsieur!" At the same instant there was a click of handcuffs, and he was dragged away.

Blinking and coughing from the dust, he rose to see close at hand a second scene of violence. Jeanne, her muscles rigid as those of a maniac, a long murderous knife in her hand, was hurling herself on Bernard, who in the nick of time managed to pinion her wrists in his bony grasp.

"Ah—the she-devil! She would have that in his heart!"

There was a swift blow from Bazin's fist across the taut knuckles, the knife clattered to earth, and another click sounded as a second pair of handcuffs slipped into place.

Even then the woman made a dive to bury her teeth in the agent's hand, but the other two shook her off and dragged her towards the Commissariat car.

A minute more and the maid and Blom were both securely trussed with a rope abstracted from the tool-box. As he tightened the last knot the inspector cast an inquiring glance towards the still figure lying a little distance off.

"That one will give us no trouble," he remarked with meaning. "Now! That business is finished. Shall we turn our attention to mademoiselle?"

Geoffrey drew a long breath. Since the three plotters had climbed out into the open, no sound or movement had come from the Rolls. Did that indicate that the black cavern was empty? A devastating dread seized him as he went slowly towards it, fearing to look through the window.

She was there. He saw at the bottom a huddled mass, of which in the darkness he could discern nothing more than a heap of clothing.

"Permit me, monsieur. You can do little with that arm of yours. She has probably fainted."

It was a matter of extreme difficulty to extricate the inert body, but at length they did so, laying it gently upon the ground. With shaking fingers Geoffrey removed the shapeless green hat, revealing, above thick bandages which concealed all the lower portion of her face, a forehead greyish-white and sunken, closed eyes. Not a flicker of an eyelash altered her complete immobility as, heavy and limp, she rested in the roadway. A lock of dark hair matted with blood clung to her brow, accentuating her dreadful pallor.

Geoffrey uttered a groan.

Fainted? She was dead.

CHAPTER FORTY-ONE

THE inspector was cutting away the encircling bands of gauze. Kneeling beside him, Geoffrey watched with a stony expression, fatalistically certain that rescue had come too late. Either the poor girl's jailers had slain her outright during the long drive, or death had come five minutes ago when the car overturned. The heavy sag of her head made him believe her neck was broken.

As the last fold of material came away, the two men bent forward, dreading the disfigurement which threatened to meet their eyes. None appeared. Only the tight gag was revealed, together with sundry creases where the skin had been long compressed.

"Look what has been done to her!" murmured the officer with a savage click of the tongue. "Now we begin to see. . . . They have much to answer for, those two!"

So saying he severed the gag, and drew it cautiously from between the swollen lips. Beyond the head wound there was no visible mark of injury, yet the cheek which Geoffrey touched remained cold as ice.

"The hands, too—bound to her body! See how the strips have cut into the flesh! Those bruises would have told a story. . . ."

The loosened hands dropped upon the ground, like two weights.

"She is dead, of course?"

Geoffrey expected no reply to his toneless utterance, which was less a question than a statement. For a moment he looked on while the inspector, without replying, pressed his ear over the girl's heart.

All at once, with the movements of an automaton, the young man rose, picked up the revolver which lay in the road, and took a step towards the two bound figures propped against the dusty hedge. He scarcely heard the astonished cry which burst from Bernard.

"Monsieur! Are you mad?"

He stared stupidly as a lean hand shot out and wrested the weapon from his grasp.

Perhaps he was mad. At any rate it was not a self he knew which had yielded to that instinctive urge towards revenge. He came slowly to his senses to hear Bazin calling to him sharply:

"Monsieur—quick! There is a flask in the flap-pocket of the car. And bring a cushion, so we can raise her head"

He complied, sure that no stimulant could bring back the spark of life to that senseless form. All hope was dead as mechanically he lifted the limp body and watched while the inspector tried to force a few drops of brandy into the mouth.

"It's no use," he heard himself muttering.

Seconds passed. He saw both the other onlookers shake their heads, then no longer able to bear the sight before him, he closed his eyes. . . .

A cry roused him.

"Monsieur! Look!"

He obeyed in time to catch the faintest discernible twitch of the eyelids. Only a mere trace of movement, but it was sufficient.

"Catherine!" he cried in a frenzy of love and longing.

"Catherine—!" and seizing her cold hands he began to chafe them vigorously.

For a single second the eyes opened, gazed blankly at him. Then the lids drooped again before there had been any sign of recognition.

"She is not dead, monsieur, but we must lose not an instant in getting her to a doctor. That wound has probably bled a great deal, besides which she has suffered terribly from shock."

Leaving the young man to continue the work of resuscitation, the inspector hastened to inspect his damaged car, which by a miracle was still fit for service. Finding this to be the case, he then held a hurried consultation with the agent, as a result of which it was decided that the latter should remain behind with the prisoners while the injured girl was conveyed to Aubergenville as quickly as possible in search of medical aid.

As they had supposed, the Portuguese was dead—shot through the back. They dragged his body to the road-side, then returning to the unconscious victim, gently raised her and placed her within the car.

Geoffrey's last glimpse of the scene of wreckage showed him the butler's glazed eyes and blood-stained features upturned to the moon-lit sky, and a few yards off the two living accomplices, glaring and livid, while Bernard, mounting guard, leaned against the hedge, a vulture-like figure etched in black, his bony fingers philosophically extracting a cigarette from a battered yellow packet.

After her brief flicker of animation Catherine had sunk back into a state of coma. As her head rested heavily against Geoffrey's shoulder, it seemed certain that she was in no degree aware of her surroundings. Indeed, she scarcely appeared to breathe, but she had given proof that she was alive, and at that knowledge a passion of thanksgiving welled up in her lover's heart. She was here, in his arms, her hair brushing his lips at a time when but for the most extraordinary good fortune, she would have been at the bottom of the cold whirling stream. Perhaps she had been unconscious all the latter part of her terrible drive. The wound on her head was no recent one by the look of it, nor had any fresh injury, beyond a few bruises, resulted from the collision. Wedged between Jeanne and Blom and with her face thickly covered, she had even escaped cuts from the shattered window.

In the sleeping village they managed to knock up a doctor, who quickly attended to the gash in her scalp and made her as comfortable as possible on a couch in his dispensary. She was suffering from slight concussion, which, combined with shock and exhaustion, had reduced her to a fairly serious state. He shook his head gravely over her as he applied restoratives, but offered no objection when Geoffrey suggested sending for an ambulance to take her to the American Hospital at Neuilly, merely stipulating that she should not be moved till the following day. He then set the young man's broken arm, dressed the bullet wound in his shoulder—luckily no more than a graze—and, providing him with a glass of cognac, left him to get what rest he could.

Meanwhile the inspector returned to pick up his prisoners, after promising to communicate with the elder Macadam as soon as he reached Paris.

Geoffrey spent the rest of the night in acute anxiety. During long hours the poor girl remained dead to the world, now wholly unconscious, now raving with delirium. Visions of brain fever filled the watcher's mind, and for a time he seriously feared that her reason would suffer as a result of what had happened in the past forty-eight hours. However, by seven o'clock in the morning she had drifted into a more or less normal slumber, and when the doctor entered bringing hot coffee and the news that the ambulance was on the way, Geoffrey himself had succumbed to exhaustion and, his head fallen forward upon the couch, was sleeping soundly.

Catherine opened her eyes upon a tiny bare room, over-looking a walled garden. Birds were singing in the trees outside, a nurse in uniform was bending over her with a keen but kindly scrutiny. For the moment she had not the remotest idea where she was, and while a thermometer was inserted into her mouth, lay examining her new surroundings with slight curiosity.

"That's better," she heard her guardian say in an honest middle-western voice as she shook down the little tube and placed it in its case. "That's decidedly better. . . . By the way, there's a young man walking up and down the corridor begging for a look at you. Shall I let him in for one minute? He's feeling rather badly used."

Catherine stared. By an ironic twist her thoughts leaped back to Miles Waring, her former fiancé. Who but he could think himself badly used? Then realizing the absurdity of this, she gropingly came a little nearer the present situation.

"Why, of course," she replied weakly. "Let him come in. . . ."

The next instant Geoffrey stood beside her. He was ghastly pale, she thought, and had his left arm in a sling.

"What's happened to you?" she whispered wonderingly. "Have you hurt yourself?"—and she stretched out a hand which he grasped in a hungry clutch.

"Only a fractured arm. Nothing at all," he replied awkwardly, his gaze devouring her. "It's you I want to know about. How do you feel?"

"Rather groggy," she murmured. "I've just waked up. Have I been ill long?"

As she spoke she raised her other hand to her head uncertainly and encountered the rim of a bandage. Astonishment overspread her face.

"Why—am I hurt, too? What is all this?"

For a second she was completely bewildered. Then recollection began to dawn on her.

"Of course! Now I remember!"—and the pupils of her eyes dilated. "It was that beast Eduardo. He banged me over the head with a candle-stick last night—or was it last night?"

He did not tell her that the thing she mentioned had happened four days ago.

"Eduardo is dead," he said shortly. "He's paid for his sins"

"Eduardo dead?" She stared at him. "And the others?" she ventured fearfully.

"Locked up, waiting for their trial. There's nothing for you to bother about now."

She struggled to take it in.

"Germaine," she whispered faintly. "She's dead, too. They killed her, you know. They set fire to her room and locked her in. I tried to stop them, but they were too much for me. They—"

"S'sh—don't talk," he commanded soothingly, stroking her hand.

"Better go now," cautioned the nurse, coming forward. "She's run on like that for hours, ever since she was brought here. We mustn't let her excite herself."

But Catherine's hand stayed her with an imploring gesture.

"Don't send him away just yet," she begged, while tears started to her eyes and spilled over her dark lashes. "I won't say any more if you'd rather I didn't."

And so, without speaking, they sat hand in hand during a long interval of perfect peace.

CHAPTER FORTY-TWO

TEN days passed before Catherine was considered well enough to discuss recent events without undue agitation, and while Geoffrey saw her each afternoon for a short time, their conversation was limited to commonplaces. At the end of that period, however, she showed a definite improvement. Her nerves calmed down, she was able to sleep the night through without a sedative, and exactly a fortnight from the memorable Saturday night she described to Geoffrey all that had happened, from her arrival at the flat till the shock of the collision, when she lost consciousness for the final time.

Geoffrey in turn related his experiences during the corresponding interval—the sudden knowledge of Blom's motive, his discovery that she was missing, his suspicion of the servants, the false telegram which had thrown him off the scent, his vigil in the room across the street, and last of all, the wild race with death, when every moment had been torture, lest she should be consigned to the river before the pursuers could overtake her.

She listened absorbedly. All this time she had been completely ignorant as to the mainspring of the plot, and she could scarcely contain her astonishment when she heard of Blom's intended marriage to the woman he planned by his villainy to turn into an heiress.

"Honorine!" she gasped. "That poor, middle-aged, down-trodden woman? I feel quite sure she never dreamed of the relationship any more than Mme. Bender did. I don't suppose they ever heard of one another. I can't believe she was a party to any wrongdoing."

"I am sure she was not. Well, in all probability she will inherit your cousin's money, though she still is ignorant of the fact; and the outcome of this has spared her tying herself up with a scoundrel who would have used her fortune and neglected her for the first pretty face that came his way."

She mused a little over this, then turned back to the night which had so nearly ended everything for her. It seemed that the drive had taken place in almost total silence, Blom, who had evidently studied a road-map, only speaking to issue commands, and every few minutes pushing her aside to peer through the window at the back to see if they were being followed.

"It was only a precaution, though, for they all believed they had come away unobserved. However, on the bit of road before we came to that last town—"

"Aubergenville," he told her.

"He remained looking out for some time, then swore horribly in German and called through the tube, to Eduardo, telling him to drive like hell."

"That was when he saw us."

"You may imagine my feelings when I knew that rescue was close at hand and heard the loathsome creature beside me scheming to throw you off the track. We pulled up in the town to ask a direction, then tore off again, only to double back and take two or three turnings till finally we got into a sort of narrow lane, very rough."

He explained what must have happened, how her captors had made the detour in order to avoid returning to Aubergenville, and how they were in the act of entering the lonely road leading to the Seine when they ran headlong into the very car they were endeavouring to escape.

"I never knew what hit us," she said. "I felt a terrific jolt which made me see stars, but if there was any thought in my brain it was that it was better to die that way than by drowning."

She repressed a shudder, and yielding her hand to his seeking one, lay back among her pillows.

"I forgot to tell you," she remarked presently when the nurse had brought tea and retired again tactfully, "that I had a visit from Hermione this morning. Poor thing, she is quite broken up, and has positively lost weight. Her clothes hung on her. Do you know, she never mentioned Germaine's money, nor the pearls, though surely she knows they are gone?"

"My father had a talk with her after the safety-box was opened. It must have been a great blow to her, but she was quite dignified about it."

"She seemed to me rather stunned. I don't believe she has grasped it all yet. The only comment she made about Honorine's getting the fortune was that heaven knows where she would go now to have her old hats made over!"

They laughed a little at this.

"The wretched part about it is that I am positive Germaine would have left her something if she had not been interfered with by Jeanne. Isn't it damnable? I am afraid the poor creature has almost no money."

"As a matter of fact," he replied, "things won't turn out for her at all badly. It is she, after all, who will furnish us with particulars regarding Mme. Bender's family, and the commission she will receive for her services will be quite enough to provide for her comfortably."

Her eyes brightened.

"Is that true? I'm glad you told me. I've been bothering about her. She is miserably unhappy, you know. She told me she has not slept since the night of the murder, thinking of Germaine and her awful end."

Her voice trembled as she whispered the last words. Geoffrey set down his cup and sat upon the bed beside her, raising her chin with his hand so that he could look into her troubled eyes.

"Catherine," he said. "I can see you are letting that dwell on your mind, too. Isn't that so?"

"It haunts me," she admitted. "Every time I close my eyes I can see that flaming room and poor Germaine lying in the midst of it. I wish I could forget it."

He thought for a moment.

"But at the time you were pretty certain she was already dead?"

"I believed she was. I had only a glimpse, though, before I was dragged away."

"Well, you may take it for granted that she not only did not suffer, but that she was never even aware of the fire. She simply went to sleep as usual and died before anything happened."

She looked at him with painful eagerness.

"Oh! If only I could believe that!" she cried with intense longing. "Do you think it is possible?"

"More than that. Since the post-mortem we are quite sure of it. Her organs were found to contain sufficient veronal to have killed her quietly and without pain. The fire was merely to cover things up. If the doors were locked it was only because Jeanne, having failed in her previous attempts, was unwilling to take any chances."

A sigh of thankfulness escaped her.

"Then there will be no difficulty about proving it was murder?"

"They will put up a fight, of course, you may depend on that. You see, veronal happens to be a drug which accumulates in the system, and it is undoubtedly true that your cousin had taken considerable quantities of it for months on end. They will swear that death was due to heart failure."

Her face fell a little.

"But do you think the courts will accept their theory?"

He hesitated slightly. Up till now he had not mentioned the part she would be obliged to play in the trial.

"Not when they have heard your evidence," he answered. "But don't let's talk of that now."

Watching, he saw a stoical light come into her eyes.

"I shall be equal to it when the time comes," she said intrepidly. "When I think of what those two have done, I could go through fire myself to bring them to justice."

"One tremendous point in our favour is their attempt to do away with you," he reminded her. "They'll find it pretty hard to explain that away."

"That was Eduardo's stupidity," she replied. "When he came in and saw me struggling with Jeanne, he lost his head and let go at me. But for that they might have pretended they were merely anxious to prevent my harming myself by going into the burning room. I shouldn't wonder if they could have got away with it, too—Jeanne is so abominably clever! By the way," as a sudden thought struck her, "what was the hammering on the front door which I heard just before I lost consciousness?"

He told her it must have been the *locataire* from the third floor, trying to wake up the servants.

"But for that interruption they would probably have allowed the fire to go on much longer. In fact, it was probably their plan to let the whole apartment be consumed, just managing to escape with their lives. In that way Mme. Bender's body would have virtually disappeared, as well as every trace of their various thefts."

"I see. So it was that unexpected hitch which altered things for them. It must have been an awkward moment. What did they do with me, I wonder?"

"I should say they moved you into one of the back rooms for the time being, then while the man ran out to give the alarm, Eduardo must have carried you up in the lift and through the trap-door on to the roof. Certainly there was only a short interval before the place was inundated with people, so they had to work quickly. It was probably Jeanne's shadow I saw on the blind in your room. She must have been busy putting your things back into the bags ready for removal. By the time the engines arrived she and Eduardo were both back at the scene of action, making a great pretence of rescuing their mistress's body."

She stared in blank amazement at this arrangement of facts.

"Then I spent the remainder of the night on the roof?" she said wonderingly.

"With your luggage," he replied. "It's the only solution I can think of. You were not in the apartment next day when we searched it, and except for that possible quarter of an hour of which I speak, Eduardo had no free moment to get you out."

"Then how did I come to be in the other flat?"

"The inspector has been investigating that. The flat belongs to a Chilean family, who went off to Rome, leaving their butler in charge. The butler took the week-end off, leaving the key with the concierge, whom he had sworn to secrecy. But the concierge mentioned the fact to Blom, who it seems was his man of business, as well as Eduardo's. He admits all this now."

"Yes, go on."

"Our theory is that when Eduardo told Blom what had happened to you and the danger they were in, Blom, knowing the Bender apartment would be searched, advised him to steal the key to the empty flat, which he must have done during the time Bernard found him with the concierge. After this he came home, took the lift straight to the top of the building, climbed on to the roof, carried you across and down into the other house, and returned by the same route. Previously he had garaged the car elsewhere in Blom's name, so that all the latter had to do was to claim it, drive to the Square Lamartine, and drop in for a friendly call on the concierge at the right moment to engage the old man's attention while you were being brought out. The whole thing was timed to a second, and would have gone off without a hitch if Bernard had not been watching the premises. So you see," he added, "you owe your life to Bernard."

"Only partly. What about your finding out that the telegram was faked? But for that you wouldn't have been on the spot at all."

"There was a good deal of luck about it. If I had not felt I could not sit still in the Commandant's study another instant I should never have seen Bernard at all, and alone he could hardly have accomplished much. If he had set upon the scoundrels single-handed in that quiet square, they would probably have stuck Jeanne's knife into him and left him in the gutter."

The trial of Jeanne Laborie and Adolph Blom became within the next few weeks a *cause célèbre*. Both prisoners stuck woodenly to their plea of not guilty, and throughout a rigorous cross-examination preserved an unbroken stolidity of bearing. Their *avocat*, a sharp if somewhat shady lawyer from Montmartre, displayed diabolical cunning on their behalf, so that only after a prolonged tussle did his defence break down under the weight of accumulated evidence. In the end, as Geoffrey had foreseen, it was the attempt to remove Catherine which turned the balance.

The truth, when all was known, may be summed up in this wise:

Shortly after Mme. Bender's return from America, Jeanne, hitherto an irreproachable servant, realized the extent to which her mistress's will had become weakened, and resolved to profit by it. At first she did not venture beyond petty thefts—juggling with household accounts, the occasional sale of some small article of value—but emboldened by success she soon began operations on a more extensive scale. She dismissed the other servants, engaged the stupid cook, who in exchange for liberal outings and a minimum of work fell in blindly with her plans, and by dint of many ruses was speedily putting away a substantial sum of money. At this period she probably thought of nothing worse than keeping Mme. Bender in a helpless state so that she could continue her pilfering. However, after nearly a year of this, Blom forced his way into the game, and the whole scheme was materially altered.

The *notaire*, through whose hands the stolen money passed, began eventually to wonder at the large sums which the maid regularly brought to him for investment. It did not take him long to discover the source of this surprising wealth, and, once sure of his facts, he pounced upon Jeanne and her fellow-thief, Eduardo, and informed them brutally that either they must admit him to a share of their gains or else he would lose no time in reporting them to the police. It was useless for the two to protest innocence; he had them in a cleft stick. From that time on both servants were reluctantly obliged to submit to his terms.

Now entered the sinister element in the plot. Some months previous Jeanne, in one of her talks with the *notaire*, had happened to mention her mistress's maiden name, in conjunction with the fact that Mme. Bender possessed no known heir. Blom had said nothing, but had noted that by a curious coincidence the name had also been formerly borne by one of his humble clients—Mme. Baron, known to her customers as Honorine. He resolved quietly to ascertain if a blood relationship might exist between the two Dieulefits, made the visit to Bordeaux, and hit on the astounding truth that the milliner was indeed not merely a connection of the wealthy woman, but actually her sole heir—a cousin in the seventeenth degree!

This gave him his cue, and he forthwith prepared his plans with cold-blooded thoroughness. He offered Jeanne and Eduardo a definite choice—prison, or conniving with him at the murder of the invalid, at whose death he, as Mme. Baron's husband, would be in a position to recompense them amply for their services. At this stage it is probable that Jeanne, the mastermind of the two servants, while hating to submit her will to another, yet realized that it served her best interests to do so. She began to think that her mistress might not have long to live, in which case her income was likely to be cut off at any moment. Better, from her point of view, make certain of a single large sum and have done with it. That she was quite conscienceless and devoured by avarice was only too apparent.

The decision made, Blom lost no time in making sure of his widow, who, regarding him as a desirable partner, accepted his proposal with astonished alacrity. It now remained to prevent Mme. Bender s making a will, and to bring about her death, in such a manner as to suggest accident or suicide. Jeanne's gradual instillation of the insanity idea—begun to serve her private ends—was an admirable aid to both these projects. It discouraged the invalid from venturing a disposition of her property which the courts might set aside, and at the same time hoodwinked the outside world into believing her capable of self-destruction. The one annoying obstacle was Miss Cushing. However, that unfortunate lady, by displaying anxiety as to her own inheritance, played into the crafty maid's hand, with the result already seen.

The train was carefully laid when the plotters were thrown into confusion by Catherine's approaching visit. Deeming it best to hasten things, they arranged the first known attempt on the victim's life by substituting the extra strong solution of disinfectant—actually the dangerous Burnett's Fluid—for the glass of water with which she was about to take her veronal tablet. The plan failed, was interpreted as a foiled effort at suicide, and for the time being nothing further was done, Catherine's presence acting as a deterrent. The truth about Mme. Bender's trying to jump out of the window was never revealed, but it was almost certainly an invention of Jeanne's to lend colour to her assertions. Here again she killed two birds with one stone. She influenced public opinion, deceiving even the doctor, and by placing the bars across the window shook her mistress's faith in herself to a terrifying extent. Indeed, her cunning foresaw and allowed for every contingency. In but one respect did she err, and even here her stupidity would have passed unremarked had it not been for Catherine's arrival on the scene. However, her ruling passion, greed, was too strong to withstand, and it was greed which indirectly brought about her ruin, even though it confused the issues and argued potently against a motive for murder.

Knowing that, once her mistress was dead, she and Eduardo would have to content themselves with what Blom was willing to pay them, she resolved to make the most of her present opportunity, and from the moment she agreed to the *notaire*'s terms, set about quietly stripping the apartment of saleable objects. Bibelots, antique silver, tapestries and finally paintings, disappeared. Catherine's suspicion regarding the thefts gave her a bad fright, but she had a worse adversary to reckon with. Blom himself was incensed at the loss of what he now regarded as his own belongings, the scene in the lower hall being due to his discovery of what was going on. At this stage he could do little but threaten; the trio were in it now up to the neck, and stood or fell together; but he managed to insist that Mme. Bender's death should no longer be postponed, ordering his tools to proceed with the business of dispatching her quickly.

The conspirators were now faced with an embarrassing situation. Catherine had become a positive menace. She was resolved to make an indefinite stay, and showed signs of her intention to oust the servants from their positions. Drastic action must be taken without delay, consequently the maid hit on the idea of making her enemy ill so that she would either be confined to her room or else forced to go away. Thereupon she administered to the unsuspecting girl small daily doses of a drug which brought on the attack, later supposed to be ptomaine poisoning, throwing the young doctor off the track by hinting that the patient had given herself some violent medicine. The drug employed was in all likelihood the digitalis kept for Mme. Bender's occasional heart seizures. It was the one noxious substance at the woman's disposal, it could be partially disguised in coffee and *tilleul*, and the result was calculated to produce precisely the symptoms noticed in Catherine's illness—acute nausea, cramps, and fainting. Mrs. Baxter's invitation happily came at the right moment, as did Geoffrey's insistence on its acceptance. The field was cleared, and all went smoothly up to the moment of the visitor's untimely return.

Geoffrey's theory regarding the fire was probably correct. Having got all she could hope to obtain, Jeanne did not in the least care if the whole building was destroyed. It meant safety for her, and although Blom might be furious over the needless loss he could not say anything. Indeed, his only possible course was to remain steadfastly behind the curtains, go ahead with his humble marriage, which would have included the customary drive in the Bois in a char-à-banc, accompanied by his friends, and then subside until the moment when more than anyone else he would express amazed gratification at his wife's stupendous luck.

The pearls, disposed of piecemeal, were never recovered, nor were the Aubusson carpet and tapestries; but when Jeanne was taken to the prison a packet of bank-notes, representing many thousand francs, was found strapped around her waist, no doubt the proceeds of various sales. The Manet was eventually traced to South America, whence it had been smuggled by an obscure dealer, and a Claude Monet, a Dégas and a small Renoir turned up finally in the French provinces, where the same person was holding them till a safe time.

The two criminals received the death sentence.

Catherine's sister knew nothing of what was happening till the excitement was past. Even then, for an anxious day or so Catherine feared that the zealous Barbara would dash across the ocean to take charge of her—an event she particularly dreaded. However, a series of reassuring cables set matters right, and she breathed again, secure in her independence. It required but little persuasion on the Baxters' part to induce her to spend her convalescence at Fontainebleau, where she rapidly gained strength, soothed by a sense of blessed security, and happy in the knowledge that almost every evening would bring Geoffrey to her side.

One afternoon towards the end of May, when Catherine was well enough to walk and Geoffrey's arm was free of its sling, the two strolled out into the forest and sat down upon a fallen beech-trunk in an open glade. The slanting sun-rays streamed through a canopy of leaves, dappling the ground with shadows and playing on the tender green of the girl's frock. The hush of the hour held them spellbound, and they were silent so long that a thrush in the nearest thicket resumed its interrupted song.

Catherine for her part was feeling curiously shy. During the past weeks she had thought of her lover with a calm and steady affection, but somehow this evening she was disturbingly aware of his masculinity, which all at once struck her as a force to be reckoned with. As she watched him poking among the dead leaves with a stick, and noticed once more the dark hairs upon the backs of his muscular hands, a tremor of nervousness seized her. Tension was in the still air, the approach of a crisis which she longed for, yet dimly dreaded.

Presently it came.

"Catherine," he began abruptly, "do you remember what you said to me that evening after the cabaret? That you'd never consent to be engaged again, but that one day you'd make up your mind to marry quite suddenly?"

"I remember. . . ."

"Do you still mean it?"

She coloured with confusion.

"I—I suppose I do," she faltered uncertainly. "Only I'd have liked to let my hair grow to a more decent length first. I'm such a fright like this!"—and she rubbed her fingers ruefully over the ruffled crop she had spent hours trying to train into subjection.

"As if that mattered!" he cried impatiently. "Besides, it will take just over a fortnight to comply with the French regulations. That ought to be long enough, surely. What do you say? I could start the process to-morrow."

The practical firmness of his tone startled her a little. It was some moments before she could meet his gaze, and when she did so she was still unable to frame a response.

Suddenly she uttered a cry.

"Speaking of hair," she gasped, "did you know you have got a patch of grey over each ear? Geoffrey! To think I never noticed it!"

"Have I?"—indifferently. "It doesn't matter. You haven't answered my question."

"But it does matter," she replied obstinately. "You hadn't them before. Tell me—is it because of—me?"

Evading her importunity, he lifted her two hands in his and kissed the open palms.

"At any rate," he said half-seriously, "you realize now what you are able to do to me if you like. For instance, if ever you should change your mind—"

Through a sudden mist fire flamed in her eyes.

"I shan't," she murmured quickly. "I—"

But whatever she might have added was stifled by the pressure of his lips.

THE END